Scarlet Wilson wrote he[...]
and has never stopped. She's worked in the health
service for more than thirty years, having trained
as a nurse and a health visitor. Scarlet now works
in public health and lives on the West Coast of
Scotland with her fiancé and their two sons.
Writing medical romances and contemporary
romances is a dream come true for her.

Kate Hardy has always loved books and could
read before she went to school. She discovered
Mills & Boon books when she was twelve and
decided that this was what she wanted to do.
When she isn't writing, Kate enjoys reading,
cinema, ballroom dancing and the gym. You
can contact her via her website: katehardy.com.

Also by Scarlet Wilson

Cinderella's Kiss with the ER Doc
Her Summer with the Brooding Vet
Nurse's Dubai Temptation

Christmas North and South miniseries

Melting Dr Grumpy's Frozen Heart

Also by Kate Hardy

Mills & Boon True Love

A Fake Bride's Guide to Forever

If the Fairy Tale Fits… miniseries

His Strictly Off-Limits Ballerina

Mills & Boon Medical

Paediatrician's Unexpected Second Chance

Yorkshire Village Vets miniseries

Sparks Fly with the Single Dad

Discover more at millsandboon.co.uk.

HAWAIIAN KISS WITH THE BROODING DOC

SCARLET WILSON

THE SURGEON'S TROPICAL TEMPTATION

KATE HARDY

MILLS & BOON

All rights reserved including the right of reproduction in whole or in part in any form. This edition is published by arrangement with Harlequin Enterprises ULC.

This is a work of fiction. Names, characters, places, locations and incidents are purely fictional and bear no relationship to any real life individuals, living or dead, or to any actual places, business establishments, locations, events or incidents. Any resemblance is entirely coincidental.

Without limiting the author's and publisher's exclusive rights, any unauthorized use of this publication to train generative artificial intelligence (AI) technologies is expressly prohibited. HarperCollins also exercise their rights under Article 4(3) of the Digital Single Market Directive 2019/790 and expressly reserve this publication from the text and data mining exception.

® and TM are trademarks owned and used by the trademark owner and/or its licensee. Trademarks marked with ® are registered with the United Kingdom Patent Office and/or the Office for Harmonisation in the Internal Market and in other countries.

First published in Great Britain 2025
by Mills & Boon, an imprint of HarperCollins*Publishers* Ltd,
1 London Bridge Street, London, SE1 9GF

www.harpercollins.co.uk

HarperCollins*Publishers* Macken House, 39/40 Mayor Street Upper, Dublin 1, D01 C9W8, Ireland

Hawaiian Kiss with the Brooding Doc © 2025 Scarlet Wilson

The Surgeon's Tropical Temptation © 2025 Pamela Brooks

ISBN: 978-0-263-32511-9

07/25

This book contains FSC™ certified paper
and other controlled sources to ensure responsible forest management.

For more information visit www.harpercollins.co.uk/green.

Printed and Bound in the UK using 100% Renewable Electricity
at CPI Group (UK) Ltd, Croydon, CR0 4YY

HAWAIIAN KISS WITH THE BROODING DOC

SCARLET WILSON

MILLS & BOON

This book is dedicated to my whole family
after the hardest year of our lives.
Love you and appreciate you all. xx

CHAPTER ONE

Jamie Robertson stepped off the plane and let the wave of warm air hit him. Perfect. It was moist but rich with scents. Whether that was mountain greenery or the aromas from the sea he couldn't tell, but he also couldn't wait to find out. As he climbed down the steps from the aircraft he could see that the baggage handlers were already moving into position to unload the plane and he prayed that his surfboards would still be in one piece.

His flight had been delayed twice, meaning he had around two hours to present at Honolulu General Medical Center for his new job as Infectious Disease Consultant. He'd taken over from someone who'd had to leave in a hurry due to family issues, and he still wasn't sure he knew everything he should about this place, or his role.

His key motivation for coming here was the fact his best friend from medical school, Joanne, had spotted a cardiology post for herself, and then seen the short notice advert for a tropical disease consultant and encouraged him to apply. Since they worked in such differing fields, they'd always joked if they ever found a hospital offering a job for each of them, they would jump at a chance to work in the same place again. One video-streamed interview later, and he'd been offered the post in a place he'd never even have dreamed of as a kid.

The cold, rainy weather of Scotland was a million miles from the sun-drenched beaches of Hawaii. Sure, he knew they could have rain too—and a number of storms or freak weather events, but the chance to work out here was thrilling.

He'd exchanged a few messages with one of the surf instructors at his nearest beach and agreed to meet later this week. Jamie was no fool. He loved surfing, but the sea and its hidden contents could be dangerous. He planned to gather as much local knowledge as he could before he settled into his own plans for surfing on a regular basis.

The airport was busy but the conveyor belt for the luggage was already moving as he got inside and he collected his luggage and headed to the exit, where a car was waiting for him.

He knew that Joanne was arriving later today, and since he'd been supposed to get here first—just much earlier—he grabbed some things for her and left them at her apartment en route, along with a note, so she could settle in.

The driver was polite, pointed out a few local places on the way to his home and waited outside while Jamie dumped his belongings, washed his face and changed his clothes.

The hospital was as modern as any other city hospital he'd worked in. But it still felt as if he was living a slightly unreal life as he strode through the main entrance. A whirlwind of meetings with staff from HR, bank details, identification badges, white coats, office and a meeting with a very jolly woman who could easily have been Santa Claus's wife in a kids' TV movie—but was apparently his secretary and was called Merry—made him actually look over his shoulder and check for some hidden camera.

Maybe he and Joanne were part of some elaborate con? There were no jobs, and this was actually some reality TV show. All he prayed for, in amongst these bizarre thoughts, was that it was a mystery kind of show instead of a romance kind. Jamie Robertson didn't do romance. Not after two failed relationships, and a stinging outburst from his last girlfriend as she'd packed her bags and told him he was quite possibly the grumpiest man alive.

Maybe it was the Scotsman in him. Weren't they meant to be grumpy? He didn't purposely mean to be that way, but he also would never walk around with a forced smile on his face all day. What was the point?

He always had too much else to think about, too many things on his mind to worry about smiling at people. Especially in his own home.

Home. He hadn't even had a chance to look around the place today due to the delays. But he'd taken over the lease, just like he'd taken over the guy's job. The only thing he'd really been interested in was its proximity to the beach, and luckily it wasn't too far from one of Honolulu's lesser-known beaches. Jamie would have to figure out everything else at a later time.

Indira, one of the HR staff, gave him a thick envelope. 'A copy of your contract, where to pick up your laptop. All the log-in instructions and passwords are included. You'll have to attend an induction tomorrow to get electronic prescribing privileges and complete the mandatory online training. Tonight, at one of the local bars there's a meet and greet, which I suggest you attend. And here's a map of the hospital, with details of key contacts for you. If you go to your office, Merry will take you along and introduce you to the staff on your ward. Please let me know if you have any questions.'

The young woman gave him a bright smile and then left him standing at the double doors she'd just escorted him out of.

Before he had a chance to ask if Merry was really his secretary's name, she'd disappeared back through the doors—which, he now realised, were only accessible with some kind of keycard.

HR, the mysterious gurus of the hospital who kept everyone firmly in their places. Consistent the world over.

Jamie sighed and ran his hands through his dark hair. Although the hospital was air conditioned, his body was still adjusting to the overall temperature rise. He might need to go a little shorter with his hair.

He sent a text to Joanne about the welcome drinks so she'd know too before he walked back along to his office. He actually had one. It didn't have a view of the ocean or anything like that. But it had four walls, a desk, a phone, a comfortable chair and some shelves and stacking units. Back in the UK, he was sometimes lucky to find a corner. Most times he shared office space with a number of other consultants, who all fought over one secretary. Jamie had never been that demanding over his admin staff. As long as they could find him if they needed to and keep notes on his patients, he was happy.

Merry met him at the door. She was a large woman in her fifties with a bright multicoloured sarong that reached almost to the floor, glistening skin and big curls.

'Lenny assures me you'll be no trouble,' she said in her Hawaiian accent, watching him carefully with her dark eyes.

Lenny. The consultant who he'd replaced.

He gave her a careful glance. Jamie might be known by some as grumpy. But he also knew how important his colleagues were. And since he was new here, Merry could likely save him from a million wrong turns, a careful nudge to the local processes, and steer him away from any inadvertent faux pas.

He held out his hand towards her. 'Hi, I'm Jamie Robertson. I'm pleased to be working here. Indira said you would be able to give me a tour of the hospital and the wards I'll be working in.'

Her brow furrowed and her gaze narrowed for a second, before she gave a laugh and a wave of her hand. 'Fifty percent.'

He frowned. 'What?'

She was still laughing. 'Fifty percent. That's what I got of what you said.'

It took him a few seconds to process because he was concentrating hard on her accent—a favour she was currently not returning.

He raised his eyebrows at her. 'Try harder.' His voice had an edge to it, and he knew it. But if he could concentrate hard to understand her accent, then she could do the same.

Merry walked over to her desk, her hand still waving at him. 'Either feisty or snide. I haven't decided which,' she shot over her shoulder.

'Me either,' he replied just as quickly.

She stopped as she dropped some files on her desk

and let out a deep belly laugh that seemed to bubble up all the way from her toes to her mouth. Several heads in the secretarial pods all rose above their section dividers, a bit like meerkats.

She had a sense of humour. He could work with that.

'Come on.' He gestured with his head. 'Show me around this place and let's see if anyone else can understand my accent.'

The hospital had nearly eight hundred beds, with a variety of specialties, along with theatres, intensive care, its own laboratory and the only level one ER and trauma centre in the Hawaiian Islands.

And it seemed that Merry knew something about them all. She hadn't stopped talking from the second they'd started their hospital walkaround. In a way, it was good. He was definitely concentrating, not just on her accent, which he was getting used to, but all her attention to detail.

He halted her near the cardiac unit and asked to go in. She raised her eyebrows. 'We don't go in there.'

'You mean no one having a cardiac event could also have a tropical disease?' He let the words hang in the air like a challenge, before she let out a sigh and pushed open the doors.

'I'm looking for my friend,' he admitted.

'She talk like you?' was the immediate question.

He laughed and shook his head. 'She's English, but we trained at medical school together. She's just started here too; her name is Joanne Meadows.'

Merry's sweeping view took in the area surrounding the nurses' station. 'Her name's not on the board yet. Usual start day is Monday.'

He gave her a quizzical glance. 'Why am I starting on a Friday then?'

There was another hand wave. 'Because we have no cover. Remind me to pick you up a pager.'

'Lenny had no backup?'

'He has a trainee. And she's good.' She wagged her finger at Jamie. 'Don't you go scaring her off. But consultant cover is on another island. In an emergency, we do it by video link.' She gave an amused shrug of her shoulders. 'Tropical diseases can be quiet.'

Jamie stopped walking and stared at her. He closed his eyes. 'You didn't just say that.'

'Say what?'

It was his turn to throw up his hands. 'How long have you worked in a hospital?'

'Forty years. Since I was seventeen.'

'And you don't know never to say the Q word?' He pushed open the doors back out into the corridor.

'Your friend—Joanne? Something happening there?'

He wasn't surprised by the question; he'd been asked it plenty of times before.

'No, absolutely not. She's been my best friend since medical school. We just hit it off. More like a sister to me. I never had a sister, and Joanne fits that role. She tells me the truth about things, occasionally laughs at my clothes, can be vicious with me.' He gave a sigh and a smile. 'But would also fight to the death for me—just like I would for her.'

Merry quirked an eyebrow. It was clear she didn't quite believe him—but she wasn't the first colleague he'd met who struggled with a male/female friendship.

Not his problem.

Merry was talking again, moving onto her next subject area. 'So, you can cover in the ER if you're not particularly busy,' she said. 'Most of the people that end up in your ward come through the ER anyhow. If you hang around, you might save a few people being misdiagnosed.'

Jamie had started shaking his head already. 'Lenny did this?'

She nodded.

He was trying to wrap his head around this. He'd done a six-month stint in the ER as a junior doctor, but 'hanging around' there hadn't really been on his radar.

'What if I got stuck in the middle of a road traffic accident, or a cardiac event? I'm not a specialist for those eventualities. Surely, this would lead to more issues?'

'Then phone a friend,' said Merry in a dry tone.

'What?'

'You just said your best friend works in Cardiac. If you have a cardiac case, page your friend.' She shrugged, and Jamie noted that she seemed to do that quite a lot. Maybe it was just around him?

As she pushed open the doors to the ER, she led him to a whiteboard. 'Let's make it easy for you.' She smiled with a gleam in her eye. 'Lenny always checked the board. Unknown rashes, gastric cases, unusual symptoms that might fit with a tropical or infectious disease. Those were the ones he generally reviewed.' She tilted her head to the side. 'Although he did deliver a baby once.'

'What?'

Jamie had stopped walking now. 'Not a single chance,' he said—just in case anyone around and listening got any kind of idea.

His eyes took in the layout of the ER. It was calm, organised. No shouting, no badly behaved patients. It certainly didn't resemble the ER in Glasgow that he'd spent his six months in.

He asked a few more questions as Merry showed him around. Finally, she took him to the ward. He almost let out a sigh of relief as soon as he set foot in the place.

Sixteen beds, properly staffed. An efficient charge nurse, good charting and recording systems, a constantly revolving list of tasks to be completed and a really pleasant atmosphere. He smiled. This was his new place of work. He might actually like it here.

There was a loud laugh along the corridor and a woman with blonde curls, a white shirt and a bright pink skirt came out of a room, putting a lid back onto a container.

She was actually singing as she came out of the room and doing a few dance moves. As she got further along, she shot a look over her shoulder and gave a wave to the patient in the room.

Was she a relative? Jamie glanced at the board next to him. The patient was Charles Eroka, eighty-two. He'd need to check the notes.

Merry got in there first. 'Piper, this is Jamie Robertson, our new Tropical Disease Consultant.'

'Oh, hey,' Piper said with a smile, surprising him with her English accent, then opened the container and pushed it towards him.

It was stuffed full of something he was sure his mother used to call traybakes, a variety of squares of covered oats, marshmallows, cookies and cereals all coated in chocolate. If a hospital dietitian were in the vicinity, they would likely let out some kind of shriek.

'Want one?' she asked. 'I made them for Charlie. They're his favourites.'

Jamie blinked. She hadn't stopped smiling yet.

'You're my attending?'

She licked her lips and straightened her back, letting her shoulders fall back and inadvertently showing off her long neck, and body curves. 'Piper Bronte,' she replied.

Green eyes. She had green eyes. And not just a dull or wishy-washy green. No, these were a decidedly look-at-me-and-pay-attention sort of green.

He gave a half-smile that he didn't even mean. 'Good English name,' he remarked.

'And you're Scottish. I was hoping for a William Wallace, or a Robert Burns.' She smiled again, clearly teasing him.

She pushed the container towards him again and he shook his head. 'I'm still acclimatising and hopefully will fall asleep at some point tonight.' He gestured to the container. 'My body still thinks I'm a toddler and sugar tends to keep me awake all night.'

Those green eyes fixed on him for a few seconds. 'Noted,' she said. 'I like to have blackmail material on those I work with.'

For the briefest of seconds his mind went somewhere it shouldn't. To a place where he could actually appreciate her smooth skin, green eyes, pink lips and curves, then it rebounded straight back to reality.

'We should talk about your learning objectives.' It came out much more abruptly than he'd intended.

She was silent but gave a nod and handed the container over the nurses' station to the people sitting beyond, where it was eagerly accepted.

She glanced at the clock and he realised it was nearing six p.m. 'Do you want to do that now?'

His jet lag and delays had brought him to the present day and time. It was a Friday, and the majority of the hospital staff would finish at six tonight. He was on call for special circumstances, but just because he was working didn't mean that everyone else had to.

He shook his head. 'No. We can do that on Monday morning. We'll go over all the current patients, their planned tests and treatments, and look at what experience you still need to gain.'

Someone nearby let out a soft laugh and he realised immediately how that might have sounded. 'No, no,' he said hastily, waving his hand, but Merry saved him.

She plucked something from the noticeboard and set it down between him and Piper. 'Tonight,' she said. 'Eight o'clock at the Pirate and Spear. Welcome drinks for all newcomers to the hospital.' She looked pointedly at Jamie. 'If you haven't found Joanne by then, I'm sure she will be there.'

'I'm on call,' he said, thankful to have those words to excuse himself.

'A third of the people there will be on call,' said Piper easily. 'Welcome drinks don't have to be alcohol.'

It was a simple statement. And, just like that, his reason to not attend vanished into thin air. If he hadn't been so tired and jet-lagged he would have made up another excuse there and then. But it seemed that his brain didn't have the capacity for that right now, so he just gave a small smile and nodded—promising himself it would be the first and last time that he was caught out.

Socialising with work colleagues wasn't usually on his

bingo card. He would have to keep reminding himself of that while he was around Piper.

Merry nudged him with her hips. 'Don't worry, you'll get the hang of all this soon enough.'

Jamie looked around him, wondering if he'd made a big mistake by upending his life to try and spend time in the same place as his friend. Guess he would soon find out.

Piper wasn't new. She'd been here for six months. But going to the welcome drinks was something they were all encouraged to do. She'd already met the one person she was interested in seeing, and he seemed a little grumpier than expected. But he was Scottish. Was that just normal?

Hawaii had been a dream come true for her. She loved the climate. She loved the people. She loved the island paradise. Tropical and infectious diseases weren't expected to be a specialism for a UK doctor, and she hoped to eventually head to the CDC in the US for a job. But to get there, she had to be fully qualified with some practical experience under her belt.

She'd studied at the London School of Hygiene and Tropical Medicine, and also done a placement there. They'd encouraged a further placement in a more tropical environment and that was why she was here.

At least that was what she told people when they asked. While Piper might have a very English name, she didn't exactly have any roots. Her parents had died when she was a child, then she'd stayed with first an elderly aunt and then a distant cousin. She'd never been maltreated, but she'd never really felt as if she had a family.

Her brain drifted back to a memory of someone coming to say that her mummy and daddy couldn't come back and pick her up. The whispers of adults outside as it was decided she would stay the night with the friend she'd been playing with, before finally packing a suitcase of clothes and being taken to her aunt's. The memories of the smell of Aunt Matilda's house invaded her senses. It was like being back there again. It wasn't that the house was dirty or smelly. To a small child it had just smelled… old. Then there was the day she'd found Aunt Matilda on the floor and had to phone for an ambulance. She'd been cared for by a neighbour for a few days before being sent to a distant cousin, a woman she'd met once at her parents' funeral.

Lynne had been awkward whilst trying to be kind, as if she couldn't wait for the years to pass by and for Piper to finally turn eighteen. Her delight at Piper doing well in school and being accepted at university for medical school had been like a giant sigh of relief. There had been the occasional offer to visit again, but Piper had known she wasn't really wanted. Her parents' inheritance had made her self-sufficient, and when she'd finished training she'd just moved from place to place, following job after job.

It was part of the reason she kept her bright, sunny demeanour on the outside. There was no one to fall back on. No one to rely on. So Piper had learned to try and make friends in every place she went. She kept her smile plastered to her face and generally did what most people asked.

People liked her. And she lived for that. Because there was nothing worse than feeling alone in this world. University had been great. Six years with the same people and a key circle of friends. But since they'd all picked specialties, she barely knew where anyone was any more. It was isolating. And with this training programme, with the encouraged moves, it almost felt as if she was meant to be on her own. Piper had learned resilience the hard way.

Lenny, Jamie's predecessor, had been a good teacher, and easy to work with. But Lenny's wife was pregnant with twins—one of whom would need in-utero surgery—and that surgery wasn't available in Hawaii. They'd had to go to a teaching hospital in Boston. That was why he'd left at short notice.

Would Jamie Robertson be a good teacher? She wasn't entirely sure. He was certainly good-looking enough, and there was no ring on his finger. But there had been mention of someone else—Joanne. Maybe they'd come here together. It didn't generally take Merry long to find out everything about the people around her. And Merry would likely fill Piper in. She seemed to have taken Piper under her wing.

It was a shame, but Jamie was the first guy she'd met since she'd got here who had actually made parts of her tingle. He'd dropped a potential mark for not eating any of her home baking. It had won her fan clubs in previous hospitals—but maybe Jamie Robertson was a harder nut to crack. It would be interesting to find out.

Piper had changed into a red dress and short red cardigan. The Pirate and Spear had a beach setting and a thatched roof, with lots of sand kicking around the floor. Even though the sun was setting and the temperature had dropped a little, it was still warm.

She made her way down towards the pub, meeting several work colleagues en route. At the entrance was a tray of red drinks with no label. Piper picked one up and gave a small sniff. Watermelon? She took a tiny sip. Yip. It was fine. She kept a hold of her glass and moved inside.

It was busy already. There were lots of standing tables with people gathered around them and some low-level music played in the background. She could also see other trays with coloured drinks. She'd stick with red. It seemed pretty safe and some of the local hooch around here was deceptively strong.

As she moved amongst the crowd she caught sight of Jamie Robertson, sipping a cocktail the same as hers, just as a woman shouted and wrapped her arms around him in a giant hug. The woman was blonde-haired and very attractive and the way that they interacted made it very clear that this wasn't their first meeting. 'Did Dick and Dom make it?' she said, laughing. Even from here Piper could see that Jamie's tense shoulders had relaxed and his face had brightened. They leaned on a nearby table together and started chatting—both at the same time, immediately.

Piper felt awkward. Jamie had a connection with someone, and she was instantly a tiny bit jealous. Not because she had plans for him, just because it was clear there was someone he cared about, and someone who cared about him. Watching other people connect always made her feel a bit unworthy, because she didn't have those connections to people. She'd planned on saying hello, but didn't want to interrupt something that looked as if it might be private.

She turned, planning to head back in the other direction, when someone came barrelling into her. The momentum meant she was flung backwards, arms in the air, cocktail vanishing and landing heavily on the floor. Piper was average height and build, but because she'd been partly turned the other way, the landing was awkward and made her yelp in pain.

She didn't know which part of her hurt most, her hip, her wrist, her ankle or her pride. As she drew in a deep breath a face appeared down next to her. Jamie Robertson. Jamie—whose white shirt was now covered in red liquid, some of which was still dripping off the end of his nose.

'Piper, are you okay?'

She blinked again, wondering if the vision would disappear. But it didn't. No, she really had just spilled a drink over her new boss. Wonderful.

His voice dipped lower as he held out a hand to her. 'Are you drunk?' She could hear the hint of distaste in the question. It brought her straight back to her senses.

'Of course I'm not drunk!' she said quickly. 'The drink—that you're wearing—was my only one.'

He slid one arm behind her back as she took his other hand and he helped her up. She winced for a second as she put weight on her ankle, but although it was a little tender, she could tell it was fine.

She glanced around. 'Where did the guy go that barged into me?'

Jamie pointed over to the bar. 'Oh, he just practically rolled his way to the bar.'

She was conscious that at this point she had one arm around his shoulder and was pressed against his very wet, never-to-be-white-again shirt. She could feel the outline of his body next to hers. It was clearly defined, with little fat and lots of muscle. Did this guy work out? And why did that give her a hot flush?

His companion was laughing at him and also talking to another guy at her side, who Piper recognised from the cardiology department.

'I'm so sorry,' she said quickly, looking him up and down. 'I've ruined your evening.'

'You haven't,' he said, but he glanced back over to his companion and she could almost see that he was holding in a sigh. He looked back down at the arm she held against her chest.

'Let me look at that.'

'It's fine,' she said automatically as he took her wrist in his hands and she let out a hiss.

'Fine?' he said back, as he gently touched her bones.

She winced. 'I must just have sprained it. I'll find an elastic bandage for it.'

He raised his eyebrows. 'Or we can walk back to the hospital and get it X-rayed to make sure you haven't fractured your distal radius.' It was the most common type of wrist fracture, often occurring when people put out a hand to break their fall.

'I'm not seventy,' she said quickly, since it was more frequent in women who'd gone through the menopause.

'I didn't say you were. But let's get it checked anyhow.'

Before she could refuse, he took a few steps back to the tall table and put his hand on the lower half of his companion's back, speaking in her ear. She gave a nod and shot a sympathetic glance at Piper.

'Let's go,' he said, steering her through the crowd and back out the entrance of the pub.

'So much for the meet and greet,' she sighed.

He laughed and looked down at himself. 'Here's hoping I don't get paged while you're waiting on an X-ray.' He peeled his wet shirt off his chest then wrinkled his nose.

'I'll get reported on my first shift for being inappropriately dressed and smelling of alcohol.'

Piper stopped short, her eyes wide. 'Oh, no. You can't come into the hospital like that. You're right. People might talk. You don't want to trash your reputation before you've even got started.'

His face darkened. 'Don't worry,' he muttered under his breath. 'I don't need any help trashing my reputation. Apparently, I can do that by just being me.'

Piper's head filled with a hundred different thoughts. What on earth did that mean? And she wasn't entirely sure she wanted to find out. This guy was her brand-new boss. For any job reference in the future, he would be the person that would back up her knowledge, expertise and the ability to put both into practice. She was definitely pushing the fact that he was handsome from her head right now. And even though he was wearing her watermelon cocktail, she could still grasp the scent of the woody cologne she'd noticed on him earlier.

That first sighting on the ward had sent a little shiver down her spine, which she'd ignored then and she was ignoring now. Going out with your boss was definitely not a thing. Particularly when he was already taken.

'I should never have worn white,' he said, shaking his head at himself. 'It's like an automatic beacon for any dirt or spills.' He wrinkled his nose. 'I mean, who did decide that doctors should wear white coats? A ridiculous idea. They're just designed to get manky.'

She burst out laughing. 'What? What did you just say?'

'Manky.' He looked surprised at her, then gave the tiniest shake of disapproval that she didn't know the word. 'A good Scottish word meaning dirty.' Then he gave a hidden kind of smile. 'Well, really a bit more than dirty. But you get my gist.'

She stared at him. 'It's like you just fell from *Trainspotting*.'

Now it was his turn to look confused. 'What?'

'Your whole accent just got thicker and more bewildering by the second.'

'I don't know what you mean,' he said, and she wasn't quite sure if he was joking or not.

They approached the door of the ER and Piper nodded to go down a corridor. Midway, there was a large grey storage trolley filled with pale blue scrubs. She decided not to even guess his size. 'Do you want to grab a pair of these?' she asked. 'Changing rooms are on your left.'

He gave a nod and started rummaging through the pile.

Piper strolled back down to Reception to register. The admin assistant recognised her and saw her holding her wrist. 'I'll get one of the staff to come and see you,' she said, and within five minutes one of the ER nurses came out with a smile.

'This is what happens when I miss all the fun,' he declared as he looked over her wrist and wrote up instructions for an X-ray. 'I think it's just sprained, but let's be sure.'

Ten minutes later, her X-ray was complete and even though she wanted to look at it herself she decided to behave and sat back in the waiting room.

Jamie appeared, now dressed in blue scrubs that

seemed to have been made solely to complement his eye colour. He filled them out well with his height, broad chest and shoulders. 'Come and see,' he said, gesturing with his head to one of the bays where he had her X-ray displayed.

'You working in the ER now?' she asked in amusement.

He rolled his eyes. 'You missed the Merry tour. She practically told me if I had a spare minute I should just come here and help out.'

Piper pulled a face. 'I have picked up some interesting cases down here,' she admitted.

He sighed and nodded. 'I guess. Now, look at your wrist. What do you see?'

Was he testing her?

'It's fine,' she said quickly, willing it to be so. 'Just sore.'

He folded his arms across his chest. So, she stepped forward and peered. Hard. For a few seconds, before finally pulling a face.

'I don't see a hairline fracture,' she said, wondering if she'd just failed his test.

'Then consider yourself lucky,' he said. 'Painkillers, rest, elevate and some strapping or a splint for some support for the next few days. If there's swelling, you should ice it.'

She turned to face him. 'I have a new boss. There's no way I'm taking time off.'

He raised his eyebrows. 'I'm sure your boss will understand.'

She gave a half-smile as she shook her head. 'Oh, I

don't know. First impressions count, and I don't know that I've made the right kind.'

'What do you mean? Like spilling drink all over him? Ruining his first welcoming drinks? Trying to overdose him with sugar? Making him work in the ER on his first on-call shift? Or just in general, because you're trying to denigrate his accent?'

She held up her not sore hand and counted off. 'Wow. One, two, three, four, five, and hey, I've run out of fingers. Even I couldn't have guessed I'd won the award for the worst first impression. I thought I was only one, or maybe two, of those.'

He tapped the side of his head. 'Mind like a steel trap.'

She wrinkled her nose. It was late. She was tired. And she just couldn't get any sense of what kind of guy her new boss was. Apart from attractive. But that didn't count.

'Is that another Scottish saying?'

'It's a worldwide one.'

She shrugged. 'Must have missed it.'

At that point, Kel, the nurse, came back in and pointed at Piper's wrist. 'Want me to wrap that up for some support meantime? Can't have my favourite baker hurting her wrist.'

Her eyes flashed and she turned to Jamie. 'See, some people appreciate my hard work.'

He threw up his hands and headed for the corridor. 'She's all yours, Kel. Good luck.'

Her stomach gave a strange little squelch as she watched his retreating back. Six months. That was how much longer her contract was.

Things had been really easy with Lenny. Jamie Robertson seemed like a whole new ballgame. And she wasn't quite sure she was ready.

CHAPTER TWO

'MERRY, WHAT SINS did I commit in a past life that you've been sent to punish me for?' asked Jamie as he stared in bewilderment at his desk.

He practically couldn't see it. It was awash with files, papers, letters and results.

She appeared at the door, shaking her head as she dumped another pile on his desk. 'I've put them in order,' she said with her brow wrinkling. He noticed a few random coloured Post-it notes adorning the piles.

'Pinks are all to be reviewed, blues are current patients in the ward, yellows are those that are used as teaching opportunities for students, greens are those being queried at the moment to see if they fall under your service.' Her finger landed on the biggest pile. 'And oranges are those that all need final approval before the letters go out. They were Lenny's cases and he didn't get to approve them before he left.'

Jamie swallowed. That was the danger of accepting a post at short notice. It left him in the middle of a dozen things he wasn't fully sighted on. It wasn't that he was a control freak, but he'd learned enough lessons along the way that he realised that this was how things could be missed. Jamie Robertson wasn't the type to miss things.

Anyone else would assign some of this work to his trainee consultant. But Jamie hadn't had time yet to determine Piper's knowledge, skills or experience. Sure, she appeared to be Miss Sunshine in this place, and he only hoped his own natural demeanour wouldn't dampen her spark, but he'd have to find a way through this in a methodical manner.

He stared at the pile, then glanced at his watch. Ward round first. He wanted to get to know all the staff who worked on his ward and who were affiliated with it. Teamwork was important to him. He gave a small smile at the white coat hanging up next to the door, remembering the fate of his shirt on Friday night, and decided to leave it there. He then had a quick check of his phone.

He'd felt bad abandoning Joanne at the meet and greet on Friday night and she hadn't answered his texts until the following morning. She'd said everything was fine, but he was still a little worried about her. They were both in a new place, making first impressions. And whilst Jamie was certain he wanted to succeed, he was equally sure he wanted his best friend to succeed too. She was a brilliant cardiologist and she deserved to shine. But he knew that Joanne didn't drink much alcohol at all, and she'd seemed at ease with the man she'd been speaking to, so unless he heard differently, he'd assume she was fine.

He walked through the doors of the ward and stopped. There it was. That hum. The hum of quiet activity. Everyone knowing what their job was, and doing it without drama. It gave him a little confidence in this place.

He moved down to the nurses' station where the charge nurse, Kiana, was looking at him with amusement as he carried in the pile of notes.

'I should warn you that Lenny used to occasionally come and hide from Merry and work in the office behind the nurses' station.' She nodded over her shoulder and then looked at the notes. 'And we're in the process of moving to all electronic records.' She flicked through the files. 'Ones that have a large blue sticker have already all been scanned and moved over.'

He frowned. 'So why did Merry give me all these?'

Kiana shrugged. 'She thinks all the electronics will fail, so she makes sure both sets are always up-to-date.' Kiana leaned over and lifted up a clipboard. 'On this you will find a current list of patients with brief notes of reviews completed, tests ordered and anything Piper is worried about.'

'She's already reviewed all the patients? I thought we might do it together.'

'You'll need to get up a bit earlier then. I swear that woman never sleeps. She was paged to the ER. You might catch her there.'

Jamie paused for a moment, wondering if it was all a giant trap to lure him down to the ER and get him to do someone else's work. He lifted the clipboard, read everything and pointed to a few of the notes. 'Piper wants me to review these patients. When does it suit?'

Kiana looked at the list. 'Mr Burns is getting some physio right now, and Ms Kerr is down at X-ray. Maybe in around an hour?'

He gave a nod and a rueful smile. 'Guess I'm heading to the ER then.'

Piper was keen to make a good impression at work, since she'd already failed in real life. She'd been on ward early to review all the patients and had been a little disappointed when she'd received a page for the ER and Jamie hadn't been at the ward already.

She wondered exactly how much Lenny had told him about her, and her past. She knew that things had been rushed and was kind of hoping that Lenny had left some things out. It wasn't that she didn't plan on being honest, she just felt it was easier to tell your own story, rather than hear it from someone else.

She checked in with the desk in the ER and picked up the chart of the patient she'd been called down to see. She read quickly over the notes and was making a list of questions she wanted to ask when Jamie came up behind her.

'How's the hand?' he asked straight away.

She held up the strapped wrist. 'It seems good. Just a little sore. I iced it and kept it elevated for the rest of the weekend, and it seems to have done the trick.'

'Anything you can't do at work I should know about?'

'A handstand?' she said with a smile.

He blinked but didn't say anything and she had that tiny wave of momentary panic that she'd had on Friday night. She really didn't know her boss well. Maybe he just didn't have a sense of humour. Maybe she should always be serious around him. But that really wasn't in her nature. Despite what had happened in her past, she always tried to have the best day possible at work. Being a medic was hard. But seeing things as a glass half-full instead of a glass half-empty had always just been her way.

'What have we got?'

Her stomach gave a flip. Partly because she'd wanted a chance to assess the patient herself and partly because he'd just completely changed the subject. Was he letting her know that he didn't really do small talk?

He leaned over her shoulder and looked at what she was writing, giving a slow nod. She noted a tiny flare of panic in his eyes.

'Do you want to do this one?' she asked immediately. 'Or are you happy for me to assess and you to observe?' She had to add the last bit, because she really did want to do the assessment on the patient herself, not just stand around like some bystander. But she had to give him his place. She was here to learn and she wasn't quite sure what his teaching techniques would be as yet.

'You start,' he said cautiously. 'If I think you're missing something, I'll jump in.'

'Okay,' she said, trying to appear casual when her insides were churning. It was like being under a microscope, and she knew right now if she missed anything she would kick herself later.

They walked over to the nearby cubicle and pulled the curtains. 'Arlo Quinn?'

The young man nodded, lying back against his pillows and looking distinctly unwell. He was accompanied by an older woman who Piper assumed was his mother. 'Mrs Quinn?'

The woman nodded and sighed. 'We've already been to this ER. They sent us away and my son is clearly worse.' Her face was tight and it was clear she was annoyed, but maybe she had a right to be.

'I'm Piper Bronte, I'm a specialist doctor. This is my colleague, Dr Robertson. Are you okay if we go over a few details?'

Even though he'd closed his eyes, Arlo nodded.

'You're on holiday from New York, and you've been here for fourteen days?'

Arlo nodded again. Piper continued. 'I can see you were in here two days ago with a temperature, headache and muscle and joint pains. I'm assuming things have got worse since then?'

'He's been vomiting,' Mrs Quinn said quickly. 'He can't get out of bed and was barely eating or drinking.'

'Arlo,' said Piper in a low voice, 'I'm just going to examine you, okay?'

Once he'd nodded again, she examined his chest and arms, listening to his lungs, checked his back, and indicated a rash for Jamie to glance at. She then continued down his limbs, noting another few marked spots on his legs around his ankles.

'I'm assuming you know you've been bitten?' she asked both of them.

'Darn mozzies,' said Mrs Quinn. 'They've hardly touched me, but they love Arlo.'

Jamie's voice cut in quickly. 'Did you take any treatments for mosquitoes before you came to Hawaii? Or have you started any since you got here?'

It was a standard and routine question here. The Aedes mosquito were native to Hawaii and could carry a variety of diseases. Not everyone took them seriously, and travellers frequently didn't take any treatments or didn't complete them thoroughly, not understanding how important they were.

Both Arlo and Mrs Quinn shook their heads.

'Have you tried any mosquito avoidance measures?' asked Piper quietly.

'What, come all this way and spend the whole time covered up? Why would anyone do that?' asked Mrs Quinn.

Piper took a breath and continued her assessment. 'Arlo, your skin feels quite cold to touch. I'm just going to recheck your temperature.' She did this quickly. 'Tell me, what else has got worse over the last few days?'

He reached his hands to his abdomen. 'Stomach pain.'

She turned her head to Jamie. 'I could hear some fluid in the chest,' she said calmly, and then pressed her hand against Arlo's ribcage and then withdrew it. His skin blanched, leaving an imprint of her fingers for a few moments.

She mouthed the word 'Dengue' to him. She looked to him for confirmation and he gave a nod. Her stomach flipped in relief. The symptoms were all there, but she would have hated to get her first diagnosis wrong in front of her new supervisor.

'Mrs Quinn, we're going to have admit Arlo for the next few days. It looks like the mosquito bites have resulted in dengue fever for Arlo. Most people have only mild symptoms like Arlo did a few days ago, but unfortunately, some people—around five percent—can go on to develop a more critical phase.'

Jamie stepped forward. 'It's important we monitor Arlo carefully. Sometimes people with dengue can go into organ failure. We're going to take some more bloods, monitor him for any bleeding, get him on some IV fluids and pain relief and watch his breathing and blood pressure.'

Mrs Quinn looked shocked and angry. 'But couldn't you have picked this up days ago? This is your fault this has happened.'

Jamie spoke in a calm and reassuring manner. 'Two days ago, if he'd been diagnosed with dengue, we would have sent you home, told you to monitor him and come back if anything changed. That's exactly what you have done. The disease only progresses in a very small percentage of people.' He moved around the bed next to her. 'And dengue is caused by mosquito bites. The only way to really avoid the disease is to do your best to avoid mosquito bites.'

Piper felt a little shiver as if a breeze had just danced across her skin. Jamie could have handled this woman in so many other ways. Her instant attribution of fault wasn't unusual in patients. Jamie hadn't seen this patient two days ago, but someone had. But he'd just circled in the most unswerving way to ensure the woman knew this disease wasn't the fault of the medics. She'd already heard rumours he was grumpy. It looked like he also took no prisoners when dealing with difficult patients or relatives.

But Mrs Quinn looked confused. 'You mean if we'd taken malaria tablets we'd be fine?'

Piper was trying to make sense of the conversation in her head. She wasn't sure Mrs Quinn was listening, but Jamie seemed completely unpanicked by her. He sat down next to the woman.

'Malaria tablets could have saved you from malaria. But not dengue. Not Zika, and not chikungunya—the other disease caused by mosquito bites. Mosquitoes are dangerous creatures. It's not just about getting a bite that causes a scratch and an itch. It's about all the diseases that they carry, and taking the threat of mosquito bites seriously.' He took a breath, giving the woman a few seconds to take things in. This was the problem with tropical diseases. Often people were blinded by the sun and sea and the idea of a perfect holiday. They frequently ignored the fact there was health advice for the area to which they were travelling. Piper had dealt with ten members of a family back in England who'd travelled on a wonderful South African safari, and all came home with malaria, after ignoring the advice about clothing and mosquito nets and tablets.

Jamie started talking again. 'There is a new vaccine that you could consider for yourself or other family members in future.'

Piper could see her starting to breathe a little easier, and finally start processing what she had been told.

She carried on with her job. She spoke gently to Arlo as she inserted an IV line and wrote up instructions for the next few hours.

'What happens next?' asked Arlo sleepily.

'We'll take you up to the tropical disease ward. Dr Robertson and I will keep reviewing you, and if you get any worse we'll move you to the ICU.'

Arlo blinked, those words getting his attention. 'Why would I need to go to the ICU?'

This was one of those moments for a doctor. No doctor liked to tell a patient that there was the potential they could die from their particular disease or ailment—indeed, that could often cause panic with some patients. Piper would never deliberately lie, but she wouldn't knowingly cause distress either.

'We would only take you to ICU if we thought your condition was getting worse and you needed some extra support. But don't worry, Dr Robertson and I will be keeping a close eye on you.'

Arlo closed his eyes again and Piper hoped she'd done enough to allay some of his fears.

Jamie nodded at Mrs Quinn. She was biting her bottom lip, as if she'd finally realised the risks the family had been taking. 'Do you have any questions for me?' he asked.

She shook her head.

'Is there other family with you?' asked Piper.

She nodded. 'My husband, his brother, my other son and my in-laws.'

Piper handed over some of the paperwork. 'If you can fill in some of the information for Arlo I'd appreciate it. Would you like us to call your relatives, or do you want to do that yourself?'

Mrs Quinn reached for the paperwork and started completing it. She glanced over at Arlo. 'I'll come up to the ward and get him settled, then go and tell my family. When's visiting? It's likely one of us will want to stay with him.'

Piper jumped in, unsure if Jamie would know the rules as yet. 'There's open visiting—you can come any time between eight a.m. and nine p.m.'

Jamie had moved around next to Piper. She caught a whiff of his aftershave. He held out his hand for the electronic tablet and she watched as he ordered a few more tests, mentally making a note to ask him about them later.

They spoke for a few more minutes, and Piper phoned the ward to notify Kiana of the admission. They waited until the hospital team had taken the Quinns upstairs before Jamie turned to her.

'Let's go up and talk in my office.'

What did that mean? Had she done something wrong?

'Sure,' she said, swallowing the lump in her throat. *It's just because he's new*, she thought to herself. But Lenny had never made her feel nervous. Not like this anyhow.

But she'd also never been remotely attracted to Lenny. He was a happily married man. Jamie Robertson was handsome in a rugged kind of way, had an accent that reminded her of a current Hollywood star, but she'd no idea if he was single or not. When his eyes fixed on hers...it was distracting.

As they walked up the stairs he ducked into the first-floor cafeteria and bought them both coffee. She nearly opened her mouth to tell him that she'd brought chocolate mint slices with her, but changed her mind. She didn't need another sugar lecture—even though she'd made sure to cut the pieces smaller this time around.

By the time she reached his office she felt a little jittery. Merry looked up with her all-knowing brown eyes and handed her a packet of cookies from her desk.

'For you both,' Merry added, without even looking at Jamie.

Piper tried not to smile. She wondered if he'd realised yet he was actually in charge around Merry. But truth be told, she wasn't sure Lenny had realised that either.

'Let's go over the cases from this morning, then we'll go and review the two patients you left notes about, then we'll go over a care plan for Arlo.'

She gulped. It was like being a medical student all over again. But under a much smaller microscope.

He seemed to notice her anxiety and said quite clearly, 'I need to understand how much background knowledge you have, in order to decide how much supervision you require. This is just a formality.'

'Didn't Lenny leave you any notes?'

He shook his head. 'Lenny barely had time to say thanks for me agreeing to start at short notice. I imagine he hoped everything would just fall into place.' He watched her carefully with his blue eyes. 'But I also imagine if he had any concerns he would have given me a heads-up.'

She was sure her shoulders just sagged in relief, and she didn't want to be quite so obvious. Of course she'd known Lenny was worried about his wife and twins. Piper had probably been the least important thing on his radar. But she just wasn't sure if he would have passed on any info about her at all—particularly the disastrous relationship that had almost affected her work.

It wasn't exactly a flag she wanted to wave. Having a new boss was like having a clean slate. But the hospital gossip trail didn't seem to forget anything; she was painfully embarrassed that at some stage some of her past would reach Jamie's ears.

He picked up the notes with the orange tabs. 'But first—' he gave a pained smile '—I have a pile of letters to sign off for patients that I am completely unfamiliar with. So we'll do these ones together. You start—give me any additional information that you remember, or concerns that were left over for these patients, and I'll see if I can agree to sign them off or not.'

She frowned. 'Lenny must have thought they were ready if he dictated final letters for Merry?'

Jamie held up his hands. 'But lots of consultants do this, even though we might be waiting for one final blood test or lab result. We're confident everything is fine, dictate the letter, but would normally have a chance to check again before we sign it. I don't want to take things for granted. That's how mistakes get made, and I don't make mistakes.'

She swallowed nervously. The grumpy rumour was proving to be true so far.

'Okay.' She nodded, staring at the pile of orange tabbed notes.

They worked through them methodically. She read, scribbled the odd thing on a Post-it before passing it on to him. Some were just given a clear tick from her and he signed them off. Others had a query, because she did remember the odd test or follow-up. Two he ended up changing completely because the patient had been re-admitted, another because the patient took an irregular discharge and didn't wait for a hospital prescription to finish their meds.

Piper opened the packet of chocolate chip cookies and ate two while they worked. After a while she noticed him taking one himself.

'Arlo's mum,' he said in a low voice.

'Yes?'

'It's important we reinforce to people their own responsibility for their health. She more or less told us that she'd disregarded the advice around mosquitoes. She didn't want her holiday spoiled, but she also wanted to blame the medic who'd seen her son a few days earlier.'

Piper nodded slowly.

Jamie looked at her. 'I don't have time to pander to people. She's made a decision that's affected her son's health. For all we know, it could also have affected her other son's.'

Piper nodded again; his gaze was stern.

'I need to know that you can have these conversations with patients. Things in the US are very different from the UK. Everyone wants to blame someone else. Sue someone.' He took another breath. 'If I thought a member of staff had done something wrong that's different. But when a patient has made a deliberate decision you have to be clear with them. Decisions often carry risks. It's our job to make sure patients and families understand those risks. It's not being unkind, it's being honest, and I expect that from you.'

Piper said the only word she could find at that second. 'Okay.'

She knew he was right. He wasn't being unkind. And she did see that Arlo's mum had been trying to apportion blame. But being that direct would be new to her.

He leaned back and looked out of the window of his office. It almost had a view of the ocean in the distance—you had to squint a little to see it, but it was definitely there.

She was desperate to try and lighten the mood in the office.

'You had time to visit the beach yet?' she asked.

He rubbed the back of his neck. 'Nope, and I'm desperate. I have a date tonight that will hopefully sort things for me though.'

'A date?' It came out much more surprised than she intended it to.

He raised his eyebrows. 'You think I'm incapable of getting a date?'

'No.' She shook her head quickly, feeling the heat rise in her cheeks. 'I just wondered if you were already in a relationship with the doctor I saw you with on Friday.'

He leaned forward. 'Joanne Meadows? She's my best friend. We did our training together at Sheffield. Hawaii is the first time she's been able to find a job in her field and I've been able to find one in mine so we can actually be in the same place at the same time.'

'Oh,' said Piper, letting that information fall into place as she now realised that, theoretically, her boss was single. Interesting.

Her heart did give a little pang though. She'd been right about the connection between them. Best friends. And close enough they'd wanted to work in the same place together. It must be nice to have a friend like that.

'So, she does cardiology?'

'How do you know that?' He looked amused.

'I don't. But the guy she was standing next to when we left the meet and greet was Guy Sanders, the cardiothoracic surgeon. So I suspect she was finding out more about the department.' She gave a shrug and a smile. 'I'm just guessing.'

Her head was guessing more things. First one was that she'd thought her boss was good-looking at first sight. But she'd also seen him with his hand on his friend's back and she'd noticed they looked close. Maybe they were best friends. But what did that mean?

'She is a cardiologist. She's a very good cardiologist. I'm hoping that now she's here she gets a chance to shine and show just how good she is.'

Now, that did sound like a friend. Or at least someone who was protective.

'You think she hasn't had that chance?'

He blinked, as if he hadn't really realised what he'd

just said out loud. 'I think sometimes it can take a while for someone to get their chance. Any of us.'

Those words were a bit heavier. She wondered if he was now meaning himself.

'So, you're going on a date tonight?' She circled back to the previous subject.

He gave a soft laugh and shook his head. 'I'm not going on a romantic date. It's the wrong choice of word really. I've got a meeting arranged with one of the local surf instructors. He's going to drive me around, show me the beaches, tell me about the reefs, the riptides and the best times.'

'But you're from Scotland.'

'You think people don't surf in Scotland? It's got its own best beaches and waves. People visit Scotland to surf, you know.'

She leaned back. 'No, I didn't. It didn't even occur to me.' But a smile was spreading on her face. And it shouldn't. Of course it shouldn't. Because it sounded as if her boss was implying he was single.

But it seemed as if he hadn't noticed the smile. 'I even brought my own boards here to see how they would fare in the Pacific.'

There was a little spark in her brain. 'You brought boards?'

'Yeah. Why?'

She took a deep breath and narrowed her eyes a little at him. 'Tell me you don't have names for your boards.'

He folded his arms across his chest. 'Doesn't everyone?'

She put her head down on the table. 'Oh, no.'

'What does that mean?' She could hear the amusement in his voice.

She looked up through her blonde curls. 'It means I've been here a few more months than you and I've met people—guys—who name their boards.' She shook her head as she lifted it slowly. 'It's not good.'

He narrowed his gaze in a teasing manner. 'You're going to hurt Dick and Dom's feelings.'

There was a second of silence, a flash of recognition, and then she burst out laughing. 'You didn't.'

'Didn't what?'

'Name your boards after TV hosts when we were kids. That's just too funny.' Then she wrinkled her nose. 'No, wait. Just how old exactly are your boards?'

'Not that old. I replace them every now and then. I just don't change the names. Plus—' he shrugged '—no one over here will have heard of Dick or Dom. I think I'm safe.'

She looked at him closely and drummed her fingers on the table for a moment. 'What were your other possibilities?'

'For my boards?'

She smiled. 'Yes.'

He lifted his hands. 'Kevin and Ian. Willie and Phil. Greg and Drew.'

'And who were they?' she asked, bemused.

'Footballers, quiz show hosts, or school mates who all thought they were worthy of being named.'

'I'm kind of glad you stuck with Dick and Dom.'

'So am I,' he agreed. 'Plus, like I said, no one in Hawaii will know who they are.'

'Does this mean that you're the kind of guy who

names his car too? Because I'm reassessing you as a boss right now.'

He held up one finger. 'I won't have a word said against my Jess.'

She put her head in her hands. 'Who on earth is Jess?'

'My refurbished VW Beetle—only sorry I couldn't bring her with me.'

'And who is Jess named after?'

Her stomach curled for a few moments as she realised it could be some kind of teenage ex-girlfriend.

'How can you even ask? The world's most famous TV detective Jessica Fletcher that was on every Sunday afternoon when I visited my gran.'

It took a few seconds longer for the recognition to set in. She pulled a face. 'Might be a little before my time.'

'Don't bet on it. I'm pretty sure there's a satellite channel that plays it all day, every day.'

'Next time I'm sick—' she smiled '—I'll be sure to look it up.'

He glanced at his watch and stood up quickly. 'Come on, let's review these two patients and see how Arlo is doing.'

She was almost caught off-guard by the quick change from relaxed talking to back-to-work.

'Of course,' she said, looking around for more notes, before realising that they would be on the ward.

Merry gave her a wink as they left and Piper handed her the cookies back with thanks. Piper wondered what Merry thought of their new boss, but would never dream of asking. It would be unprofessional. Plus, if Merry decided she didn't like him, then the whole hospital would surely hear about it.

* * *

Jamie's first full day wasn't working out how it should.

He had no problem with how his trainee was shaping up. She'd taken the lead this morning reviewing patients, and had managed most things down in the ER with no problem. Dengue was difficult to diagnose—which was why it probably hadn't been picked up at the first visit. A number of tropical diseases could often be mistaken for each other in the early stages, so he was pleased that Piper had asked the right questions and known the progress of dengue in order to make the right decision.

What wasn't working out how it should, was what had just happened in his office. Most places he'd worked before, he'd been nicknamed Dr Grumpy by others. Even his mother had once remarked on what was called his 'resting bitch face' and habitual demeanour. Jamie had just accepted it, and had probably embraced it even more since the trouble at a previous workplace.

It wasn't that he'd done anything wrong. But he—along with others—had been under suspicion for a while and he'd hated that. Eventually, they'd discovered that a locum doctor had been acquiring some doses of controlled drugs through a variety of methods. But from the moment the spotlight had shone on him and his colleagues he'd been furious. The investigation had cast a cloud over all of their names, and even after being exonerated it still didn't stop the anger and bitterness that remained.

He remembered how people had looked at him. At how, when he'd required pain relief for a patient, he'd been questioned multiple times about why it had to be a controlled drug. So not only had his morals and ethics been questioned, but also his abilities and decision-making as a doctor.

It had taken three months before the guilty party had been found. But even after, Jamie remembered how some staff from other wards had looked at him and his colleagues, and how they'd all been treated. Thirty people being under suspicion in a hospital with eight hundred staff was not easy. And it had taken its toll on them all.

Some had retired, some had left nursing or medicine. Some had had job offers withdrawn during the investigation. And all of it still stayed with Jamie.

His first long-term girlfriend had left him during that investigation. She'd been a firefighter he'd met on a night out, and things had progressed quickly. The investigation had blown up only a month after they'd moved in together, and had ultimately led to their downfall.

Or maybe not ultimately. Because that might have been Jamie. He wasn't good at sharing. He kept things bottled up. And the more Sarah had asked, the grumpier and more frustrated he'd become. He knew the investigation was causing him strain at work, and at home. He'd hated that it had all seemed out of his control. Just saying, 'It wasn't me,' wasn't having any impact. The hospital needed a suspect, and eventually a guilty party. Sarah had left in a fit of fury and frustration that had been entirely justified. The whole episode had impacted on him more than he'd ever really acknowledged.

It was why he tried not to make friends at work any more. Knowing that at any moment, for any reason, it could all be pulled away. He'd leaned on Joanne a lot during that time, and she'd been great. Talking him down, listening to his frustrations and offering him hugs through the phone. She'd never doubted him for a second and had been just as angry as he was at what he was being put through.

But just there, in his office, he'd let part of his guard down without meaning to, and he wasn't entirely sure why.

Piper was easy to be around. She clearly worked hard and wanted to learn. He could see why Lenny hadn't left any notes—because there was nothing to worry about. There were plenty of occasions over the years where he might have left notes about a trainee himself, but for Piper there was no need.

But apart from work, she also seemed to be getting under his skin. Dick and Dom? Jess? Things he would never normally share with anyone at work. Of course Joanne knew. But that was different. That was a long-term friendship. Not someone he'd known for barely five minutes. And when he'd noticed himself leaning across the table towards her, or her to him, he knew he had to draw the meeting to a close.

Of course she was attractive. Those green eyes and blonde curls were hard to miss. But there had to be a line between them. No, there had to be a *wall* between them.

He couldn't afford to give anyone at the hospital reason to talk about him. Not when he'd only just arrived. Hawaii could shape up to be the place he wanted to work for ever. And he could hardly do that if he ruined his reputation as soon as he got here.

So he was going to ignore what was right in front of his eyes. Her clear skin, bright eyes and clothes that matched her personality. The fact she was a good doctor. And the fact she was friendly. Because that was all he could think of.

The big thing he was going to ignore was the way her scent lingered when she left the room, and the way his nose occasionally picked it up in a corridor and then he wondered where she was.

Because being distracted at work was the absolute last thing he needed here. Not when he was trying to earn a reputation as a good and reliable doctor.

CHAPTER THREE

JAMIE FELL INTO a routine that involved five a.m. starts and a call from the Pacific Ocean. The surf instructor had been as good as his word, showed him the best beaches, told him the best times and given him warnings about a few things to look out for.

Jamie had surfed enough places to know all the fundamentals but assistance from a local with years of knowledge was what he always valued most.

He loaded up either Dick or Dom early and hit the beach sometimes when the sun was just rising. It was magnificent. He'd seen a lot of sunrises. But Honolulu, Hawaii, was something to beat. The way the orange and red rays streamed across the blue water was magical. It looked like the start of some movie. And Jamie Robertson was getting to live it every day.

The waves were good first thing in the morning, and after a few weeks he started to recognise fellow surfers. What he liked most was how much of a mixed bunch they were. There were a few surf instructors, a cop, a barrister, a couple of students, a few shop assistants from the beachfront cafés, a teacher and a garbage collector. There was an older woman who'd been an Olympic rower at one point in her life, and her daughter who worked in the local library.

Sometimes he chatted, sometimes he just closed his eyes, sitting astride his board in the middle of the ocean, and other times he just rode the waves as often as possible before he had to head for the hospital.

Now he knew his way around a little better, he'd timed dropping his board back off at the house, picking up a coffee from the local shop, then hitting the showers at work before changing into his clothes and being on the ward for seven-thirty.

Piper generally arrived around the same time he did, carrying a cup with lemon tea. And no, she didn't like the fancy teabags, she preferred old-fashioned black tea with a slice of lemon in it.

Today she was wearing a bright pink shirt and a pair of black trousers with matching pink shoes. Her lipstick matched her shirt even though he tried not to notice. Her wrist had now healed and she no longer needed the support.

He'd only just finished his coffee when he got a page from Maternity Services. He glanced down and gave a nod to Piper. 'Ready for Maternity?'

She gave a look of surprise and then joined him as they walked down the corridor. 'Have they told you what it is?'

He shook his head. 'Could be anything.'

They arrived at Maternity and were introduced to one of the obstetricians, who had concerns over one of his patients.

'Maybe I'm overcautious,' he said. 'But my patient is twelve weeks pregnant, has a history of a rash and bite marks some days ago. She's also had some vague symptoms that she put down to the early stages of pregnancy. Fatigue—'

'Did she have prenatal bloods done?' Jamie broke in.

'She did. But the lab doesn't have them any more.'

Jamie nodded. In some countries prenatal bloods were kept in case any additional tests needed to be run at a later date. But every country was different.

He turned to Piper. 'What're your first thoughts?'

'I need to take a full history,' she said, then pulled a face. 'But I'd also like to know if she's had an ultrasound already that might have shown any other signs.'

They weren't near the patient so she could speak freely. 'If the baby has been infected by Zika virus, it may show up on the ultrasound. There could be brain development issues or microcephaly.'

Jamie gave a nod. He would expect her to know this, but was glad that she could demonstrate it.

The obstetrician spoke. 'We're taking her for a scan now. Would you like to come along? It may be too early to tell, but if it is Zika, I would expect some of the indicators to be present.'

'What does the patient know?' asked Jamie.

'She knows we need to investigate. She raised the concerns about the mosquito bites and rash herself.'

'Can we take a fresh blood sample too? It's the easiest way to confirm if the virus is in her system.'

'Absolutely. Come along and meet her.'

The young woman looked serious. At her early stage of pregnancy she virtually had no bump to speak of, but she was wearing a strappy top so they could already see her rash. He let Piper take the lead.

'Hi, Marie, I'm Piper, one of the specialist doctors for tropical diseases. Do you mind if I take a look at you?'

Marie leaned forward. 'Please do, this rash is everywhere.'

And it was. It had clearly started on her face, but was also on her trunk and limbs—there was a mixture of raised and flat areas that were red and obviously itchy, as Marie kept scratching. Her palms and soles of her feet were also slightly swollen.

'How long ago did you start to feel unwell?' asked Piper.

'Just a few days. It started with a headache and a temperature, and then this...' She held her hands out over the rash on her body.

'Any other symptoms?' asked Piper.

'Some joint pain.' Marie rubbed her elbows. She shook her head. 'This is Zika, isn't it? I've read about it. I've got all the classic signs.' Her hands went to her belly. 'I know it affects pregnancy.'

'It can do,' Jamie broke in. 'And we're going to do a scan of your baby now, to see how things are. Because this looks like a brand-new infection, your baby might not show any obvious signs. But we're going to take some bloods from you too, to see if we can confirm if this is Zika, or something else.'

'If it is?' Her eyes were wide and she looked at them all.

Her obstetrician gave a slow nod. 'If we get confirmation, then we would have to monitor you very carefully during your pregnancy. We would likely scan you every few weeks, keeping a careful eye on your baby's brain development and skull.'

'So my baby will be affected?'

Jamie glanced at the obstetrician, seeing if he wanted him to take the lead here. The man gave the tiniest nod. 'I can't tell you that for sure,' said Jamie. 'You are near the end of your first trimester. There is no good point in a pregnancy to catch Zika virus, but some of your baby's development has already taken place. Zika can affect the placenta and your baby's growth. There is still much brain development to take place, and that's what we have to monitor carefully. Every case is different.' He put a hand on her arm. 'Let's wait for the blood results, and do your scan now.'

The obstetrician made sure Marie was comfortable and then lowered the lights in the room. As Jamie suspected, the ultrasound showed an eleven week and four days foetus that—at that moment—was developmentally normal. They confirmed dates and measured the nuchal fold, noting no abnormalities.

Marie appeared to breathe a sigh of relief. Jamie could see the flicker on Piper's face but she didn't speak up, and they all agreed to meet later, once the blood tests were back.

As they walked back down the corridor he could sense Piper was uneasy. He glanced at his watch and stopped, picking up a nearby phone from the wall and calling up to the ward to see if there were any issues. Once he'd confirmed everything was fine, he left instructions to be paged if he was needed.

'Come on,' he said to Piper, leading her to the main entrance and out of the doors into the bright sunshine.

'Where are we going?'

'Just along the street for some lunch. It takes us away

from the hospital and gives us a chance to talk about the case.'

She gave a nod and followed him down the street to a popular café on the main street.

'Inside or out?' he asked.

The temperature was warm, but the tables were shaded. 'Outside,' she said, and they grabbed a few seats and checked the menu.

The waitress appeared almost immediately, taking their orders of iced tea and a mixed omelette, and crepe with ham and cheese.

As soon as the waitress left, Piper turned to him. 'So, if the blood test is positive, and it likely will be because her symptoms are textbook, we have to be honest about the outcome for her baby.'

He wondered if she realised this was a kind of test, due to what he'd said to her after meeting Arlo and his mother. He'd told her he needed her to be direct. And somehow, he knew she would find this hard.

Jamie nodded. 'And we will be, but let's base things on facts. The truth is, we have no treatment for Zika. Marie is going to spend the next two years potentially in a wait-and-see state of mind. Even if her scans go well and there are no obvious abnormalities of her baby, it could be that he or she will have a developmental delay that won't be apparent until they are older. On the other hand, they could develop the microcephalic skull and facial features. His or her brain development could be badly affected. We just don't know. And we have no reason to scare our patient more than she's already scared herself.'

Piper sat back and sighed as their iced teas were placed

in front of them. The worry lines were deep across her brow. 'Could there be another diagnosis?'

'Of course. But Zika is the most likely right now.'

She shook her head. 'That poor woman. I don't know if could spend the next thirty weeks so worried.'

Jamie agreed. 'It could be a really stressful time for her. What's worse, she could push all that anxiety onto her baby. Which won't help the pregnancy or the baby.'

'So, what's the right answer here?' She threw her hands up in frustration.

She had passion. That was clear. And Jamie liked that. She was concerned about the wellbeing and outcome for a potential patient of theirs. That was good. He could see it in the tiny worry lines across her forehead and around her green eyes. From the way one of her hands was currently squeezing and releasing the white cloth covering their table.

He'd worked with colleagues in the past who really didn't care what happened to their patients long-term. They wanted the flash diagnosis or surgery. The interesting case so they could write a research paper for publication. But Jamie had never been like that. His work had always been about the person and how a diagnosis might impact on them and their family. It looked like Piper might have a similar process. As her supervisor, it was his job to guide her in that direction.

'It's not up to us to find the right answer. It's up to us to give Marie the information she needs, in a way that she and her family can deal with. It could be that we'll spend the next five or six months working alongside her obstetrician, and likely a paediatrician, to keep monitoring this baby.'

She licked her lips as the waiter placed their plates in front of them. 'I didn't get enough of a history,' she said critically. 'I don't even know what potential supports are in place for Marie. Surely it's crucial she has family around to support her at a time like this.'

Jamie took a bite of his crepe. 'There's still plenty of time for that. Think of this as a long-haul project.'

She was clearly interested and her green eyes studied him closely. 'So, if the baby is affected—or even if not—you would still want to be involved with the paediatrician around the outcomes for the baby?'

He took a sip of his iced tea. Delicious. Just the right refreshment for a day like this. The breeze had picked up a little around them, but it was still extremely warm. He smiled at her.

'Of course I would. Zika is lifelong for these children. As a tropical disease consultant, I'd like to know what Zika does to children, teenagers and adults who have to live with the long-term effects. It gives me a better understanding of the disease, and all the impacts it has. It means if I'm faced with this situation ten years down the line, I have better knowledge to answer questions a mum like Marie might have.'

She put down her fork. 'I can't imagine what the next thirty weeks might be like for her. Imagine, every time you go for a scan, holding your breath to see if the sonographer might think the skull size isn't quite right, or there're signs of calcifications or abnormalities of the brain.'

He got what she was saying, but now he was beginning to wonder if she was too emotionally invested here.

'But you have to take a step back,' he said carefully.

'Because we are here as Marie's doctors, as part of her team.'

Her head lifted sharply. 'What's that supposed to mean?'

'It means that I want you to have empathy for our patients, but to also respect their decisions.'

'And you think I don't?'

He took a careful breath. 'I need you not to get too emotionally involved. I need to know that your own feelings and compassion won't get in the way of being a doctor to them.'

She opened her mouth to speak again, but stopped and set down her knife and fork. 'You want me to pretend that I'm not going to think about poor Marie and her baby all night?'

His heart gave a little pang for her. He reached over and touched her hand. 'I'm your supervisor. I've got to look out for you. If you get too emotionally involved with our patients, you'll burn out. They need your expertise.' He let his shoulders give a small shrug. 'They need your compassion. But they also need your professionalism. And I need you to be a fellow tropical disease consultant for the next thirty years, not for the next five.'

Her brow wrinkled and he could tell a million thoughts were spinning through her head. She took a sip of her iced tea and sat deep in thought.

He liked that she was taking the time to consider things. He'd seen too many colleagues crash and burn because the job consumed every part of them. It was difficult to find the balance, and he knew that himself.

She finally gave a huge sigh and nodded. 'I understand

what you're saying.' She gave him a half-smile. 'But I will still think about Marie all night.'

'Okay,' he said. 'Can't stop your brain from functioning.' He said it in a light tone, not wanting this conversation to become confrontational or for her to think he was criticising. He really was concerned about her.

A little question appeared in his brain. Would he be like this for any colleague? He hoped he would. But there was something about Piper. Was he being protective because she was a fellow Brit? Or was it just because she was in his specialty? He'd like to think so. But something deep inside told him this was a little more personal.

'Have you got any kids?'

The question seemed out of the blue and it took him a moment to find the words to answer. 'What? No, not me. Not yet anyway.'

She was staring straight at him. He supposed it might be a natural question after what they'd just discussed, but he hadn't expected something so personal.

'You haven't mentioned any, so I'm assuming you don't either?' Was he overstepping?

She shook her head. 'Hopefully on the horizon in the future,' she said, taking another bite of her omelette. 'Of course—' she gave a nod '—after I've qualified as a consultant, after I've finally found a job that I want to stay in, once I've bought a house, and once I've found a man I want to spend the rest of my life with.' She said the last one with a smile.

He raised his eyebrows. 'Not much to do then. All in a day's work.'

She waved her hand. 'Easy.'

She was single. She was definitely single. Even though

he'd already got that impression, now he knew. His mind was going places it certainly shouldn't.

'What about you? Do you have the same plans, minus the get to the consultant stage and find a job stage?'

She was still smiling at him and made it sound like the most natural question in the world, instead of an all-out way to ask him if he had another half.

Or maybe it was only him that thought like that.

'Lenny's house is pretty good,' he admitted. 'It's close to one of the beaches I can surf at, seems to be in a nice neighbourhood and walking distance to a few shops, cafés and bars. I think I'd struggle to find anything nearly as good.'

She was still watching him, and he was conscious he hadn't answered all of her question. 'As for a person to spend the rest of my life with—' he laughed '—give me a chance. I've just arrived. I barely know anyone.'

'You've worked lots of places—never met anyone you thought of inviting along?'

'Are you always this nosy?'

She was completely unperturbed by his response. 'Absolutely.'

That was it. The sparkle in those green eyes. Could these moments of attraction be a two-way street?

'Well, no.' He paused and tried not to smile right back at her. 'Not yet anyhow.'

Her gaze narrowed a little. 'Definitely not your friend Joanne?'

He felt a little stung but answered easily. 'Definitely not my friend Joanne.' He picked up his fork. 'However, anyone potentially being considered for the position will need to get her approval.' He stabbed at his crepe.

Her frown relaxed a tiny bit as a gleam of amusement appeared in her eyes. 'You don't think that's taking things too far?'

He shook his head as he quickly ate a small piece of ham and cheese crepe. 'Not at all. She has good judgement. And she's like a sister to me. I'd expect anyone I was seeing to get along with Joanne as if she were my actual sister.'

Piper leaned her head on her hand. 'You could be setting anyone up for automatic failure!'

He gave a soft shrug. 'Hope not. But I expect to know anyone that Joanne decides to date too.' He raised one eyebrow and gave a rueful smile. 'And I'd *better* like them.'

'You haven't heard the rumours then?'

His body gave a little jerk. 'What rumours?'

It must have been his response because Piper automatically held up her hands. 'Hey, just locker room wishy-washying.'

He couldn't hide the smile. 'You and I are probably the only people on this island that would use that expression.' Then he looked a little more curious. 'So, what is the rumour?'

Piper sat back a little and took a final sip of her iced tea. 'Well,' she said, setting her glass down, 'it looks like your friend Joanne might be getting friendly with her colleague Guy.'

'Guy Sanders, the cardiothoracic surgeon?'

Piper shrugged. 'It's just a rumour. People say they've noticed sparks between them, and they seem to be getting along well.'

Jamie felt himself acting instinctively and jumping to

his friend's defence. 'Maybe they do just get on well.' He knew that hospital rumours could be damaging on occasion. Plus, surely Joanne might have said something if there were sparks between her and her boss?

And as soon as he had that thought, his stomach gave an uncomfortable twist. Had he told Joanne that Piper was invading his thoughts more than she should? Of course he hadn't. He hadn't been able to work out how he felt himself, so he wasn't likely to share. And neither was Joanne. He knew her. She'd tell him when she was sure.

'Rumours can be harmful,' he said more seriously than he intended. 'Here's hoping they stay in the locker room.'

He stood up quickly and moved to settle the bill. If he'd just made Piper uncomfortable she didn't say anything but appeared at his side and opened her purse. He shook his head. 'It's on me.'

They walked back along the pavement to the hospital. A few people glanced at them and Jamie noticed—just because of Piper's latest comment. Could people also be looking at them and surmising something?

That made him uncomfortable. Because he knew how quickly inappropriate gossip could spread in a hospital. He consciously took a step away from Piper as they walked down the corridor. If she noticed she didn't say anything, and by the time they'd made their way back to their own department he was feeling like a fool.

They walked back onto the ward and one of the nurses approached. 'Dr Leiu asked if you could give him a quick call.'

Dr Leiu worked on Hawaii, nicknamed the 'Big Island', which was ironic since Oahu—where he was based—served a much larger population. Since he'd got here, he'd learned that they often cross-covered for each other as their area of medicine tended to have fewer specialists than others. Jamie had learned the art of video consultations and of peering at a screen and asking to see a variety of rashes in different lights.

Jamie gave a nod to Piper and she followed him to his office as they connected with Dr Leiu. Frank Leiu was local to the islands but had spent a few years at the CDC in Atlanta, gaining more experience in tropical medicines, then had a spell in Samoa. Jamie was already confident in his colleague and was sure he had plenty to learn from him.

'Hi, Jamie,' came the warm accent. Then, after a moment of recognition, 'Hi, Piper.'

She gave a smile as she took the seat next to Jamie.

'Hi, Frank,' said Jamie. 'What have you got?'

'I've sent you a set of results.'

Jamie opened his emails and went to check, blinking before sitting back up. 'And where did these come from?'

Frank had a resigned look on his face. 'It's from a cruise liner that's just left Hawaii and is on its way to dock in Honolulu.'

Jamie put his head in his hands. 'Norovirus—perfect. Do you have any idea how many are affected?'

Frank pulled a face, and Jamie could tell what was coming. 'When I saw them yesterday, it was just one family and one other individual. The family are currently inpatients on IV fluids.'

'The other individual got back on the boat, didn't they?' said Jamie. This wasn't so uncommon. Many holidaymakers had paid huge amounts for their cruise holidays and didn't want a bit of sickness or diarrhoea stopping their fun.

'He did,' said Frank. 'At least we think he did. We don't even have irregular discharge papers for him. The gentleman just disappeared.'

Jamie rolled his eyes. 'If only the average person knew just how extremely infectious it is.' He leaned back in his chair. 'Okay, thanks, Frank. I'll let you know if we need assistance at our end. Send me the missing patient's details.'

They ended the call and Jamie pointed at the computer. 'Check out the vessel sanitation programme online. You'll find definitions and instructions for an outbreak. In the meantime, I'll contact the ship's doctor to put him in the picture.'

They spent the next hour making arrangements around whether the cruise ship would be safe to dock. The missing patient was a staff member of the cruise ship, and clearly hadn't wanted to be left behind. Thankfully, he didn't work in the kitchen and hadn't reported back on duty, and had instead stayed in his cabin. But since he was still actively unwell, he would remain infectious.

Piper looked out of the window. 'I've never cruised. But often wanted to. I've always thought how wonderful and luxurious it looks. A different port every day, chilling by the pool, admiring the views and drinking cocktails.' She gave a sigh and a shudder.

Jamie stood alongside her and gave her a sideways glance. 'And now you're thinking that it's just a giant tin can and petri dish?'

She burst out laughing and put her hands to her face. 'Yes!'

'We'll be meeting the cruise ship as it docks at seven

a.m. tomorrow morning. We'll meet with the captain and ship's doctor before any decision is made about disembarkation of the passengers.'

'People might hate us,' said Piper, actually looking a bit worried.

He nodded. 'I don't think it will come to that. But we will look at the evidence we have, we'll find out how many more have symptoms, and it's likely we'll be asking the ship to have a deep clean. The cruise company are already organising for that, and it's likely the ship will have to stay docked for another day.'

'Yip,' she said, nodding, 'we're going to win the popularity contest.'

'Can you call the labs? It's likely we'll be presented with some samples by the ship's doctor tomorrow that we'll need tested quickly. They need to be ready to process as it's usually a twenty-four-hour turnaround.'

'Sure,' she said, turning around and picking up the phone again.

Jamie gave a nod of appreciation. Whilst he'd been worried about her earlier today, now Piper had just jumped into doctor mode easily. Tomorrow could be a nightmare day, or it could be relatively straightforward. It would all be based on the numbers involved.

Part of him was glad this had happened—not for the people on the cruise ship, but definitely for himself as her supervisor. It would give him a chance to see how quickly she could learn new processes and put them into practice, recognising what her role was in the big picture.

The Hawaiian Islands could be at risk from a number of disasters. Most people only considered the environmental kind. Hurricanes, volcanoes, wildfires, earthquakes, severe storms and floodings. But there were also these kinds of human disasters. This cruise ship carried just over seven hundred passengers and three hundred crew. Potentially one thousand people who could be affected by this debilitating infectious disease.

He gave her a final nod. 'I'm going to go and do a final check on our ward today. Read as much as you can about the procedures and I'll meet you here tomorrow at six. That will give us a chance to go over things before we meet the captain and ship's doctor. Are you okay with that?'

Those green eyes fixed on his. There was something about them. A sense of determination and a steely nerve. He liked it.

She swept a strand of blonde hair away from her eyes and behind her ear. 'Perfect.' Then she gave him a half-smile. 'Now, go away and let me study.'

CHAPTER FOUR

PIPER WAS A tiny bit scared but determined not to show it. It wasn't that the details of the outbreak prevention and response plan were complicated. It was everything else that seemed complicated.

What left her wondering most was both Jamie and Frank's response yesterday. They'd both just seemed to accept the situation and move forward. Calm. No panic. All the while it had felt as if she had a trapped bird in her chest scrabbling to get out. Would she ever manage to feel like they did? She wasn't entirely sure. Maybe she'd picked the wrong specialty after all.

It had led to hours of her searching for just how many outbreaks there were on cruise ships every year and left her reeling at the possibilities.

And in amongst all that was the conversation and lunch that had taken place between herself and Jamie. She'd been surprised when he'd suggested lunch away from the hospital, then later felt a little insulted that he was clearly checking to see if she understood what her role was here.

In other circumstances she might have got up and walked away. But Jamie had a style about him. A sense of burden that clearly sat on his shoulders for some unknown reason. She had no idea why. He made the odd comment that made her suspect something might have happened in the past, but since the only connection to that past that she knew of was through Joanne Meadows, that really didn't help at all.

His reaction to the apparent rumour about Joanne had been understated, and it seemed as if he might have wanted to ask more—but since she didn't know any more, that wouldn't have been useful. It did make her wonder about the friendship. Was it really possible for a guy and girl to be best friends with no underlying romantic interest from either one? She struggled to think of anyone she knew who was in a similar position, but there was just no one.

And it bothered her. Much more than it should. Because she liked Jamie Robertson, even if he was a bit grumpy. Yesterday, as they'd sat together at the café, she'd felt comfortable. No, more than that. She'd been interested in finding out more about him. She enjoyed being in his company.

His accent was to die for. If she closed her eyes she could see him as a past Highlander, part of a Scottish clan, or in some Hollywood film saving a president or king from terrorists or aliens. Sometimes her imagination took her to places that were entirely inappropriate for a colleague.

But...it seemed she'd kind of established there was no other half. And she liked that. It made her feel free to notice just how handsome he was. It left her able to let her eyes linger for longer on his muscular forearms if he was wearing his scrubs. To notice the little lines at the corners of his eyes, or to wonder if his teeth were naturally that straight and white.

She gave herself a shake. This was dangerous territory. It could even end up being embarrassing. There was every chance in the world that Jamie Robertson wasn't the slightest bit interested in her, and all these thoughts could just be ridiculous.

Plus, she'd already had one embarrassing incident here. And for a few weeks she'd been the talk of the place. She'd met a guy who was a locum—who'd apparently worked at the hospital a few times—and dated him for a few weeks. He'd been anxious to keep things quiet at first and she'd accepted that, ignoring all the other red flags that were raised. It had felt nice to have a connection. It had been great to be part of something. She hadn't worried too much that he didn't want their relationship made public—particularly when he told her he'd had a nasty breakup at work before and wanted them both to be sure about their relationship before it was made known.

It had all been lies, of course, and hindsight was a wonderful thing. When they'd gone on a date to a popular restaurant it turned out one of the hospital departments was having a night out there too, and there had been lots of slightly disapproving glances. Piper had no idea why. Until Lenny had quietly had a word in her ear the next day and let her know that her date was actually married with two kids. Piper was horrified. The guy had certainly never mentioned a wife or children to her—but then again, she hadn't told anyone about their relationship. So, no one could have warned her. It hadn't stopped the glances for the next couple of months, and she'd been self-conscious even having any kind of conversation with anyone else who was married, in case the staff thought she was flirting.

It was clear that people within the hospital didn't realise how deep the hurt went. And it had made her question herself. Was she really so desperate for a connection—to find someone for herself—that she might overlook things that other people would have noticed? Maybe there had been telltale signs that she'd missed—all because she just wanted to find a connection for herself that she could trust.

It was hard being that person. It was awful that colleagues might think her desperate. She'd cried for a week, trying to ground herself again, telling herself the rejection she felt was natural and not deliberately personal. She hated that he might have picked up on her vulnerability, and had been determined not to willingly expose that part of herself again.

Dating anyone else work-related was probably not a great idea—particularly someone who was her boss. But she didn't want to rule it out altogether.

This morning had been precise and illuminating. They'd met at the hospital, checked the status of all beds, run over the plans, grabbed a coffee, arranged to meet at the dock.

As she climbed out of her car she could see the luxury liner was already in place. Instead of the usual gangway that the passengers would normally use to disembark, a much smaller ramp was in place.

As she headed towards it she could see Jamie was already waiting. They each had a bag with protective clothing which they both donned before entering the ship. The meeting with the captain and ship's doctor was short and to the point. 'I've potentially twenty passengers for assessment for hospital admission. The ship's infirmary is full and we are using an additional five cabins. I also have another twenty showing symptoms.'

'Staff or crew?'

Jamie turned, a slightly amused expression on his face at her question.

'Only two crew members at the moment,' replied the doctor. 'The one who came back on board is still having symptoms, but isn't in a state to require admission, and his roommate is now infected too. I've set up a makeshift quarantine for them meantime.'

'Would you like assistance assessing the patients for admission?'

He nodded. 'Much appreciated. I've also collected some samples for testing.'

'Let me check they're labelled the way they require to be for the local lab, and I'll arrange transport for them,' said Jamie. 'We're looking at a twenty-four-hour turnaround.'

The captain looked annoyed. 'Twenty-four hours?'

'It's the quickest time scale possible.' Jamie pointed behind him. 'Your cruise company has arranged a deep clean, as per international regulations. Let's get that started. No one disembarks until we've assessed the situation.'

For a moment, Piper wondered if the captain might argue. But the ship's doctor gave him a nod, and she and Jamie finished donning all their protective equipment and went on board.

Several of the affected patients were elderly and had already been commenced on IV fluids. Norovirus could be very debilitating for the elderly, and could cause dehydration and confusion. Piper started another few IVs and could see Jamie do the same. They started a regular dialogue with the physicians back at Honolulu General Medical Center, arranging transport for those that needed to be hospitalised.

Piper moved onto a young baby, who was very lethargic and clearly unwell. She listened to her heart and lungs, took a history and checked her skin. After a few moments, she walked over to where Jamie was finishing with another patient.

'I'm really worried about this baby,' she whispered. 'I need to take some bloods and get a cannula into her for some IV fluids. Can I have the specialist bag, please?'

Jamie frowned. 'Have you done many paediatric lines?'

She gave him a casual glance. Did he think she was not capable? 'I've done a few. I mean, I'm not a paediatrician but I've always managed.'

'Do you mind if I do it?' he asked straight out—no excuse or niceties.

She looked back over to the baby and nodded immediately. The baby was the priority here. Not how she felt about things.

'Perfect,' he said. He crossed the room in a few strides and positioned a light above the baby's arm, angling things so it would be easier to pick out the veins.

The mother was shaking at this point and Piper asked quietly, 'Would you like me to hold Amy? I know it can be hard to watch something like this.'

The mother blinked and nodded, handing her baby over to Piper, who cuddled the baby in and turned one little arm so Jamie would have easier access.

To her amazement, Jamie knelt down and started singing as he rubbed the little arm to try and encourage the veins to show. It was difficult. This little one was already dehydrated.

She held her steady. Jamie kept singing in a low, melodic voice, getting Piper to reposition the baby so he could look at both arms. Finally, once he was confident, he inserted the cannula, first draining a small amount of blood required for sampling and then fastening the line to the IV to start some fluids into her small body.

It was the first time that she'd ever seen Jamie with a child. And he was a natural. His focus was clear, and his whole attention was on the baby. It made her stomach a bit wobbly. Even though she should probably be annoyed, she knew inside that he'd probably got that vein more quickly and easily than she would have. There was no shame, he was more experienced and that was fine.

'Good call,' he said in a whisper. 'This little one needs to be admitted and monitored closely.'

Great. Her stomach gave another wobble. Any more and it would be like jelly.

She gave a nod and disappeared to talk to the hospital paediatricians so they were ready to receive this baby, and another three-year-old who also had norovirus.

Between herself, Jamie and the ship's doctor, they ended up admitting seventeen of the passengers to Honolulu General Medical Center. The numbers were lower than expected. They didn't need a mass casualty plan for the hospital and that was a relief.

The cleaning crew—all suitably protected—proceeded with the deep clean of the entire ship. There were a large number of them, all needed to ensure the correct procedures were followed across such a large area, and Piper had some thoughts about adding additional footfall to an already infected area.

The majority of passengers and crew were only a little annoyed by the disruption. The captain had made an announcement to keep them informed. By the time all the patients were assessed, they sat down for a recap.

A few patients were still causing some concerns. The question was whether to wait or admit them. No one wanted to be offloaded during their holiday, but it was difficult to monitor patients safely on a cruise ship—particularly when there could be other incidents at any moment which would take up the staff's time.

They agreed to wait another six hours and reassess some of the patients then. In the meantime, Piper and Jamie headed back to the hospital.

First thing Piper did was head to the staff showers. Even though she'd worn protective clothing, norovirus was such a tricky thing and she wanted to be sure every inch of her was scrubbed and there was no chance she was bringing it back to the hospital.

A ward area had been screened off to isolate the adult patients, with the few paediatric cases held in a separate area.

Jamie scanned all the charts and made a few decisions. 'Mr Imbago—his dehydration and general condition look as if he's going into heart failure. I'm going to call Joanne for a consult. Mrs Underwood has vascular issues in her legs. I'm calling them for a consult since she appears to have less circulating volume, putting her extremities at risk.'

Piper held up another chart. It was from a teenager.

'Tyler Miller definitely has norovirus, but I think he might have mono too.'

Jamie raised his eyebrows and looked at her in surprise. 'Okay.' He took the chart. 'Not entirely surprising for a teenager. What's made you go down that road?'

She pointed at a few elements on the chart. 'Mainly his history. He wasn't feeling well prior to the cruise. His symptoms fit with mono, and if that's underlying it could contribute to why he's been so poorly with the norovirus. His body is fighting two things.'

Jamie read over the notes. 'You could be right. Let's send him for some further testing. Can we check him over again?'

Piper gave him a nod. She didn't care that they had to put protective clothing on again. When there was a norovirus outbreak in a hospital, staff could be in and out of protective clothing all day, it was part and parcel of the job.

'Tyler,' said Jamie as they moved to his bed. He was on his own which was unusual for a teenager, but his mother was back on the ship with his younger sister and his father had also been admitted to the Honolulu General Medical Center with norovirus.

Jamie examined Tyler and asked Piper to take some notes. 'Swollen lymph glands, potentially enlarged spleen, and a rash on his abdomen and back.'

He looked over at one of the nursing staff. 'Can I get a temperature and a blood pressure check, please?'

Tyler was lying back against his pillows looking exhausted. His chart noted he was vomiting continuously and his IV fluids had already been increased.

Jamie came and stood at the bottom of the bed and

spoke in a low voice. 'I think you're right about the mono, but I also think there's something else going on.'

'I've already ordered the monospot test and EBV antibody test. Is there something else you would like?'

'A throat culture to check for strep and a full blood count, please.'

The nurse appeared back, bringing a cardiac monitor with her. As she connected the heart monitor, Tyler gave a shudder.

Jamie turned to Piper. 'Can you look for his urea and electrolyte levels, please?' It wasn't the words, it was the tone and urgency.

She called for one of the phlebotomists to come and take bloods and he came in, taking the samples in only a few minutes before rushing them to the lab.

Piper felt a little confused but didn't want to admit it. She moved over closer to Jamie, her arm brushing against his gown's sleeve. 'What is it?'

Jamie's eyes were fixed on the monitor, watching the higher than normal heart rate. The nurse met Jamie's gaze. 'Blood pressure eighty over fifty. Temperature thirty-nine, five.'

'Sepsis,' said Jamie, his voice practically a whisper. 'The blood pressure and temperature fit. This poor kid is in the wars right now.'

He turned his head to the nurse. 'Contact the ICU. See who is on call today and ask them if there is a bed available.'

Piper was taking everything in. 'Norovirus, mono, and now sepsis?'

Jamie nodded and she could see just how worried he

was. 'Which parent would you like me to speak to? Tyler's mother or father?'

'I think his mother and sibling should get off the boat. Tyler won't be well enough to re-embark, and we have no idea how the sepsis will progress.'

Piper gave a nod and went to make the call. Her stomach was churning. Sepsis could kill. It could be treated, and Jamie had picked things up early, but sometimes when the body was fighting infection there was a chance that all the organs could just shut down. And now that they realised Tyler was fighting more than one thing it was important he was treated quickly.

It took a while to get connected to the ship's officer, and then for them to find Tyler's mother. Around fifteen minutes later, she finally got to speak to her. She explained how things had taken a turn, and that it would be best if she could come to the hospital with her daughter.

The woman was very upset. She started to panic, fussing about their luggage and how long it would take to pack up the cabin. Fortunately, the ship's purser was available to take over the call and assured Piper that they would make those arrangements, plus transport to the hospital and a room at the nearby hotel. The purser was a miracle-worker and passed Piper back to Tyler's mother, where she had to explain everything all over again.

As she'd moved to the office she'd taken off her gloves and disposed of them. She could feel her heart beating in her chest as she explained things in the clearest language that she could, her fingers drumming on the desk. All the time she was remembering what Jamie had told her about being honest with a relative, while ensuring she still remained empathetic.

A warm hand closed over hers, enclosing her fingers and settling her. She took a deep breath and looked up in surprise. Jamie was right at her shoulder. She could feel him there, even though they were both still wearing their long-sleeved gowns. He'd taken his gloves off too, and the warmth from the palm of his hand sent a little buzz up her arm.

She met his gaze.

'Are you okay?' he mouthed.

She nodded, her mouth instantly dry. Was this the closest they'd ever been? It felt like it. She could see every single one of his eyelashes, a few tiny freckles around his eyes and all the different shades of blue in his irises.

She tried to keep her voice steady even though she could hear the tremor as she kept talking to Tyler's mother, nodding even though the woman couldn't see her. 'Of course we'll be waiting for you when you get here.'

She glanced at Jamie, her eyes widening in question, and he nodded. Piper took a breath and ended the call.

She hadn't moved her hand and neither had he.

Part of her was annoyed. She'd vowed not to let anyone see her vulnerability. But Jamie could clearly see through the mask she kept in place.

'I just came to see if you were okay,' he said. 'I know that was a difficult call to make.'

She licked her lips and nodded, blinking back tears. 'She's really upset and wasn't really taking in what I was telling her. I think we'll need to explain everything to her again.'

Jamie gave the tiniest nod. 'The intensivist is here. He's reviewing Tyler right now. How soon do you think she will be here?'

Neither of them had moved their hand. There was comfort here. She could feel it. A connection. And although she'd been thinking about Jamie as attractive, and she'd admired how he looked in his scrubs, this was something else.

After her disastrous secret romance she'd steered clear of everyone else. She'd been here for six months. And all of a sudden it struck her how lonely she was.

And this? A simple hand on hers was making her crave an even deeper connection.

She took another breath and gave him a smile. 'Thanks for checking on me.'

It was almost as if he hadn't realised what he had done and he glanced down at their hands and pulled his back. She instantly felt the space in the air around her—and didn't like it.

It almost made her laugh out loud. This was ridiculous. They were in a serious situation. They had patients to see and then a cruise ship to review again. Any personal thoughts or feelings right now were inappropriate and ridiculous.

But that was easy to say. Turning off her thoughts and feelings was much harder than she could have imagined.

'Come and see the intensivist,' he said. 'He'll be in charge of Tyler's care while he's in the intensive care unit. We'll check in daily.'

She gave a nod. Jamie had turned away. It was as if the moment hadn't happened and he'd gone back to doctor mode. For the patients that was good. Just not for her.

Jamie was trying to stay focused and keep things on track. But certain parts of his brain, and his body, were in other places. His touch hadn't meant anything. At least, not initially. He'd only meant to offer some support and comfort with a call that he knew would be difficult. But as soon as his hand had touched hers, he hadn't wanted to move it.

Her skin was as soft as he'd imagined. There had been a rose-tinged scent in the air. Since they were both enclosed in disposable gowns he'd known it hadn't come from there—but perhaps from her hair, her clothes or her skin.

For whatever reason, it had made him stop in time. He must truly be losing his mind as he could picture himself in that kid's cartoon movie where the snake hypnotised those around him. That was how he felt, even though no one else would ever see the connection.

He imagined trying to explain this to Joanne, and just how hard she would laugh at him. She'd likely throw the nearest cushion at his head.

He had to keep putting things into place in his brain. He couldn't act on an attraction to someone he was training—even though they were both adults. His experience of conflict at work had stung. He didn't want to go down the road of forming friendships and attachments with those at work, when his past experience meant that could all be blown up and destroyed through no fault of his own.

Even though the drug investigation and the failure of his first serious relationship had gone hand in hand, the failure of his second long-term relationship had been entirely his own fault. He could make a connection to a woman fairly quickly. Both of his former long-term girlfriends had been nice people. There had been no hidden agendas except his own. While he could connect quickly with someone, he couldn't maintain a lasting relationship. The hospital investigation had damaged him—made him more closed-off, less likely to trust. He was naturally grumpy, and usually saw the glass half-empty. He knew it didn't help things. But when Jill, his second long-term girlfriend, had challenged his behaviour and the fact he couldn't open up to her, it had made him all the more defensive. She'd ultimately left too, and now he'd heard she was happily married with a little boy.

So, even though he could feel the pull of attraction to Piper, what was the point? He'd proved twice he couldn't see relationships through. He couldn't open up. He couldn't properly share how he felt about things. Why try again?

A nurse appeared at the door and gave them both a nod. 'The intensivist wants to move Tyler straight away.'

Jamie's stomach clenched. He must have deteriorated even further.

Both of them hurried along the corridor. The intensivist had just finished listening to Tyler's heart and lungs. He looked up. 'I'll take him straight along. I agree, this is definitely sepsis and I want to try and delay its progress as much as possible.'

'Is there anything we can do to assist?'

He shook his head. 'I'll check in with you a few times a day in case his two other diagnoses further complicate things.' He pointed to the tablet next to him. 'You've run all the tests I need. I'll just wait for the results and take it from there.'

The staff moved quickly, getting Tyler ready for the

move and calling some others to help wheel all the equipment along to ICU.

By the time they came back, both Jamie and Piper pulled off their disposable gowns and caps.

'It's so hot wearing all this,' breathed Piper as her hair fell around her shoulders. Her face was flushed and Jamie was sure that his own must mimic hers.

Another nurse appeared. 'Tyler's mom is making her way up here. I thought you might want to speak to her first, rather than send her straight along to ICU.'

Jamie reached over and touched Piper's arm. 'Let me do this.'

She shook her head. 'I'm perfectly capable.'

'I know you are, but you made the phone call, let me do the face-to-face part. Then we can walk her along to ICU and she can speak to the intensivist.'

Piper frowned. 'I feel as if you don't think I can do this.'

'I think that telling a mother there could be a potential that her son's life is in danger isn't a job that either of us want.'

Piper sat down for a minute and took a breath.

'You know how serious sepsis can be,' he said in a low voice.

'I do,' she said. 'But he's a young, fit and healthy guy. If anyone stands a chance, it's got to be Tyler.'

'I agree.' He licked his lips and considered his words carefully. 'But his body has already likely been weakened over the last few months with his undiagnosed mononucleosis. Now he has norovirus on top of that. A healthy teenager could get over both, but still be unwell for some time. But both, alongside sepsis? It's a big deal.'

Piper closed her eyes for a second. He wanted to reach out and hug her, but he knew that wasn't appropriate. He watched as she took some long, slow breaths. Her eyes opened. She looked determined. 'To be the best doctor I can be, I can't be afraid of the hard conversations,' she said.

'I agree.'

'Then we should do this together. Tyler's mum deserves a team that can answer her questions, and give her empathy for the situation that she's in. We should also talk to Indira in HR, and ask if she can put some patient support in place for the next few days.'

'She can do that?'

Piper nodded. 'In special circumstances, where family members are in a different country and might be unsupported, she can put things in place.'

'Indira? I thought she was a bit scary, to be honest. What kind of things?'

'She could probably arrange some childcare for Tyler's little sister. A child won't be allowed in ICU and I imagine that the mum won't know anyone to take care of her.'

Jamie gave a nod. 'That's a great idea. I had no idea Indira could arrange things like that.'

Piper tapped the side of her nose. 'She likes to keep things like this low-key.' Then she gave him a little wink. 'And I'd better ask her.'

Jamie stood up and rolled his shoulders. 'I knew she didn't like me.'

'I didn't say that.' Piper walked towards the door. 'I think she just couldn't understand everything you said. I'll be back in two minutes.'

By the time Piper came back, Jamie had already escorted Tyler's mother into one of the offices. The poor woman was fraught. Her hair was dishevelled, her clothes crumpled and she had a bag in one hand with a variety of things poking out of it. Her six-year-old daughter was just as bewildered-looking.

Piper slipped into the room and put a hand on Tyler's mother's shoulder. 'We understand that things are difficult today. I've arranged for some childcare within the hospital, so you have time to see both your husband and your son. Is that okay with you?'

There was something about watching Piper with relatives and patients. There was a genuine warmth that seemed to just glow from her.

Indira came inside with one of the staff from the paediatric ward and introductions were made. Tyler's sister seemed happy to go and watch the promised movies and eat the food that was on offer. And once Tyler's mother had some time to make herself happy with the arrangements she agreed.

Jamie knew that by taking Tyler's sister, and the stress of her care, out of the equation it would give his mother some time to think. He gave Piper a nod and she sat down next to Tyler's mother as Jamie started to explain the circumstances to her.

It took some time. She was tired, worried about both her husband and son. She revealed that her husband had a heart condition and hadn't been able to take his medications properly while he had norovirus. He'd been too unwell to give his proper history but, while they were in the office, Jamie phoned Joanne, giving her all the details she needed and asking her to review Mr Miller's condition with a particular slant on his cardiac condition.

Piper took Mrs Miller's hand in hers as they explained sepsis and what it meant for Tyler. They tried to prepare her for how he might look in the intensive care unit, with the possibility of him being ventilated at some stage.

Then, before they took her along, Piper made her some tea and produced a storage tin filled with chocolate traybakes. She seemed to know that the woman hadn't had any time to look after herself for the last day or so, and wanted her to be ready for ICU.

The aroma from the storage tin drifted towards Jamie and his stomach gave an inappropriate groan. He gave a half-smile. 'If you tell me that it's good I might try some later.'

Mrs Miller gave the first smile he'd seen from her. She held out the napkin Piper had given her. 'If I ask for some more to take with me, will that tell you enough?'

He gave her a smile and they both walked her along to ICU, waiting with her while she spoke with the intensivist, and staying as she broke down a little while first seeing Tyler.

The best thing they could do right now was assure her that Tyler was in the right place and would have the best possible care. A further message had come through from the ship's purser that they'd contacted other relatives, who would be coming to support the family.

Mrs Miller shook her head. 'This was supposed to be a quick family celebration before my husband starts a new job. I never thought things would turn out like this.'

Piper gave her hand a squeeze. 'We'll check in on you and Tyler.'

Mrs Miller gave a grateful nod as they left the ICU and made their way back down the corridor.

'Ready to get gowned up again and head back to the ship?' Piper asked.

Jamie gave a nod. 'Even though I'm already too hot and sticky, we need to check on those last few patients. I suspect we might need to admit another two of the older patients.'

Piper agreed. 'I know the two you mean. I just want to run and check on our baby before we head back to the ship. Will I meet you there?'

'Sure,' he said, admiring her constant enthusiasm. She wasn't showing any signs of tiredness or strain. It had already been a long day, both physically and emotionally, and his shoulders were aching.

As Piper dashed down the corridor Jamie's stomach growled again. His feet automatically took him back to the office where the storage tin had been left. He washed his hands and inhaled. Chocolate and mint. He couldn't pretend he wasn't interested.

He grabbed a slice and took a bite, pausing for a moment as the sensation hit his tongue. This was what he'd been missing out on? Since he hadn't eaten all day, he practically finished it in two bites and reached for another slice. This was good. Better than good.

Now he was wishing he'd accepted whatever had been in the tin that first day on the ward. No wonder the nurses always swept in quickly.

Jamie bent back and cricked his neck. This day wasn't over. He still had to spend the rest of the day with Piper, who was slowly but surely getting under his skin.

And he wasn't quite sure what he planned on doing about it...

CHAPTER FIVE

PIPER COULDN'T HAVE described how tired she was. The norovirus outbreak had been full-on. They'd admitted another two passengers to the hospital. Spent another six hours on the cruise ship that night, and then gone back to the hospital to deal with all the patients.

Tyler had been really sick for a few days, before he'd finally turned a corner. His father had taken five days to show no further symptoms of norovirus, and some of the older patients had ended up in hospital for ten days. They were lucky that they'd managed to keep the norovirus contained, with no other cases in the hospital.

Tyler and his family had finally flown home yesterday, after he had spent fourteen days in the hospital.

She'd also spent some time following up on their pregnant patient who had Zika virus.

In the end, she'd worked seventeen days in a row and desperately needed some down time.

Going home at night to her apartment was supposedly great. It was a nice place, comfortable. But for Piper, the walls seemed to echo loneliness back at her. It had always been like this for her. Any more than six months in a place meant that the newness had vanished, the initial friendships had been carved, but because she wasn't there permanently people always viewed her differently. They were nice, and mainly kind. But they would forget about her as soon as she moved on. It was a hollow existence. And the older she got, and the further along in her training, the more amplified the noise.

It didn't help that she kept looking at Jamie and wondering. There was something between them. But what was the point of acting on something when they could both be moving along soon? Finally finding that connection then being forced to break it could end up breaking her.

And she couldn't tell him any of this. Because then he'd realise how lonely she was. How she'd spent her whole life looking for family. And he would probably run a million miles, instantly scared. Who could blame him?

Jamie had offered to give her time off but she'd refused, knowing he would be working himself. Now, finally, they'd managed to get the next two days off, with Dr Leiu covering from the 'Big Island'.

Even though she'd longed to lie in bed until midday, it seemed as if her body clock was working differently. She woke up just after sunrise, finally deciding to go and get some breakfast. She had a list of things to do in her head, but a huge priority for today was to relax. So she changed into her beach gear, grabbed the latest paperback she was reading, slathered herself in sunscreen and dug her sunglasses out of her bag.

She walked slowly down the street. It was a fifteen-minute walk to the nearest beach, where one of her favourite cafés was situated. She found a table that was shaded but faced the small beach and ordered a spinach and tomato omelette with bacon on the side, toast and a large black lemon tea. She stretched her legs and flipped open her book, losing herself in the pages of the slightly scary space horror story.

Every now and then she looked over at the beach. There was a fitness group working out. That might be fun. She should try it some time. There were the normal hard and fast surfers out on the waves, some swimmers and a few families setting up large umbrellas, clearly set on staying here for the day.

It was a smaller beach, with a string of cafés overlooking the sea and a beach patrol of lifeguards to keep everyone safe. There was also a siren system if any sharks were spotted, but in the last eight months that she'd been here she'd never heard it sound.

That was a little reassuring. Because every time she looked out at the waves she did honestly hear the *Jaws* theme tune playing in her head. She'd never swum in the ocean and had absolutely no plans to. Paddling was fine. If she wanted to swim, she'd find an enclosed swimming pool where she could clearly see the bottom and its contents.

She gave a shudder and let out a short gasp as one of the characters in her book was accidentally sucked out into the dark void of space, and with perfect timing a few ice-cold drips landed on her arm.

The inadvertent scream that left her lips made a good few people whip their heads around for a better look. She brushed the cold drips from her arm, letting her book close without marking her place.

'What are you doing?' she said as she looked up.

Jamie Robertson had a broad grin from one side of his face to the other—he was almost unrecognisable. It also didn't help that his wetsuit was peeled from his chest and shoulders and hanging at his back. His right arm was around a slightly worn surfboard.

'Dick or Dom?' she asked, willing her eyes not to focus on his bare chest and dark chest hair.

'Dom,' he said as he propped his board up against the side of the café. 'Hey, Joel,' he shouted. He looked down at her table. 'Mind if I join you? Or are you meeting someone?'

She shook her head and pointed at the chair opposite. 'Help yourself.'

He sat and then leaned down and picked up the book that had landed on the floor. He glanced at the title. 'So, this makes you scream in public?'

She raised her eyebrows at him. 'You made me lose my place. This might not end well for you.'

'Are you a serious reader?'

'At least two or three books a week. I love reading.'

'And is it all sci-fi?' He asked the question as the café owner came out and put a plate in front of him.

She frowned. 'When did you order?'

He shrugged. 'I have a standing order now. Breakfast burrito. Can't beat it. Well, I like a side of toast too.'

Joel appeared with the toast and Piper looked at her empty plate. 'Can I have a fresh fruit bowl, please, and another tea?'

'Shouldn't you be reading your namesake?' And then he rolled his eyes. 'Stupid question. Feel free to kick me under the table. You've probably been asked that a million times before.'

She rolled her eyes too, but smiled. 'I preferred the first half of *Jane Eyre*, where things were pretty miserable. I was bored after that. I didn't mind *Wuthering Heights*, and I didn't really enjoy *The Tenant of Wildfell Hall*.' She held up her hands. 'So, you see, I'm pretty much a disgrace to the Bronte name.' She couldn't tell him the truth. That the underlying themes about families and isolation and loneliness were actually just too tough for her. She'd read those books as a teenager and actually given away all her copies. Maybe as an adult she would feel differently, but the feelings that had been imprinted on her had stayed. She gave him a smile and held up her book. 'Hence the sci-fi.'

As Joel left, Jamie nodded at her book again. 'So, are you one of those folks who watches every episode of *Star Trek*, all the *Star Wars* films and obsess about *Firefly*?'

She stared at him for a moment, then couldn't help but smile. 'I read everything,' she said. 'Fiction, romance, historical, murder mystery, horror and sci-fi,' she added, then shrugged. 'But maybe yes to all of the sci-fi stuff.'

Jamie started on his burrito. 'How on earth do you make time?'

'I don't sleep,' she said simply.

One of his eyebrows raised. 'You'd better be joking.'

She laughed. 'Already thinking about having a sleep-deprived doctor working with you?'

'Maybe,' he admitted.

'In order to make me sleep, I have to do some reading. It helps quieten things down for me, and gives me some space. My primary teacher told my mother I didn't read books, I inhaled them.'

It was one of her key memories of her mother. And she held it dear because there were so few.

He continued with the burrito as Joel reappeared with

the tea and fruit for Piper and a large orange juice for Jamie.

She leaned back in her chair and sighed. The sun had started to shift slightly and she wasn't quite in the same amount of shade she had been earlier.

'Do you come here every day?'

He glanced over at the beach. 'Most days. I go twice a week to one of the other beaches too, but this is my nearest and my favourite.'

'Hence why Joel knows your order.'

'I usually eat and run and he has things packed up for me.'

She pointed at his plate. 'So, that breakfast burrito is why you turn your nose up at my traybakes?'

There was a tiny flush in his cheeks. 'Yeah, about them…'

'What about them?' She was automatically defensive. Was the man with a half pint of orange juice in front of him really going to give her a lecture about sugar?

He pulled a face. 'I might have eaten half the contents of that tin on the day we went back to the cruise ship.'

'Aha.' Now she was secretly pleased and folded her arms. 'So now you actually like them?'

He leaned forward and kept his voice low. 'That mint chocolate thing? That's addictive.'

She laughed. Since he'd got here, he'd definitely got some sun on his face and body. It was likely due to his surfing. The light scattering of freckles suited him. Made him look a little warmer than the normal frosty exterior.

'Well, I'm pleased to hear that you actually like something. Mr Eroka's—Charlie's—favourite is rocky road. I also do a peanut crunch, a krispie cake, an orange version of the mint, flapjacks, and I'm experimenting with a version with everyone's favourite cookie.'

He said the name out loud and she nodded.

He waggled a finger at her. 'Not sure about that one. Destruction of those cookies is questionable.'

Now she leaned forward. 'Well, let's just wait and see. You might like it. More than that,' she joked. 'It might actually put a smile on your face.'

A deep furrow appeared on his brow. 'What does that mean?'

She pulled a face. 'You can sometimes be a little grumpy at work.'

For a moment he looked tense, but then she noticed his shoulders relax as he sank back further into the chair. 'And you think you'll win me round by telling me this?' There was a hint of amusement in his voice.

She kept things light. 'Well, I figured you already knew anyway.'

He let that hang for a few moments. 'Maybe. I just don't like to get too friendly with people at work.'

Wow. How to sting. She tilted her head and contemplated him for a few minutes. 'You spend more than eight hours a day at work. Sometimes you can be there for more than twenty-four hours. Why would you want to have no friends?'

'It's complicated.'

He didn't expand. But she wasn't going to let it go.

'You're not grumpy all the time. At least not around me.'

She met his blue gaze straight-on. It was a challenge. They were out of work now. And she had to know if the flirtation, the glances, and that touch the other day, was all just a figment of her imagination. This—whatever it was between them—seemed like a two-way thing to her. If she was wrong, she wanted to know. Before she became the talk of the hospital again. And before she started to get her hopes up.

His fingers started drumming slowly on the table. Was he nervous?

'I'm trying to teach you. There's no point in being grumpy,' he finally said.

She licked her lips and shook her head. 'No, I don't think it's that.'

His head gave a little jerk of surprise. 'So,' he said slowly, a smile starting to appear on his face. 'What do you think it is?'

Her skin prickled. Okay, now her stomach was somersaulting and she didn't feel quite so brave. Couldn't he meet her halfway?

'I think that sometimes you might be lonely.'

He blinked. 'I just got here. Why would you say that?'

'Because you sometimes have the same look on your face that I do, and I've been here eight months.'

'So, what does that mean?'

'That maybe we're both lonely?'

Did she sound desperate? She hoped not. But none of this was planned. And she wasn't entirely sure she'd steered this conversation in the right direction.

Jamie leaned forward, his voice low. 'Do you have a suggestion as to what we do about it?'

She leaned forward too because she couldn't help it. 'Maybe we should hang out a little. Do you have plans for the rest of the day?'

Had she just asked her boss out on a date? If he said

no in the next thirty seconds, she swore she would try and find somewhere to hide.

He stretched his arms above his head. This time she didn't hide the fact she was looking at his bare chest. If surfing was his only workout, it certainly seemed to keep his body in shape.

'Want to learn to surf?' he asked. 'I could go and pick up Dick.'

She lifted one hand and shook her head. 'There's no way I'm going out there to be shark bait.'

He laughed out loud. 'Come on.' He waved a hand at the ocean. 'You must know you're much more likely to be in a car accident than to be bitten by a shark.'

She pointed to the pole on the beach with the red siren on it. 'They have sirens,' she said. 'It's a real threat. I'm not making it up.'

His brow wrinkled. 'You're actually worried?'

'Oh, I'm not worried, I'm terrified. There's no way I'm setting foot in that ocean.' She held up one hand. 'Well, not any more than ankle deep.'

He swept out his arm, taking in the whole beach area and the view of the ocean to the side of them.

'Piper Bronte, you do realise that you're on one of the Hawaiian Islands, right?'

She could feel her chin tighten in indignation. 'Of course, I know that. But I came here very safely. On a plane.'

Jamie looked thoughtful for a moment. 'You do know that the oceans around the Hawaiian Islands contain some of the most beautiful marine life known to man? You're prepared to miss all that?' He shook his head. 'Honestly, when you're out there—there's nothing like it. That pull of the ocean, that feeling of being part of something.'

Piper straightened her back and swallowed. 'I don't mind boats. Well, reasonably sized boats. But I'm not swimming, or going on a surfboard.'

Jamie gave a slow nod. 'How do you feel about a glass bottom boat?'

She took a moment to think. 'That sounds…okay, I guess.'

He looked down at the table. 'Are you finished?'

She nodded.

'Let me settle the bill then take you on a trip.'

Piper glanced down at her beach clothes. 'Do I need to change?'

He gave her a smile. 'Absolutely not. You're dressed perfectly. I've got a T-shirt and shorts in my bag.'

Jamie disappeared for a few moments, then came out and carried his surfboard inside the café. His wetsuit had disappeared and she was a little sorry.

'Joel will keep Dom safe for me. Let's go.'

They headed to Kewalo Basin Harbor.

'Don't we need to book in advance?' Piper asked as they made their way through the crowds of sightseers.

'All done online,' said Jamie, waving his phone. 'We just need to get there on time.'

They passed a few colleagues from the hospital who gave them a casual wave, one lifting a drink towards them.

Was this a date? Had she asked her boss on a date and he'd accepted, or was this something completely different? Maybe he just felt sorry for her and had decided to keep her company. A pity date. That would actually be worse than anything. What could be worse than dating a married man? Possibly, the whole hospital finding out that your boss took you out on a pity date. Maybe Piper should just accept the fact that dating wasn't really for her.

She could turn into Miss Havisham, the old recluse that wore her tattered wedding dress in *Great Expectations*. Hopefully by then, she'd be too old to care what anyone said about her. And, to be honest, now that she was here, she would prefer if her mansion was in the Hawaiian Islands, instead of in England. Pity Charles Dickens wasn't around to rewrite the story for her. Though with her surname, that thought alone was probably a criminal offence.

'This will be fun,' said Jamie as he pointed at a sign advertising the sightseeing trip they were about to go on. He did actually look happy about it. She hadn't meant to be so bold earlier, when she'd said he seemed quite happy around her. But maybe it was actually true.

She liked that. It made her feel warm inside.

They joined a line of tourists and climbed onto the impressive fifty-foot catamaran. It did have a glass bottom on the middle of the floor of the boat. But the rest of boat seemed sturdy. There were built-in benches around the edges, with a permanent roof to keep off the heat of the sun.

The guides were extra friendly, asking everyone their name, where they were from, and if they wanted anything to drink on the voyage. They also did a quick check for any medical conditions they should know about, before letting everyone know they would be out at sea for just over an hour, and would hope to see as much sea life as possible. They checked for any special requests and basically told everyone to enjoy the ride, relax and ask any questions they wanted.

Piper wasn't sure whether she was comforted by the life vests on the boat—enough for everyone—or secretly terrified.

Jamie saw her expression and slung his arm around her shoulder. 'Stop panicking. Everything is going to be fine.' He handed her a bottle of beer. 'Why don't you just relax and enjoy the view? These guys know what they are doing.'

As the boat left the harbour and the guide started to give them an overview of the Hawaiian Islands, Piper did start to relax. She leaned into Jamie. It was comfortable. He hadn't removed his arm and she liked it there.

They learned that the people next to them were visiting from Texas, and the family on their other side were Italian. When someone else enquired about them, Jamie answered easily, saying they both worked at Honolulu General Medical Center. It was obvious that people assumed they were a couple, and neither of them said otherwise.

The boat continued out, giving spectacular views of the Waikiki shoreline and Diamond Head, the volcanic tuff cone on Oahu. Every now and then the guides would stop the boat and gesture for the guests to view the floor of the boat, or to look around at the surrounding sea. Piper was fascinated. It felt safe in the boat and they saw a monk seal, a whole host of sea turtles, and finally stopped at one of the vibrant coral reefs with multicoloured tropical fish.

She sipped slowly on her beer and enjoyed the vibe of the boat ride. Of course, during the trip, she and Jamie moved positions, sometimes leaning over the side to watch the sea creatures and then moving closer to the glass bottom to get a better view of what was beneath them.

It was the most relaxed they'd been around each other, and she liked it. As they looked at some final views of the impressive Diamond Head again, she murmured, 'Can you imagine how things were thousands of years ago when these volcanoes were active?'

He grinned. 'You imagining some kind of sci-fi movie, jumping back in time?'

She leaned her head on his shoulder. 'Oh, if we're jumping back, it's definitely for some dinosaurs. We might only get one chance.'

She paused as their gazes connected, the ocean breeze blowing her hair between them. Jamie reached up and pushed some strands behind her ear. They were so close. She could see every eyelash, every detail of his skin, and she realised she was every bit as exposed as he was. But it didn't matter to her. She was comfortable around him.

The boat gave a jerk and she realised they were coming back into the harbour. Jamie's voice was low. 'There's never just one chance,' he said, moving his arm from her shoulder and taking her hand in his.

Her heart skipped a few beats. The one thing that she was sure of was that she didn't want this day to end. 'Have you had a chance to explore Chinatown yet?' she asked.

His brow wrinkled and he shook his head. 'I've been to Chinatown in San Francisco, but didn't even know there was one here.'

'Then let me show you around, and we can eat at my favourite place. Did you have plans for dinner already?'

Her insides were in a little knot in case he said yes, but her body sagged in relief as he shook his head. He glanced downwards at them both and their casualwear. 'We're still dressed okay?'

She grinned. 'Don't worry. No one will care what we're wearing. Let's go and have some fun.'

Jamie was wondering how on earth he'd got here. This morning, his only plan had been to surf. His other plans for the day certainly hadn't been glamorous. He had some laundry to do, a house to clean and a fridge that was crying out for a food shop—none of which he'd done.

Instead, as soon as he'd glimpsed Piper sitting at his favourite café, everything else had gone out of the window. But he wasn't quite sure what he was doing around someone who'd announced they'd never swim in the sea.

On paper, they might be polar opposites. But in person, the chemistry was definitely there. And out of the hospital environment, he didn't have as many reservations as he had enclosed in the medical centre, surrounded by their colleagues.

Breakfast had been interesting. His Dr Grumpy nickname had clearly followed him, and that was entirely his own fault. But Piper's comment about being lonely had struck a nerve in a way he hadn't expected.

He did generally keep himself to himself, and that was deliberate. He was still stung by the investigation. Why invest in people and relationships when they could all turn on you in the blink of an eye?

He'd examined it so much in his head that he'd convinced himself to lock it in a box and push it to the back of his mind. But the fact that people he'd considered good friends didn't have his back at the time, he'd never forget that. Particularly when he'd known that he would never have acted like that towards someone else.

Part of him wondered if she was maybe insulting them both, hinting that maybe this attraction wasn't real, and linking together might just be convenient. Because he knew that wasn't how things worked for him. But he was still cautious about the fact he did find initial attraction easy, and what came next much harder. He'd failed twice after all.

And why was someone like Piper lonely? She was the happiest, friendliest person he'd probably ever met. He imagined she had a shedload of friends.

If he was misreading this buzz between them, his instincts were clearly so wrong he should pack everything up and head back to Scotland. Because it wasn't what he read in her eyes, or felt as her body relaxed against his. Both of those gave him an entirely different message.

And her invitation for the day to continue? He would gladly accept. He kept her hand in his as they made their way on the local bus towards Chinatown.

As soon as they neared the area, he could see the change in tone and temperament. Chinatown was bright and vibrant. There was music playing, the streets were more crowded than other parts of Honolulu and the smells that permeated the air were delicious.

'Do you care what we do?' asked Piper. 'Or—' she raised her eyebrows '—can I decide?'

He knew exactly what his answer was supposed to be. 'You decide.'

She grinned at him, and pulled him across the street.

'First up, dim sum. This is my favourite no-nonsense place.'

He could smell the food and see the line snaking around the corner as they crossed the street. Before he had a chance to put his hand in his pocket, Piper had got them two small plates, crammed with food.

'This place opens at eight in the morning,' she said. 'Lenny introduced me to it after a particularly bad night at the hospital. Said he sometimes came here after a night shift, before going home.' Jamie raised his eyebrows but she gave him a casual wave. 'Now tuck in, because we've got some walking to do.'

They perched on a bench nearby and ate the delicious food, then purchased some bottles of water. 'Should I be afraid?' he asked, as she led him down the street.

Piper was animated. 'Absolutely not. We're continuing the theme of relaxing today, and I'm going to take you somewhere equally as beautiful as the ocean.'

Jamie tried to be convinced as they walked past some raucous bars, even though it was still afternoon, and some shops and street vendors that were crowded with both locals and tourists.

Finally, they got to an entranceway of the Foster Botanical Garden and he looked at Piper in surprise. 'I didn't know you were a garden fan.'

She smiled and shook her head. 'I like anything beautiful and that makes me think, and there's lots of things in here to make you think.' She gave a tug of his hand, then pulled him closer and whispered in his ear. 'It's also a great place to go when you want a change of scenery and a quiet place to read.'

He looked at her in appreciation. He was finding out

more and more about her all the time. He wondered if she hadn't made too many friends at the hospital. It seemed odd that a young woman would spend time by herself in the botanical gardens. But then maybe he was judging when he shouldn't.

Piper picked up a glossy leaflet and map of the gardens. 'There are tropical plants here that some people only ever read about. And there are some really rare things too.'

Plants had never really been Jamie's thing. He'd admired some extravagant flowerbeds in the past, but had absolutely no knowledge about what had been in them, or how to look after any of the contents. But he listened and watched patiently as Piper led him around the gardens.

'This is the Hawaiian loulu palm.' She pointed at the tall, broad trees in front of them. 'They have thickly pleated leaves and while they're native to the islands they only grow in certain places.' They moved onto the next tree, which had white and yellow flowers. 'I can't even say this one,' said Piper, pointing to the words in the leaflet, *East African gigasiphon macrosiphon*. 'It's almost extinct in the wild,' she said, 'and this one here is the only flowering tree outside of Africa.'

They wandered through the rest of the gardens, stopping to rest occasionally and sip water on a bench beneath some trees, then continuing along the self-guided tour which celebrated all the plants and trees found across Hawaii. There were a number of oddities which made them laugh. The sausage tree, the cannonball tree and the double coconut palm which was capable of producing a coconut of fifty pounds.

'What would anyone do with a fifty-pound coconut?'

murmured Jamie, which made Piper roll her eyes and laugh.

They finished by passing the vanilla vines and cinnamon trees, stopping to breathe in heavily, letting the scents pervade their senses. Jamie pointed to a sign as they made to leave. 'What? You aren't taking me to see the poisonous plants? Is that because you already know them and have got them stored away, ready to go in the traybakes if people annoy you?'

She widened her eyes in fake surprise. 'Well, now you've spoiled all my future plans!'

She slid her hand through his arm and they walked comfortably together back to the main area in Chinatown. Two hours had passed in a flash.

She pointed to some of the restaurants as they passed. 'Don't think it's only Chinese restaurants here. There's Vietnamese, Mexican, Korean, a charcuterie place, a brilliant vegan restaurant and lots more.'

'So, where are we going for dinner? We're not exactly dressed for anywhere posh.'

She looked down and laughed. 'We will be fine, I promise. Just like I knew the best place to get dim sum, I know the best place for genuine Chinese food.'

She took him down a side street, into a small dark restaurant that was mainly lit by candles. Since the restaurant was small, the tables were arranged a little differently, meaning that they ended up sitting side by side instead of across from each other. The waiter was attentive, bringing them the cocktail of the evening. Instead of a menu, he asked them their likes and dislikes, then brought them an array of small dishes to share, with a variety of appetisers, then a range of main courses with chicken, beef, noodles and rice.

The first fruity cocktail turned into a second, followed by a bottle of wine. His senses were on full alert. Piper was becoming more animated as the night continued. He lost count of the number of times their hands and arms touched as they reached for the bowls of food.

Eventually, their hands just settled on top of each other. She gave him a smile. It was all he needed. Their bodies naturally turned towards each other as they continued to sip their drinks.

The dim lights added to the atmosphere. It struck him that they'd spent all day together, with no real planning or intent. But he liked this. He liked her.

'We should try the Korean place next,' said Piper. 'But we might need to book it.'

He liked that even more. The certainty that they should do something like this again.

'When do you think we'll actually get time off together again?' he joked.

'Oh, I'm sure Dr Leiu could be persuaded,' she said with a smile, leaning in towards him. Her hair had fallen in front of her face again, and he reached up and tucked a strand behind her ear, his fingers brushing the soft skin on her cheek.

This time she reached up, her own hand closing over his. 'How many times today has this happened?' she whispered.

'I told you there would be more than one chance,' he whispered back, smiling at her.

She leaned forward, pressing her lips against his. He

could taste the sweet fruit of the cocktail on her lips. As she leaned her body next to his, he could feel her soft breasts against his chest wall. It sent a shockwave of impulses through his entire body. He could feel all the cells waking up, calling their neighbours to attention.

His other hand threaded through her hair, pulling her face even closer to his. He could feel her eyelashes on his cheeks. Her other hand wound around his back, pressing him even closer.

Thank goodness it was dark. It was only a kiss, but it was still a restaurant.

She gave a half laugh as they kissed and he stopped, speaking against her mouth. 'Okay?'

They hadn't moved apart. 'Yes,' she breathed. 'But I might have thought about this a few times,' she confessed.

'You have?' His heart leapt in a way that surprised him. He wanted to hear that. He wanted to hear that she'd thought about him just as much as he'd thought about her. Even though he didn't want to admit that to anyone else.

'I might have too,' he admitted. His finger stroked her cheek again. 'But people might have something to say about this,' he said. 'I am your boss.'

She nodded as she kissed him again. 'Then let's not tell. I'm a consenting adult and I won't have anyone tell me who I can or can't kiss.'

'Are you sure?' Even though it had been hours since they'd both got ready this morning, he could still smell the scent of her perfume. It was tantalising. He knew he wasn't going to forget this scent.

She kissed the side of his face. 'Yes, I'm sure. Now, let's get out of here.'

It was all he needed to hear. He put some cash down on the table, grabbed her hand and led her back out into the warm, noisy Hawaiian night.

CHAPTER SIX

WORK WAS DIFFERENT. At least in her head it was. Everything still functioned exactly as it should. Piper still did ward rounds, reviewed patients, accepted referrals and continued to learn in her specialty.

But a million other little things changed. Every time they sat next to each other or brushed arms while standing at the nurses' station it felt as if her whole body was on high alert.

The night had ended perfectly. He'd walked her back to her apartment and—after some more kissing—he'd left her at the door. She'd toyed with the idea of inviting him in, but they'd both decided to take things slow. And that was fine. It suited her. Because part of the thrill was letting the attraction build between them.

She'd wondered why he'd agreed so easily. But the day had been so perfect overall that she didn't want to think too much about it. Jamie Robertson was just as attracted to her as she was to him. That was enough to know.

The hints of flirtation and lingering glances hadn't been in her imagination and that was partly a relief. Now, she didn't hesitate to let her gaze linger on him. To share secret smiles and whispered comments.

But one thing bothered her. She'd been the one to suggest they kept their relationship a secret. It went against all her principles, and she wondered if she'd just drunk too many cocktails and too much wine that evening. And Jamie had agreed—in principle, apparently, because he was her boss. But what if it was something else?

There was still a tiny alert in her brain. About trusting someone. About letting them close, when she knew just how fragile her heart really was. A small voice still whispered that his contract was for ten more months, and hers only for another almost four months. Was it wise to form any kind of relationship when neither of them knew what the future held?

And was it wise to keep it a secret? That didn't make her comfortable and she knew she would have to bring it up soon.

But she still felt the pull. The emptiness or hollowness that had seemed to follow her faded into the background when Jamie was there. And she preferred that life, preferred that feeling.

The ward had been quiet today and Jamie was involved in an online international teaching session, so Piper decided to go back to the ER. She scanned the board for the word 'rash'. There were a few kids in the department, so she reviewed an infected nappy rash, a five-year-old with chickenpox, and contacted Obstetrics to arrange immunoglobulin for the five-year-old's pregnant mother.

One of the charge nurses gave her a shout. 'You trying to win points with Paeds?' she joked.

She held up her hands. 'Any rash, any time. Just so happened it was kids this time.'

The charge nurse handed her a chart. 'So, can you make-believe this fifty-year-old's sore is actually a rash for me then? I've been waiting for someone to see him for a while.'

'I'll have a look,' she agreed. 'But it might not come to much.'

She wandered into the cubicle and introduced herself to the patient. She glanced at the address. He was thin, a little unkempt, and his address was in one of the poorest parts of the city.

She took her time getting some history from him, checking his obs, and then looking at the sores on his skin. There were four, on both legs, on the lower portion. To be more accurate, they were ulcers, open and looking extremely painful. The man also had a low-grade fever.

Piper sent a message up to Jamie, and wasn't surprised when he headed down as she waited for some blood tests. 'What do you think?' he asked.

'I think I've got a local with cutaneous leishmaniasis. I know it's a parasitic disease and caused by sandflies. He doesn't use any kind of repellent. He works on the beach, and is generally in quite poor health.'

Jamie nodded. 'How did you come across this one?'

She gave him a quick rundown of her morning in the ER and he shot her a smile. 'Don't let it be said that you ever take ten minutes to sit down.'

She gave a shrug. 'It's fine. I like to learn, and I like to help out. Anyway, I've picked up a case that should have been ours anyhow. That's good, isn't it?'

'Of course it is. Let's talk to him while we wait for his blood results to confirm his diagnosis. This is a lot more unusual here. It's more common in Africa and Brazil. Things can get tricky with this disease. These ulcers can take months to heal, and if he's already in poor health it will take even longer.'

Piper gave a sigh. 'Should we expect more cases if the sandflies carry it here?'

'Definitely a possibility. Let's ask about the area he works in at the beach, and about his companions. If anyone has similar ulcers, we have to encourage them to come in.'

Piper checked her notes. 'He could have an enlarged liver or spleen. But I'm not sure we'll be covered to run those tests.'

Jamie nodded. 'You're right, but we can start him on some antifungal medications meantime to try and treat the condition. We need to let him know he's in for the long haul.'

Piper finished her documentation. 'I hate that this is considered a sometimes forgotten disease. I think it's mainly because it affects the poor, and has high numbers in some of the poorest countries in the world. It seems unfair.'

'It is, and his poor nutritional state won't help. But we can treat the disease as best we can, continue to monitor his condition and see if there is anyone else around him we can assist.'

The patient was admitted to the ward and Jamie came to find Piper again. 'Ready to get out and do some local visits?'

She was surprised. 'What?'

'Mr Leong has told me that some of his workmates have similar ulcers. He also got very quiet when I asked him if any of his family or neighbours might be affected.'

She gave a slow nod. 'So, what are we going to do?'

He gave a half-smile. 'I've spoken to Merry about what food banks are open in the area, and if there's a local free clinic.'

'And is there?'

He nodded. 'Merry knows everything. I've got some supplies, both food and medicines, and some protective equipment and some information. While folks might know about sandflies, this case is unusual. Hopefully, there will only be low levels of cases, but I'm just conscious that not everyone affected might come to the hospital.'

Piper got ready and when they left the hospital Jamie surprised her with a brand-new car. 'When did you get this?'

'Yesterday,' he said. 'It's just a leased car. I figured I might need one, and decided to lease so I can hand it back if I need to leave.'

She clicked her seat belt into place. 'Why would you need to leave?' It was as if even the thought of him leaving had kicked off all her defences.

He glanced over at her. 'What if Lenny decides he wants to come back?'

'Isn't that unlikely? Surely he'll want to stay in Boston once his baby has its surgery?'

Jamie started the car and pulled out of the lot. 'It makes sense to be near your kid's surgeon for the first few months. But that doesn't mean they need to stay in Boston for ever.'

'Isn't the job yours?' she asked, feeling strangely annoyed that she didn't have this information already. 'What kind of contract did they give you?'

'A year.'

'Oh.' She had known that, but had wanted him to say it out loud so it was confirmed. It shouldn't matter to her. After all, her own contract only had a few months left to run. After that...who knew? Her training post was at an end and she would be looking for a consultant post of her own.

'You might be sick of me by then.' Jamie gave her a smile as he pulled out into the traffic.

'Only if you annoy me,' she quipped back, before taking a look around. She was keeping her mask in place all the while, wondering if he was having this conversation with her for another reason. Maybe he didn't want to continue the relationship that they'd started, and this was his easy way of letting her down. Her heart sank. Please don't let it be that. 'Where are we headed?'

'We have a few stops. Several local businesses regularly donate to the food bank and we'll pick up their supplies on the way. Both the food bank and the free clinic are in the same street.'

Healthcare was different in the US than it was in the UK. But the Honolulu General Medical Center had a variety of different funding streams that could be used for those with no health insurance. They regularly supplied items to the free clinics.

When they reached the food bank, one of the workers came out to greet them, helping them unload all the supplies. The place was well-stocked and friendly. As they were there, Piper watched a number of families appear to collect what they needed.

The worker was curious as Piper handed over some leaflets. 'We've had a few cases of a disease caused by sandflies. Instead of just disappearing after a few days, the bites can cause ulcers. Hopefully, it will just be a few people, but can you give out the leaflets, and direct anyone to the free clinic next door if they think they could be affected?'

The worker nodded. There were a number of health posters up around the food bank walls covering a variety of issues, and the staff seemed happy to help.

As they went back outside, Piper looked at Jamie. 'It's not a notifiable disease, should we be chasing people down?'

Jamie gave her an interested look. 'Good question. You're right, it's not notifiable here, but it's still a tropical disease. I often feel like it's quite neglected. And while right now I expect this to only affect a few people, if a higher number of people were affected I would still talk to infectious disease consultants in surrounding areas.'

She gave a nod as they climbed back into the car to drive to the end of the street. She already knew it was one of the most deprived areas in the city. It was widely known that people who lived in areas of deprivation usually suffered from poorer health.

The public health principles of inequalities in health had been part of Piper's studies and she wished it had been covered years earlier when she'd done her first medical training. It gave her a broader perspective on her job, and made her take all a person's individual circumstances into consideration when she contemplated their care and treatment.

As they climbed back out of Jamie's car, he popped the boot and lifted out a whole host of packages she hadn't seen. 'What's that?' she asked.

'Mosquito nets and insecticide,' he said. 'I picked them

up from the store at the hospital. At the very least we can try and encourage people to sleep under them at night. Prevention is the best protection.'

She gave him a smile at the phrase she'd heard countless times in her tropical disease studies. 'I didn't even know we had those. You'll need to show me the store some time.'

He gave a smile. 'There are also some prescription medicines for the clinic, and some instructions on how to treat anyone that comes in. Let's take the rest of the supplies in.'

They headed into the clinic and spent the next half hour talking to the staff who worked there. The staff were friendly and competent and glad to have some instructions on the relatively unusual disease.

They climbed back into the car. 'I've booked that Korean restaurant that you pointed out,' he said.

She felt a rush of warmth across her skin. 'You have? When for?'

'Friday night. You said it was good, and I thought we might want to dress a little better and enjoy the night.'

She couldn't help the smile that spread across her face. 'Are you saying we looked like beach bums the other day?'

He laughed. 'Maybe just a little. I promise you I have at least one good shirt.'

She rolled her eyes. 'And I have at least one dress that would be entirely unsuitable for hospital wear unless I wanted Indira to chase me down the corridor waving a contract in her hand.'

He leaned forward so their faces were almost touching. 'Now *that* I like the sound of.'

She liked the sound of it too. The other day had been completely casual and unplanned. This...this was more... more like a real date. Something that a couple might do.

It was all very well keeping things to themselves in the hospital, but that didn't mean they had to hide away completely. She liked the idea of dressing up and going for a really nice dinner with a guy who made the blood race around her body. She remembered that people from the hospital had seen them on their previous day together, too. There had been no whispers. No stares. So, maybe things weren't quite so quiet as they thought. That made her feel better. She'd hate to think that Jamie had anything he wanted to hide from her.

'Me too,' she whispered, and he gave her a smile that sent those delicious tingles across her skin. She could get used to this.

Jamie was trying to stop smiling. He really was. But being around Piper was infectious.

She'd left to go home for the evening after he'd told her he was meeting Joanne for drinks. He would have invited her along, but that might be a bit awkward since he hadn't told Joanne he was seeing anyone yet, and she would suss him out in two minutes flat.

Even though he'd taken this job to spend more time with his best friend, they'd honestly been like ships passing in the night. They'd arranged to meet in a bar near to her apartment for drinks. He thought he was early, but when he arrived she was already waiting, sitting in a booth with a beer for him and a soft drink for her.

He slid in opposite her and gave her a suspicious glance. 'What?'

She pushed her hair behind her ear. 'What do you mean?'

He narrowed his gaze like some kind of comedy villain. 'You're early, you've bought drinks—you're itching to tell me something.'

He sat back and looked at her, unable to help the amused expression he was sure was on his face. She was giving off a vibe. He couldn't tell if she had spectacular gossip, a revolutionary new research idea or she was just up to something.

For a moment he had a flash of panic. Had someone told her about him and Piper before he even had a chance? No, she would have killed him straight off if that was news.

She tilted her head and frowned. 'Okay, I was ready to tell you something, but you're deflecting already. Don't think I don't notice. What have you got to tell me?'

'You go first.' He took a sip of his beer.

'Nope,' she said, smiling stubbornly at him.

He bit his bottom lip, hating he might actually be a bit nervous about this. 'I might have met someone.' The words seemed to fly out of his mouth.

Her eyes widened, but then she had the good grace to look a little sheepish. 'I might have met someone, too,' she admitted.

'What?' he snapped. 'Why didn't you tell me?'

She raised her eyebrows and pointed at him. 'Why didn't *you* tell *me*?'

He sighed. 'Okay, I need to know who he is, so I can decide if I like him or want to kick his ass.'

She burst out laughing. 'You will not "kick his ass".' She waggled her fingers in the air.

It was his turn to point at her. 'You don't know that.'

Then he shrugged. 'I might have to. You know I'm going to ask questions.'

She kept her focus on him. 'And I'll do the same. Who is she?'

He pulled a face. 'That's the thing, and that's what makes this not so great. She's the doctor I'm training.'

Joanne opened her mouth and closed it again. She waited a minute, took a sip of her soda and then sighed, lifting her glass towards his. 'And this is why we are best friends.'

Jamie lifted his glass and clinked it, but was still confused. 'What are you talking about?'

She sighed. 'Sometimes you're such a dum-dum. Guy—' she sighed again '—is training me.'

His brow wrinkled. Piper had mentioned the rumours about Joanne and Guy to him weeks ago, hadn't she? He wondered if his friend knew that people had noticed their attraction. And were their colleagues also gossiping about him and Piper?

'So, it's Guy Sanders, the cardiothoracic surgeon, who you are seeing?'

She nodded, at first looking sad but then smiling. 'And what's your woman's name?'

'Piper. Piper Bronte.' He took in her expression. 'I know, a classic English surname.'

He ran his fingers through his hair. 'But officially, I'm her boss. That isn't a good look. Which is why we'd prefer to keep things quiet.'

'Okay, I get that. It is kind of awkward. Are you sure about this?'

'Are you?'

She held up one hand. 'Stop. We're going to get nowhere if we just keep batting things back to each other.' She gave him a smile. 'I want to know how she makes you feel.'

He held up his beer. 'And that is why when you ask some questions, I take the fifth.'

'You're Scottish. You can't take the fifth.'

'I'm on American soil, I can.'

'Keep going like this and we'll give each other a headache.' She drank her soda then set it down. 'So, I'll start. He annoyed me at first. I thought he might have taken advantage of me.'

'What?' His voice rose and he leaned closer to her.

'Calm down. You know me. I can't handle drink. I thought I was drinking a virgin cocktail and it turned out I wasn't. He practically had to carry me home to make sure I was okay. When I woke up, I might have jumped to some wrong conclusions.'

'Why didn't you tell me? Why didn't you text me?'

She put her hand on her chest. 'Because I got things wrong enough without dragging anyone else into it. He's a good guy. It just wasn't a great first impression to create.'

'For you, or for him?'

She rolled her eyes at him. 'Oh, please.' She waved her hand. 'Anyway, I like him now. And I'm not sure where it's going or what might happen. But I wanted to mention it to you before you noticed, or anyone else noticed something.'

Jamie took a few breaths. 'Snap.'

'What? And that's it?' She couldn't keep the hint of laughter out of her voice.

But he was looking at her seriously. He reached over

and touched her hand. 'Thanks for telling me. I know you find it hard to trust people. But just know that I'm always going to have your back. No matter what else is going on.'

She reached over and put her hand over his. 'Thank you. I know that.'

It was odd. How different it was to touch Joanne as it was to touch Piper. People didn't always understand. But with him and Joanne, it was deep down friendship. No attraction. No romance. Just complete respect and love for the other person in a completely companionable way. Straight talking when it was needed. Hugs when required. Someone who would always answer the phone if he needed it, and someone who he could be honest with—even when he didn't like it.

It was Joanne who'd held his hand—virtually—when he went through the whole drug stealing agenda. At one point he thought she was going to get on a plane and take people out on his behalf—her conviction of his innocence had never wavered for a second and he'd be eternally grateful. Maybe he could be a little more honest with her.

'I like Piper. I like her a lot. I don't want to put her training programme at risk. I don't want anyone to think I'd give her an easy time or pass her because I'm dating her. She's a darn good doctor and doesn't need any special treatment.' He looked at Joanne. 'Just like you. I want you to shine while you're here. I don't want anyone to think Guy is favouring you. You don't need that.' He leaned back. 'You're probably better than he is.'

She burst out laughing. 'Why, thank you, my friend. Feel free to trample anyone who threatens to get in the way of my career.'

Jamie blew on his knuckles, then rubbed them on his chest. 'Of course. That's what I'm here for.'

She lifted her glass again. 'So, we're good?'

He clinked his glass against hers. 'We're good.'

They chatted for another hour, gossiping about past class mates and where they all were in their careers, before finally leaving and he walked her home, gave her a hug and started back to his place.

It felt good to talk. He certainly didn't want Joanne to hear anything from anyone other than him, and it was kind of weird that she'd met someone around the same time, in similar circumstances. But life was strange sometimes, and Jamie had always just accepted that.

The walk was good. Part way through lit streets and part way near the ocean. Close enough to smell the scents and hear the waves crashing on the beach.

He loved it here. The island was beautiful and he wanted a chance to explore more of it. There were at least one hundred and twenty-five beaches—not all he could surf at, and he might already be sure he'd found his two favourites. But he was still new here. It had only been two months since he'd stepped off the plane and been drenched by Piper's cocktail at the drinks party.

It wasn't long to have feelings like this.

His stomach clenched. The locum doctor he'd worked with that had stolen the drugs—he'd known him for six months. Never for a second had he had any reason to suspect him, but it turned out there was lots he didn't know about the man.

It was entirely different to his relationship with Piper, but it made him realise he didn't know that much about her. He told himself that his instincts were normally good.

Maybe if he'd spent longer in that doctor's company, he might have realised something. He'd spent too long second-guessing himself about this—at the time—and even months after. He had to let it go. He knew that. But it had caused an impact on his life, and the lives of those around him, that he couldn't pretend hadn't happened.

He pushed himself to focus on Piper. She'd been wearing a red dress today that flared around her hips, and she'd spent all day saying, 'It has pockets,' much to the pleasure of all the females around who wanted to order one too. She had a remarkable sense of style, an ability to know what clothes and colours suited her, all which added to her sunny demeanour. Did she ever have a bad day?

Jamie wasn't sure he wanted to know. He liked the fact she always looked on the bright side of life, and the cup was always half-full instead of half-empty. But she had made a comment about being lonely. Was that something he should explore—push further on? How would he feel if she pushed him on elements of his past?

He wondered how she actually tolerated him. But for some reason, she did. The spark was there. And he wasn't sure that anything would ever erase that.

A warm sensation spread over him. He just had to take a leaf out of her book and try to adopt a happier approach. He had to learn to trust people again. To have a little faith.

Joanne had stood by him. There must be other people in this world with the same set of morals and principles. Just because he'd been let down before didn't mean he would be let down again.

It was time to let his guard down. How could he hope to form any kind of relationship with barriers in place?

And was Piper worth it? He thought so. She even made him smile.

He laughed out loud as he walked along. Would anyone even recognise him? He would just have to wait and find out.

CHAPTER SEVEN

Piper was contemplating whether it was appropriate to ask Jamie to join her for breakfast. She knew that he surfed. She knew they both reached the hospital around seven-thirty. But even though she'd have loved a leisurely breakfast, she'd settle for a fifteen-minute one.

It was pathetic really. She'd seen him only yesterday, but it seemed like too long ago. This was like being a lovesick teenager again.

Lovesick. The word hit her straight in the chest. She gave herself a shake. Was she ready to go there yet? Maybe, not quite.

She sent the text before she gave herself any more time to think about it, or second-guess herself.

The dots appeared on her screen and her heart gave a little jump.

Meet you at Don's. Order me a breakfast burrito.

She smiled. The café just along from the hospital where they had lunch. Close and convenient.

She walked swiftly down the street, ordered for Jamie, then added tea and scrambled eggs for herself.

He jogged up a few minutes later, his slightly damp,

just a bit too long hair wetting the collar of his pale blue shirt. She could smell the body wash he'd used to dull the scent of the ocean, but somehow there was still a bit there. The remnants suited him.

The food arrived quickly and Jamie signalled for a coffee too. 'Will the beach café be mad that I stole you?'

His cheeks flushed a little and he smiled. 'Well... I might have eaten that breakfast burrito too.'

'You did not.'

He shrugged. 'I did. Who knows when, or if, we'll get lunch today?'

She shook her head and ate her scrambled eggs. 'I'm hoping to dial into that seminar on measles later.'

'Did you ask for some vaccination figures for the island?'

Piper nodded. 'And I spoke to some of the staff at the clinics around reasons for refusal. The vaccination uptake around here is quite good, but there have been a few isolated cases of measles over the last few years. Two were related to trips to Florida where there was an outbreak at the time.'

Jamie nodded. 'Well, if I don't look busy, Merry will send me down to the ER.'

'To work with Joanne?' She couldn't help it. She was curious about their drinks last night, even though he'd told her where he was going. It was the easiest way to bring it up.

It was almost as if he could read her mind. He gave her a halfway kind of knowing smile. 'I'll need to introduce you. You'll like her, and she'll like you too. She's dating that guy you told me about.'

Piper was momentarily confused. 'What guy?'

'Guy Sanders—the cardiothoracic surgeon you said she was with the night of the drinks party.'

Piper couldn't pretend the world hadn't just got a little brighter.

'Oh.' She looked at him questioningly. 'Did you know?'

He shook his head. 'Rumours that you'd mentioned aside, I didn't have a clue. We've hardly seen each other since we got here—even though that wasn't the plan.'

She hesitated, wondering if she should ask the question. 'Did you tell her about us?'

'Of course.' He was halfway through his burrito. His eyes fixed on hers. 'Why? Wasn't I supposed to?' He wiped his mouth. 'She won't say anything.'

Piper held up her hand. If she'd had pom-poms she would have done a cheerleading routine, even though she'd never tried one in real life. 'No, of course it's fine.' She licked her lips. 'Did she say anything about me?'

A frown creased his brow. 'No, why would she?'

Piper shrugged. Curiosity was definitely killing her here. 'Nothing. I just wondered.'

Jamie pushed his plate away and took a sip of his coffee. 'Piper, you know you have nothing to worry about, right?'

She could feel heat rush into her cheeks. Was she really so obvious? Apparently so.

'I didn't mean anything.' Even she knew it was a weak response.

He signalled for the bill. 'Honestly—' he stood up '—Joanne will love you when she meets you, just—' His words stopped dead, and he gave a half laugh and made his way to the counter to settle the bill.

She hadn't managed to stand yet. Was that sentence going where she thought it was? *Just like I do?*

No way. It was far too soon. They were still getting to know each other, and even though it had slipped into her thoughts earlier, she hadn't expected it to slip into his. She was being ridiculous. Of course she was.

By the time Jamie came back he looked a little less flustered. 'Ready?'

It was as if it hadn't happened. She swung her purse strap over her shoulder, letting it settle in front of her. 'Sure.'

They walked back to the hospital and climbed the stairs to their floor. Every time they passed someone on the stairs or in the corridor she wondered if they were looking at them as if they were a couple. It felt like they had an array of blazing stars above their heads, even though she knew that wasn't true.

Did she look at every couple who passed her in the corridor or canteen and make assumptions about them? Of course she didn't.

But that still didn't stop the laser focus of Merry as they walked into the office together. Her eyes went from one to the other as she lifted a green sticky note. Merry had a system. Each day of the week was designated a particular colour of sticky note. Vengeance came for the doctor who hadn't done everything on the sticky notes on the day they were given them.

'Good. Strange one. A local just came back from vacation. Claims he was bitten by a raccoon that might have rabies.'

Jamie tensed next to her. 'He didn't get a jab before he got on the plane?'

Merry tutted. 'Apparently not.'

Piper could almost immediately feel his stress.

'Come on,' he said, striding down the corridor at such a pace Piper struggled to keep up.

The man was in the ER and looked quite relaxed. He lifted his trouser leg to reveal an angry bite. Jamie leaned over the wound.

'It's deep,' he said. 'Down into the muscle. Are you sure it was a raccoon that bit you?'

The man gave a half laugh. 'Absolutely. We'd been chasing the critters for a few days. They swarmed our camp at night.'

Jamie picked up his chart and checked it, flicking to the previous vaccine information. 'You didn't have any rabies shots before you went?'

The man, Kai, shook his head. 'Too expensive.'

Jamie took a breath. 'Where were you?'

'Kansas. It was a hunting party.'

'Do you go on hunting parties often?' Piper could hear the edge to his tone.

'Every year if I can.' The man looked decidedly pleased with himself.

'And if you hunt every year, do you never get a set of rules you should follow if something like this happens? You didn't consider rabies shots?'

The man wrinkled his nose. 'Well, sure. But no one ever really follows them rules and none of the other guys got rabies shots.'

Piper could tell that Jamie was trying to keep a lid on his temper right now.

She stepped forward to get a better look at the wound area. 'You do know that there is rabies risk in Kansas? Particularly around raccoons.'

'That's why I'm here.' He made it sound obvious, but Jamie's face was a picture.

He spoke, his voice rising a notch, louder but definitely clear. 'You do know that if you are scratched or bitten by a creature that could possibly have rabies, your first step is to get medical attention?'

The man waved his hand. 'We didn't have time for that. We had the hunt to finish, and then head for the plane.' He winked at Piper as if she were some kind of co-conspirator. 'We were in the middle of nowhere.'

Jamie spoke again. 'Is there anyone still in the area you can contact to see if the animal that has bitten you definitely has rabies? Reason I ask is it's likely the animal will be dead by now.'

That captured the man's attention. He considered Jamie for a moment, then held up his hands. 'It's the wild. We found dead raccoons throughout our trip.'

Jamie closed his eyes for a second and sucked in a breath. 'Rabies was probably what killed a high percentage of them.' He glanced at the clock. 'We need to work out from the time you were bitten how many hours have passed.'

'Why do you need to do that?'

'Because most people should get rabies immunoglobulin in the first twenty-four hours after being bitten. You need a rabies shot on day zero, day three, day seven and day fourteen. This is serious. Rabies can be lethal.'

Kai wrinkled his nose. 'People just say that to frighten others.'

Jamie put his hands on his hips. 'Up to seventy thousand people die every year from rabies.'

'Well, aren't you just the bundle of fun.' Kai blew a

bit of hair out of his face, but it seemed he was finally taking things seriously.

Piper felt a little nervous. Jamie's face was currently like thunder. She'd never seen him look so angry, and she partly understood it. If the man could afford to go hunting in Kansas, he could afford rabies shots.

'When, *exactly*, did you get bitten?'

'What does it matter, just give me the shot.'

Piper decided to step in. 'It's important because the first treatment should be given in the first twenty-four hours. If that's not possible, then it should be given by seventy-two hours. We need to work out if you're still in the treatment window.'

'Rabies is one hundred percent fatal, Kai.'

Kai's face finally paled. 'I don't believe that, there's always a treatment.'

'Once symptoms appear, it's one hundred percent fatal,' Jamie repeated. 'I need the date and time of when you were bitten.'

There was silence for a few moments, then Kai looked as if he was concentrating as he counted things off on his hands. 'It was Wednesday, no Thursday, and it was first thing in the morning. About four a.m.'

Piper swallowed and tried to calculate the hours, including the time difference. 'We're four hours ahead,' she murmured.

Piper and Jamie exchanged glances. They were past the seventy-two hours. Not by much. But by enough to worry them both.

'Let me prepare what we need,' said Jamie, disappearing to the emergency dispensary within the ER department.

Piper followed him. 'This might not work.'

He nodded. 'But better to give a rabies vaccine than not. I'll give him a vaccine, sign him up for the other three that he'll need and put some immunoglobulin in the wound. Worst case scenario, we'll have to give the immunoglobulin IM. But that's not the most effective way.'

'Rabies can incubate for sometimes as long as a year. How are we going to know if this has worked?'

Jamie shook his head. 'It's a wait and see. We have to go over the signs and symptoms with Kai, make sure he understands them and tell him to come back.'

Piper took a deep breath. She was watching Jamie take the medicines out of the fridge and prepare them. He was so cool, calm and collected, even though she'd felt the tension emanate from him earlier. She usually liked watching him work.

He was easy to watch. Today he was wearing a pale blue shirt and navy trousers. He always had the look of just-about-ready-for a haircut, but he suited the longer style. And with the blue shirt today, his eyes just popped. Should she even be thinking any of these things?

'But if we tell him to come back with symptoms, what are we actually going to do to help?'

He set down the vial he was holding and turned to her, taking a step closer so she could smell his aftershave. Right now, she could reach out and touch his chest. But she didn't. The chance of another staff member walking in was too big. She didn't want them caught in a compromising situation. She just tilted her head up to his.

'We're going to watch and learn.' His voice was deadly serious. 'Hawaii has been rabies free for a while. Any case we ever see will have been contracted somewhere else in the world. We know it's one hundred percent fatal.

We also know they are researching a cure. But this is a horrible disease, and those affected die a horrible death, seizures, neurological damage, pain, paralysis and difficulty breathing. All we can do is make someone suffering more comfortable.'

Piper's whole body shuddered. 'But's that just so… so…useless.'

She flung up her hands and Jamie caught one in his. 'It is. But it's part of our job. Not everyone has a good outcome and we need to be here for the good and the bad outcomes.'

She gave a nervous laugh. 'You make it sound like wedding vows.' She wasn't quite sure where those words came from, but what she was absolutely sure about was the way heat rushed into her cheeks. She imagined they were so red right now they could probably light up this room.

He gave her an amused look. 'Well, I'm not quite sure my head was there, but you could be right. We do pledge to do no harm.' He still had one of her hands in his, and for the briefest moment he pulled it to his lips and kissed it.

She could have sworn it was an electric shock. Something that zapped straight to her heart, but also to her brain.

This guy had got under her skin more than she'd ever imagined. Maybe those words had been a weird kind of Freudian slip. But even if it had been, it wasn't as if he'd bolted from the room.

In fact, he was still there, right in front of her.

Those blue eyes stared straight at her. 'Tonight,' he said. 'Do you want to come over to my place?'

She froze for a second. They'd been taking things slow, and it had been nice. But she couldn't pretend that her mind hadn't been racing ahead.

Her pause must have flustered him. 'You don't have to,' he said, breaking eye contact with her and focusing back on the vials.

Her hand slid over his. She smiled at him. 'I'd like that.' She didn't add anything else. She didn't need to. They both knew what this meant.

The next few hours floated past. Kai's wound was treated with immunoglobulin, the remainder being injected, and a rabies vaccine given in his arm. Piper went over the details of the signs and symptoms of rabies with him at length. It seemed horrible, telling someone the potential signs of their impending death, but she had to make sure he understood. She gave him appointments to come back for another three doses of the vaccine and the consequences of his actions finally started to sink in.

'How will I know if the raccoon that bit me actually has rabies?'

Piper licked her lips. 'Unless it has been kept somewhere it can be observed, you won't know. The fact that you told us you saw other dead raccoons in the area mean it's likely the rabies infection is present. Once a raccoon has the virus it will usually die within two weeks. We can't know for certain either way whether the raccoon that bit you was infected or not.'

She hated these kinds of conversations. But she had to be honest with her patient. In truth, she wished he'd had the sense to look at vaccinations before his trip. She asked the name of the tour operator and vowed to email them later. They should let anyone know who was booking with them that rabies was present in the area they were hunting and they should seek a vaccination before they came on the trip. She understood that vaccinations were a choice, but it sounded as though the risks associated with the trip hadn't really been outlined thoroughly by the tour operator.

By the time she'd finished writing up her notes she was exhausted. Jamie had gone to do a final ward review before they left and her nerves started to play up.

Should she go home first? Get showered and changed? Or did that ruin the spontaneity of the invitation? Did that make her seem too much of a control freak?

She glanced down at her clothes. Her dark trousers and yellow shirt were crumpled. She was sweaty. And not in a good way. A quick glance in the mirror told her that her hair was limp. Before she could give herself a chance to think about it any longer, she dashed off a message to him.

Going to freshen up—meet you at your house.

And in the blink of an eye, she was out of the hospital and gone.

Jamie wasn't entirely sure what was going on. Was that text message actually a quiet rejection—or did it mean exactly what it said?

He stayed at the office, finishing some notes, and then had a moment of mad panic that Piper might turn up at his house and he wasn't actually there.

How could he start trusting someone and loving them

if he wasn't actually there? That stopped him dead. Loving her?

He swallowed, his mouth dry; that sense of panic was increasing. But he took a breath, willing himself to relax, and found the corners of his lips turning upwards. Yes, Dr Grumpy was smiling.

Maybe this invitation had been a mistake. He could do the attraction part. That was the easy part. And to be truthful, that was where he still was with Piper.

But what about the bit that came next? He'd messed things up twice before. Was he really in a position in life where he could open up and share? Even the thought made him catch his breath.

Was he even being fair? He could see the vulnerability in Piper. If this didn't work, he got the feeling she wouldn't be able to just walk away and shake the whole thing off. She wasn't that type of person—at least, he didn't think so.

This wasn't just anyone—this was Piper Bronte, the woman he suspected was just as lonely as he was. He could sense she wanted a connection. Was he really ready for that? Or was he about to ruin everything? He wished he could predict the future. He wished he could look into a crystal ball and see the next five years. But unfortunately, the universe hadn't granted him that superhero gift so far.

He took a deep breath and tried to concentrate on the night ahead. Just one night. He could do that.

The evening temperature was pleasantly warm and he toyed with ordering in, or cooking something. Even though he didn't know all of Piper's like and dislikes, he knew what she'd eaten the last few times they'd been together so stopped at the deli and picked up some ingredients.

He showered, changed and started preparing the food, all the while wondering if she would actually show. Had he been too forward?

The whole boss/trainee thing was just so complicated too. And it made him determined to ask a few more questions.

The doorbell rang just before eight and he swung the door open. 'Come in.'

She gave him what looked like a nervous smile as she pushed a chilled bottle of wine into his hands. 'Here, I didn't want to come empty-handed.'

Her blonde hair was sitting just below her shoulders in natural curls, and she was wearing an orange and yellow swirly-patterned dress. It might have looked too busy on someone else, but suited Piper perfectly.

He bent to kiss her cheek, inhaling her amber scent and taking the wine from her hand. 'Come through to the kitchen.' He signalled with his head. 'You can watch me burn things.'

She followed him through, and he could see her looking from side to side as they moved through the house.

'It's still all Lenny's décor. The only things that are really mine are the two surfboards on the porch.'

'They look a little well worn—am I allowed to say that?' she asked as she perched up on one of the stools around the kitchen island and hob.

He popped the cork on the wine and poured some into the glasses, passing hers over to her. 'Surfboards are like guitars. You have to wear them in.'

She raised her glass. 'If you say so.'

He put some oil in a large pan, waited until it sizzled then tossed the ingredients in.

'What are we having?'

'Chicken stir-fry.'

'Perfect.' She smiled, sipping her wine.

'And there's dessert, if it sets,' he said warily, glancing at the large fridge.

'You made dessert?' There was a hint of humour in her voice. 'The guy that judges my traybakes?'

He tossed the ingredients around the pan. 'Hey, you're not the only person that can make things. My dessert is legendary.'

'Where?' she joked.

'In my own mind?' He laughed as he took a sip of wine himself. 'Honestly, I don't mind if you say it's hideous and don't eat it.'

He opened the fridge door. Top shelf was full of fresh fruit and veg, second shelf might have held some beer, but on the third shelf there was an elegant cheesecake, topped with peach and passionfruit.

Piper moved over and inspected it, inhaling deeply. Her eyes were sparkling. 'All this effort,' she said with a smile.

'You're worth it,' he replied without even thinking. There was a moment of silence that Jamie wanted to fill.

He glanced through the patio doors to the back garden. 'Do you want to eat in here or on the deck?'

The skyline was dimming, giving a warm purple shade to the sky. 'Let's eat outside,' she said.

Jamie kept cooking the stir-fry for a few more minutes before serving it up onto plates and carrying them outside. There was a white table with four regular chairs and an outside sofa with comfortable cushions.

He set the plates on the table as Piper followed with the wine glasses and cutlery. She automatically chose the sofa so they would be side by side.

Jamie sighed as he sat down next to her, relaxed into the cushions and lifted his plate. 'You know what I like most about this place?' he said in a low voice.

'What?' asked Piper, green eyes on his.

'This.' His voice was almost a whisper and he held out his hand to the world around them. Even though they were in a city, sitting in this garden they would never have known it.

As they listened in what seemed initially like silence, he could see Piper's senses go on alert. All around them was noise. But it was quiet noise, the leaves brushing together in the wind. The birds in a few trees and insects clicking around them. The scents of the flowers in the garden mixing with the eucalyptus leaves, lavender and chamomile. It really was like a little paradise.

Once he knew that she'd got it, he smiled at her. 'I came out here for a beer the first week I got here, and just listened. It's magic. There's a whole ecosystem in this garden alone. You just have to pay attention and listen.'

She gave him a warm smile. 'Well, there's a whole new side to you I didn't expect.'

He held out his hands. 'It's just like being part of the ocean.'

She shook her head firmly. 'Nope, there're sharks in there. This is entirely different.'

He laughed. 'You don't think there could be dangerous animals in the garden?'

She set down her wine glass. 'Spiders and scorpions are not the same. I can deal with them.'

He laughed as he topped up both of their wine glasses. 'Our world is part of the reason I went into tropical diseases. There are a million organisms that can do you harm, or help us live healthy lives together. In the correct set of circumstances, they can be all good, or all bad.'

Piper swallowed some food. 'That's simplistic.'

He waved his fork. 'Would you like to be part of a sci-fi experiment, so that you could go back in time to the Jurassic period and see some of the dinosaurs and plants that were around then? Or even go back to the Ice Age and wonder at how anything actually survived that?'

She comically narrowed her gaze at him. 'We've been down this road before. You know I'm a jump back in time for the dinosaurs girl. But you seem to have kept your interests a little hidden.'

He kept fork-waving. 'Yeah, yeah, trying to decide what university course to do was hard. Archaeology, climate change, physics, plants, space.'

'And you settled on medicine.'

He shrugged. 'Seemed like a good idea at the time.'

She moved a little closer to him. 'So, if you could go back in time and change that, would you?'

He frowned. 'Yes…and no. I wanted to be Indiana Jones, or Buzz Aldrin, or David Attenborough, or maybe even Stephen Hawking.' He liked the feeling of her body next to his. It was as if it was meant to be there.

'Don't let it be said that you're unambitious,' she joked. He slid his arm around her shoulder, pulling her even closer.

'Instead,' he sighed, 'I became a doctor.'

She knew he was joking, so she gave him a nudge in the ribs. 'Yeah, the easy choice.'

He set down his glass and brought his free hand up next to her face, one finger tracing down the side of her cheek. 'Yeah, the hours of hard work and study were simple.'

He kept his finger on her face. 'Do you ever think you picked the wrong career?'

She lifted her hand, folding it around his. 'Only for a second, on days like today, when you have to tell someone something you know they don't want to know or hear.' She gave a weak smile. 'Then I wonder why I didn't go into dermatology, or something that might be simpler.'

'But then we wouldn't have the opportunity to work together. Do you regret coming to Honolulu?'

She smiled. 'Not for a second.'

'And this?' he asked. 'Do you regret this? Because I need to know that you don't feel pressured. I'm your boss. Your trainer.'

Piper lifted her own hand to run a finger down his cheek, his skin connecting with where the stubble was starting to poke through. He would swear electricity sparked around them. 'I am here of my own free will. If you hadn't invited me over soon, I might just have broken in.'

He smiled, wondering if he was brave enough for the next part. 'I don't make connections easily,' he started. 'I've had two failed relationships in the past, and have been told I'm grumpy—you might not have noticed. Where do you want this to go?'

She blinked and he could see a waver in her eyes. For

a moment she looked away, focusing her gaze on one of the orange birds of paradise in the garden.

'Two failed long-term relationships?' He watched her swallow. 'Well, I didn't have that on my bingo card. What happened to them?'

'Me,' he said honestly. 'Both of them walked away but—' he took another breath '—it was entirely my fault.'

She licked her lips slowly. 'Why was it your fault?'

He paused, knowing this was his chance to be honest. To let Piper know what she could be getting into. But part of him really didn't want to tell her. And the realisation that he didn't want to give her an excuse to leave him hit hard, and deep.

He sighed and looked into those green eyes, hoping he wasn't about to sabotage everything. 'The initial stuff—the attraction, the romance is all fine. It's the bit that comes next that I'm not too good at.'

'And what bit is that?' She blinked. She was studying him closely. He'd put himself under this microscope. He had to see it through.

'The opening up stuff, the honest stuff, the staying for the long haul.' He tried a smile. 'Some people say I'm grumpy and that's hard to live with.'

She ran a finger down his cheek. It was the lightest of touches. 'But why are you grumpy?'

He shook his head. 'It's me. It's my natural tendency.' He stared out into the garden. 'And then some stuff happened at work. An investigation.' He sighed. 'I hadn't done anything, and they found the person responsible but—' he ran his fingers through his hair '—people I thought were friends at work disappeared, and I couldn't bear the thought that some people might have considered me guilty.' He gave a rueful shrug. 'I got grumpier, and angrier, and I couldn't shake it off, even when it was all over.'

She looked at him carefully. 'For both relationships?'

He sighed. She had a right to ask. He just didn't like talking about it. 'I guess so. I just couldn't shake things off. It's difficult to trust people when others have walked away. I guess I was just waiting for it to happen again—and it finally did.'

He watched her swallow.

'I don't make connections easily either.' Her voice faltered a little. Then her green eyes met his. 'But I want to. I want this to be something. I'm not the kind of person to get involved in something short-term. I want to be in it—' she paused and pressed her lips together as if she was scared to say the words out loud '—for the long-term. So, if this is us, you'd better be prepared to work. To stay, and try harder.'

He watched as a single tear slid down her cheek. 'Family is important to me,' she said. 'Because I've never really had that. My mum and dad died when I was quite young, and then I went to one relative and eventually another.' She put her hand on her chest. 'It feels like I've really been on my own for ever, and it's not what I want. It's not who I am.' She took another long, slow breath and gave him the sincerest look he'd ever had. 'I want to be in this.'

In a flash, his head was filled with a million thoughts. Pieces fell into place. His instincts had been right, and this connection was more than real. And he knew in a split second how he felt. Where he wanted this to go.

And who he could see himself spending the rest of his life with.

'I want to be in this too,' he said in a soft, gentle voice. 'In fact, know that I am in this. I'm in this for you. This is where I want to be.'

A smile broke out on her face as he brushed the tear away from her cheek. Her lips connected with his. Soft and sweet, with an insistence all of their own. One hand moved down her back and the other threaded its way through her silky hair. Their kiss deepened, more than any they'd shared before. This had meaning. This had purpose.

In case he had anything to wonder about, she shifted position, pushing his shoulders back against the sofa and moving her leg so she was sitting astride him.

As he took a breath, she started to unbutton his shirt. She leaned forward, the skin of their cheeks connecting. Her voice whispered in his ear, 'Do I get to see any other rooms in your house?' He could hear the mischief in her voice.

His hands had started unfastening the zip at her side, inching it down a little. He paused, smoothing his hands around her breasts as he kissed her again. 'Maybe I need you to specify which room, exactly, you want to see.'

Her hands were on his bare chest now, skin exposed to the warm air. He knew she could feel other parts of him as she smiled and pushed herself against him.

'I guess the room I really want to see is your bedroom.' Her voice had lowered—it was husky now and he didn't need any other sign.

He stood, holding her in place, carrying her easily back through the house and into his bedroom. This room also faced out onto the garden. The patio doors were open, white curtains flapping in the light breeze. But there was no one overlooking this property from the back. The garden was entirely enclosed by the dark green trees and bushes.

He laid her down on the bed. 'Are you sure about this?' he asked, before he moved.

Her hands wound around his neck. Her green eyes met his. 'Absolutely,' she replied as she pulled him to her and left him in no doubt of her intentions.

CHAPTER EIGHT

LIFE WAS A BUBBLE. At least that was how it felt to Piper. They dressed up and dined at the Korean restaurant, toasting each other with cocktails and returning to Jamie's.

She'd been secretly terrified that night at his house. When he'd finally opened up to her and told her about his past relationships, for a second her brain had told her to run. A man who wasn't prepared to work at a relationship wasn't someone she wanted.

But she'd known as she'd sat there, the very fact he was telling her this was his way of opening up. Or at least starting to.

She'd had a chance to run, or jump. And her heart had made her jump right in. She only hoped she wouldn't have reason to regret it.

After a few weeks, she had a toothbrush at his house and a change of clothes. Then, little by little, she started leaving her mark on his house. At first it was just a pair of cushions. Then it was a little carved wooden ornament on one of the shelves. Then she added a few books to the bedside table.

None of it was actually discussed, but it seemed to happen organically, and they were both comfortable.

After another few weeks, Merry raised her eyebrows at them as they walked into the office. 'Isn't it time you made this official?'

Both of them started and stopped walking. Jamie looked from Piper to Merry and back again. 'What do you mean?'

She made a scornful sound. 'What I mean is, you need to talk about this before someone else does. Have you met the barracuda in HR known as Indira?'

Jamie gave a sigh. He looked back at Piper. 'She's right. I'd better go.'

'*We'd* better go,' said Piper, smiling at him.

Merry held up one hand. 'No, go separately. She'll want to ask you questions.'

Jamie nodded, leaned over and gave Piper a kiss on the cheek, and left.

Indira was as impressed as he'd thought she would be. He reassured her that this was a normally developed relationship with no collusion, and would not impact on his decision-making, or Piper's training.

She made him sign something similar in legal speak.

Then Piper was called to the HR offices and asked similar questions, ending with a signed declaration from herself. For a few seconds, she had a wave of panic, wondering if Indira would tell her something about Jamie that she didn't know. But no. Nothing was said. There was no secret wife or ten children. And although she'd known that, it was still a relief.

By the time they met in the hospital canteen later, they had both been through the wringer. Ideally, they were there to talk over patients, but they ended up sitting out in the staff gardens on a bench sheltered from the sun by large trees.

Piper was eating a fruit salad and drinking some water. 'I thought at one point she was going to ask for your inside leg measurement.'

'Would you know it?' he quipped.

'I could have a guess,' she replied with a shrug.

They looked at each other and smiled. 'You okay with all this?' he asked.

She closed her eyes and breathed in. 'Couldn't be happier.'

A surge of warmth suffused him. It took him a few minutes to say the words out loud. 'Me either.'

She reached over and squeezed his hand. Neither of them had mentioned the immediate future. Jamie still had no idea what he'd do when his contract was up, or where he might want to go and work next. If they wanted a future together, they'd have to work all that out, and it could add complications. For now, he was happy they'd reached this place.

Piper opened her eyes. 'We have work to do.'

'We do? I thought we were just here for decoration?'

She laughed. 'Okay, we had a message from Tyler's primary physician back in Baltimore. I sent him all the details digitally, then spoke to him on the phone. He's going to have a long recovery. He's still exhausted and it looks like they plan to home school him for a while.'

'Poor guy,' said Jamie. 'The ultimate bad luck on the holiday of a lifetime.' He shifted in his seat. 'Kai still isn't showing any symptoms of rabies and he's completed his four vaccines now. I'm still not entirely sure the seriousness of this has sunk in.'

Piper lifted her eyebrows a fraction. 'I had a very interesting and sharp conversation with the tour operators. The words "potential liability" and "leaving themselves open to litigation" seemed to do the trick. They have assured me they will be clear about risks for anyone else booking a hunting trip in the area.' She paused for a moment. 'What about Marie? Did you see how her latest scans went?'

Jamie breathed in and nodded slowly. 'You know the sixteen-week scan showed some evidence of microcephaly?'

Piper nodded.

'Well, the twenty-week scan measurements were a bit more reassuring. There is still some evidence of microcephaly but at the moment it's not too severe. You know the baby does a huge amount of growing from this point onwards and she will be monitored every two weeks.'

'She?'

He smiled. 'Yes, Marie is having a girl. She seemed happy when she found out.'

'It's a long road ahead,' said Piper resting back against the bench with a sigh. 'Can I go along to the next one?'

'Sure, I'll put the date in your electronic diary.'

'Thank you.'

They made their way back upstairs and Jamie paused on the stairs. 'I'm surfing at a new beach tomorrow. I'm going with one of the surf instructors that I've met. So I'll be leaving a bit earlier than usual.'

She gave a nod. 'Meet you at work?'

He nodded. 'Meet you at work.'

* * *

She woke early, wondering if Jamie leaving had disturbed her. The doors remained slightly ajar and the gauze curtains were blowing in the breeze. It was like being in the pages of a romantic novel.

She stretched and showered, dressed and wandered through to the kitchen. She looked at the contents of the fridge and decided to pick something up. Her phone pinged and she picked it up. There were two alerts.

The first one was a picture of Jamie and Dom at the new beach, sent more than forty minutes ago. The second one was from a dog shelter she'd signed up to. It was showing a white and brown mongrel with big dark brown eyes that had apparently come into the shelter after its owner had died. Her heart twisted in her chest.

She hadn't had the dog conversation with Jamie yet. But she was prepared to go there. Millie, the dog, was already toilet trained and was seven years old. A rescue would be more practical than a puppy, but she would need to see what he thought of the idea.

By the time she'd picked up breakfast and made her way to the hospital she could already see things were busier than usual.

She walked through to the ER. All the boards were full.

'What's happening?' she asked.

'Multi-vehicle pile-up,' one of the charge nurses replied.

She looked around the busy department. There was also a group of suits.

'Who are they?'

The charge nurse sighed. 'Investigators. We've had

some issues with our controlled drugs. They are here to look into things at the worst possible time. The likelihood is we'll be in that cupboard all day.' She glanced at Piper. 'Would you mind seeing some of the minors and helping us clear things?'

'No problem,' said Piper, grabbing an apron and some gloves. 'I'll text Jamie to join us too when he arrives.' She didn't like the sound of being watched by investigators but knew it was necessary. These things happened in hospitals but she'd never been directly involved before.

'Brilliant. We need all the hands we can get.'

Piper sent the text and glanced at the board. There were a number of patients she could see easily, so she put her head down and got to work.

Jamie stretched his back after the forty-five-minute drive to the beach outside Honolulu. He patted Dom—he'd made it safely and he could see the rest of the guys unloading for the early morning surf.

The beach was rockier than others, which meant it was a little less popular. But there were still a fair number of surfers here at this early hour. There was no tower, which meant this beach had no lifeguards, but that was fine with him. He met the surf instructor on the shingle beach and listened as he talked him through any danger zones, the riptides, rocks and coral around the area.

He was already jealous of those out in the surf. The waves were hitting the beach perfectly and it wasn't long before he was in the water, paddling out.

This was one of his favourite parts. The feel of the water against his skin. The pull of the waves as he pulled himself through against the tide. The burn in his arms as they worked harder and harder to get him out to the perfect spot. It was tougher than it looked, and some mornings he only had time to do this a few times.

This morning had been even harder. He had a routine, which he loved—for his own physical and mental health. But waking up this morning and having to tear himself away from the warm body lying next to him? It was much harder than he'd ever predicted.

He'd surfed when he'd lived with his two previous girlfriends. But he'd never felt the same attachment, love and comfort that he did around Piper. That actually embarrassed him now. That both of those women had eventually left him because they knew his feelings better than he knew his own. He'd shortchanged them.

Yes, he'd had affection for them both. But he'd never felt like he did with Piper. This was totally new, all-enveloping. It meant everything to him, and he wondered when to have that conversation with her. The one that said, *This is it. Let's stay together. Let's plan on for ever.*

Would he scare her away? She'd revealed part of herself to him. And it all made sense. He could understand her loneliness. It made him ache. That she'd experienced such an unfortunate set of events that had left her feeling like she'd never really had a family.

Might he have been a little bit scared? Funnily enough, not for a second. Piper was precious. Of course she would seek out connections for herself. Jamie had been lucky. His mum and dad were still in his life back in Scotland. They were both still working, were proud of their son, and didn't smother him in any way. He'd been lucky enough to discover found family with Joanne. Their connection might not be understood by everyone, but Jamie knew they would still be friends into their pension years.

He couldn't imagine how lonely life would be without these people. Piper deserved it all. She deserved love, she deserved happiness and he only hoped he could be the person that could give it to her.

His body had been on automatic pilot, his arms powering through the water, until he became conscious of other specks in the ocean around him. It was odd—no matter how giant the ocean, surfers all seemed to know the correct distance to wait and catch the best waves and all congregated in the same areas.

He climbed onto his board, turned around to face the shore and sat astride, waiting and watching. Another of his favourite parts. Those moments just before.

Sometimes he would sit here for five to ten minutes. Sometimes he would sit here for half an hour—particularly at sunset times.

The guy on his right started paddling, getting ready to start riding a wave. Jamie turned his head to watch his fellow surfer. He wasn't the type to try and ride someone else's wave and impinge on their enjoyment. He preferred to watch and admire.

But something else caught his eye. At first he blinked, not sure he had seen anything at all. And then he adjusted his position on the board, squinting in the light reflecting off the ocean and trying to get a better view.

Was something else out there?

The ocean was full of a myriad of different things. Bottles, parts of fishing nets, broken surfboards, sometimes parachute remnants from parasailing that had gone wrong. Clothing, discarded life jackets, and any paraphernalia left on beaches could all be dragged out to sea.

He blinked again. Was that something? Panic gripped his chest. Was that a hand?

He stood on his board, shielding his eyes and attempting to get a better view. The guy who'd been on his right was already gone, and the guy on his other side was concentrating on the shore.

'Hey!' Jamie tried to attract his attention. But he was a fair distance away and voices didn't always travel well out on the water.

He focused his attention again. Fear gripped him. Yes, that was definitely a hand, and was that another next to it?

'Help! Someone needs help!' he shouted, lying down on his board and starting to move as quickly as he could towards the hand.

He didn't carry a phone or any kind of alert when he surfed. He had his surfboard leash, his wetsuit and a very basic life jacket, but that was it. He always told someone else when he surfed and never went that far out.

His muscles burned as he powered towards the hand. It wasn't just one hand. It was two. And the closer he got, the more he could see just how much trouble they were in.

One person was clinging to the other, essentially dragging them both down.

The temptation to dive in was strong. But Jamie knew the surfboard he had right now was their greatest chance of floating and survival.

'Grab on,' he shouted as he came towards them.

Teenagers. It was teenagers. Both looked exhausted. As soon as the girl grabbed hold of the side of his board she vomited into the ocean. She was wearing a wetsuit and a very unsuitable life jacket. Her counterpart was similarly dressed and Jamie could see he was in the midst of a full-blown panic attack.

'Hold on. Hold the board,' he instructed.

The girl was already failing and he bent over and grabbed the neck of her wetsuit, determined to keep a hold of her.

'What on earth are you two doing out here?'

'Surfing,' spluttered the boy.

'Where are your boards?'

'Gone.' The boy held up an exhausted hand, showing a tether still around his wrist. 'Sharks,' he gasped. 'There were sharks and she panicked.'

Jamie frowned, trying to make sense of what he was hearing. He scanned the ocean for any immediate danger. In the distance he could spot a few fins, but couldn't say for sure what they were. There was nothing in the immediate vicinity.

Sharks didn't really attack people. Shark attacks were extremely rare. They could be hungry, they could be curious. But shark attacks were usually put down to mistaken identity. Some people believed that sharks could be attracted by bright colours but Jamie wasn't entirely convinced, though the girl did have a bright pink wetsuit.

He made an attempt to steer the board back towards the shore, but manoeuvring wasn't easy with two people holding on. He glanced back to shore, hoping someone might have noticed, but so far he could see no help coming.

He kept trying to move, sideways, then turning the full board in the correct direction. As he lay down to move forward his board tipped, nearly sending him into the ocean.

'Careful,' he said. 'Try and hold on near the back of the board so I can move us towards the shore.'

It was difficult for his arms to power through the ocean if there was no room for them to move. It didn't take a genius to note that if he had to stay astride the board, paddling back ashore would be extremely difficult depending on the tides.

But as he started to make progress the board tipped again and he realised the girl had let go. She just didn't have the strength. Jamie didn't hesitate. He dived straight in, and under, at the point she'd disappeared. It wasn't that her life jacket didn't work at all, but it was clearly old and needed to be replaced. Its float capabilities were definitely limited.

He gasped as he pulled her up to the surface. Should he take off his life jacket and try to put it on her? It seemed like the best idea, but wasn't practical. He wasn't sure he could hold her, hold the board and shuffle himself out of the life jacket and get it on her without putting them all at more risk.

He held onto the side of the surfboard. 'Kick to shore!' he instructed the boy.

The girl bobbed in the space he'd left for her between the board and his body. Every few seconds she slipped and he had to make a grab for her again. This was useless. They needed some help.

He waved his arm, trying for a few moments to capture someone's attention. But the sun was in the wrong direction, meaning he wasn't sure if anyone saw them.

Just then he felt a swell and a pull and his heart sank.

Riptides could be deadly and he knew exactly what this was. They were strong, unpredictable currents that flowed across each other. Ocean swimmers were all schooled on what to do if they felt themselves in a riptide, but Jamie wasn't sure if the same rules applied to three people clutching onto a surfboard as their only real buoyancy aid.

He could hear the rules in his head. *Don't swim against the current. Relax. Raise. Ride.*

But which way was the current actually going? This riptide could push them hundreds of yards offshore.

And then he saw something else out of the corner of his eye. A rock. The surf instructor had pointed it out to him, warning him to stay away from it. Riding this riptide would be dangerous, even deadly. People were told to swim parallel to shore, but swimming parallel right now would let the riptide take them straight into danger.

Although he could see one, he knew there were many rocks and coral reefs in the same vicinity. This riptide could take them straight into it, where they could all be torn to shreds.

Already he was struggling to keep the girl afloat. So, after a few seconds consideration, he took his life jacket off. It was dangerous and it was stupid. But she was practically unconscious. He slid one of her arms into it while trying to keep a hold of the board.

It seemed to take for ever to get her other arm inside and finally fasten the clips to secure it in place. His energy was depleting. They weren't swimming against the riptide at all, just floating along in it. Jamie lifted his arm again, doing his best to signal to the shore for help. But the waves around him were getting stronger, gaining momentum from the fact they were now crashing off the nearby rocks.

'Try and push backwards!' he shouted to the boy. 'This current is going to take us into the rocks!'

If only they could get out of the pull of this water. He was struggling. He could feel his limbs starting to feel heavy. He started to be aware of how cold he was. If he'd been by himself he would have tried to remain on top of the surfboard. But there wasn't room for three atop the surfboard. Any attempt to try and push the girl on top failed dismally. He also considered putting his own tether on her, but it didn't make sense. She could barely open her eyes. If she fell off the board he was sure she wouldn't be conscious enough to pull herself back on top.

As his limbs grew heavier and cold started to overtake his body, his mind went to Piper. He didn't want to leave her. He wanted to be part of her future. She'd already had enough bad experiences in her life without her boyfriend drowning in the sea.

He should have stayed in bed this morning. He should have just cuddled into her and realised just how lucky he was.

Everything about the ocean right now was wrong. His legs used every available ounce of strength he had left, trying to push them backwards out of the riptide. He didn't care about being far from shore. He just cared that they wouldn't be pulverised against the rocks and coral and end up like Swiss cheese.

There was a thud at his back. A crash. His heart rate quickened. They hadn't made it out of the riptide. They were practically on the rocks.

He felt a sharp pain in his calf. A tear. There was

coral beneath them. He knew the damage coral could do. Every surfer did. It had clearly come straight through his wetsuit.

His hand still held the board and he wondered if it was worth it. Wouldn't he be better trying to hold the two teenagers and keep them alive?

I'm sorry, Piper was the thought that rushed through his head.

She didn't deserve this. He wanted to be with her. He wanted to be her family. He wanted to spend the rest of his life with her. If only he would get the chance.

His hand caught a hold of the teenage girl. She hadn't even told him her name and he pulled her to his chest, wrapping his arms around her to try and shield her from the rock and coral.

His foot connected with something that made every pain sensor in his body scream. But his mouth couldn't follow as the waves were crashing over his head.

Something caught at the side of his head with a thump. He knew it was Dom. There were stories of surfers being knocked out by their own boards, but Jamie hadn't expected to be one of them.

He thought he heard another noise, a scream, but his brain didn't really have time to compute because all of a sudden everything went black.

CHAPTER NINE

THE ER WAS CHAOS. Piper was struggling to find some of the patients she was trying to clear and eventually found them still in the waiting room.

All of the patients from the multi-vehicle road traffic accident had been brought in. They included children on a school bus, and now the ER waiting room was rammed with angry parents trying to find their children.

HR had called for extra staff and diverted admin staff from other areas to man the front desk and Piper could see they were trying their best.

Piper had now assessed and cleaned fifteen wounds, putting local anaesthetic and stitches into seven. One would wait for Theatre due to the positioning and depth of their wound, and another few had a variety of temporary stitches.

She wiped the sweat from her brow as she dumped the latest apron and gloves, then stood and scrubbed her hands again at the sink.

One of the suits from earlier stuck something in front of her nose. 'Piper Bronte?'

'Excuse me?' She bumped him with her elbow, pushing him away from the sink until she'd finished washing. He stared at her and she could swear he didn't blink. 'What do you want?'

'Can you verify these entries for me?' He showed her a list of dates with her signature, all done while she was countersigning for using controlled drugs. Morphine was frequently used for patients in severe pain and she knew she'd prescribed and administered the drug to a number of patients in here, alongside one of the nursing or medical staff.

'Can't actually tell you,' she said truthfully. 'I'd need to double-check all the dates against the electronic prescriptions. It looks like my signature, and I've certainly signed for and administered morphine in this department, but I can't verify these entries for you right now. Look at this place.' She held up her hands and shook her head. 'This is hardly the time.'

The man glowered at her. With spectacular timing, she heard one of the charge nurses shout over to her, 'Piper, can you check this with me?'

Piper strode over. She checked the prescription, counted the drugs in the cupboard. Took out one vial, pulled up the medicine, watched the cupboard be locked, signed the book and then went with the nurse to witness the administration to a man with a badly broken leg. They checked his identification band, checked his prescription again, then administered the medicine. They countersigned and returned to the treatment room to dispose of the needle, syringe and empty vial.

She was conscious of a dark-suited person following them around. She was about to say something when she glimpsed Indira. Her voice was quiet but clear.

'She's being difficult?'

Piper was ready to cross the room in two strides but what she heard next stopped her cold. 'Jamie Robertson? Yes, he's not reported for duty yet. There was an incident and investigation at another place he worked.' She gave a hollow laugh. 'It was all investigated and he wasn't implicated. Someone else was guilty.'

So why mention it? Piper felt a chill across her skin. Was this what Jamie had been telling her about? The investigation was around drugs? But he wasn't implicated. And she was pretty sure that Indira was out of line right now.

She moved quickly. 'You think I'm being difficult. I've not been, but I can be. Whatever and whoever you're investigating is not appropriate in this instance. The ER is slammed. There are patients here with very serious injuries and you're getting in the way. An investigation shouldn't get in the way of patient care.' She looked directly at Indira. 'I'm sure our HR manager can find you a more appropriate time to interview staff about this. After all, I'd hate the hospital to be open to the possibility of failing patients because clinicians were being pulled away from their care responsibilities. The litigation would be horrendous, not to mention the bad publicity.'

She turned on her heel and left. She was mad. And where was Jamie? The words *not reported for duty yet* stuck in her mind. That wasn't like him at all.

She pulled out her phone and called him. It went straight to voicemail. Something skittered across her skin. A bad feeling. Something wasn't quite right.

She started walking through the ER, her head going from side to side. It was chaotic. Maybe he was actually here but had just dived straight into work. But every room she looked in had busy staff, but no Jamie.

She stopped and picked up one of the phones from the wall as she heard the wail of yet another ambulance siren. The phone only rang once. 'Merry? It's Piper—is Jamie with you, or on the ward?' Her racing heart filled the silence and she swallowed against a dry throat as she listened. 'No, not since first thing this morning. He was going surfing. I just expected him to be here. Will you page me if you hear from him?'

Merry's agreement didn't settle her as she hung up the phone. Because she wasn't a real ER doc, Piper never triaged any of the ambulance patients, particularly not those who came in under a blue light. Usually, she just took a patient from the board when they'd already been clerked in.

But today the voices made her stop as soon as she heard the name of the beach.

'Near drowning, trying to rescue two teenagers. Male, around thirty. No ID at the moment. Police are talking to others at the beach. Got caught in a riptide and was smashed off the rocks. Multiple injuries—possible fractured ribs, tib and fib. Unconscious with head injury. He's not orientated to time or place. Breathing spontaneously after resus. Tachycardic, hypotensive, multiple wound contusions.'

'And the other two?'

'Girl is hypothermic, following in ambulance behind, and the boy is conscious with multiple similar wound contusions. The coral was rough on them.'

Piper's legs had started moving towards the gurney. The paramedic continued. 'He really saved them both, apparently shielded the girl from the rocks and coral, taking all the hits himself.'

There was a sharp noise. 'He's one of ours.' Before she had time to think, she heard the shout. 'Lira, Mark, Ben—get over here! It's Jamie Robertson. And someone find Piper!'

The gurney was moved automatically into one of the trauma bays. And everything became a blur. She wanted to help, but knew she wasn't the best person. So, she stood with her back pressed against the wall in the trauma room, not getting in the way of her colleagues.

They moved like the slick, well-oiled machine they were. She wasn't an ER doc, she didn't have that skill set. But when she heard certain shouts: *'Call for X-ray!'* She picked up the phone next to her and made the call. *'Get these bloods to the lab!'* She grabbed the nearest porter. *'Get another IV line in!'* She picked up a cannula and had it in place in less than a minute. One of the nurses tapped her shoulder and handed her the line for the IV bag she'd just run through and Piper connected it. The whole time her heart was racing.

'What's going on?'

Merry had appeared as if by magic, and had her hand on Piper's shoulder. Her voice cracked with emotion. 'Is he alive?'

'Yes,' Piper said quickly, instantly allowing herself to be swamped with relief. 'He's alive. They're just assessing his injuries.'

Merry stood for a moment, clearly taking the news in. Her brown eyes turned to Piper. 'Do you need anything?'

She shook her head and felt the warm hand on her arm.

'I'll go and take care of things for the ward, and for any referrals. Phone me if either of you need anything.'

And in a sweep of gold, she was gone.

Piper tried to catch her breath. The X-rays were over quickly. Multiple fractures were confirmed. CT called to say they were ready just as Jamie started to come around. He'd been breathing on his own, but the contusion to the back of his head had caused concern. She followed the gurney to CT, waited until he had been positioned in the machine and waited outside the reporting room. She didn't ask questions. She didn't want to compromise any of her colleagues. But Mark stuck his head out of the room, clearly looking for her, met her gaze and said a few words. *'No permanent damage.'*

He was good. Or at least he would be. She closed her eyes to give herself a moment. Seconds later, he was wheeled back out, and this time into a cubicle instead of the resus room.

She waited until he was settled, attached to the monitor again for his heart and blood pressure, before she went into the room.

Lira gave her a nod. 'Perfect timing.' She lifted a wound pad and Piper winced at the angry abrasion wounds. They were on his back, his legs, his feet. The wetsuit had provided little protection.

She spoke automatically. 'All these wounds should be flushed out with clean water for five minutes. Any obvious contaminants should be removed and then some iodine applied, and some antibiotic cream.'

'You don't want to watch and wait for any signs of infection?'

Piper shook her head. 'I can almost guarantee it, with

this many abrasions, what's in the sea, and his exposure getting resuscitated on the sand. Let alone to being in here.' She gave a nervous laugh. 'This place has probably been a petri dish today. Let's not wait. Let's just start.'

Lira gave a nod. 'No problem. I'm just going to sort out some analgesia for him.' She pointed a finger at Jamie. 'Three broken ribs, all these wounds, a fractured tibia and a small intracranial haematoma. Don't move until I get back.'

She disappeared through the curtains and Piper tried to swallow. Tears had already pooled in her eyes.

'Hey...' His voice was scratchy and he reached out towards her.

Piper had never moved so quickly, grabbing his hand with both of hers and letting herself feel his skin against hers. He was still cold and she automatically started rubbing his hand between hers.

'Resuscitated?' she said.

He closed his eyes. 'I'm sorry. I had to go and help. I couldn't leave those kids out there.'

And she knew that. She knew who he was. She wouldn't be with him if he'd been the type of guy to leave those kids to drown. But the weight of that settled on her shoulders like a giant elephant. 'I know,' she croaked.

'And now an intracranial bleed?'

He winced and tried to touch the back of his head. 'It should all get reabsorbed—at least that's what Mark told me. He just said they'll observe me over the next few days.' He blinked and for a second she was so glad he was lying down because he looked wobbly.

His hand was starting to slowly but surely heat up.

'When I said to meet me at the hospital, this isn't what I had in mind.'

He gave a half-smile and nodded. 'I know. What's going on?'

'Major road accident,' she replied, and as she went to add something else the curtains swept back and one of the dark suits entered.

'Dr Jamie Robertson?' he said.

Piper felt every hair on the back of her neck rise. She could feel Jamie bristle too.

'Yes—what?' he replied, trying to sit a little further up in the bed but his face distorted with pain.

'We're undertaking an investigation into the disappearance of some controlled substances from the ER. We need to interview anyone who has worked here. Can you look at this and verify your signature on these recordings?'

Both Jamie and Piper spoke at the same time.

'This is completely wrong. Dr Robertson is a patient. He's not working and he's just suffered a head injury...'

'No! I won't verify my signature. How on earth am I supposed to do that? What's this about? I want to know exactly what's been happening. Why am I under suspicion? I won't speak to you unless I have legal representation.'

There was a long silence. Piper stared at Jamie wide-eyed. She'd never heard such a fierce reaction from him. It was out of character.

The suited man tutted. 'Why would you require legal representation? We do understand you've been part of an investigation in the past.'

It was the way he delivered the words. The hint of accusation.

Jamie's voice was icy. 'Get out. I'll give you the name of my lawyer when I'm discharged from hospital.'

He pulled his hand away from Piper and she looked at him in confusion, before gathering her thoughts as quickly as she could. 'Did you clear this interview with Jamie's doctor? Mark Bellingham? I'm sure he wouldn't have agreed.'

The dark-suited man turned and left, muttering under his breath.

Jamie looked at her, his eyes blank. 'Did you know about this?'

Her skin prickled. 'They tried to interview me earlier. I refused.'

'Did you know about me?'

She hesitated, wondering how on earth to tell him. 'I heard something earlier, but this is what you were telling me about before—you just didn't tell me it had been a drug investigation,' she started as the curtains swept back and Lira appeared with the dressing trolley and medicine. A junior nurse was with her.

'Can you give me ten minutes, please?'

Piper gave a nod. 'Of course.' She glanced back at Jamie, but he didn't look at her. It was almost as if his mind was someplace else.

As she walked away her legs wobbled and her stomach gave a flip and she knew what was coming. She ran to the nearest restroom and vomited, letting her head hang over the sink until she was sure it had passed.

She washed her face and her hands. She had the bathroom to herself so slid down to her haunches for a few seconds, letting the cool tiles at her back soothe her racing heart.

She could have lost him. She could have lost him today. All because he loved surfing. She'd known this when she'd got together with him, and even though she didn't have the same interests, she would never ask Jamie to give up something he loved.

But this could happen any time. No matter how careful he was. It was always a risk. And asking him to live a life without risk wouldn't be fair. Even she knew that.

But it swamped her. That feeling of almost having a perfect life. The start of a family. Someone to share with. To plan with. To be with for ever. To have all that—and then to have it snatched away. Again.

She really didn't know if she could handle this. When she'd decided to trust Jamie and let him in, she'd known she was opening herself to a world of potential hurt again. But the truth was, she'd never thought Jamie would ever do anything to hurt her. But he had. Unwittingly, but it was just who he was.

He'd said it himself. He couldn't not have helped those teenagers. But could she live with that? What kind of selfish human being was she, that she would have preferred it if he'd walked away?

As for his reaction to the drugs question? She had no idea what that was about, and didn't really care. They'd ambushed her too, and she'd also said no. She hadn't thought about getting a lawyer, she'd just wanted a chance to verify things herself, but there was no opportunity to do that.

She took another breath. The walls around her seemed to make this small space echo. Everything was getting too much for her.

Her thoughts drifted back to being told that her mummy and daddy couldn't come back and pick her up. The overwhelming sensation of being alone in this world.

The horrible need for resilience in a child who should never have had to learn that lesson. She was back there. Right now. Right back in the middle of all those emotions.

It wasn't a life. It wasn't a life she wanted. But when she'd finally got what she wanted—and realised it could be gone again in a fraction of a second? It was just too much.

Tears flowed down her cheeks and she struggled to breathe. This was all so wrong. The timing couldn't be worse. What kind of person would break up with her boyfriend after he'd been injured? When he'd likely need someone to care for him for the next few weeks.

But all of that would just impinge on her heart more. She'd dreamed of the perfect life. She'd found it. And was now realising she wasn't emotionally equipped for it. The risks were just too high.

She walked back through to the cubicle. Lira had clearly finished as Jamie was positioned on his side, with fresh wound dressings, his face still twisted, either in pain or anger.

She moved to the side of the bed. 'I'm sorry, Jamie,' she said in a whisper. 'I have to go.'

His eyes opened. 'What?'

She shook her head. 'This—us—it's just not working out. I wasn't ready for this. I wasn't ready for today.'

He stared at her. 'You believe what they said? You doubt me?'

She frowned. 'What? What have they said?'

'About the drugs,' he snapped.

'This is nothing to do with the drugs,' she replied. 'This is about us. This is about me staking my heart and my life on a guy who might not come home one day.' She pressed her hand against her heart. 'I thought I was ready. I thought I was ready to find and build a family. But I've realised I'm not. Maybe I'm just meant to be alone. I can't cope. I can't let myself be broken again.' She shook her head. 'It's happened too many times. And I just can't let myself go through something like that again.' She took a deep breath and looked him in the eye. 'I'm glad you're safe. I'm glad you'll get better. But I can't do it. I can't watch. I'm sorry, I don't have it in me.'

He looked confused now, and even though she knew he'd had painkillers and he had the mild bleeding, she couldn't wait until he was clear of this to tell him. She had to do it now. Because she had to walk while she still could.

'You trust me?' he asked in his croaky voice.

She reached out and touched his face. 'Of course I trust you,' she said. 'But I have to do what's best for me right now.' She gave him a sad smile. 'Find someone who will make you happy. You deserve it, and I want it for you more than anything.'

And before she could change her mind, she turned on her heel and left.

Jamie was stunned. His chest was so tight he felt as if he couldn't breathe. It was as if the world had planned a disaster for him, and if one part of the disaster didn't go the way it should have, another part would just be revealed.

He'd nearly died today. He'd nearly died—and all his thoughts had been about Piper. About the life they could have together and what he could potentially lose.

And then he'd lived. He'd lived, and got here, only to have another part of his life implode.

He'd done this before. He couldn't do it again.

Piper had looked at him and told him this wasn't about the drugs. But what else could it be?

People had walked away before, and it was about to happen all over again. He couldn't take it. He just couldn't go through all that again. The looks on people's faces. The wide eyes whenever he wanted to prescribe a controlled drug. The double and triple checking. The questioning of his abilities and if he was looking after his patients correctly or just prescribing something so he could have a chance to steal it.

No. He couldn't survive that again.

He almost let out a wry laugh. At least he didn't need to wait to see if Piper would stay. Because it was apparent she wouldn't. The first whiff of scandal and she was gone. He actually couldn't believe it of her.

He'd thought he'd got things right this time. He'd thought he'd picked the person he could invest a whole life in.

Why could he ever have thought things might be different? He'd thought he'd known Piper. He'd thought she'd revealed the biggest parts of herself to him, and he'd thought he'd be able to trust in her.

But the trust was apparently one-sided.

She'd gone. She'd left.

And he'd been a fool. A fool to finally believe in love, and to believe he had found it when, in fact, the whole world was laughing at him.

His head was still fuzzy. Things still weren't entirely clear to him. But one thing was clear.

Piper was gone. And the world was echoing around him.

CHAPTER TEN

MERRY WAS SITTING next to his bed. This was not how he'd imagined his future. Was this actually some kind of drug-induced nightmare? Because it felt like it.

'What is it?' he croaked. His voice still wasn't quite back to normal. They'd tried to intubate him at the beach, but he'd responded by vomiting water all over them.

She gave him her best frown. 'Sit up.'

He gave himself a shake and sat up in the bed. He pulled a face, remembering the lightweight cast on his leg, and many other sensitive areas, as he adjusted his position. 'What is it?'

She set down a letter on his bedside table and slid the table in front of him. 'Read.'

He picked it up, feeling Merry's glare. It was Piper's letter of resignation. He sighed. 'She's gone?'

'She's gone,' Merry confirmed.

'I thought it was all just some crazy dream—or nightmare.'

'Well, apparently not.'

He took a deep breath. 'I don't know what to do. I'm not even sure entirely what I said to her. I think I can remember what she told me. How she didn't feel ready. She wasn't designed to be in a relationship. How things were just too hard. That she was afraid of being broken.' He waved one hand in the air. 'And in between all that there was some drug investigation and I was shouting for a lawyer. But as soon as she found out about the drugs—she just left.' He shook his head, trying to put all the pieces together in a way that might make sense.

Merry frowned and shook her head.

He looked at her and sighed. 'I didn't do anything wrong with drugs. But I've been down this road before. My first girlfriend left too, when I was in the middle of an investigation.'

Emotions swept over him. Anger, resentment, disappointment and despair. 'I know I'm not the easiest guy to be around, but I need the other person in my life to support me.'

He noticed the multiple coloured Post-it notes in her hand. She set them on the table too. 'All from Joanne. Answer her. Soon. I feel like I'm her secretary.' Then she gave a big sigh. 'What Piper, and you, don't realise is that we're all broken. All of us, at different parts of our lives. And we can break again, and again. You just need to find the right person to help you build yourself back up.'

She eyed him sceptically. 'Maybe you're not the person for her.'

'I am!' he shouted immediately. 'Of course, I am. I just have to be conscious long enough to convince her.' It came out of nowhere. Through the doubts and reservations like a tidal wave. It was overwhelming and told him what was, deep down, in his heart. The realisation had been there for the last few weeks, and certainly in the last day, when he'd thought he might never get a chance to see her again. And all he knew for certain was that, no matter what, he wanted to see Piper again.

Merry gave a sly smile and nodded approvingly. 'Just checking.' She stood up and pointed to the crutches in the corner. 'I'm going to get the physio. He'll get you on your feet.' She placed one more purple Post-it on his table. 'And this one? It's your lawyer. Recommended by me, because you need someone local. Someone to talk to your investigators, *and* to a certain someone from HR who shared information she shouldn't have. Because you do have people in your life to support you. I'm one, Joanne is clearly one, and I'm predicting Piper is another.'

'Are you telling me to go get them?' He put his hand on the note.

Her hand closed over his. 'I'm telling you to go get your girl. The rest can all wait.'

CHAPTER ELEVEN

TRYING TO CHANGE her designated trainer in a specialty was a lot harder than she'd imagined.

Everyone's placements were confirmed—just like hers had been. But there had to be circumstances that meant that people might request a change? A family emergency? A change in circumstances? A broken heart?

She put her head back in her hands. Nothing made sense to her. And that was all she wanted—her life to make sense for the first time in for ever.

Her apartment was starting to echo around her again, the space and lack of personality amplifying in a cruel and taunting way.

Her doorbell rang and she glanced at her phone. Her delivery of four doughnuts, a tea and two cream cakes wasn't due for another ten minutes. Maybe the driver was early.

She walked over to the door and pulled it open. It was truly the last person she'd expected to see.

Jamie was decidedly lopsided, a large padded bag in one hand and leaning heavily against one crutch. 'You need to let me in. I'm going to fall down,' he said, his thick accent dancing across her ears.

She automatically stood aside, and he moved slowly

in on his crutches. She could feel herself enter doctor/patient mode and she pointed to a chair for him.

He sat down with a sigh and then, strangely, started rooting about the padded bag. 'Only one tea?' he asked.

It took her a moment to click. 'That's my delivery?'

He grinned as he pulled out the cream cakes and doughnuts. 'Wow. Sugar rush. Met the guy outside. He asked if you could put the carrier back outside your door.'

She sucked in a breath, trying to keep her temper. She grabbed the empty carrier and stuck it in the corridor outside her apartment. She'd already tipped the guy online, so he wouldn't be mad with her.

But she was mad with someone else. She folded her arms as she closed the door. 'What are you doing here?'

'Eating cake,' he answered promptly.

She paused, taking in his appearance. His colour wasn't good. He'd definitely struggled with those crutches. And she had no idea how he'd got here.

'Should you even be out of hospital?'

He pulled a face. 'Yeah, well, it was a bit of a debate. But I had motivation to get out of there.'

He met her gaze and she let her arms drop. She moved back across the apartment and picked up a doughnut and sat down next to him. He winced.

'What?'

'Sorry.' He grimaced and pointed to his thigh that she'd just grazed. 'Coral wound.'

She could say so much, but she could already smell his aftershave and the soap that he used. It was catching somewhere in her chest.

'What are you here for, Jamie? I told you everything I needed to at the hospital.'

He gave her a nod. 'I know you did. But I didn't get much of a chance of a response, and I thought I had a right for you to hear me out.' He pointed to his head. 'Plus, head injury. So, my recollection is kind of faded, because in my head you heard I was under investigation for drugs, and left.'

'Not true,' she spat out instantly, aghast. She hadn't even considered that. The drug investigation had meant literally nothing to her. Of course Jamie wouldn't have had anything to do with that. She hadn't given it even a fleeting thought.

She shifted uncomfortably now, looking at the expression on his face and being careful not to brush against him again. 'Okay,' she said eventually. 'I'll hear you out.'

She sensed him relax a little, sit a bit further back into the seat and take a breath to prepare himself. She wasn't entirely sure she was ready for this.

He pulled something from his jacket and handed it to her.

'What's this?'

'It's your resignation letter. Merry told me to give you it back.'

She stared at it and shook her head. 'We can't work together, Jamie. It's just not going to work. I have to move and train someplace else.'

'Why?'

She met his gaze for a fraction of a second. 'You know why.'

He nodded. 'Do I get a chance to speak?'

She gave the smallest nod.

'You told me you were broken. And what I'm here to tell you is that we're all broken.' He took a deep breath.

'You might have noticed that something else was going on the day I tried to be superhero.'

'Okay,' she said, her answer almost a question.

'The drug stuff. I've been involved in all that before.'

She licked her lips, wanting to ask questions but telling herself just to listen.

'I told you about the investigation, but I never told you the details. One of the places I worked, controlled drugs went missing. A bit like what has just happened here.' He ran one hand through his hair. 'And honestly, it's like the worst part of my life has come back to haunt me.'

She turned a little to face him more as he continued.

'We were all questioned and investigated. It went on for months. At one point they started to say none of us could prescribe or administer controlled drugs. It caused an uproar because it would have affected patient care. Everything was fine to begin with, but as time went on I noticed people from other departments looking at me differently. It was the same with the rest of the people from our department. No one would sit with us in the canteen. We stopped getting invited to events. People that would have spent half their day talking to you would walk past without so much as a nod. It was horrible. It was isolating, and it was like having a big accusatory finger on your back.'

'But they found the person?'

He sighed. 'They did, and it was a locum doctor who'd worked there for more than six months and who I really liked.' He gave a sad smile. 'I'm a bad judge of character.'

'You're not,' she said automatically before she could stop herself.

He looked at her. 'It wasn't just the investigation that

mattered. It was here,' he said, pressing his hand against his heart. 'Afterwards, people tried to pretend they hadn't treated me differently. But I could never let things be the same again. It had been guilt by association. No one wanted to be friends with anyone in the department. It didn't matter how close you'd been in the past, or how much you'd done for them, it all came down to the investigation.' He shook his head. 'I've never got over it. The only person who knows how much it affected me is Joanne. She was my own personal cheerleader who phoned me time and time again to try and talk me into getting my confidence back. She never doubted me for a second, and it made the world of difference. So you can imagine how I felt the other day, knowing it all might start again.'

Piper swallowed. He'd only shared the tip of the iceberg, not all the details.

He slid his hand over to hers. 'I didn't tell you this for pity. And I didn't tell you this because I think it compares in any way to what you've gone through. I told you this to let you see that I'm a bit broken too. And honestly, I don't know that those feelings will ever go away.'

She sat for a few minutes, letting his words and their meaning wash over her. Her heart squeezed. She tried to imagine being in that situation and feeling as if your colleagues no longer trusted you, through no fault of your own. It was truly horrible.

'Why did you only tell me a little of this?'

He hung his head and shook it, eventually looking back up with his blue eyes. 'Because this is the part I'm not good at. The hard part. The sharing part. The part where you let your guard down and let someone see how truly broken you've been before.' He put a hand to his chest. 'I'm a guy. I'm supposed to be able to handle all this without it impacting on me.'

'That's ridiculous,' she said softly. 'It doesn't matter what sex you are. You're allowed to be hurt. You're allowed to be vulnerable. And you're allowed to admit that things have had a lasting impact on you—something you need to work through.'

Jamie fixed his eyes on hers. 'I love you, Piper Bronte. I have since probably a few weeks after I met you. But I didn't want to tell you because I wasn't sure I was really worthy of you. You give off this sunshine personality, and I love it—everyone does. But really, you're just as insecure as the rest of us. But, Piper, just because you have resilience in spades doesn't mean you have to live your life being ready to use it.'

His hand ran down her arm. 'It's okay to be vulnerable. It's okay to be scared. Can you imagine if we eventually get around to having kids? I can tell you right now I'll be scared to take them anywhere or do anything with them at all. But we can't live our lives like that. We have to risk loving. We have to risk being loved. We have to open our hearts to the potential of being hurt, because it's part of life.'

She gave a soft laugh. 'What makes you think we'll be having kids?'

His blue eyes fixed on hers. 'Because I'm yours, Piper. And you're mine. You probably deserve better, but if you'll let me I'll fight to the death for you.' He put his hand on his chest. 'Right here tells me that we're meant to be. Tell me your heart doesn't tell you the same. There's no one else I want to live my life with. And I'm sorry I scared you. And I'm sorry I tried to be a superhero. It didn't work out too well for me. But it made me realise how lucky I was to have you. And if I'd drowned out there, Piper, I wouldn't have been sorry for a second of me and you. I would only have been grateful that you let me love you.'

She let out a sob. She couldn't help it. How could he say those things? How could he speak about something terrible happening as if it happened every day?

And then her breath caught. Because it was likely that somewhere in this world, someone could be losing someone they loved.

She shook her head. 'That's the bit I can't do. I can't let my head go there. It's too hard. I've been there, and I've done that. It's not the life I want.'

He held out his hands to her apartment with the blank walls. 'But is this what you want? Because this isn't you, Piper. This place isn't the Piper that I know and love. You have so much love, so much vibrancy, deep down in here.' He pointed to her chest. 'You need to let it out. You need to let it shine. You might be broken—' he pointed to himself '—I'm *definitely* broken, but together we can find the pieces to put each other back together. We can work on this. We can work on this together.' He shook his head. 'And I can guarantee you that if I—or we—have to go through a drug investigation we will need to be right at each other's side. Because it's hard. And both of us will need support. I'll need support from you, and you'll need support from me. We shouldn't have to do this alone.'

She was shaking now. At the hospital the other day she'd been overwhelmed. It had all been too much for her.

But that was because she'd only been thinking about

herself. She hadn't considered asking anyone else for help—because she'd never had that opportunity. She'd learned to live her life without those sorts of people around her.

Now, Jamie was offering her something new. Something that meant she wouldn't always be on her own. He was also telling her that he needed her. And that made her feel more balanced. This wasn't just about her needing and wanting something, it was about him too.

'But what if I put all my trust in you and something does happen?'

He nodded and took both her hands. 'You'll have my family, my mum and dad, who I guarantee you will love and in return they will adore you. You'll have Joanne, who will be like a sister to you, and will love and support you if something happens to me. She might also have someone else too, and it will just expand our family more and more. Because if you marry me, Piper, you get a whole family, not just me. And we get you.'

She started to cry again. Because this…this was giving her the building blocks to know she should take a chance on Jamie, take a chance on love.

'I love you,' she whispered. 'And it's possible I might just lock you in that house of yours to stop any chance of anything happening to you at all.'

'Do you promise to lock yourself in with me?'

She let out her first little laugh and some of his words just connected with her brain. 'Did you just ask me to marry you?'

'Of course I did. I don't plan on you getting away from me for a second longer. Will you give me an answer?'

He brushed her tears away with his fingers as his blue

eyes locked on hers and she could see the sincerity and love shining in them.

'I think I might take a chance on saying yes,' she whispered.

'And I'm going to make you the happiest woman alive,' he replied, bending closer and sealing their promise with a kiss.

EPILOGUE

THE SUN WAS splitting the sky and the guests' jackets were littered like coloured confetti on the white chairs in the atrium. Scotland did sometimes have really hot days and today was one of them.

The bagpipes started with only the tiniest hint of a wail as the piper piped in the bride.

Jamie, in his kilt, was already waiting at the top of the aisle, his best woman—Joanne—dressed in a particularly striking suit was next to him. Both of them were grinning down the aisle towards Piper.

'Come on, girl,' whispered Jamie's dad. The pride in his voice was evident and he held out his arm for her to take. He'd cried the second she'd asked him if he would escort her down the aisle a few months ago.

She held her bunch of orange birds of paradise flowers next to some dark Scottish ferns. Her dress was lace, straight, with short sleeves and a round neck, finished with a satin ribbon around her waist. She'd decided to go without any veil or headdress and just left her natural blonde curls to do their own thing. After all, her husband-to-be loved her hair just the way it was.

Jamie held her gaze the whole walk down the aisle. His dark Argyll kilt jacket with dark blue and green checked kilt made him look more handsome than ever. And no, he hadn't changed his hair either. It was just how she loved it—long enough to run her fingers through.

She beamed at him as she walked with his father. She truly had a new family, and it was the best feeling in the world.

She and Jamie were leaving Hawaii, having both secured jobs in Atlanta at the CDC. They were both excited to move to Atlanta, Georgia, but had decided to come back to Scotland to get married first.

The drug investigation had disappeared just as quickly as it had begun. Both she and Jamie had used the lawyer recommended by Merry to answer any questions. Further questions had been raised around the pharmacy supply not being documented properly during a handover, and just like that, everything was verified and new processes agreed. Indira had seemed to vanish in a puff of smoke.

Piper met Jamie at the top of the aisle, his father kissed her on the cheek and then went to join Jamie's mother.

She turned to Jamie and they joined hands as the celebrant began the ceremony.

Her heart was full as she promised to love, honour and cherish her husband-to-be. They included a handfasting ritual in their ceremony, where their hands were tied together and held up for the guests to see, as the celebrant explained that the physical ties would be removed, but the internal ties forged would remain for ever. When they pulled their hands back, an infinity knot was formed and their guests let out a huge cheer.

When Jamie pulled her in for the kiss he paused for a second. 'I am going to love you for ever and ever,' he smiled just before their lips connected.

He tilted her back as the guests cheered again. Her hands were around his neck. 'For ever and ever,' she whispered back before moving in to kiss her husband, now and for always.

* * * * *

*If you enjoyed this story,
check out these other great reads
from Scarlet Wilson*

Nurse's Dubai Temptation
Melting Dr Grumpy's Frozen Heart
Her Summer with the Brooding Vet
Cinderella's Kiss with the ER Doc

All available now!

THE SURGEON'S TROPICAL TEMPTATION

KATE HARDY

MILLS & BOON

For Scarlet—always a joy working with you

CHAPTER ONE

HAWAII. LONG WHITE sandy beaches, turquoise water, surfers and palm trees. Gorgeous flower garlands and hula dancing. Tropical breezes, turtles and volcanoes.

Joanne couldn't wait for her plane to land in Honolulu.

Best of all, the secondment to Hawaii meant that she would be working in the same hospital as her best friend, Jamie Robertson—something they hadn't managed to do since they were medical students in Sheffield, six years ago. She had spotted the ad for a secondment in Hawaii at the Honolulu General Medical Center, and checked it out before messaging Jamie with the link. Although he'd originally started out in the Emergency Department, he'd become interested in tropical medicine—and where better to work in tropical medicine than in the actual tropics?

They're also looking for cardiac specialists. I'm applying. Why don't you come with me? Months in the sun.

She knew why Jamie wanted to go, and not just because he'd get a lot more experience in his specialty. She'd teased him that it was a chance to wear seriously loud board shorts and catch the kind of waves you just didn't get here in the UK, though they both knew what she hadn't said: it was also a way for him to leave behind a seriously dark patch of his life.

It wasn't just the chance for them to work together again

that had tempted her; it was the place. As Jamie knew, Hawaii had been on Joanne's bucket list for years.

You could actually visit Mauna Loa and Kīlauea, while you're here.

Mauna Loa, the biggest volcano in the world; and Kīlauea, the most active volcano in the world. A thrill went through her at the thought. She'd been fascinated by volcanoes ever since she was tiny and her grandmother—a Reception class teacher—had helped her make her own volcano out of clay, then mixed red powder paint with bicarbonate of soda and added white vinegar to make 'lava' froth up from inside the clay volcano and run down the outside. She'd loved it...until her dad had smashed it in a fit of drunken temper and her mum had thrown it away.

But she wasn't that scared five-year-old any more.

Her grandparents had made sure of that. A few weeks after the volcano incident, they'd realised how bad things were at home—despite Joanne's mother's best attempts to cover it up—and they'd scooped her up to live with them. They'd arranged a court order to become her legal guardians, and they'd stepped up to give her the love and security she needed. They'd been there to support her during visits to her parents, and dried her tears when her parents had neglected to turn up for a prearranged trip, or hadn't shown up when they promised to come and see her in the school nativity play, or had forgotten even to send a card on her birthday. Her grandparents had supported her, too, when Joanne had reached the age of fourteen, finally realised that her parents were always going to put alcohol before their daughter's needs and would always let her down, and decided to go non-contact with them.

Joanne had seriously considered a career in vulcanology,

until she was sixteen and her grandfather had developed atrial fibrillation; then she'd known without a shadow of a doubt that she wanted to become a doctor specialising in cardiology, so she could spare other families from the worry caused by a loved one's heart problems. Luckily she'd been a straight grade-A student and her teachers had let her switch her geography A level to biology in the middle of her first term; she'd done well enough in her exams to be accepted to study medicine in Sheffield.

Which had been the perfect choice, because on her first day at university the boy in the room next to hers had knocked on her door. Jamie Robertson was spontaneous, where Joanne was controlled; funny, where she was sometimes too serious; and he loved eating cake, while her go-to stress relief was baking.

They were made to be best friends.

And, even though several of their fellow students had scoffed and said men and women could never be friends and surely they had to fancy each other, they'd proved that their friendship was platonic—and it had lasted. All the way through their undergraduate years, all the way through their hospital training—even though it had been in separate hospitals—and beyond. As far as Joanne was concerned, Jamie was like the twin brother she'd never had.

She pushed away the thought that she wished his parents had been hers. After all, she'd had her grandparents. And her grandmother had encouraged her to take the chance to work in Hawaii, even though it took an entire day to get there from London and there was no way she'd be able to see them during her secondment.

'You go, and you send us photos of that amazing blue sea

and the volcanoes,' her grandmother had said. 'Enjoy those tropical breezes and take the time to smell the flowers.'

'I'm going there to work, Gran,' Joanne had protested.

'You won't be working twenty-four-seven. You'll have time to have some fun.' Her grandmother's eyes had twinkled. 'And you never know. Those romantic sunsets might wake you and Jamie up and make you realise you're more than just good friends.'

'It won't do anything of the sort. We're best friends, Gran, and that's all we want from each other.' No way did she want to entrust her life and her happiness to someone else, even Jamie.

But now, as Joanne looked out of the plane's window, she began to wonder if her grandmother might just have a point—because Hawaii looked an incredibly romantic place. The volcanic rocks of the Hawaiian islands rose from the bluest sea she'd ever seen in her life. Towns hugged the bays, and the volcanic rocks were covered with lush green jungle. Then, as they drew nearer to Honolulu itself and the plane began its descent, she could see the huge crater of Diamond Head, looking exactly like the volcanoes she'd drawn as a child, but with amazingly green grass in its centre instead of bubbling lava. There were wide sandy beaches edged by turquoise waters; the neat, white and silver high-rise buildings of the city; and finally it felt almost as if they were going to land on the sea itself when the plane set down on the runway.

When Joanne stepped off the plane, Hawaii turned out to be everything she'd dreamed it would be. The vivid colours of the ocean and the jungle-clad mountains were even brighter without a plane window to obscure her view; she could feel the warmth of the wind curling round her, and smell the most amazing floral scent on the breeze. It really was the tropical paradise she'd always longed to visit.

As soon as she switched on her phone to let her grandparents and Jamie know she'd arrived safely, it beeped with a message from Jamie.

Welcome to Hawaii! Hope the flight was good. Welcome drinks for all the new doctors tonight in the Pirate and the Spear. Going straight from work so see you there. J x

His second message gave her the address of the bar and told her the dress code was casual, and his third message told her he'd persuaded the concierge to let him leave some bits in her kitchen so she could make herself a coffee and something to eat and wouldn't have to drag round the shops until she'd had some rest.

She smiled. It was exactly what she would've done for him, if she'd been the one who'd started right after arriving.

Once she'd collected her luggage and was through customs, she took a taxi to the third-floor flat she'd arranged in a block near the hospital. It was quite a bit smaller than her flat in London—a little kitchen at one end of the living room, plus a bathroom and a bedroom—but she knew that most of the time she'd either be working at the hospital or out exploring the island, so it didn't matter that the flat was tiny.

The kitchen was square, with a granite countertop on one side with four tall stools that was clearly used as a dining table, and a tiled floor. There was a bowl of fresh tropical fruit on the countertop—a pineapple, a guava, a papaya and a dragonfruit. Jamie had also left her some milk, butter, cheese and a punnet of tomatoes in the fridge; and a pack of local ground coffee, a loaf of fresh bread and a box of pineapple-shaped shortbread biscuits on the countertop next to the kettle.

She found a mug and a cafetiere in the cupboard, put water in the kettle and switched it on, going to explore the rest of the flat while the kettle was boiling.

The living room had wooden flooring, with a large cream rug in the centre. There was a cream-coloured sofa on one side and two comfortable chairs, with a light-wood coffee table set on the rug between them. At the end were sliding glass doors leading to a balcony, and to her delight she discovered that if she looked one way she could see the mountains, and if she looked the other way she had a view of the ocean and palm trees.

Two doors led to the bedroom and the shower room. The double bed looked comfortable, and again there was a sliding door leading to the balcony, plus plenty of cupboard space.

She glanced at her watch. Technically, she could squeeze in a power nap before the drinks thing, but after all the travelling the chances were she'd sleep through her alarm. Maybe it'd be better if she simply pushed through the tiredness, unpacked, had a shower, changed and headed out to the Pirate and Spear. Everyone would surely understand if she didn't stay as late as people usually would on a Friday night, because she'd been travelling since yesterday lunchtime.

After sending her grandparents pictures of her views, she made herself a coffee and a sandwich, unpacked, and found a pretty dress. The welcome folder in her flat included the number for some taxi firms; she booked one, and then a shower and splashing her face with cool water helped to wake her up again. A bit of make-up, and she was ready five minutes before the taxi arrived.

The bar was busy, and full of people she didn't know; it was almost like being a student again, she thought, pasting an awkward smile on her face and asking everyone which department they worked in, how they were enjoying their stay in Hawaii, and if there was anywhere they really recommended her to visit. The long hours of travelling and lack of sleep meant that nothing anyone said to her actually sank in, so she really hoped she hadn't asked the same questions of the same people already.

But at last Jamie arrived and greeted her with a hug and the familiar twinkle in his blue eyes; although she still could barely remember a thing anyone said to her, she didn't have that fish-out-of-water feeling any more. She was among friends—or at the very least friends-to-be; that, and the pineapple-and-coconut deliciousness of the virgin chi-chi cocktails she'd been sipping, put her in great spirits. A local band was playing the kind of music that always made her want to dance, and soon she was in the middle of the dance floor, having a great time. It didn't even matter that Jamie said something to her about needing to pop out for a bit; she could manage on her own, now. Everything would be just fine.

One more drink, Guy promised himself, and he'd done his duty in welcoming the new doctors to the hospital—as well as being able to tell his brother that he'd kept his promise and was partying and having fun.

Then again, Jordan wouldn't believe him without evidence, so Guy posed for a selfie, holding up a cocktail that he hadn't sipped yet, and making sure there were people dancing in the background. He smiled, hoping that the low light would hide the fact that it didn't quite reach his eyes, took the snap, and sent it to his brother with the caption *Hipahipa!*

The reply came back almost immediately. Good to see you're having fun. Hipahipa??

It means 'cheers' in Hawaiian, Guy texted back.

Got you. Hope you're going to dance with the gorgeous blonde.

Gorgeous blonde? What gorgeous blonde? Guy checked the photo. How crazy that he'd been so focused on making himself look bright and cheerful for his brother, he hadn't even noticed the woman in the background of the shot.

He noticed her now. And he definitely hadn't seen her before at the hospital, because he would've remembered. Jordan was right: she was gorgeous. When Guy swivelled on his bar stool, he could see that she was still in the middle of the dance floor, her arms raised and her eyes closed, smiling her head off and clearly abandoned to the music.

And for a moment it felt as if everyone else had faded out of the busy bar. It was just the two of them, with the lights sparkling round her, and he could feel himself being drawn towards her...

He shook himself, and the noise and the crowd surged back into his attention.

Maybe, he texted back, having no intention whatsoever of dancing. He was just going to take a sip of his cocktail, so he could truthfully say he'd made the effort to party, and then he'd slip quietly back to his flat, where he had a stack of journals awaiting his attention.

Stop texting me and dance, Jordan's text demanded.

On it, Guy responded. Again, to keep himself truthful, he stood up and moved his feet to precisely three beats, then waggled his fingers by his sides. But, before he had the chance to leave quietly, the gorgeous blonde from the dance floor was right beside him.

'Why dance over here all on your own, when you could come and dance with me?' she asked.

Guy didn't even get the chance to say no, because she'd taken his hand and was towing him off to the dance floor.

Oh, no.

This wasn't the plan.

But somehow he ended up staying on the dance floor with her. Really moving his feet instead of faking it, the way he had when he'd texted his brother. He was matching her move for move. And...was he actually enjoying himself?

Guy had never really been one for partying—which was what half the problem with Imogen had been. And it had been so long since he'd metaphorically let his hair down that he couldn't quite remember what having fun was supposed to feel like.

'What's your name?' he asked.

She said something he couldn't hear over the music, even though he'd leaned closer to her in an attempt to hear—close enough to become aware of the sweet vanilla scent she wore. A scent that made his pulse leap unexpectedly and his breath catch.

It was pointless trying to have a conversation over loud music.

Maybe he should forget it and just smile and dance, like everyone else was doing around him.

Given that this was meant to be a welcome drink for the

new medical staff, he assumed that she was one of the new doctors. She probably thought he was one, too. She hadn't asked him to elaborate on what his speciality was, or offered any information about her own, but that was fine by him. He wasn't looking to start a relationship with anyone. A few minutes dancing together and then saying goodnight meant that he'd kept his promise to his brother—and, more importantly, he'd kept his promise to himself. No involvement, no complications, no more broken hearts.

So he just danced with her.

Until he became aware that she was staggering slightly.

She'd clearly been knocking back the cocktails from the welcome table. Unless she drank a lot of water or juice to hydrate herself, he thought, she'd have the most horrific hangover tomorrow. 'Let me buy you a drink,' he said, and drew her off the dance floor to a quieter area of the bar.

'I c'n buy m'own drink,' she said, lifting her chin and slurring her words in a way that told him she was definitely drunk.

Yeah. He'd been here before. He'd managed it then, and he'd manage it now.

'Humour me,' he said, and ordered her a fruit juice.

She took a sip, then smiled. 'Oh, 's nice. Wha's innit?'

'It's a POG,' he said. At her bemused stare, he explained, 'Passionfruit, orange and guava juice.'

''S *nice*,' she said again.

But one glass of fruit juice—even a large one—wasn't anywhere near enough to sober her up.

And he noticed that none of the people she'd been dancing with earlier had come over to check on her. Which irritated him: OK, so most of them had probably only just met, but surely if you'd formed a kind of group on your first night in a place you kept an eye on each other and made sure nobody was left behind? It wasn't as if they were eighteen-year-old medical students with a lot of growing up still to do.

'Where you do live?' he asked. If it was close enough, they could walk; otherwise he'd call a cab and go back with her to make sure she got back home safely. Hopefully one of her new colleagues would have a flat in the same block and could look after her.

She thought about it and her huge grey eyes widened. 'Don't know.'

What? How could she not know where she lived? Was she really that drunk? Oh, dear God. If she was that careless with herself, there was a good chance she'd be careless with the patients, too—making her a real liability to work with. Please don't let her be on the cardiac team.

'My phone,' she said, after a really long pause. ''S on there. My 'dress, I mean.'

Except, when she took her phone from her glittery clutch bag, it refused to switch on.

'Oh, no,' she said, looking horrified. ''S out of charge!'

It was the same make of phone as his own, so he knew his charger would fit. Maybe he should take her back to his place, put her phone on charge for long enough to fire it up again and find her address, make her some toast to soak up the cocktails. Then he could persuade her to drink some strong black coffee—enough to sober her up. And then he could see her safely home. He certainly couldn't leave her here. Especially as, he realised when he glanced at the dance floor, most of the people she'd been dancing with seemed to have left the Pirate and Spear.

'Don't worry. I'll sort it out for you,' he said dryly. 'Trust me. I'm a doctor.'

She smiled. 'So 'm I!'

One who got drunk enough to forget where she lived, and who didn't pay enough attention to detail to keep enough charge in her phone to last for the evening. Not the kind Guy wanted to have to work with. Hopefully she'd be working in an area he didn't have much contact with.

A couple of hours, and this would all be over, he thought.

'OK. The plan is, we'll go back to my place, charge your phone, then find out where you live and get you home safely,' he said.

''S very kind ofya,' she said. 'Thank you.'

She gave him another of those smiles that made his stomach swoop.

Not now, he warned himself silently. Been there, done that, and made the biggest mistake of his life—one that definitely wasn't going to be repeated. He'd learned his lesson about relationships.

It didn't take long for him to sort out a taxi and get her back to his place. He settled her on his sofa, plugged her phone into his charger and went to the kitchen to make coffee and toast. But when he went back into his living room with a plate and a mug for her, she was asleep.

Really asleep.

When he put the plate and mug down on the coffee table and shook her shoulder gently, she didn't wake. Her eyes screwed more tightly shut when he called, 'Hello!', so thankfully she wasn't unconscious; but it was pretty obvious that this particular sleeping beauty wasn't going to wake before morning.

He could put a blanket over her on the sofa, but he didn't want to leave her there alone in case she woke in the night and was disoriented and sick. Plus he didn't fancy sitting up all night in a chair watching over her and getting a crick in his neck, when he knew he had a long stint in the operating theatre tomorrow. He owed it to his patient to be at the top of his game.

Which left him only one choice: to share his bedroom with her. Then, if she woke and was ill, the sounds would wake him and he'd be able to help. And the bed was enormous. It wouldn't be like having to share a student's single bed with her and cuddle in close. They were adults. It was perfectly possible to share a bed with someone and not have sex with them.

Thus decided, Guy put the toast and coffee back in the kitchen—he'd clear up in the morning—scooped her up, and carried her to his room.

What now? If he left her fully clothed and she was sick everywhere, she'd be stuck here until he could launder everything for her. He wasn't comfortable with the idea of undressing her without her consent; but, given that even carrying her the length of his flat hadn't woken her, he didn't have a lot of choice in the matter.

In the end, he decided to treat her as he would an unconscious patient. Give her some dignity. He took a T-shirt from his drawer, removed her dress and replaced it with his T-shirt. Then he tucked the top sheet over her before putting her dress on a hanger, going to the bathroom and changing into a pair of pyjama shorts. He climbed into bed beside her, checked that she was still breathing, and turned off the light. Tomorrow, when she'd sobered up, he'd suggest maybe choosing her friends a bit more carefully.

But it was the first time he'd shared his bed—even in circumstances such as these, where he would never lay a hand on someone who couldn't give consent—with anyone since his ex-fiancée. It made way too many memories churn through his mind. And it was a long, long time before he could fall asleep.

CHAPTER TWO

JOANNE WOKE, HER head throbbing, her tongue feeling as if it had been coated with sand and then stuck to the roof of her mouth with superglue, and nausea roiling in her stomach. Why hadn't anyone ever warned her that jetlag felt like a hangover? She had some paracetamol in her bag, she was sure. Hopefully they'd stop her feeling so sick and achy. A big glass of water might help, too. Flying long-haul was dehydrating. And tiring. Just as well that the bed was so comf—

The bed.

She was suddenly, horribly aware that she wasn't alone.

Someone was lying next to her. Breathing evenly—presumably asleep.

She froze.

What the hell?

She didn't remember taking anyone home with her. In fact, she even didn't remember leaving the bar. She'd had a single alcoholic cocktail—a mai tai, which was apparently *the* Hawaiian cocktail—and then she'd switched to drinking virgin chi-chis, which someone had told her was like a pina colada but without the rum. She remembered seeing Jamie, but he'd disappeared somewhere while she was dancing. And she'd seen the shy guy on his own in the bar, clearly responding to the lure of the music but not having the confidence to strut his stuff on the dance floor.

That someone who looked like a young Brad Pitt—all scruffy blond hair and gorgeous blue eyes—was on his own was surprising. But, being a fixer, Joanne had gone over to him, taken his hand and invited him to come and dance with her and her new friends. She remembered all of that.

But *then* what had happened?

She couldn't remember. It was just a blur.

Cracking open her eyelids was a bad move. Although the curtains were drawn, the light in the room was still too bright.

She shifted slightly so her face was turned towards the body lying next to her, and half-opened the eye closest to the pillow. Yup. She hadn't imagined it. There was a man lying next to her—turned away from her, but his hair was blond and scruffy. Mr Brad Pitt Lookalike? Or, worse, was it someone else—someone she couldn't even remember meeting?

And she was…

…no longer wearing her dress.

Oh, dear God.

A really nasty thought struck her as another memory flooded back. She'd been almost falling over with tiredness when he'd taken her to the bar and bought her a drink. An utterly delicious drink—he'd told her it was a mixture of tropical fruit juices.

But was that true?

Had he put alcohol in it?

Because of her father, Joanne barely drank alcohol. She always had the one drink and then stopped: to prove to herself that she *could* stop at just one. Even now, she was scared she might have inherited an addict's gene, and if she didn't keep her usual iron control she could end up being an alcoholic like her father was.

She'd been so sure that she was in control; but maybe over the years she'd made herself vulnerable, instead. Because she didn't ever have more than one alcoholic drink, it meant she wasn't used to the stuff and couldn't hold her drink, the way her friends could. If this man had slipped a couple of measures of spirits into her drink, disguised by the sweetness of the fruit, then the alcohol would've affected her much more than it would any of her colleagues back in London. And a lot faster.

Was that why her head was banging, right now? Because she was actually suffering from a hangover rather than jetlag?

How stupid was she?

She'd just spent the night with someone and didn't remember a thing about it. *She'd slept with a stranger.* She had no idea whether he'd used a condom or not. She could be pregnant, or have picked up an STD. How could she have been so stupid and reckless? Angry with herself, she clenched her fist and banged it into the mattress in frustration.

And she instantly regretted her action when a deep voice said, 'Good morning.'

Clearly the movement had woken him.

Why, why, *why* hadn't she just got up quietly while he was still asleep, dressed, grabbed her stuff and run?

'I...' What did you say in this kind of situation? She didn't have a clue.

'Hangover?' he asked. 'I can get you some water and some paracetamol.'

Was he *laughing* at her? That grated, particularly when he was the one who'd caused this. Her temper flared. 'And you think that makes up for the way you spiked my drink and took advantage of me?'

'Excuse me?' His voice was icy.

'You heard,' she said. 'You must've spiked my drink. Because I assume I'm in your bed, and I don't remember getting here, let alone taking my dress off.'

'Yes, you're in my bed. And not because anyone spiked your drink. You're here,' he said, 'because you'd been downing cocktails all evening, to the point where you couldn't even remember where you lived. I bought you some fruit juice in the hope it might sober you up enough to help you remember, but it didn't work—so I brought you home with me instead, to keep you safe. And the reason you're wearing my T-shirt instead of your dress is because if you were sick in the night you would've been sick over your only clothes. I can assure you, I treated you in the same way that I would've treated an unconscious patient. Respecting your dignity. I thought you'd be more comfortable here than on the sofa, and I stayed purely so I could hear if you were ill in the night and needed help. Though as I'm working today I'm afraid I didn't sleep on the floor. I'd rather be fresh for my patient.'

Oh, God.

He'd *rescued* her.

And she'd just accused him of taking advantage of her.

Shame and guilt burned through her in equal measures, and her face felt as if it were on fire.

She was about to apologise when he added, his tone going from icy to positively arctic, 'Maybe you need to be a bit more careful about how much alcohol you consume, in future.'

He was lecturing her about how much she'd drunk? 'I had *one* cocktail,' she said through gritted teeth.

'I'd say you had a lot more than one,' he said.

'Yes, I did—but, after the first one, they were virgin cocktails,' she said, stung. She was the daughter of a drunkard with a mean temper, not a drunkard herself. She never, ever, *ever* got drunk. 'The coconut and pineapple thing.'

'From the jug on the welcome table?'

She nodded, and regretted that immediately as pain lanced through her head. 'Yes,' she muttered.

'Newsflash. Those ones were all alcoholic,' he said dryly.

'But they can't have been. I asked. I *checked*. I was told...' Her voice faded. She couldn't believe that anyone would have deliberately lied about something like that. Whoever had reassured her that the cocktails were non-alcoholic obviously hadn't realised, either. Or maybe someone with a very irresponsible sense of humour had added some kind of flavourless alcohol to the supposedly virgin cocktail jug. And she'd drunk at least three. Way, way more than she usually drank. No wonder she felt so terrible.

Though she was also aware that she was in the wrong, blaming him. Even though she was angry with him for thinking she was a lush, she knew she owed him an apology. 'I apologise for blaming you,' she said tightly.

'Apology accepted. And maybe think about choosing better friends in future,' he said. 'If you want a shower, use whatever you like in the bathroom. There's a fresh towel. I hung your dress up. And I've charged your phone.'

Another memory seeped into her head. Him asking her where she lived. Her not being able to remember, and saying she'd check her phone. Except she hadn't been able to, because her phone had run out of charge.

Joanne was about to tell him she wasn't usually this scatty—but it sounded like the kind of weak excuse that someone scatty would give. *The lady doth protest too much.* Of course he wouldn't believe her.

'Thank you,' she said quietly, feeling awkward and embarrassed and ashamed.

A shower made her feel a bit more human, as did squeezing a little toothpaste onto her finger and rubbing it over her teeth.

But she'd made a real fool of herself. She'd leapt to conclusions and been rude to someone who hadn't deserved it. Worse still, she didn't even know his name. He was probably a member of staff at the Medical Center, but the hospital was big enough that their paths weren't likely to cross again.

She'd thank her rescuer, grab her stuff and go.

When she walked into the kitchen-cum-living room, she could smell the coffee. Ohhh. She could *kill* for a coffee.

As if it was written all over her face, he said, 'I made a pot. Help yourself.'

'Thanks.' She poured herself half a mugful and added enough cold water from the tap that she could drink it straight down, then risked a glance at him. He'd clearly got dressed while she was in the shower—a plain black T-shirt, faded jeans. And he looked even more like a young, gorgeous Brad Pitt. She'd just bet women threw themselves at him all the time.

He gestured to the breakfast bar. There were two white tablets on a plate, and a glass of water. 'Paracetamol,' he said.

'Thank you.' He was being kind, polite and efficient, and she wanted to squirm.

'Toast?' he asked.

This time, she didn't make the mistake of shaking her head. 'Thank you for the offer, but I can't face eating anything.'

'It might help.'

She grimaced. 'I don't think so.' She took a deep breath. 'Thank you for—well, coming to my rescue. It was very kind of you.'

'I could hardly leave you in a place where you clearly didn't know anyone.'

'Oh, you could,' she said. 'Plenty of people would've done. For all you know, I could've been a scammer, and you could've woken up this morning to find me gone, along with your wallet and any pocketable valuables.'

'You weren't in any state to burgle anyone, last night,' he said. 'Can you remember your address, this morning?'

Her toes curled with embarrassment. 'Yes,' she said. 'Though I'm shakier on the code to let myself into the building, as I've only done it once. That's on my phone. Heavily disguised.' She paused. 'You said you charged my phone?'

He walked into the living room area, retrieved it along with her handbag, and handed them to her.

'Thank you,' she said. 'If I'd lost my phone, I would've been really stuck.'

'Indeed,' he said dryly.

She knew he was still judging her. But what could she say to convince him that normally she was the most sensible person on the planet? Instead, she switched her phone on. There was a barrage of messages from Jamie. *Where are you? I came back to the bar and you'd gone. Went to your flat and you didn't answer. Concierge checked for* me and you weren't there. Are you OK? Ring me as soon as you get this!!!! xx.

She wasn't sure she was up to a conversation, so she simply typed back, Cocktails not quite what I thought they were. Made a fool of myself and have the hangover from hell fighting with my jetlag. Someone kind looked after me. I'll be fine. Just going to sleep it all off. Catch you later xx.

That little smile as she read what was obviously a concerned text and tapped out a swift reply—a bit rueful, but clearly very affectionate—made Guy's heart feel as if it had done a backflip. A backflip that he, as a cardiac surgeon, knew was anatomically impossible, but he felt it all the same.

'Your friends noticed you'd gone missing?' he asked.

'Uh-huh,' she said. 'I've let Jamie know I'm an idiot, but I'm OK.'

Jamie?

Her boyfriend, Guy assumed, though he wasn't going to ask because it was none of his business. And it was ridiculous of him to feel disappointed. He wasn't looking for a relationship; even if he had been, the fact that she'd been happy to leave the bar with him last night, despite the fact that she had a boyfriend, proved that she was as faithless as Imogen. 'Maybe your boyfriend's learned from this to keep a better eye on you in future,' he said.

She didn't say anything out loud, but her expression said it all for her. *Judgy, much?*

Well, hey. She was the one who'd drunk all those cocktails, last night. She'd said she thought they were non-alcoholic, but surely she'd realised after the first couple that they were fully loaded?

But he didn't react by snapping at her. There was no point.

'Thank you for looking after me,' she said again. 'And for the coffee, the paracetamol, and charging my phone.'

'You're welcome,' he said, knowing that he sounded a bit stuffy—but, really, what else could he say?

'I'll get out of your hair, now,' she said. 'And I'm sorry for—well, everything.'

Jumping to the conclusion that he'd taken advantage of her: that had really stung. Maybe she'd had a bad experience before; but then again, surely that would've made her much more careful about drinking?

Not that it was his place to judge.

'You're welcome,' he said, as unemotionally as he could. 'I, um—do you want me to give you a lift home?'

'That's kind, but you've done more than enough for me already,' she said, lifting her chin. 'Thank you again. Enjoy the rest of your day.'

And, very quietly, she walked out of his flat and out of his life.

Joanne tapped her address into the maps app on her phone, and discovered it was a twenty-minute walk from her rescuer's flat. If she'd been wearing normal shoes, it would've been fine; but she'd be stupid to do it in party shoes, get blisters, and end up limping everywhere on her first day at the hospital on Monday.

Luckily her app for a cab worked in cities all across the world; she booked a cab, which arrived three minutes later and took her back to her flat. She was careful to drink three large glasses of water before heading for her bedroom, closing the curtains and sinking onto the bed.

Talk about making a fool of herself.

She'd better hope her rescuer wasn't the chief of the hospital. Well, he'd looked a bit too young for that. Probably around her own age; maybe a couple of years older. OK. She'd just hope that he worked in an area she was likely to have minimal contact with, to save future embarrassment.

And, as she closed her eyes, a hot wave of shame rolled over her again. Because she didn't even know her rescuer's name.

What a start to her so-called Hawaiian adventure.

Come Monday, she'd just have to hope that her behaviour last night wasn't the hot topic of the hospital grapevine…

CHAPTER THREE

Monday definitely started better than Saturday had, Joanne thought. And spending most of Sunday catching up with her sleep helped to shift the remainder of her hangover and the jetlag; when she discovered that some of the city's supermarkets were open twenty-four hours, even on a Sunday, she nipped out to buy supplies, including fresh blueberries and oats so she could bake the muffins her old department had loved as a welcome present for her new team.

On Monday, she was up early to bake; and then she was ready to start her tropical adventure properly.

It was a fifteen-minute walk to the hospital from her flat, and she had instructions to arrive at the reception area at eight to collect her staff ID card and locker key. Once all the admin was sorted, she headed for the cardiac care unit with her box of home-made muffins.

'Hello,' she said with a smile to the woman manning the reception desk. 'I'm Joanne Meadows, your new cardiologist. I made some muffins as a way of saying hello to everyone, and I wondered if you could direct me to the staff rest room, please? And to the cardiology suite—I believe I have my first patient at nine-thirty,' she added.

'Sure! Welcome to Honolulu GMC. I'm Patty,' the receptionist said, smiling back. 'If you go down the corridor behind me, the rest room's on the left. The changing room and lockers are opposite, and the cardiology suite's at the end.'

'Thank you,' Joanne said.

She found the rest room, and had just placed the box of muffins on the countertop next to the kettle, along with a note saying, *Hi, I'm Joanne, the new cardiologist, and I baked blueberry muffins for you—please help yourselves*, when a voice said, 'Good morning.'

She turned round to face the newcomer and groaned inwardly.

Of all the departments in the hospital, it would have to be *this* one where her rescuer worked.

'Good morning,' she said, squirming inwardly.

How awkward was this?

Then again, if she acknowledged the situation, maybe they could agree to move past it—because clearly they were going to have to work together for the next few months.

'Thank you again for rescuing me on Friday night,' she said. 'I, um, don't think we introduced ourselves.' If they had, she didn't remember it. All she could remember was the embarrassing mess of the next morning: waking up in a stranger's bed, leaping to conclusions, and making a total fool of herself. 'I'm Joanne Meadows, the new cardiologist.'

'Guy Sanders, cardiothoracic surgeon,' he said.

His accent was definitely English. There was a slight burr that she couldn't quite place—West Country, perhaps? 'Are you on secondment here, too?' she asked.

He inclined his head. 'I've been here six months.'

'I'm here for four months,' she said, giving him her best professional smile. 'I'm over my jetlag—and other indispositions,' she added with a rueful smile, 'so I baked muffins this morning as a kind of hello to my new team. Please feel free to help yourself.'

She'd baked muffins? This morning?

'They're low-sugar and high-protein,' she added. 'Full of oats.'

Spoken like a cardiac specialist. 'Beta-glucan,' he said. Soluble fibre that was good for blood sugar control, satiety and lowering cholesterol. Exactly what a cardiologist—and cardiac surgeon—would recommend to patients.

'Well, hey. We have to walk the talk, don't we?' she said. Her eyes crinkled at the corners as she smiled. 'Blueberries, too. For the anthocyanins. And they're still warm.'

Warm cake.

One of his favourite things.

Which was one of the reasons why he ran five miles every morning on the beach, with the sound of the sea clearing his head; it staved off the effect of any cake he'd scoffed, the previous day, and it also set him up mentally for the day ahead.

He was about to thank her and take a muffin when she added, 'I really am sorry about Friday. Can I maybe buy you dinner?'

Dinner.

He could've been tempted, except he'd heard something on the grapevine yesterday as he was coming out of Theatre. About Jamie Robertson, the new secondee to the tropical medicine department, and how his girlfriend from England was coming to join the hospital in the cardiac department.

Joanne Meadows was the only new person in the cardiac department, which meant she had to be the girlfriend they'd been talking about.

Since she was already in a relationship, why was she asking him out to dinner—or at least why wasn't she asking him out to dinner with her *and* Jamie? Surely she wasn't naïve enough not to realise that it would look like a date? And, having been at the sharp end of a cheating relationship, no way did Guy want to get involved.

'No need,' he said, slightly more abruptly than he intended.

The smile was still on her face, but it didn't reach those gorgeous grey eyes any more. 'Uh-huh,' she said.

And now he felt guilty. This was her first day at the hospital and he ought to be welcoming her, not letting his own past colour his reaction to her. She was a colleague. They were going to have to work together. Even if it *was* a bit awkward, given that on Friday night she'd been so drunk that he'd had to take her home with him to keep her safe. Which also begged the question where her boyfriend had been when she was clearly incapacitated—but he didn't actually know Jamie and was trying very hard not to judge other people.

'You've got a cardioversion this morning, haven't you?' he asked.

'Three, actually,' she said. 'I have to admit, it's nice to come in straight to see patients rather than spending a morning doing admin, or dragging through an induction course; in my experience, most hospitals work in pretty much the same way and it's more important to meet your colleagues and focus on your patients.'

He agreed completely.

'The first cardioversion's at nine-thirty,' she said. 'I'm going to say hello to the team, then see my patients to check if they have any questions before the procedure and reassure them.'

'Mind if I join you for the first one?' he asked.

Her eyes narrowed. 'I know we got off on the wrong foot on the weekend, but I'd like to assure you that it was a one-off, and I'm perfectly capable of doing my job. I'm fully qualified, with several years of experience.'

From the crispness of her voice, she'd clearly taken it that he didn't trust her. Given how stiff he'd been with her, that wasn't surprising. Worse still, she was right and he was being a stuffy idiot. The hospital wouldn't have hired her if she wasn't good at her job. 'I... That came out a bit wrong,' he said. 'I'm a surgeon; you're a cardiologist. We're new to each other, so I thought it might be useful for both of us to see how the other works—given that you'll probably refer patients to me, and after I've done any surgery they'll come back to you for follow-up testing. It's your first morning and it might be nice for you to have a familiar face—someone who can introduce you to the team and show you around. And maybe you'd like to come into Theatre during one of my procedures, so you get to meet my team.'

She blushed, and Guy forced himself to ignore how pretty she looked. She was in a relationship, which made her off limits. He'd just have to suppress the attraction he felt towards her. Besides, even if she hadn't been dating someone else, he wasn't looking for any relationship other than a working one. Hawaii was all about getting his balance back.

'That's kind of you to suggest it,' she said. 'But don't you have surgery?'

'Not this morning. I have a pile of admin,' he said with a shrug. 'Which needs to be done, admittedly, but I can catch up with the paperwork later today.'

'All right,' she said. 'If any of the cardioversions don't work and my patients end up being referred to you, then yes, it'd be useful for them to meet you, too.'

He took her to the cardiology area and introduced her to the nurses; then they walked over to where her cardioversion patients were waiting in cubicles with the curtains drawn back.

Joanne quickly scanned the three sets of notes the nurses had given her, then went to the first cubicle.

'Hello, Mrs Lee. Nice to meet you,' she said with a smile, and shook the patient's hand. 'I'm Joanne Meadows, your cardiologist, and this is my colleague Guy Sanders, our surgeon on the team. How have you been feeling?'

Joanne was good at this, Guy thought. She'd introduced them both, her manner was open and friendly, and she showed concern for her patient's feelings. Exactly what he wanted from a cardiologist.

'Dreadful,' Mrs Lee said. 'I struggle to walk anywhere, I get out of breath walking up the stairs, I can't get down on the floor and play with my grandchildren—and it makes me feel as if I'm ninety, not fifty-five.'

'That's rough,' Joanne said sympathetically. 'I see you're on medication to control the rate of your heartbeats. Has it helped?'

Mrs Lee shook her head. 'I've been on the tablets for three months now, and I feel worse instead of better.'

'Then I think we'll change your medication after the procedure. I can prescribe something that might help a bit more,' Joanne said. 'Would you like me to take you through what happens?'

'Yes, please.' Mrs Lee looked awkward. 'The doctor I saw last did tell me what to expect, but it went straight out of my head. All I could think about was that it's an operation and I need anaesthetic. And I—well, I'm a bit worried.' She bit her lip.

'I know that waiting for an operation can be really scary, because this is a step into the unknown, but you'll feel so much better afterwards,' Joanne said, her voice kind. 'Tell me what's worrying you most, and then I can hopefully reassure you.'

'I'm just scared that I'm not going to wake up from the anaesthetic—and I didn't say goodbye properly to the kids or the grandkids.' She looked miserable. 'Or my husband. He couldn't stay because he had to get to work. I should've kissed him goodbye. In case I...'

In case she didn't make it back from the operation, Guy thought. A lot of his patients had that worry.

'I can understand why you're worried, but cardioversion is a procedure that doctors have been doing for a lot of years—more than half a century,' Joanne said. 'I've done quite a few, in my time, and I've never lost a patient yet. You're right in that all operations do carry a risk, but for this procedure it's less than one in a thousand.' She glanced over at Guy.

He nodded. 'She's right. You're more at risk of dying from a stroke or a heart attack if we don't get your heart beating at the right rhythm and rate again, than you are of dying from the cardioversion procedure.'

Mrs Lee wrapped her arms round herself. 'I read somewhere that it's more likely to be a problem if you're overweight—and I know I'm fat. I've struggled with my weight my entire life.' She looked miserable. 'I've put on fifteen pounds, these last three months. But it's so hard to do anything about your weight when you just don't have the energy to do any exercise.'

'First off, we wouldn't offer you a cardioversion if we didn't think you'd come through it,' Joanne said. 'So please try not to worry about that.'

'And secondly, you'll definitely have more energy again after the cardioversion,' Guy added, 'though we'd rather you didn't go straight out with a surfboard or start training for a marathon this afternoon.'

Mrs Lee gave them a rueful smile. 'I'm hardly going to do that!'

'It's best to take it easy for a couple of days, to let yourself get over the operation—when you have an anaesthetic, even though it's going to be a short and light one, it always takes a little while to get over the procedure,' Joanne said. 'And then I'd recommend gradually increasing your exercise, doing a little bit more every day.' She smiled at their patient. 'Can I just check that you haven't eaten anything since ten o'clock last night, and have only drunk a little water and your tablets this morning?'

Mrs Lee nodded.

'And you haven't missed even one dose of your blood thinners in the last four weeks?' Guy asked.

'No. I take one every evening, just before I go to bed,' Mrs Lee said.

'That's perfect,' Joanne said. 'Now, I'll tell you what's been happening and why you've been feeling so rough lately.' She drew a quick diagram of a heart. 'Normally, a special group of cells starts an electrical signal here at the sinus node, telling your heart when and how to beat, so it's all coordinated. When you have atrial fibrillation, the electrical signal gets jumbled, so your heart beats irregularly and doesn't get time to fill up with blood between beats and can't send enough blood round your body.'

'That's why you're out of breath and struggling,' Guy added.

'We're going to put some pads on your chest and your back, and administer a shock—it's a bit like the defibrillation you see on TV dramas when someone has a heart attack, but it's not such a strong current. The shock will disrupt the jumbled electrical signal and reset your heart. Sometimes we have to give you two shocks or even three to get the reset,' Joanne added, 'but in most cases it's successful.'

'What if it doesn't work?' Mrs Lee asked.

'Then we'll try another procedure—we can do something called an ablation, which stops the signal going down the wrong pathways. And if that doesn't work, we might need to give you a pacemaker,' she said. 'You might end up seeing Dr Sanders here. So you've got plenty of options. But for now let's focus on the cardioversion. What we'll do this morning is give you a light sedation, so you'll be asleep for the procedure and it won't hurt. The whole thing takes about five to ten minutes. I'll put a defibrillation pad on your chest over your heart, and another on your back, and they'll be connected by wires to the defib machine so we can monitor what your heart's doing and give the shock. The nurse has already put a butterfly in the back of your hand to give us easy access to your veins, so we'll give you some medicine through that to put you to sleep. It might feel a little bit cold, but it won't hurt. Then I'll press a button on the machine to deliver the shock, and check the rhythm and rate of your heart's what I want them to be.'

Joanne was really good at explaining, Guy thought, keeping it simple without being patronising. Mrs Lee was already looking much less worried than she had been.

'The anaesthetist will keep a check on your vitals and make sure your airway's kept clear, and they'll hold the oxygen mask in place between shocks,' she said. 'Anaesthetists have very strong hands, so you might feel a little bit sore and see a little bit of bruising under your jaw in the next couple of days, but it'll clear up pretty quickly. You might also find your skin's a bit sore where the pads were, a bit like sunburn, but some aloe vera gel will help soothe that. We'll check there aren't any complications; then we'll wake you up again, and keep an eye on you for a couple of hours.'

'You might feel a bit sleepy for the rest of the day,' Guy said, 'and you definitely can't drive yourself for a couple of days, but you should be able to go home today, as long as you've got someone who can keep an eye on you for the next twenty-four hours.'

'My sister's on her way to the hospital now,' Mrs Lee said.

'That's great. I'm going to review your medication,' Joanne said, 'and I'd like you to keep taking the blood thinners after the operation—I'm pleased to see you're on the new direct oral anticoagulants rather than warfarin, so you don't have to have your blood coagulation monitored every week.'

'My dad was on warfarin,' Mrs Lee said. 'He had heart problems, like me. He died in his forties.'

'Heart problems often run in the family,' Joanne said. 'But I promise you that it doesn't mean you're going to die early—and you'll feel a lot, lot better in a few days. You'll be well enough to play with your grandchildren and walk upstairs without being out of breath.'

A tear trickled down Mrs Lee's face. 'That's all I want. To feel *normal* again.'

Joanne squeezed her hand. 'You will. I promise—and I don't make promises I can't keep. Now, I need to have a chat with my other two patients, and in the meantime the anaesthetist is going to come and see you and prepare you for the operation.' She smiled. 'I'll see you again very soon. And in an hour's time you'll be sitting up, having a cup of tea and wondering what on earth you were worrying about.'

Joanne was just as meticulous with her next two patients, Guy noticed, paying attention to their worries and making sure she reassured them and they knew what to expect from the morning. However chaotic she was in her personal life, he was relieved to see that definitely didn't spread to her professional life. And she made sure the patients were comfortable with him, too. Weirdly, it felt as if he'd worked with her for years, and what they said to the patients seemed to dovetail easily. If it hadn't been for Friday night, he would've thought her the perfect colleague.

When it came to the procedure itself, she was just as careful as she'd been pre-op, making sure everything was documented and checking everything. She was friendly and professional with the anaesthetists, the nurses and the support staff, and invited all of them to help themselves to the blueberry muffins in the rest room. And her follow-up with the patients was good, too. Mrs Lee was in tears, but they were clearly happy ones.

'I can't believe I feel so much better already,' she said, mopping her eyes with a tissue.

'That's great to hear,' Joanne said with a smile. 'We can send Dr Sanders back to his operating theatre now, then.'

It was a dismissal, but a nice one. He smiled. 'I'm glad

you let me stay this long. It's always lovely to see a patient so much happier in such a short time.'

'Oh, I'm happy, all right,' Mrs Lee said with a wide smile.

'I want you to stay here for another hour, just so we can finish monitoring you,' Joanne said, 'but your sister can come in and wait with you, if you like. And I'm going to change your beta-blockers to some that might suit you a bit better, so you'll need to wait for the pharmacy to bring them up to you.'

'All right.' Mrs Lee was smiling through her tears.

'I'll walk you out, Dr Sanders,' Joanne said with a smile. At the door of the cardiology unit, where nobody could hear them, she said, 'I hope this morning has reassured you that what happened on Friday won't happen here at the hospital.'

Guy winced. Had he been that obvious? 'Sorry.'

'Don't be. In your shoes, I would've felt the same—wanting to be sure my new colleague wasn't a total liability,' she said. 'I hope you're feeling more confident in me now.'

'I am,' he said.

'Good. Thank you again for rescuing me. I never have more than one alcoholic drink, and I really did think the cocktails were virgin ones—they didn't taste of alcohol. But in future I won't trust anything unless I see it being made in front of me.'

'That's a good plan,' he said.

'You and I got off on the wrong foot,' she said, 'and I like my working relationships to be easy, so all the attention's on the patient instead of dealing with personality clashes. Can we start again, starting with me buying you lunch?'

Didn't she want to have lunch with her boyfriend? Or maybe his shifts didn't work out, today. 'All right,' he said. 'Do you know where the canteen is?'

'I'm sure I can find it,' she said.

'It'll save time if I collect you. I can maybe show you the bits you need to know about at the same time. Does half-past twelve work for you?'

'That'd be great,' she said. 'Enjoy your paperwork.'

'As much as anyone does.' Guy inclined his head. 'See you later.'

CHAPTER FOUR

TWO MORE CARDIOVERSIONS LATER, and with all three of her patients released happily to the care of their family, Joanne sat down in the office to write up her notes on the computer. She'd just finished when there was a knock on her open door.

'Is now a good time for you to take your lunch break?' Guy asked, smiling at her.

Weirdly, Joanne's stomach felt as if it had flipped.

She never, but never, reacted to anyone like that. Not to the heart-throb actors in movies or TV dramas; not to pop singers or rock stars, the way her gran still sighed over Robert Plant and Bryan Adams; and definitely not to people in real life.

But here he was. Smiling at her. And it made her feel decidedly *odd*.

'Now's fine,' she said, striving to be as professional and detached as she could. But she noticed how blue Guy's eyes were: the same deep blue of a Hawaiian summer sky.

Oh, for pity's sake. Since when did she describe anything in such a soppy way? If she said any of this to Jamie, he'd roar with laughter and accuse her of being on a sugar rush.

'How were your other two cardioversions?' he asked.

'Both successful—one was first time, which is always

nice.' Most cardioversions needed two shocks. 'How was your paperwork?'

'Dull, but it's sorted,' he said. 'Let's go to lunch. The canteen's good—the coffee's excellent, the fish is fresh, and they also do sandwiches if you're up to your eyes in paperwork and need to grab something to eat at your desk.'

'That's useful to know,' she said, following him into the corridor. 'Are there any local specialities I should try?'

'There's loco moco,' he said. 'Which is two scoops of white rice, a hamburger patty, brown gravy and a fried egg.'

'Fried egg and gravy?' she asked, trying and failing to imagine a fried egg as part of a Sunday roast dinner, covered in gravy. 'Are you sure?'

He grinned. 'It's the language difference. In the same way that American biscuits are more like what we'd call scones and they call our biscuits "cookies", gravy isn't the same as English gravy,' he said. 'It's actually sauce. Being Hawaii, it's fusion food—there's chilli, garlic and soy in it.'

Egg with a savoury sauce. That made a lot more sense to her. 'Not that I'm too fussy to try it,' she said, 'but I'm not a huge fan of burgers.'

'How about Spam sushi?' he asked.

She rolled her eyes. 'What's this, tease the newbie day?'

'No, it's a real thing. Spam musubi—marinated cooked Spam, served on a block of sushi rice and with a sheet of nori wrapped round it. You'll see it in practically every shop.'

She blew out a breath. 'OK. Maybe I'm not as adventurous as I thought I was. Sushi, I like. But Spam?' She wrinkled her nose. 'Gramps likes the Monty Python skit about Spam. That's as close as I'm going to get.'

'I'll admit, it's not my thing, either,' he said, his eyes crinkling at the corners.

He was laughing with her, rather than at her, and Joanne found herself relaxing with him. Guy the surgeon seemed a lot more light-hearted than Guy the man she'd met in the cocktail bar on Friday—and a lot easier to talk to than the slightly forbidding man who'd offered her coffee with a side of lectures, the following morning. She liked the way he was with her, right now. Maybe they could become friends, which would be a bonus.

'You did ask about local specialties,' he reminded her. 'But if you like sushi, you might like a poke bowl. The marinated tuna ones are very good. Lots of veggies, with a bit of spicy mayonnaise drizzled over the top. Or maybe Hawaiian barbecued chicken—which includes pineapple.'

'Yes to chicken and fish,' she said. 'And I love pineapple.'

The canteen was bright and airy; she was tempted by the chicken and pineapple, but opted for a poke bowl, as did he. To drink, she chose a fruit juice—which definitely didn't have alcohol in it, because this was the hospital canteen and hospital canteens didn't tend to have a drinks licence. 'Is this like the juice you bought me on Friday night?' she asked.

'Passionfruit, orange and guava,' he said. 'Yes. You remember that?'

'I do.' She sighed. 'I know you're convinced I'm a lush, but I'm really not. My bad habit is coffee, which I guess is true of most medics.'

'Pouring half a cup and topping it with cold water so you can drink it straight down, on a busy day?' he asked.

'It's practically the first thing you learn in your foundation year training,' she said with a grin. 'Especially when you're in the Emergency Department. Anyway, I'm buying you lunch. No arguments.'

'Bossy,' he commented.

'Efficient,' she countered.

'I'll give you that,' he said, 'as you brought warm homemade cake in this morning. Which was excellent, by the way.'

The compliment made her feel warm all over, and much more at ease in his company, because she knew from experience he wasn't one to mince his words or say something he didn't mean.

'And thank you,' he said. 'Both for lunch and the cake.'

'You're very welcome.'

They found a table in a quiet corner and sat down.

The poke bowl was absolutely delicious. 'This was a good choice,' she said.

'Fresh and local. It doesn't get better than that,' he said. 'So what brought you to Hawaii?'

'It was my idea and I told Jamie about it,' she said. 'I don't know if you've met. He's in the tropical medicine department.'

'I know him by sight, but we haven't worked together,' Guy said.

And it sounded as if they hadn't socialised together either, Joanne thought. Which could be because Jamie was a bit cautious, given the problems in his previous job, or it could be because Guy wasn't one for socialising. Her clearest memory of Friday night was seeing him standing in the bar, awkwardly moving to the music and looking a bit lost; then she'd towed him off to the centre of the dance floor with her and her new friends—none of whom had stuck around, and none of whom she could actually remember.

Certainly none of them had made themselves known to her since Friday.

She shook herself. They were moving past that. He'd asked about why she came to Hawaii. 'It's the first time we've had a chance to work together properly since we trained. He's here for the surf, and I'm here for the volcanoes. How about you?'

'I wanted a change from England,' he said.

Seven thousand miles or so away, and a minimum of eighteen hours travelling? That kind of distance, plus the way his face had suddenly shuttered, made her wonder if Guy had needed some space between himself and a difficult situation. Not that she would ask. It was none of her business. 'Quite a change,' she said, keeping her tone as anodyne as possible. 'Let me see—a choice of a grey and rainy summer's day, or tropical sunshine and jungle?'

'And the bonus of being able to run by the sea every morning,' he said.

'You don't live near the sea in England?' she asked.

'The nearest sandy beach is about a forty-minute drive from the centre of Bristol,' he said. 'And even the river's a twenty-minute cycle from my house. I normally run on the common, not far from my house, so it's good to hear the waves swishing.'

Bristol: so she'd been right in picking up that West Country burr. 'I have to admit, I'm not a runner, and you'd never get me on a treadmill at the gym,' she said. 'I'd rather do weights or a dance class any day. Though I like walking in the park near Alexandra Palace, especially with Gramps and Dexter, his spaniel.'

'You're a Londoner?'

She nodded. 'I trained in Sheffield, but I moved back to

London when I qualified. My grandparents live in Muswell Hill, and I was lucky to get a job at Muswell Hill Memorial Hospital. I live just round the corner from them.'

'You're close to your grandparents?' he asked.

'Yes.' She wasn't going to tell him that she'd lived with them since she was a small child, because that would mean explaining about her parents, and she didn't want to do that. Better to head him in a different direction. 'Gramps was diagnosed with atrial fibrillation when I was sixteen,' she said instead.

'Is that why you chose cardiology?'

'Yes. I wanted to work in something that might help him—and might help other families not have to go through the kind of worries that we went through.' She smiled. 'Before then, I'd planned to be a vulcanologist. I've visited Iceland and Sicily, and seen a tiny bit of steam coming out of Vesuvius when I went to Naples, but I've never managed to visit Hawaii or seen actual lava. It's why I chose a secondment out here, because it means I'll get to see the one of the places I always dreamed about as a teenager.' She bit her lip. 'Though I'm not so happy about being quite so far from my grandparents. Gramps is stable, but obviously he's older now and getting more fragile, so I worry about it. I was going to turn the job down, but he and Gran sat me down and insisted I should take the chance and not worry about them. They say they'll be fine for the next four months. I guess I can videocall them any time the worry really gets to me, provided I remember the time difference,' she finished.

'You haven't got a brother or sister who can keep an eye on them? Or your parents?'

'I'm an only child, and no,' she said. And she needed to shut down this avenue of conversation right now, before it got sticky. 'What about you? What made you pick cardio-thoracic surgery?'

'I'd always been drawn to the precision of surgery, and I was going to work as a general surgeon—but then I got to scrub in and assist with a heart transplant when I was a student,' he said. 'It blew me away that we could make that kind of difference to someone's world. I fell in love with it. And luckily the lead surgeon noticed and offered to mentor me. I've never looked back.'

'It's the nearest we can get to waving a magic wand,' she said. 'They come in, like Mrs Lee this morning, struggling and miserable—and we send them out tired from the anaesthetic but already feeling so much better than they did when they came in.' She smiled at him. 'So where did you train?'

It was a fair question. He'd asked her the same thing. 'London,' he said. 'The London Victoria. When I qualified, I moved to Bristol.' And he'd met Imogen. Then he'd got engaged to her: the biggest mistake of his life.

'I thought you had a bit of a West Country accent,' she said. 'Are you from Bristol originally?'

'Bath,' he said.

'Hot springs and curse tablets,' she said with a smile.

He was relieved that she hadn't said Jane Austen. Imogen had been a huge Austen fan, and had even made him dress up in Regency costume to attend a ball. He'd hated every minute of it.

'I assume if you grew up there, you did all the touristy stuff as part of school trips,' she said.

'We did,' he said. 'We went to the baths and we all had to draw the Gorgon's head and write a story.'

'Did you taste the waters?'

'One sip. It was the most disgusting thing I'd ever tasted in my entire life,' he said with a shudder.

'I agree,' she said with a smile. 'Jamie dared me. He'd obviously done it before, because he took a video of me on his phone as I took a sip from the paper cone so he could show me my reaction.' She shuddered. 'It's daft, I know, because the baths themselves are from the hot springs, but I didn't expect the waters you drank to be lukewarm.'

The look on her face as she spoke about her boyfriend reminded Guy that he shouldn't be getting too comfortable in her company. She was already seeing someone, which made her off limits. 'It was a bit mean of your boyfriend to make you drink it, if he knew what it tasted like.'

'Jamie isn't my boyfriend,' she said, waving a dismissive hand. 'He's my best friend.'

'Isn't that the same thing?' He'd always grown up believing that your partner was your best friend, the way his parents were. Friendship was one thing; attraction was another. But love…that was being attracted to your best friend.

'No, it isn't,' she said. 'Or are you one of these dinosaurs who think that men and women can't be friends?'

'No. Of course men and women can be friends.' He frowned at her. He wasn't a dinosaur. Then again, Imogen had proved to him that his expectations had been too high. Maybe his parents' marriage was a one-off. Except he was pretty sure that his brother and his sister both described their partners as their best friends, too. 'But you're very close to him, and the hospital grapevine says you're his girlfriend.'

'Hospital grapevines—in every hospital I've ever worked in—are notorious for getting things wrong,' she said crisply. 'Jamie and I are mates. He's more like the twin brother I never had.'

So she wasn't off limits?

He stuffed down the sudden feeling of lightness. Yes, he was attracted to her, but he wasn't going to act on that attraction. He'd learned from his mistakes with Imogen. But he didn't want to put their working relationship back on a rocky footing by being gruff with her. 'I apologise,' he said. 'Sorry. I guess I'm a bit of a cynic, at heart.'

She shrugged. 'I might be naïve, but I see everyone as good until proven otherwise.'

He'd been like that, once. But then there had been Imogen. 'What happens when it's proven otherwise?'

Her grey eyes widened, as if he'd made her think about something painful, and guilt slid down his spine. Someone had clearly hurt her, in the past. It was unfair of him to have prodded a sore spot.

Before he could apologise again, she said abruptly, 'Then I stay out of their way. I was going to ask you, does the hospital run rehab clinics for cardiac patients?'

He knew this move well: deflect attention from your feelings by talking about work. He'd done it all the time, after Imogen's betrayal, until people at work gave up asking about his personal life. And then he'd escaped to Hawaii. 'Not at the moment.'

'That's something I've been working on in London.' She tucked a strand of hair behind her ear and launched into what he recognised as professional mode. 'I'd like to set up something similar here. An eight-week course—the first half of the session teaching about nutrition and healthy habits, and raising any issues people have been worrying about, and the second half doing taster sessions of different exercise classes,' she said. 'Something to help our patients' confidence. Gramps was told to build up his exercise and fitness, but everything was really vague—"see how you feel" isn't that helpful. It'd be much more useful to give people advice about which symptoms should make them ease up or take a rest, and when they can up the pace or push themselves a bit harder.'

'It's a good idea,' he said. 'It would work for my patients as well as yours. Maybe we could work together on a plan—as colleagues,' he added quickly, not wanting her to think he was hitting on her. Because the last thing that someone who'd been hurt needed was to get involved with someone who'd also been hurt badly and was still struggling to get over it. 'And the permanent staff here might have some ideas about local exercise professionals we could involve for classes. Yoga, Pilates, low-impact aerobics, and perhaps resistance bands rather than weights.'

'Maybe some aqua-aerobics, too,' she said.

'Except it's easy to overdo things in a pool,' he said. 'The buoyancy and temperature mean people underestimate how hard they're working.'

'That's a good point,' she said. 'Your heart has to work harder in the water because your circulation changes and more blood returns to your heart. And the resistance of the water makes your heart work even harder. Maybe not aqua-aerobics, then.'

'And not weights,' he said. 'Especially whole-body weight exercises like planks and press-ups.'

'Wall press-ups are better,' she agreed. 'And nothing where they hold their breath.'

'We're on the same page, I think,' he said. 'Maybe we can schedule in some time to discuss it during the week, and work up a proper project outline.'

'Including timescales and costs,' she said. 'I agree.' She

glanced at her watch. 'But I'm guessing you have surgery this afternoon.'

'I do. A CABG,' he said. 'If you don't have clinic, you're very welcome to come and sit in.'

'Unfortunately,' she said, 'I do have clinic. But I'd love to come and sit in on a procedure later in the week, perhaps.'

'OK,' he said. 'I'll take you back to the cardiology department. And we'll catch up later in the week. Lunch on Thursday, perhaps, and bring our diaries?'

'I'll look forward to that,' she said.

Her smile made a tingle start at the base of his spine, and he reminded himself to be careful. Not even a flirtation: this was going to be strictly work between them.

Strictly.

CHAPTER FIVE

'WE'RE COLLEAGUES,' Joanne told herself, pacing up and down her flat on Wednesday night. 'This isn't a date. It's a working lunch, to discuss a mutual project.'

So why was she looking forward to it as if it *was* a date?

This was crazy. She didn't want to get involved with anyone. No way would she ever let herself be in a position where she relied upon someone else for her happiness. That would make her vulnerable to being let down, the way she'd felt when her parents had let her down again and again and again. Even though her grandparents had rescued her and done their best to protect her and make her feel loved, she just couldn't quite bring herself to trust anyone with her happiness again.

But Guy was the first man she'd met in years who could make her heartbeat speed up just by smiling at her. The first man in a long time who'd made her feel like a woman rather than an asexual doctor.

Her gran had suggested that a romantic location such as Hawaii might make her look at Jamie differently. Except it hadn't. He was still her best friend, the person she trusted more than anyone else and could talk to about anything.

Well, *almost* anything.

But nothing romantic was ever going to happen between them. It just wasn't how they felt about each other. Jamie didn't make her pulse leap with excitement. She didn't want to slide her arms round his neck and tease his mouth with hers. She didn't want to slow-dance with him on a beach under the stars. And she didn't have to make a conscious effort not to think about him.

Whereas Guy Sanders...

Yeah. He was the one who made her feel what her gran had suggested.

She paced the floor again.

Guy made her feel all at sixes and sevens. And it wasn't just because he was easy on the eye. Or because he'd rescued her and lectured her at the same time.

Maybe it was because she recognised the same signs of damage in him that she could see behind her own smile. She kept people at a distance by being super-efficient and super-smiley, by making it very clear that they were colleagues and she was happy to have fun with them but wasn't looking for forever. Guy kept people at a distance by being kind and professional, and making it clear that he was in Hawaii to work.

Somehow, she had to get this all out of her system before their lunch meeting tomorrow.

But how? How, when she felt all fizzy and dizzy just because she was going to spend time with him?

She couldn't even ask Jamie to talk some sense into her, because their off-duty wasn't in sync and this needed to be a face-to-face conversation, not a series of texts or messages.

'Repeat after me, Joanne Meadows,' she told herself, still pacing. 'Nothing is going to happen between you and Guy Sanders. He's a colleague for the next four months, and then you're going back to London and you'll never see him again.'

Except it didn't help.

Because a little voice in her head whispered, 'But it's four months. With an end date. What if…?'

'No,' she told herself firmly. 'He's off limits.'

On Thursday morning, Guy went for his usual run on the beach, hearing the swish of the waves rolling onto the sand, tasting the salt in the air and smelling the scent of the incredible flowers wafting on a tropical breeze.

Hawaii really was the paradise everyone said it was. Especially at this time of the morning, when there were only a few runners, swimmers and dog-walkers around. Pristine white sand leading onto crystal-clear waters of the most amazing blue, topped by white surf; all the hustle and bustle of city life seemed to slow down here.

Except it felt different, this week. All the colours seemed brighter, if that were even possible. All because of a woman who had bright ideas that could really change the community for the better, and the sort of drive to make it happen.

He needed to remind himself that Joanne Meadows was his new colleague. She was the one who did the electrical stuff in the department, and he was the one with the scalpel. There were a couple of areas where their patients crossed over, and he was looking forward to working with her.

But.

Right now, he was running alone, and thinking about what it would be like to stroll across these sands instead. Hand in hand. Maybe tucking a tendril of hair behind her ear. Watching the stars come out together, showing her the different constellations out here. Dancing with her under the stars, each of them wearing a single earbud connected to a phone playing a romantic song, sharing the music and sharing the moment…

Oh, for pity's sake.

This wasn't how it was supposed to be. He didn't let himself get distracted. Not since Imogen's betrayal.

Until he'd met Joanne.

And suddenly all bets were off.

He managed just fine at work, because his focus had always been good when it came to his job: he could switch off everything but the steps in an operation. But if he was doing paperwork, or chores, or even just walking to the hospital from his flat, he found himself daydreaming about Joanne.

He'd almost called her last night and suggested dinner. Somewhere quiet and romantic, with a good menu showcasing the best of the local food...

Thankfully, his common sense had kicked in just before he'd pressed her name on his phone directory. OK, so now he knew she wasn't someone else's girlfriend, she wasn't off limits any more; but they still had to work together. Even if it was only for four months. It would be utterly stupid to do anything that might make that awkward.

But, even though he was trying, he still couldn't stop thinking about her.

And he didn't know what to do. He could call his brother—but Jordan would consider it a good thing. A sign that Guy was finally moving on from his ex's betrayal. And if Guy admitted that the woman distracting him was indeed the beautiful dancer from the bar on Friday night, Jordan would encourage him even more.

Right now, he didn't have anyone else to go to for a dose of common sense. So he'd simply have to manage it himself.

'It's a work relationship, and work only,' he told himself—out loud, just to drive the point home.

And he pushed himself to run a little bit faster.

* * *

When she'd finished in clinic that morning, Joanne headed for the cardiac unit and rapped on Guy's open door. 'Hey. Ready for lunch? I've brought supplies.' She waved her notebook at him.

'Paper, rather than a laptop?' he asked, glancing up from his desk. 'That's pretty old-school.'

'I think better on paper,' she said. 'There's something about brainstorming with a pen in my hand—a connection to the brain I don't get from a computer keyboard.'

'Fair enough. Just let me save this.' He saved the file, logged off, and stood up to join her. 'You bought lunch on Monday, so it's on me today. No arguments.'

'Thank you,' she said. And yet again his smile made her stomach flip.

He was being professional. She needed to do the same. But it was hard to concentrate on anything except his nearness. Especially when he sat next to her rather than opposite her at lunch, with a plate of sandwiches, her notebook and a pen between them, and her hand brushed against his. Her skin actually tingled where it had touched his—and she'd never reacted to anyone like this before. It scared her and thrilled her in equal measure but was this something she could trust? Would it be better to quietly distance herself, before it started getting complicated? She was pretty sure he was equally thrown by this thing between them, because she'd noticed him glancing at her mouth, then her eyes, then looking away.

For pity's sake. She was thirty years old, not a raw teenager. She was perfectly capable of having a good professional relationship with him—perhaps even a friendship.

She could rise above this pull of attraction and focus on her work.

And, after a mental ticking-off, she managed to concentrate on the cardiac rehab project, and they managed to get a lot done during their lunch break.

'I'll type this up tonight,' she said, 'and email it over to you to check it through—anything I've missed or any mistakes.'

'Thank you.' He looked at her. 'Didn't you come out here to—well, experience a different culture? It seems a bit harsh for you to be working at the hospital during the day and then doing more work in the evening.'

'It's fine. And it's nice to be busy while I'm settling in,' she said lightly. After all, it was only her first week. It took time to make friends—and, after her experience at the Pirate and Spear, she didn't really want to end up on more evenings of pub crawls.

'We could…' He stopped himself. 'No. That's monopolising you. And I'm sure you'll be busy seeing Jamie.'

'Jamie and I haven't managed to coordinate our shifts, yet,' she said. 'What did you have in mind?'

'If you weren't planning to do the volcanoes with Jamie, maybe we could go for a hike at the weekend,' he suggested. 'The volcanoes here on O'ahu are dormant, but the Diamond Head crater is apparently a good place to see the sunrise, and Koko Head has a botanical garden in the bottom of the crater.'

Was he asking her on a date?

'So—this is friends doing a bit of sightseeing together?' she checked.

'Uh-huh. I've not got round to visiting the craters, yet, so it's something to tick off my list. We'll need reservations and a parking permit for Diamond Head,' he said, 'and from what I've read Koko Head is a tough hike, because there's a trail of stairs made out of an old trail track—more than a thousand of them—but the views are spectacular.'

'Sturdy shoes, sunhat, sunscreen and water,' she said. 'And maybe do the hiking early in the day or late in the afternoon.'

'In the afternoon, you'd get the sunset,' he said. 'It's popular, so it might be a bit crowded, but you'd get some amazing photos to send to your grandparents from there or from Diamond Head.'

She nodded. 'I noticed the sun sets a good couple of hours earlier in Honolulu than it does in London at this time of year. Obviously because it's nearer the equator,' she added, not wanting him to think she was too ditzy to realise that.

'OK. I'll see if I can book reservations for Diamond Head, and if not we'll go to Koko Head. Would Saturday or Sunday suit you best?' he checked.

'Either,' she said. 'I don't have any plans for the weekend.'

'I'll let you know what I can get. There's also a luau at the beach for the new doctors on Friday evening, next week,' he said. 'If you'd like to go.'

'A luau being a party?' she guessed.

'With traditional foods and a hula dancing display,' he said. 'That was what happened at the one in my first month, anyway.'

'That sounds good.' She paused. 'I assume there will be soft drinks available?'

'Yes.'

And she liked the fact that he didn't bring up her mistake on Friday night. He wasn't the sort who went on and on about things, then. But again, was this a potential date, or was this a casual invitation to join a group? 'Can I tag along with you and your friends?' she asked, trying not to be too obvious but wanting to know where she stood.

'I'm sure you'll know a lot of people there, but I can meet you earlier so you don't have to arrive on your own,' he said.

Not a date, then. And she wasn't sure whether she was more relieved or disappointed. Then again, it was going to be just the two of them on the volcano trail... 'That'd be good,' she said. 'Where do I get a ticket?'

'The link's on the staff newsletter,' he said. 'If you haven't seen it, I'll forward it.'

'Thank you. That'd be kind.' And she appreciated that he hadn't leapt in and said he'd get her ticket for her. Clearly he respected her independence and her ability to sort things out for herself, which was good.

She spent the afternoon sorting out a pacemaker for Ben Palani, who'd been suffering from palpitations. The medication he'd been given to control his heart rhythm was making his heart beat too slowly, he was short of breath even when he wasn't doing much, and he'd been suffering from dizzy spells.

'A pacemaker will stop your heart beating too slowly and take the symptoms away, so we can use medication to regulate your palpitations, Mr Palani,' Joanne explained. 'It's an oval shape about the length of my thumb, and if it senses your heart is beating too slowly it sends an electrical impulse to your heart to restore your normal rate.'

'Will I feel it doing that?' he asked.

'No. You might be aware of the change in your heart rate, but you'll get so used to it happening that you won't notice it,' she explained. 'We'll fit it just under your collarbone, between your skin and the muscle of your chest, and we'll connect it to your heart with a couple of electrodes, which we put in through a vein. I'll be using an X-ray camera, to make sure I'm putting the leads in the right place and they can't accidentally come out again, and then I'll connect the pacemaker and use the echocardiogram machine to check your heart trace and see it's working properly. Then I'll slip the pacemaker into a pocket under your skin—you'll feel a little bit of pressure when it goes in, but nothing alarming—and close up the wound with dissolvable stitches, so you don't have to worry about coming back to have the stitches out.' And she wished she'd had a chance to see Guy doing stitches; she had a feeling she could learn something from him. She smiled at her patient. 'We'll give you antibiotics today, to reduce the chances of you getting an infection. The procedure takes about an hour, and although we'll keep you in tonight to keep an eye on you, you'll be able to go home tomorrow lunchtime.'

'Will I be awake for it?' he asked.

'Yes. But you won't remember anything of it,' she said, 'because we'll give you a painkiller and light sedation. You'll feel a bit sleepy and relaxed.'

He nodded. 'All right.'

'Do you have any questions?'

'Well, I've been reading up about it,' he said.

And scaring himself, Joanne thought, judging by the worry in his eyes. The internet was full of horror stories. She gave him an encouraging smile, and waited for him to tell her what he'd read that was really bothering him.

'And it works with magnets, right?' he asked. 'Does that mean I can't use my phone or my fitness watch?'

'Your phone should be fine,' she said. 'Though I'd advise you to use it on your right ear, because I'm putting the pacemaker on your left side, and don't put it in your shirt pocket. Current advice is to keep your phone six inches away from your pacemaker—and if you've got a tablet, don't prop it on your chest.'

'Got it,' he said. 'What about my fitness watch? I mean, my family doctor said it would help me keep an eye on my health.'

'It does, but it's not a medical device,' she said gently. 'There is some research being done into whether fitness watches affect your pacemaker, but as long your watch doesn't use something called "bioimpedance sending"—that's where the watch sends an electric signal into your body and reads the signal that comes back—you should be fine.'

'How do I know if it uses this bio thing?' he asked.

'It'll say in the manufacturer's leaflet,' she said. 'I'd also advise not to cook with an induction hob, because they use magnets—or, if you do, keep about two feet of space between your pacemaker and the hob.'

'Hob?'

'Ah—another word that's different in American English. The bit you'd use a saucepan on,' she said.

'Stovetop,' he said with a grin. 'My wife never lets me near the kitchen, only the grill if we cook outside, so I'm all right there.'

'Good. I'd steer clear of scales that measure body fat, too, and ultrasonic toothbrushes.'

'I'm never going to remember all this,' he said, frowning.

'Don't worry. I'll give you a leaflet, and there's a website link on there to the pacemaker's website which tells you which things are safe for normal use, where you need to take precautions, and which things you need to avoid,' she said with a smile. 'You should be able to go back to normal daily activities by the middle of next week. Don't drive for the next week, and don't lift your left arm above your shoulder or make big movements with your shoulder for the next six weeks—so that's no swimming, bowling, golf or weights.' Hopefully that covered most of his likely recreational hobbies.

'What about my guitar?' he asked. 'I'm in a band with my friends. Can I still play? Or is the magnet in the amp going to be a problem?'

Something in his expression told Joanne that this was the thing Mr Palani was most worried about. She smiled. 'I think the problem's more likely to be with the strap on your guitar feeling uncomfortable. You might need to wear it over your other shoulder. And quite a few famous rock guitarists have had pacemakers fitted and kept playing.' She named a couple from the rock bands her grandfather—who wasn't far off Mr Palani's age—liked.

'One of them's dead now,' he said, his eyes widening.

'But not because of his heart,' she said. 'He was one of my grandad's favourite guitarists.'

'Your grandfather's a man with good taste,' Mr Palani said. 'I hope he passed it on to you.'

'If there's a pub quiz and there's a question on late sixties, seventies or early eighties rock,' she said, 'let's just say people would want me on their team.'

'Good to hear,' he said, visibly relaxing.

'Give me a second and I'll check for you.' She looked up the website on her phone. 'Here we go. You can see this for yourself, if you like. Magnetic fields of guitars are very low and won't affect your pacemaker. Just keep your guitar six inches away from the pacemaker.'

'I trust what you tell me.' He looked relieved. 'Life without the band... I mean, we play mostly for fun, because we're all retired and it keeps us from under our wives' feet and stops all the bickering, but we do occasional gigs at a local bar. If I had to give it up...'

'You won't have to give it up,' she reassured him. 'And hey, if you do have a gig while I'm in Hawaii, let me know so I can come and see you play.'

He cheered up immensely. 'All right. I will. Tell me your favourite song with a steel guitar, and I'll play it for you.'

'That's an easy one. "Albatross",' she said.

'Excellent choice.' Ben smiled at her. 'We play a mix, but I love blues and rock.'

'My grandad loves early Fleetwood Mac,' she said. 'I was brought up on Peter Green and Pink Floyd.'

'Then I'll play "Albatross" for you.' He smiled. 'I'm happy to have the op now.'

When Joanne got home, that evening, she checked her email and discovered that Guy had sent her the staff newsletter. There was a link to buying the tickets for the luau, so she quickly sorted that out, then typed up the notes from her meeting with Guy and sent them to him, adding, Thank you for sending the newsletter. Have booked ticket.

To her surprise, he messaged back straight away. Great. Am sure you'll enjoy it.

She knew she really ought to leave it there—but somehow she ended up typing a longer message. You would've enjoyed my pacemaker patient this afternoon. Took him a while to tell me what he was really worried about, but he'd read up about magnets and he wanted to know if he could still play his guitar. I reassured him and he's promised to let me know when his band's next gig is. He's even going to let me pick a song for him to play especially for me. Let me know if you'd like to join me.

The answer came back swiftly, and was a little cagey. What kind of music?

Blues and rock, she messaged back. Ben Palani plays steel guitar.

I would've put you down as a Taylor Swift fan, he replied.

Was he being judgy again? No reason why I can't like Taylor Swift *and* Pink Floyd, she pointed out.

True. I listen to Daft Punk and Radiohead. Though it's always classical piano for me in Theatre. Something that keeps the beat but doesn't overwhelm.

A man with broad tastes who listened to electronica, alternative rock and classical music. Guy Sanders was an interesting mix, she thought. Bach or Einaudi?

Bach and Debussy, he replied.

They had a lot in common, she thought. Good choices. I like Satie as well.

Me, too. Couldn't get reservations for Diamond Head, so it'll have to be Koko Head. Will be busy, but maybe we could go early Saturday morning and try to beat the crowds and before it gets too hot? I'll pick you up at half-past six?

That'd be great. Thank you. Looking forward to it, she replied. Though chatting like this with him made her feel antsy. She didn't want to give him the wrong impression. They were colleagues and might become friends, but that was it. And she really needed to stop thinking about how beautiful his mouth was. Sorry, didn't mean to take up so much of your evening. Catch you later.

OK. I'll get back to you tomorrow on the project, he typed back. Goodnight.

Night, she replied.

And she was really, really looking forward to their volcano trip at the weekend.

CHAPTER SIX

ON FRIDAY MORNING, Joanne checked in with Mr Palani. He'd had a good night; although he was still a bit sleepy, he had a broad smile on his face and he was holding his wife's hand. 'Honey, this is Dr Meadows,' he said. 'She's a marvel. And she says I can keep playing the guitar.'

'I'm grateful for that,' Mrs Palani said. 'Ben would be bored stiff and driving me crazy if he couldn't jam with the boys every afternoon.'

'We can't have that,' Joanne said, smiling back. 'Especially as I can't wait to hear him play.'

She went through the discharge notes with him, ran a quick ECG to check that the pacemaker was still doing its job properly, and went through the medication with him. 'You're good to go,' she said. 'Make an appointment with Reception to see me in two weeks so I can check that the wound's healed, there's no infection, and the pacemaker's working properly. And obviously if you have any concerns before then, come straight back to me.'

'I was telling my wife how good you were yesterday. How you stopped me worrying,' Mr Palani said.

'That's what I'm here for,' she said. 'Well. That, visiting the volcanoes, and coming to see your band. Let me know where to buy the tickets, because I'd like to bring a friend.'

'We're a bar band,' Mr Palani said. 'No tickets necessary.

Just turn up, have a beer and have a good time. But I'll let you know when we're playing next.'

'Great,' she said.

At the end of her morning clinic, she checked her email and Guy had sent her his thoughts on their plan. Instead of taking a proper lunch break, she bought a sandwich from the canteen and ate it at her desk so she could go through his suggestions, then sent the file back to him.

Thanks. Doing a minimally invasive CABG this afternoon, if you want to scrub in for some or all of it, he replied.

A coronary artery bypass graft done without cracking the chest open? Of course she wanted to see it! Love to. Want to see your stitching technique—might give me ideas for my next pacemaker, she typed back. What time?

Starts at two, he said. Operating Room #2.

She glanced at her watch. The paperwork needed to be done, but this was going to be useful, too. I'll be there.

At five to two, she scrubbed in and Guy introduced her to his team, including Keanu, his intern. 'I'm doing it off-pump, by the way,' he said. 'It's a double graft, so my patient's a good candidate.'

Joanne knew off-pump meant that instead of stopping the patient's heart and diverting the blood to a heart-lung machine to take over the heart's pumping function, Guy would be operating while the patient's heart was still beating. 'Any proper reason you chose off-pump and minimally invasive?' she asked.

'Over to you, Keanu,' he said.

'It's quicker than conventional surgery so the patient's under anaesthetic for less time, it reduces the risk of a bleed because the incision's smaller and no bones are cut, it lowers the risk of a stroke afterwards because the heart doesn't stop beating, and it gives the patient a shorter stay in hospital and a quicker recovery time—a couple of weeks instead of three or four months,' the younger doctor recited. 'Plus there's less pain and scarring.'

'Textbook answer,' Guy said. 'Well done.'

Keanu's eyes gleamed. 'This is the first time I've seen one outside a textbook or video.'

'Next time, you'll do one,' Guy said. 'And after that you'll teach one.'

'Teach one?' Keanu's voice squeaked slightly. 'But...'

'That's how you learn best—see one, do one, teach one. And I'll be here as your backup. It's not solo surgery,' Guy reassured him. 'Joanne's a cardiologist rather than a surgeon, but she needs to know this stuff.' He looked at her. 'Which vein am I using for the grafts?'

'You could use one from an arm or a leg,' Joanne said, 'but I'd say you'll use a vein from inside the chest wall.'

'Yup,' he confirmed. 'Keanu—why?'

'Uh...' The intern looked at Joanne.

'Over time, radial arteries and saphenous veins tend to narrow, whereas mammary veins tend to stay open longer,' she said gently. 'Given we're doing the bypass because the artery's narrowed—stenosis—we want to give our patient the best chance.'

Guy gave an approving nod. 'Spot on. And the other reason we use those three areas, Keanu, is because we can remove them without damaging the patient's circulation. OK. Let's go, team.'

Once the patient was anaesthetised, Guy made a small incision in the left side of the patient's chest, between the ribs; then he inserted an endoscope, a tube with a camera on the end, to let him see inside the chest, and the surgical instruments he needed. As he worked, he explained to Keanu what was happening, and directed him to look at the screen which showed a magnified view of what he was doing. He encouraged the younger man to question him, and made sure Keanu understood the answers; Joanne was quietly impressed by his teaching ability.

Once an immobilising device had minimised the movement of the beating heart, Guy prepared an artery on the chest wall and surgically attached it to the aorta, the main blood vessel from the heart to the body, then attached the other end of the donor vessel to the blocked artery just after the blockage. He repeated it with the second blocked artery; once he was satisfied that the operation was complete, it was time to withdraw the instruments and close the incision.

'How many sutures do you think we need to close, Keanu?' Guy asked.

'Five per inch,' the intern said. 'So that's…maybe twelve?'

'Agreed. We can do alternate sutures,' Guy suggested. 'Unless you'd like to do some, Joanne?'

'Your call,' she said. 'But I think Keanu would learn more by doing them than watching me.'

'That's fine,' Guy said.

He placed the first suture, clearly taking it much more slowly than he usually would so Keanu could see the technique more easily. Keanu was a little hesitant at first, but with Guy's praise and guidance he gained in confidence, and ended up doing most of the sutures.

'Good work, team,' he said. 'Let's wake the patient up. Keanu, what happens now?'

'Recovery room until he's round from the anaesthetic, then he'll be in the critical care unit for a couple of days so we can monitor him more closely, then a couple of days in a regular hospital room, and discharge home if we're happy with his recovery,' Keanu said.

'Couldn't have put it better myself,' Guy said.

'That was amazing,' Keanu said.

'Seconded,' Joanne agreed. 'Because I'm a cardiologist rather than a surgeon, I don't get to see this very often. And the last one I saw was a traditional on-pump with the patient's chest cracked open.'

'The stats are pretty much the same for both approaches,' Guy said, 'but I think this approach is more patient-friendly, and it's how I'm teaching my interns—and my residents.'

'I assume that's American for F1s and registrars,' Joanne said.

Guy's eyes crinkled at the corners. 'You'll get used to the terminology. Over here, you're a resident.'

'And he's an attending,' Keanu said. 'I'd love the chance of a secondment in England, if it means I'd get to learn more about this kind of procedure.'

'I'll help you with your application,' Guy promised.

'Thank you for letting me sit in on this,' Joanne said. 'I'd better let you get on with your patient.'

'Next time you do a pacemaker, maybe Keanu and I can sit in,' Guy said.

'Sure. I'll check my schedule and let you know what's coming up, so you can see what suits you,' she said. 'See you later.'

But she was thoughtful all the way back to her office, and while she was catching up with her paperwork. This was her first time seeing Guy in Theatre—the operating room, she corrected herself—and he'd impressed her. He was undoubtedly skilled as a surgeon, his movements sure;

he was polite and clear with his directions to his team and checking with the anaesthetist; and he was good at teaching, too. He'd focused on building Keanu's confidence and knowledge rather than knocking him down—an approach she favoured, too.

Her initial impression of Guy as a slightly judgy mansplainer had vanished. He was good to work with, and his patient skills had been top notch with Mrs Lee, her cardioversion patient, helping to reassure her before the procedure. She realised now that he'd been a bit abrupt with her on Monday morning simply because he cared about the patients and his work; as soon as he'd seen for himself that she was professional and not the total mess he'd met at the Pirate and Spear, his attitude had changed completely.

She liked him.

Really liked him.

But it really wasn't a good idea to let herself get involved with him. She was here for four months, and then she was going back to her life in London. Whenever he came back from Hawaii, he'd go back to Bristol. Long-distance relationships were tricky at the best of times, let alone adding in the extra complications of the long hours a doctor worked and having to juggle shifts.

Though who was she trying to kid? It wasn't just the distance. She was rubbish at relationships. She'd tried a few times, but they never worked out. Either her partners got too intense before she was ready for it, declaring a love she didn't feel in return and making her back off because she didn't want to put her heart on the line; or they thought she wasn't opening up enough to them and ended things.

She knew what was at the heart of it. Her parents. All the times she'd convinced herself that they did love her, that this time they'd be there—and they weren't, because her dad had gone on a bender and drinking was more important than his daughter. All the times she'd cried herself to sleep, convinced there was something wrong with her because otherwise they'd love her enough to show up, wouldn't they? Even though her grandparents had done their best to reassure her, to make her know how much they loved her, every time her parents 'forgot' it chipped away at her ability to trust anyone.

In the end, she'd given up on relationships and stuck to friendships. They at least worked. So it would be better for both of them if she and Guy stuck to being just colleagues, maybe friends.

CHAPTER SEVEN

THE NEXT MORNING, Joanne was ready when Guy rang her doorbell. She pressed the intercom. 'On my way down,' she said. She picked up the light backpack she'd filled earlier with a box of home-made banana bread, a couple of bottles of water, suncream, a hat, a mini first-aid kit and a lightweight rain jacket which folded up into its own tiny pouch, locked the flat behind her, and headed down to meet him.

'That looks professional,' he said, nodding to her bag.

'It's just easier to carry stuff in it. Hat, suncream, water, snacks, first-aid kit and waterproof,' she said.

'No kitchen sink?' he teased as he ushered her to his car.

She laughed. 'No. I think you, as the muscle-bound runner, can carry that,' she teased back.

He drove them out to Koko Head; the crater rose up before them, a massive hump silhouetted against the sky.

'The profile makes it look a bit like a sleeping dinosaur,' she said. 'A dimetrodon.'

'Dimetrodon?' he queried.

Perhaps he hadn't been fascinated by dinosaurs when he was little. And she supposed a dimetrodon wasn't one of the famous ones like a T. Rex or triceratops. 'The one with a big curved fin on its back, a bit like a sail,' she said.

'Were you a dinosaur fiend as a kid, by any chance?' he asked.

'Yes. It kind of went with the volcanoes,' she said. 'Koko Head is a tuff cone, by the way.'

'A tough cone?' he queried.

'T-U-F-F.' She spelled it out. 'Diamond Head's a tuff cone, too.'

'I never did geography. A volcano's a volcano, isn't it?' he asked.

'No—it depends on the chemistry of the magma,' she said. 'The three most common ones are cinder cones, shield and composite.'

'So tuff cones are rare?'

'No. What happens is the magma rises and comes into contact with water, which forms steam and turns the lava into plumes of fine ash. The ash falls around the vent, and over time the ash solidifies into rock.' She smiled at him. 'Don't start me off on volcanoes. I can get very boring.'

'No, it's interesting.' He smiled back. 'My mum's a chemistry teacher. We used to do kitchen science experiments when we were kids, and the volcano was one of my favourites—vinegar, red food colouring and bicarb soda.'

It sounded as if he'd enjoyed it the same way that she had when her grandmother had done the experiment; except he obviously hadn't had a father who was a mean drunk and smashed it up. She shook herself. *Not now.* She wasn't going to let her parents spoil this.

'That and the giant bubbles,' he continued, 'when she added glycerine to warm water and washing-up liquid and we used a wire coat-hanger as the bubble-blower.'

'So you've got brothers or sisters?' she asked.

'One of each. I'm the baby. Jordan's a chemistry teacher, like Mum, and Melissa's a pianist. Her recordings are the ones I play in Theatre,' he said.

'Are you close?'

'Pretty much,' he said. 'Mel lives in London, so I don't see her as much as I'd like, but Jordan lives in Bath and we get together when we can.'

'That's lovely,' she said, remembering that he'd said he'd grown up in Bath. 'Do your parents still live in Bath?'

'They do,' he said. 'Mum was envious when I told her I was coming here—she'd love to visit Mauna Kea for the observatory. I haven't done it yet, but I'm definitely going on one of the night sky tours on the Big Island.' He smiled. 'Mum taught us how to recognise a lot of the constellations, when we were kids—and if there was a lunar eclipse in the middle of the night that turned the moon red, you can bet she'd be up watching it and then wake us in time to see the last bright sliver of the moon turn red behind the earth's shadow. Same with meteor showers and comets. Jordan does the same with his boys, and Mel with her daughter. Jordan lives just outside Bath, and there aren't any streetlights in his village, so we all converge in his garden to watch the meteor showers—blankets, hot chocolate and sun-chairs on the patio.'

Which sounded like the kind of thing her grandmother would love. The kind of thing Joanne herself would love sharing with her children—not that she planned to have any. Because that would mean trusting someone enough to rely on their support, and her childhood memories ran too deep.

'You never thought about being an astrophysicist?' she asked instead.

'I thought about it,' he said, 'but my interest was caught by medicine. So here I am.'

'I want to visit the Big Island to see Mauna Loa,' she said

thoughtfully. 'Maybe we could go together and do a combined trip—so we get the stars for you and the lava for me.'

'That,' he said, 'sounds like a really good plan.'

It warmed Guy all the way through that she'd thought of something that worked for both of them. If he was honest with himself, he'd put off doing the touristy things in Hawaii because it made him feel lonely, doing things on his own and not being able to share the joy with someone else. He wasn't really one for chatting to strangers and he didn't make friends that easily.

And yet Joanne had been a stranger, a week ago, and they seemed to be becoming friends. She seemed to understand him, and he felt a kind of connection with her that he wasn't used to experiencing. Even though part of him wanted to be more than just good friends, he knew it would be a bad idea. He was still healing from Imogen's betrayal, and he recognised the way Joanne clammed up about her past because he did exactly the same thing; someone had obviously hurt her, too.

Being friends and colleagues was a much better idea. So he'd be sensible and ignore the pull he felt towards her.

He parked in the small car park near the trail. 'We can maybe walk round the botanical gardens in Koko Crater afterwards,' he said. 'At least there'll be some shade there.'

'Works for me,' she said.

They headed up a concrete path from the car park, through a couple of dirt tracks and a tarmacked road, and then they found themselves at the base of the crater trail hike. There were people sitting at the bottom of the steps, looking a bit daunted and doubtless wondering if they could handle it.

'You weren't kidding about it being tough,' she said, staring at the wooden steps that led straight up the side of the volcano, divided into two wide sections with a third very narrow section on the side. Her expression was one of dismay. 'I assume one of these is up, one's down, and one's either for overtaking or for when people need to stop for a moment?'

'I think so,' he said. 'This is my first time, too.'

The staircase looked broad at the base, but at the very top it looked like a toy train track set against the side of the volcano.

'The tramway was built here during the second world war, and the trail was renovated a year or so ago,' he said. 'There are one thousand and forty-eight steps, and we'll be climbing twelve hundred feet. On average, it's meant to take about forty minutes to an hour to get to the top.'

'It looks to me as if it gets steeper, the higher we climb—and, with the change in altitude, the higher steps are going to be the toughest ones,' she said. 'A thousand and forty-eight steps.' She calculated rapidly in her head. 'That's the equivalent of seventy flights of stairs in an average house. And it's two and a half times as many steps as the ones going up the bell tower in Notre Dame, though I guess at least this is straight up rather than a spiral.'

'We don't have to do it if you don't want to,' he said. 'We can walk round the botanical gardens and go for a drive instead, if you'd rather.'

'No. It's a challenge, and I'm up for it,' she said. 'I'm reasonably fit from aerobics classes, but I think it would be a good idea to take this at a slower, steady pace.'

'I agree,' he said. 'And maybe miss out the bridge. I looked up hiking tips, earlier, and there's a short stretch halfway up where everyone struggles—it's a bridge over a ravine, and people cross it on all fours. But there's a path at the side to bypass it.'

'Spoken like a cardiac surgeon,' she said with a smile. 'And that sounds like a good idea.'

As they walked up the steps, he noticed there were markers showing how many steps they'd climbed already. But around the one hundred and fiftieth step, a middle-aged man was sitting beside the trail, breathing heavily, and a woman was talking to him, her hand on his shoulder and anxiety wreathing her face.

'Are you all right?' Guy asked.

'I...it's Geoff. My husband.' She bit her lip. 'We're on holiday. We came early so we could do the trail when it's cooler and it would be easier.'

It wasn't particularly cool, though; it was already in the twenties, Guy thought, and quite humid. The tropical heat could catch you unawares and exhaust you.

'But he's not feeling very well,' she finished.

'We're both doctors,' he said, gesturing to Joanne. 'Can we help?'

'I don't want to make a fuss.' Geoff was wheezing slightly. 'It's my fault for eating too much breakfast, a bit earlier than I'm used to. Just a bit of indigestion, that's all.'

'Do you have any pain or a feeling of pressure in your chest, or your back?' Joanne asked gently.

'Only a little bit. It's a bit better now I've sat down for five minutes. I'm just being a silly old fool, out here in a tropical paradise and forgetting I'm nearly sixty, not twenty-one,' Geoff said.

Guy and Joanne exchanged a glance. 'Do you mind if I check your pulse?' Joanne asked.

'All right,' Geoff said.

Joanne gently checked his pulse. 'A little bit fast, but that's probably because you've pushed yourself and you're a bit worried. It's nice and strong,' she said.

'Have you had any episodes like this before? A little bit of pain that you've not wanted to bother anyone about?' Guy asked.

'A bit,' Geoff admitted.

'Your doctor wouldn't have happened to prescribe you a GTN spray, would they?' Joanne asked.

'I didn't bother her about it. It was only a little bit of pain, and it went away again,' Geoff said. 'And it's so hard to get an appointment. The receptionist's a right dragon. I thought I'd be all right.'

'You don't think he's having a heart attack, do you?' his wife asked, looking horrified.

Geoff was sweaty and breathless, though that might be due to the exertion of climbing a hundred and fifty steps that were steeper and further apart than normal stairs. And he'd said that he felt better for sitting down, which meant it was more likely to be angina than a heart attack.

'It sounds like angina—a bit of discomfort in your chest because you've got a partially blocked artery that's stopping your heart from getting enough blood. A lot of people ignore the pain because it goes away again, but it's a warning sign that you might be heading for a heart attack in the future,' Guy said. 'My advice is to get yourself to hospital so they can check it out. The doctor will run some tests, including your cholesterol levels, your blood pressure and your blood sugar levels—nothing that hurts. Maybe some special X-rays. If I'm right and it's angina, they'll prescribe you a medication called glyceryl trinitrate; it's either a pill you put under your tongue, or a spray. That'll help ease the pain, and a few easy lifestyle changes starting now can help you avoid developing heart disease.'

'No more fry-ups for me, then, I guess,' Geoff said wryly.

Guy looked at Joanne. 'Your first-aid kit doesn't happen to have any aspirin, by any chance?'

She shook her head. 'Sorry. Just paracetamol.'

'I've got some aspirin in my bag,' Geoff's wife said.

'Knowing you, Sally, it's probably out of date,' Geoff joked, and then winced.

Out-of-date aspirin was better than nothing, Guy thought. 'If you could give him an aspirin to chew, that'll help prevent a blood clot. Plus, if his arteries are narrowed, aspirin helps the blood flow more easily through them.' It would also help if Geoff was suffering from a heart attack rather than angina.

'I feel a fraud,' Geoff said, grimacing. 'It doesn't hurt, now.'

'If the pain's gone away after a rest, it probably *is* angina rather than a heart attack,' Guy said. 'Forgive me for sounding rude, but with my medical professional hat on I think maybe this hike will be a bit too strenuous for you today.'

'But we were looking forward to getting to the top,' Geoff said. 'The views are meant to be incredible.' He looked miserable. 'If we just take it a bit more slowly...'

'We're both heart doctors,' Joanne said. 'I'm a cardiologist and Guy's a surgeon. So we're not being killjoys when we advise you not to do it—we want you to be safe. It's not just that these stairs are steep and you need to take bigger steps, it's the fact it's hot and humid, and there's less oxygen the higher you climb. Why struggle when you don't have to?'

'Be sensible, Geoff,' Sally pleaded.

'Let us help you back down,' Guy said. 'And we'll call an ambulance—it'll be here by the time we get down to the base of the trail.'

'I don't need an ambulance. I can drive,' Geoff said.

'What if you feel unwell when you're driving?' Guy asked. 'It's a twenty-minute drive to the hospital, and then you'll have the worry about parking, and you really don't need that extra stress.'

'But what about the car?' Geoff asked. He looked at his wife. 'Sally, it's a rental. We can't just abandon it here.'

'I'll drive it to the hospital behind the ambulance, and I'll sort it out from there,' Sally said. 'Stop worrying.'

'Worrying will only make the pain worse,' Joanne added. 'Everything's going to be fine, Geoff. We'll go slowly down the steps, and we'll stop whenever you need to. Please don't feel you have to put a brave face on—we'd rather stop every five steps to give you a breather than rush down and have you collapse halfway down.'

'It's all such a fuss,' Geoff grumbled, but Sally shook her head at him.

'I'd never forgive myself if you had a heart attack and died. The kids would never forgive me, either. Just do what you're told, for once.'

Geoff gave in and let Guy help him down the steps while Joanne called the ambulance. By the time they got to the car park, the ambulance had just arrived.

'Thank you, both of you,' Sally said. 'I don't know what we would've done without you.'

'I'm sure someone else would've stopped to help,' Guy said with a smile. 'Do you want one of us to go in the ambulance with Geoff so he's not on his own?'

'You've already done so much for me,' Geoff said. 'I don't want to take up any more of your day.'

'It's not a problem. We can come back here another day,' Guy said.

'No, really. We'll be fine. But thank you.' Geoff fished in his pocket for his wallet. 'The least I can do is buy you a drink.'

'No need,' Joanne cut in swiftly. 'If you want to thank us, listen to your wife and listen to what the hospital tells you.'

'I've learned my lesson,' Geoff said. 'That was scary.'

'Everything's going to be all right now. The ambulance will take you to the Emergency Department at the Honolulu General Medical Center—that's our hospital,' Guy said. 'So if they decide to admit you, you'll see a face you know, tomorrow.'

'And it'll be me prescribing you the GTN, if we're right about the angina,' Joanne added with a smile. 'Try not to worry. Everything's going to be all right. And if we don't see you tomorrow, enjoy the rest of your holiday.'

The paramedics took over, and Guy and Joanne headed back to the trail.

'Sorry. We've missed the coolest bit of the day,' Guy said. 'And, given this is a former tramway, there's no shade.'

'We couldn't have let Geoff and Sally struggle on their own,' Joanne said.

'I was tempted to drive him to the hospital myself—but if he becomes ill again on the way there, it's better that he has access to oxygen and someone can do an ECG,' Guy said.

'Agreed. We did the right thing, Guy.' She patted his arm, and the feel of her skin against his made a shiver of pure desire ripple down his spine. 'And now we're going to see the views—and we'll take it steady on the way up.'

By the time they reached halfway, the steps seemed never-ending, just stretching up and up and looking almost vertical. And then Guy noticed the people ahead of them moving very slowly and gingerly across the railway ties, while others were crossing them on their hands and knees.

'That must be the bridge,' he said.

Just to prove him right, there was a signpost showing the trail at the side.

'I think I'd rather do the path than—well, *that*,' Joanne said.

'I'd rather be sensible than fake-brave,' Guy said.

The ground was uneven, but the detour was well marked, and they were soon back on the trail and climbing again.

'I think we're going to feel this tomorrow,' he said as the angle of the trail got even steeper. 'I'm glad we persuaded Geoff not to try going up again. I think this would've been way too much for him.'

'It's definitely a challenge,' Joanne said. 'We've more than earned these views, so they'd better live up to expectations!'

And then at long, long last, they were at the top. One last set of stairs—this time metal ones—and they were at the viewpoint, looking out over Hanauma Bay and Waikīkī. When he leaned against the barrier, her arm brushed against his; again, he felt a jolt like electricity.

He'd never reacted to anyone like this before, not even Imogen.

He'd known Joanne for all of a week. How could he possibly feel so drawn to her, so soon? OK, she saw things the same way that he did, and she wanted to make a difference in the same way that he did...but surely that wasn't enough?

She tempted him to drop his guard, to let her into his life and risk a proper relationship again.

When you know, you know. The words slid into his head.

But *did* he know? He'd got it wrong before, and he'd promised himself not to fall head over heels for anyone again. What if he'd got it wrong this time, too? It would be terrifyingly easy to make another mistake—one that would hurt both of them. Should he take that risk?

'This is a stunning view,' she said, nudging him.

'Yes,' he said, though privately he thought that she was more stunning than the blueness of the ocean, depth of the sky, and the lush green of the jungle.

She took a couple of snaps for her grandparents; he did the same for his family. And then, unable to resist, he said, 'We climbed up here together. I think we should take a selfie together to remind ourselves that we did it.'

'Great idea,' she said.

The next thing he knew, his arm was round her shoulders, the incredible view was behind them, and she was taking a snap of them both on her phone.

He only hoped he didn't look as dazed as he felt.

'You're not smiling,' she said. 'Come on. Say cheese.'

'Cheese,' he said, and she took another snap. 'Better,' she said.

For one mad moment, he almost pulled her into his arms and kissed her. He couldn't even blame the altitude, because they weren't that high up; her nearness was what had sent him into a spin. But thankfully his common sense intervened. 'We ought to let the next lot of people have some space up here,' he said.

'True. We need a drink of water before we go back down,' she said. 'And something to eat. I made banana bread last night. With lots of oats, walnuts and pumpkin seeds, and less sugar.'

'Spoken like a cardiologist,' he teased.

And it tasted even better than it sounded. 'This is fantastic. I hope you're going to teach this recipe to our patients,' he said.

'Better than that, I'm going to make it for them,' she said. 'And once they've admitted healthy food doesn't necessarily taste like sawdust, I'll give them the recipe and get them to make suggestions about healthy swaps for their favourite foods. Patients are more likely to stick to a healthy diet if they've got a stake in it, instead of being told what to do.'

'Good plan,' he said.

After a second slice of banana bread and more water, they made their way back down the steps. Joanne slipped, at one point, and Guy caught her and held her close—even though it made his own knees feel slightly wobbly, being so near to her. 'OK?' he asked.

'I am, now. Thanks for stopping me sliding over,' she said. 'I don't think I'd dare do this trail if it had been raining.'

'Wish we hadn't done it?' he asked.

'No. That view was amazing. But I think next time we go exploring a volcano I'd like a slightly easier hike.'

She was thinking there'd be a next time?

Yeah.

He wanted to do something like this with her again, too.

'Diamond Head's meant to be a lot easier,' he said. 'And we could definitely time that for sunset—maybe one night in the week, after work.'

'I'd like that. Let's synch our schedules, later,' she said.

At the base of Koko Head, they made their way round the crater to explore the botanical gardens.

'I've never seen so many cacti or such huge ones,' Joanne said. 'I had a flatmate who loved succulents, so we had a whole windowsill of them in the kitchen—but they were all small. And I'm going to take pics for Gran.'

Guy recognised some of the cacti—the big golden ball cactus that lived up to its name, the curly agave cactus, the saguaro and the prickly pear; the greens and greys of the plants were a sharp contrast to the orangey soil.

After the cactus garden, they found the baobabs, their trunks like fat blobs; and finally they walked through a grove of plumeria trees with cream and yellow flowers back to the start of the garden.

'Frangipani,' he said. 'I've seen lei made out of these.'

'They smell like peaches, all sweet and juicy,' Joanne said, breathing in the scent.

'Stand in front of the flowers,' he said, and snapped a photo. 'I'll ping it over to you,' he said.

'Thank you.' She smiled. 'I've had a really amazing day.'

'But?'

She wrinkled her nose. 'I've been thinking about Geoff and Sally, wondering how he is.'

'Me, too,' he admitted. 'They've gone to our hospital. He'll be in *our* department. So we *could* ring Reception and see if they're still there.'

'And, if they are, pop in and see them?' she suggested.

He nodded, and made the call. 'They're still there,' he confirmed. Without thinking, he tucked her hand into the crook of his arm. 'Let's go.'

CHAPTER EIGHT

GEOFF AND SALLY were sitting in the waiting area when Joanne and Guy arrived.

'Hello. Can we get you a cup of tea?' Joanne asked.

'I know you said you worked here, but I didn't expect to see you here today! You didn't cut your date short for us, did you?' Sally asked.

'We weren't on a date,' Guy said, and Joanne was shocked to feel a twinge of disappointment. Of course it hadn't been a date. They'd gone on an outing together, as friends.

'And we didn't cut our trip short. We went to the top,' Joanne said, 'so if you'd like to see the pictures, Guy will go and get us all a cup of tea.'

'Yes, boss,' Guy said. 'And obviously coffee for you.' He turned to Geoff and Sally. 'Actually, Geoff, I probably ought to make it just water for you, for now, in case they're planning a procedure.'

'They said an angiogram,' Geoff said.

Guy nodded. 'In that case, not even water.' It was recommended to avoid food for six hours beforehand and fluids for two hours. 'Sorry. Let's forget the tea.'

'No. Sally could do with a cuppa. I'll be fine.' Geoff gave them a wry smile. 'I'll just stare longingly at you, like a labrador puppy.'

'Sure?' Guy asked.

'Sure,' Geoff said.

'In that case, do you take milk, Sally? Sugar?'

'Just milk, please,' Sally said. 'I can't believe you came here for us.'

'We were worried about you, and the only way to stop worrying was to see you for ourselves,' Joanne said. 'So how are you doing?'

'Guilty that I'm ruining our holiday, and bored waiting,' Geoff said.

'And he's a bit scared, but won't admit it,' Sally said, holding his hand and squeezing it.

'What tests have they run so far?' Joanne asked.

'They took some blood and did an ECG,' Geoff said. 'They said to keep the sticky pads on.'

'Probably because they'll do another ECG later. Are you waiting for results before the angiogram?' Joanne asked.

Sally shook her head. 'Just that.'

'Has someone talked you through the procedure?' Joanne checked.

'Yes, but neither of us can think straight or remember what the doctor said,' Sally admitted.

'I can run you through it, if you like,' Joanne said. 'It's a procedure I do all the time.'

'Would you?' Geoff looked grateful.

'Sure,' Joanne reassured him. 'It's an X-ray that looks at the blood vessels around your heart and it shows us if any of the blood vessels are narrowed or blocked—and, if they're blocked, we can unblock them,' she said.

Guy returned with three drinks, handing the tea to Sally and one of the coffees to Joanne. 'Sorry again, Geoff,' he said.

'I'll just appreciate my cup of tea that bit more later,' Geoff said.

'I'm just taking Geoff through what happens in an angiogram,' Joanne told Guy.

'That's Joanne's area rather than mine,' Guy said to Geoff and Sally. 'Though I can tell you her cath lab looks like my operating theatre but with a few extra machines.'

'We'll sedate you for the procedure, so you'll be awake but sleepy and comfortable. You won't feel any pain, and you probably won't remember any of it afterwards. What I'll do, once you're lying on my table, is numb the skin in your leg, then make a little cut and put a narrow flexible tube called a catheter into your blood vessels and feed it up to your heart. You won't feel it moving,' Joanne reassured him. 'Once it's in the right place, we'll put some dye in the catheter, which shows up on the X-rays. If there's any blockage, we can put a tiny balloon in the artery to open up the blockage, and follow it up with a little wire mesh called a stent to support the artery and keep it open, so blood can flow through it properly again. Once it's all done, we'll take the catheter out and close the incision; then you'll go into the recovery room and lie flat for a couple of hours while we keep an eye on your blood pressure, your heartbeat and your oxygen levels.'

'Put like that,' Sally said, 'it doesn't sound quite so scary.'

'And then I can go home?' Geoff asked. 'Well—back to the hotel?'

'If we're happy. There's a possibility we might keep you in overnight so we can keep an eye on you,' Joanne said. 'The main thing is that you drink plenty to flush the dye from your body, then take it easy for a couple of days—no lifting, and no strenuous exercise.'

'Which means no going back to climb Koko Head,' Guy

said. 'For the record, we were both struggling on the last bit. It's really steep.'

'And I nearly slipped and fell, coming down,' Joanne added.

'I'm not one for beach holidays and sitting around,' Geoff said. 'But I get the message. No climbing Koko Head.'

'Will he be able to fly home, next week?' Sally asked.

'If it all goes as planned, yes, though it's worth having a word with your insurance company to see if they'd rather you stayed a bit longer before flying,' Joanne said. 'Geoff, your leg might feel a bit sore afterwards, and you might have a small bruise or a bump, but it'll clear up quickly. We'll also give you some lifestyle advice to help avoid further heart disease.'

'No smoking, eat healthily, be active and watch his stress?' Sally asked. 'I've been telling him that for years.'

'Listen to your wife,' Guy advised with a smile. 'That's pretty much what we'll tell you.'

'So will he get the chest pains again?' Sally asked.

'That's possible,' Joanne said. 'Angina—the chest pains—can be triggered by cold or heat, or by stress. I'd recommend keeping active, but overdoing exercise might trigger it, so you'll need to pace yourself; and if you eat a big meal you might get angina but think it's indigestion. Eating smaller meals can help avoid that. But I mentioned earlier that there's medication you can take to help the pains in future.'

Geoff was very anxious when the nurse came to collect him. 'Can Sally come in with me?'

'I'm afraid not,' Joanne said gently. 'But if it'll help, I can sit with you.'

'And I'll stay with you, Sally, while you're waiting. We'll

go to the canteen for cake. The procedure takes about an hour,' Guy said.

'Are you sure?' Sally asked. 'I mean, it's obviously your day off, and it's not fair to make you stay at work.'

'It's fine,' Guy said. 'I'd like to think that if my parents were in your shoes and I wasn't there to support them, someone would offer to be there for them.'

'That's why I trained as a cardiologist, too,' Joanne said. 'My grandad has atrial fibrillation. I don't want any patient's family to worry the way my gran and I did when he was first diagnosed.'

Sally's eyes filled with tears. 'Thank you—both of you. I don't know how we can ever repay you.'

'That's what we're here for,' Guy said gently.

Joanne explained quietly to Meera, her colleague, that she'd met Geoff and Sally at Koko Head, and she was aware that their patients were anxious and a long way from home; she didn't want to muscle in on anyone else's work, but she thought that seeing a familiar face would help to settle Geoff and make the procedure easier for everyone.

'That's kind,' Meera said. 'So you were climbing the trail with Guy, were you, when you met Geoff?'

Uh-oh. The question sounded casual, but Joanne had a nasty feeling it could lead to speculation, and she really didn't want them to be the subject of hospital gossip. 'We both had the same idea, and it made sense to car-share. And it meant we could sneak in a bit of work on the cardiac rehab project on the way.'

'I've been meaning to talk to you about your project. My sister's a nutritionist. I could ask her to come and do some of the sessions, if you need her,' Meera said.

'Thanks—that would be brilliant.' Joanne smiled at her,

and was relieved to move the conversation back to cardiac health and Geoff, away from any hint of a relationship between herself and Guy. Because they were just friends and colleagues, weren't they?

She held Geoff's hand until the sedation kicked in, and stayed in the lab but out of the way as Meera performed the procedure.

'Good news,' Meera said. 'Come and look at the screen so you can see for yourself. There's some narrowing, but we're not going to need a stent.'

'So he'll be OK to fly, in the middle of next week?'

'Should be,' Meera said. 'I'll prescribe GTN and he needs to check in with his family doctor once he's home. I'll give him a letter to take back with him.'

'That's great,' Joanne said.

'That was really kind of you, coming here to help someone on your day off,' Meera commented.

'If my grandparents were in trouble, I'd like to think someone would help them,' Joanne said. 'So this is kind of paying it forward.'

Once Geoff was round, Sally was able to come and sit with him on the ward, and Meera suggested Sally could stay overnight at the hospital in one of the flats for relatives.

'One of us can stay with you, if you like,' Guy said.

'No. You've both done more than enough,' Geoff said.

'I'll see you in the morning, when I'm back on duty,' Joanne said. 'Try to get some rest.'

Sally hugged her. 'Thank you, love. Your parents must be so proud of the person you've become.'

Joanne hadn't spoken to them for more than a decade, but she wasn't going to talk about that here. 'Mm,' she said noncommittally.

As they left the hospital, Guy turned to her. 'I don't know about you, but Koko Head's catching up with me. I'm too tired to even think about cooking tonight. Want to grab something to eat in town? There's a place near me that does the most amazing fish tacos.'

'And that's a Hawaiian specialty? It sounds Mexican,' she said.

'Try it, and make your own mind up,' he invited. 'And that's not me coming on to you. That's tired, hungry medic talking.'

She reminded herself that she didn't need to have romantic feelings about Guy. 'OK. As long as we go halves on the bill.'

'Fine by me,' he said.

The bar was on a terrace overlooking the beach; each of the plain wooden tables had a stylised wrought-iron pineapple lamp with a tealight inside it, and a small vase with a couple of frangipani flowers. Fairy lights were strung across the ceiling, and a singer was crooning along with a guitar.

It was incredibly romantic. If this had been a proper date, Joanne would've felt swept off her feet.

But she reminded herself that Guy had suggested this place because of the food and the fact it was near to his flat, not the ambience. 'What do you recommend?' she asked, when the waiter had seated them and given them menus.

'I'm having fish tacos,' he said. 'Mahi-mahi with island slaw, lime sour cream, sweet potato fries and fire-roasted salsa.'

'Sounds good,' she said, but then she looked at the menu. 'Wait. Crab cakes, grilled asparagus and island slaw. What's the difference between island slaw and regular coleslaw?'

'They make it with vinaigrette rather than gloopy mayonnaise—plus what fruit do you associate with Hawaii?' he asked.

She gestured to the tealight lamp.

He gave her a thumbs-up. 'And it's fresh, not canned, which makes it even better.'

'The tacos sound good, but crab cakes are one of my favourites. I can't choose,' she said.

'We could,' he suggested, 'share plates. Half each. But I'm afraid I refuse to do that with pudding. The pineapple crème brûlée is amazing. And it's served in the bottom of a pineapple.'

'I wouldn't share something that sounds that good, either,' she said with a smile.

The food definitely lived up to his descriptions, and it was beautifully presented.

'Hang on. The sweet potato fries—they're not orange,' she said. 'They're *purple*.' She tried one. 'And they're delicious. I'm glad you suggested sharing.'

'My pleasure,' he said. 'I'm glad you're enjoying dinner.'

Again, his smile made Joanne's heart feel as if it had done a backflip, and she had to remind herself that this *wasn't* a date. Even if she secretly wished it was.

She enjoyed every bite—particularly the pineapple crème brûlée. 'I think I want this with every meal, from now on,' she said. 'Including breakfast.'

'Told you it was good,' he said. 'Can I offer you coffee back at my place?'

Where she'd made a fool of herself, last weekend? No chance. Although he'd ordered a beer, she'd stuck to water. 'That's kind of you to offer,' she said, 'but I think the Koko Head trail's just caught up with me, too. I'll get a cab back to my flat and have an early night.'

'I'll drop you back,' he said.

'You don't have to do that.'

'I know,' he said, 'but it would make me happier to know you're home safely. Humour me.'

He put on some classical music on the drive from his road to her flat.

'Is this your sister playing?' she asked.

'Yes.'

'She's very talented.'

'She is. And we're all really proud of her,' he said. 'When she tours, we always go as a family to the first night.'

It sounded as if they were a close family. Although Joanne knew she was lucky to have her grandparents, she was also aware that they weren't going to be around for ever. And even though Jamie's family treated her as if she was one of them, bits of her wondered what it would be like to have a proper family of her own.

Then again, that meant letting someone close enough to share her life, and she wasn't sure she was ready to give someone that level of trust. She was close to her grandparents and to Jamie, but that was different: she'd built that trust up over the years. Her past relationships had all fizzled out because she hadn't been able to let them close, thinking of her parents and not wanting to risk being let down again. What was to say her burgeoning relationship with Guy wouldn't fizzle out, too? No. It would be better to stop secretly wishing for something that had always been just out of her reach.

Something had made Joanne antsy, Guy thought. She'd just gone very quiet. The last thing he'd said was how proud they all were of his sister.

Was it the mention of family that had upset her?

He'd noticed that she only talked about her grandparents. She'd said she was an only child, and she'd changed the subject when he'd asked if her parents would keep an eye on her grandparents while she was here in Hawaii. So had she lost her parents when she was young? Not that he could ask. It was way too intrusive. And he didn't quite know what to say.

All too soon, he turned into her street.

'Thank you for today,' she said. 'I enjoyed it.'

'Me, too.' He wondered if she was going to ask him in for coffee; if she did, he'd better be polite and turn her down, because she'd made it clear that she wanted some space. And he curbed the desire to slide one hand under her hair, draw her closer to him and kiss her goodnight, because he had the feeling that would be the quickest way to make her run a mile in the opposite direction. 'Goodnight, then,' he said neutrally. 'I'll see you at work in the week. And at the luau on Friday.'

'All right. Goodnight,' she said. 'And thank you for the lift.'

'You're very welcome.'

Joanne Meadows was a puzzle, he thought as he drove back to his flat. She intrigued him. He wanted to get to know her better—and that in itself was worrying. He'd promised himself he wouldn't get emotionally invested in anyone again after Imogen. Not just because she'd cheated on him, but because of her reason: she'd told him straight that he wasn't enough for her. The barb had gone deep, and made him question whether he'd be enough for anybody.

Joanne wasn't like Imogen. Being a doctor herself, she understood the demands of the job and knew that he couldn't simply hand over to someone else in the middle of an operation, and that he'd need to decompress after six or seven hours of concentrating in the operating theatre. She didn't worry about making sure she was seen in the 'right' places or wearing the most fashionable clothes—she wanted to visit places because they were interesting, and she wore sensible shoes and a backpack if she wanted to hike somewhere, rather than something pretty that would give her blisters or expect someone else to carry everything for her.

The differences between the two women made him feel slightly less twitchy about taking the risk of getting involved with her. But then there was the fact that Joanne was guarded. She was warm and friendly to everyone, but he'd noticed that the barriers were there—wreathed in smiles, but there. If he took the risk and tried to get closer to her, would she let him? Or would she clam up and push him away?

Geoff was able to leave the hospital, the next day. Joanne updated their rehab project pitch and sent it to Guy for his thoughts, and they sent the final files to the hospital chief, but she didn't actually see him during the week—either he was in Theatre, or she was in the cath lab—though he did send her a message to remind her that he'd meet her outside her flat on Friday.

Weirdly, she found herself missing him.

He wasn't her only friend at the hospital; she'd also got to know some of her colleagues and was going to an aerobics dance class with two of them, and she never had to lunch on her own because there was always someone who suggested she joined them. But Guy…there was something about him. Something she couldn't—or maybe didn't want to let herself—pin down. Something that drew her.

She shook herself. For pity's sake. They were colleagues, and when she left Hawaii at the end of her secondment she'd be walking out of his life. She just needed to treat him as if he were like all her other colleagues at the hospital: friendly, but not close.

Just before her afternoon clinic on the Friday, it suddenly occurred to her: she didn't have a clue what the dress code was for tonight. Guy was probably already in his own clinic, so she couldn't ask him. Meera wasn't around, and the nurses she'd become friendly with were off duty, too. In the end, she went to see Patty in Reception.

'Can I ask a stupid question, please, Patty?'

'There's no such thing as a stupid question, honey. What can I do for you?' Patty asked.

'The luau tonight. I forgot to check what the dress code was,' Joanne said.

'The three Cs—casual, comfortable and colourful,' Patty said. 'A luau's about having a good time with your friends and your family. It doesn't matter what you wear, as long as you're having fun.'

'So a sundress?' Joanne checked.

'With slippers instead of heels,' Patty added.

'Slippers?' Joanne asked, confused.

Patty laughed. 'That's what we call flip flops, over here. Rubber slippers. If you don't have any, wear something you can kick off easily to dance on the beach. And bring a wrap, because it can get a little cold after sundown.'

'When you've walked across a park in London on a wet and windy winter's day, you know what cold is. What I've experienced here isn't even close,' Joanne said, smiling back. 'Sundress and flip flops it is, then. Do I need a lei or anything?'

'They'll have lei when you get there,' Patty said. 'Made with fresh flowers. And they smell gorgeous.'

'I can't wait for my first luau. Will you be going tonight?' Joanne asked.

'I'll be there, with my husband,' Patty confirmed. 'I'll see you later.'

After her shift, Joanne went back to her flat, showered and changed into a pretty and bright sundress. She left her hair loose, and added floral canvas shoes that she could kick off easily. She'd just finished getting ready when Guy texted her to let her know he was waiting outside.

She ran lightly down the stairs to discover that he was wearing light-coloured chinos, canvas shoes and a bright red shirt patterned with large white hibiscus flowers.

'You look lovely,' he said.

'Thank you—and you look…very bright,' she said. Like her, he tended to wear scrubs at work, and he'd worn muted colours at the Pirate and Spear and when they'd gone hiking.

'It's a luau. You're meant to wear something bright,' he said. 'It feels a bit like cultural appropriation, but I checked with Patty before my first luau and she said this is the sort of thing everyone's expected to wear.'

The red suited him, but at the same time it made her want to stand on tiptoe, slide one arm round his neck and draw his head down to hers so she could kiss him.

Which was *not* what she should be doing.

She didn't even have Jamie here to talk some sense into her, because he was working and unable to get to the party.

When they got to the beach, they showed their tickets

on their phones to the girl on the reception desk, who gave them each a lei made from the most gorgeous-scented flowers—bright pink for Joanne and yellow for Guy.

'*Aloha.* Welcome to Hawaii! You wear it draped over your shoulders, so it hangs down at the front and the back, not like a necklace,' the receptionist said, helping Joanne put hers in place.

'It's beautiful,' Joanne said, holding the side up so she could sniff it. 'I've only ever seen them on films and photos.'

'Enjoy the luau,' the receptionist said. 'The hula dancers are over on the right, and the food's on the left.'

'Thank you,' Joanne said. 'How do I say that in Hawaiian?'

'*Mahalo,*' the receptionist said.

'*Mahalo,*' Joanne repeated, smiling back.

The sun was beginning to set; the sky was gold at the horizon, stripes of purple and crimson across the sky, reflected in the calm waters. It was breathtakingly beautiful; she took a snap, then put her phone away.

They went to see the dancing first; the group of sixteen gorgeous women all wore matching flowing red dresses with yellow lei, and yellow flowers in their hair. Joanne was mesmerised by their graceful arm movements and swaying hips, all in perfect time and synchronisation.

'One of my Theatre nurses, Ailani, is one of the dancers tonight,' Guy said. 'She's on the front row, far left.'

'She's really good,' Joanne said. 'They're all good. Though I kind of was expecting them to wear grass skirts.'

'Stereotype,' he said, but his tone wasn't unkind. 'Ailani's taught me that it's not about women in grass skirts and coconut bras, shaking their hips to entertain tourists. It's telling a story—kind of like ballet does, except every movement and gesture has a specific meaning. And it takes a long while to learn. It's about spirituality as well as moving.' He smiled. 'I asked her a lot of questions, but I was respectful about it. She's rightly proud of her heritage.'

When the dancers took a break, Joanne and Guy joined the queue for food. 'Kalua pig is traditional,' the server explained. 'We serve it on a plate of taro leaves, but you can't eat them. The pork's slow-baked in an underground pit and then shredded.'

It was served with slices of the vibrant purple sweet potato she'd tried at the bar with Guy, sweet bread rolls made with pineapple, and macaroni salad. There were dishes of hulihuli chicken, grilled with pineapple and a tangy sauce, and lomilomi salmon with onions and tomatoes. Every bite was delicious.

'Dessert?' Guy asked when she'd finished her plate.

'The pineapple crème brûlée has ruined me for all desserts,' she said. 'But you go for it.'

He came back with two bowls, both multicoloured. 'Only a small portion,' he said, 'but it's traditional and I think you'll like it.'

'Ice cream?'

'Shave ice,' he said. 'Without a D. It's what it sounds like—ice, then flavoured with syrup. It's a bit like a slushie, but nicer. This one's pineapple, vanilla and red.'

'Red?' She tasted it gingerly. 'Oh! It's cherry.'

The fruity dessert was refreshing, the tartness of the cherry balancing the sweetness of the pineapple, and she appreciated his thoughtfulness. 'Thank you,' she said with a smile.

* * *

After another hula demonstration, the band was playing music everyone could dance to. Some people were sitting around the fire-pits, chilling out and talking; others were dancing; and still more were walking along the edge of the sea, with the waves shimmering up over their feet. A crescent moon hung in a velvety sky full of stars, its silvery shape reflecting on the ocean.

Guy couldn't resist asking Joanne to dance with him. The music was upbeat, and they were both laughing. But then, as the music turned soft and sweet, he found himself holding her in his arms for a slow dance.

And everything around them melted away.

The music, the people laughing and talking and dancing nearby, the sounds of people clearing away the food, the moon and the stars…they were all gone.

All he was aware of was Joanne.

Her gorgeous grey eyes.

The warmth of her skin.

The scent of the lei they both wore.

The swish of the sea against the soft, soft sand.

It all added up to an incredibly heady package. A tropical temptation.

He'd stooped slightly so his cheek was against hers as they danced, holding her close. How could he resist moving his face ever so slightly, so the corner of his mouth was against hers?

And it was like a flame to touchpaper, sending heat through his whole body, because she moved her face ever so slightly, too, sliding her lips against his. Warm and soft and so incredibly sweet. His arms tightened round her, and she slid her hands round his neck, parting her lips to let him deepen the kiss.

The whole universe seemed to stop, concentrated in a single kiss…

CHAPTER NINE

When Guy finally broke the kiss, he simply stared at Joanne, not knowing what to say. Her eyes were unreadable. He didn't have a clue what she was thinking. And he was shocked by how quickly he'd lost himself, kissing her.

'I... Sorry,' he whispered. 'I shouldn't have done that.' But the temptation had been too much for him to resist. The stars shimmering above them, the sweet floral scent in the air, and Joanne in his arms.

Almost at the same time, she was saying, 'I shouldn't have kissed you first.'

'It was my f—' he began, and at the same time she said in a nervy, breathy voice, 'It was my fault.'

They were talking over each other. Panicking. *Gabbling.* Both of them were clearly thinking the same thing. He took a deep breath. 'It's *both* of our faults,' he said.

And then he realised he was still holding her; he loosened his hold and took a step backwards. Time to back off.

'I'm sorry,' he said again. 'Let's pretend it didn't happen.'

'But it did,' she said. Then she blushed even more, as if she hadn't meant to say that.

So he hadn't been alone in this thing? She'd wanted to kiss him as much as he'd wanted to kiss her? 'I'm glad you did.' The words spilled out before he could stop them.

The colour in her cheeks deepened further still. 'In full view of all our colleagues? Or at least, quite a few of them?'

'They're too busy dancing, eating and drinking cocktails to have noticed one little...' His mouth went dry. It hadn't *felt* little. 'A single kiss,' he whispered. And, God help him, he wanted more. He knew he shouldn't. Getting involved with her would be a bad, bad idea. For both of them. So why did he want to wrap his arms round her and kiss her again? Why did he want to kiss her until they were both walking on starlight?

'I don't want to be the hot topic of the hospital grapevine,' she said.

Yeah. He'd been there, too, and hated it. Part of him wanted to wrap his arms round her again and tell her everything would be OK—that he would protect her. Except how could you protect anyone against gossip? Only by keeping your distance. Which he hadn't done. He'd made her vulnerable, and that wasn't fair.

'I'm sorry,' he said. 'Look—why don't we get out of here? Nobody will notice we're gone. If anyone does, we'll say you had a headache and I walked you back.'

Again, her expression was unreadable, and his skin started to feel too tight. Had he got this completely wrong?

But then she nodded. 'We need to talk. And we can't do it here.'

He picked up his shoes; she followed suit, and they headed off down the beach, not talking, until they found a quiet spot.

'Here?' he asked softly.

She nodded, and sat on the beach, her knees drawn up and her arms wrapped around her legs. He sat next to her, mirroring her position.

'I honestly didn't mean to kiss you.' So much for having good intentions. And what he'd said was insulting, as well as not quite honest. She deserved better. 'Well, not at the luau, in front of everyone,' he amended.

Her gaze met his. 'Is that a roundabout way of saying that you wanted to kiss me somewhere *not* in front of everyone?'

She'd got right to the heart of the matter. And, unless he was reading this very wrong, she was looking for a truthful answer. Well, he'd already made a mess of this. Telling her how he really felt couldn't make it much worse. 'Ever since Koko Head,' he said. 'Maybe even before that. There's just something about you that—' He shook his head in frustration, trying to find the right words to explain it without scaring her off, and came up with, 'Draws me.'

'I'm not looking for a relationship,' she said. 'I don't… I can't…' She sighed, and stared at her knees.

He guessed that she, like he, wasn't used to being so inarticulate, so at sixes and sevens with herself. Time for a bit more honesty. 'I'm not looking for a relationship, either,' he said. 'I came to Hawaii to get away from Bristol. From my family, in part.'

Her head snapped up and she stared at him. 'I thought you said you were close to them?'

'I am,' he said. 'Which is why I needed a little bit of space.'

'I don't understand.'

He felt a muscle work in his jaw. He was going to have to tell her. Of course he was. *But*. 'Promise me this isn't going to change things between us? You're not going to pity me?'

'Pity you? Why would I pity you?' Joanne asked, not understanding.

'Because that's what I've put up with for the past year,'

he said. 'From my colleagues, from my friends, from my family—well, maybe not so much pity from them as wrapping me in cotton wool and trying to manage me,' he added, wanting to be fair. 'Maybe coming here was running away from the problem—but I just want to be *me* again.'

He looked shocked, as if he hadn't meant to say that last bit out loud. As if he hadn't talked to anyone about it before. Ha. She knew how that felt. She waited, giving him space to decompress and talk.

'I'm sick of being the person everyone pities,' he said. 'When actually I'm a surgeon who does the best by his patients and works well with his colleagues.'

Did he only define himself in terms of work? What about who he was inside?

'What you said about not wanting to be the hot topic of the hospital grapevine—that's what I was,' he said. 'Everyone saw me as the poor bloke who went home with the flu, staggered up the stairs and discovered his fiancée in bed with someone else.'

'What, in *your* bed?' she asked, completely shocked. Being cheated on was bad enough, but to be cheated on in your own private space? That was really tough.

He gave a single nod, his face tight with misery.

'That,' she said, 'is a horrible thing to do to someone.' She reached out, took his hand and squeezed it once. 'And that's not pity, by the way. That's solidarity.'

'Did someone cheat on you?' he asked.

'No,' she said, not ready to talk to him about the stuff inside her head quite yet. 'But I can guess how rough it must feel.'

'It did. I thought Imogen loved me. We'd set a date for

the wedding. I was so stupid, so blind, so sure I'd got the life I wanted. A job I loved, a girl I loved...'

And it was telling that the job went before the girl, Joanne thought. Though, in fairness, it was the same for her.

'Imogen blamed me, at first. She said I was a workaholic and that I gave her no choice but to look elsewhere.' He gave a huff of laughter. 'But I was already a qualified doctor when I first started dating her. When I asked her to move in with me, she knew the kind of hours I worked. When I asked her to marry me, she knew exactly what she was taking on, and that I wouldn't be able to give her my full attention, all of the time.'

It was beginning to sound as if Imogen had accepted his proposal, but then changed the rules. 'What did she expect you to do? Give up more than a decade of training and find a job with the kind of sociable hours she approved of—even if it was a job you hated?' Joanne asked.

He gave a wry smile. 'That's what I wondered, too. So I pushed back and reminded her. And then she said...' His face looked pinched. 'Well. Never mind that.'

Clearly whatever Imogen had said had cut him to the quick, and it still hurt enough for him to find it difficult to repeat it, Joanne thought.

He lifted one shoulder in a rueful shrug. 'Let's just say the other guy she'd been seeing gave her what she wanted.'

Implying that Guy hadn't. And yet the man she'd been getting to know was kind and caring, the sort who gave rather than took. Had Imogen perhaps said something to justify her own selfish behaviour, and Guy had taken it to mean he was the problem rather than her? Did he think he was lacking in some way? Because that was crazy.

'I get,' she said carefully. 'that you can't help who you fall in love with. I'm not judging her for that. Though it also isn't a valid excuse to hurt someone. Why didn't she have the decency to end things with you before she went off with him?' She shook her head. 'And to sleep with someone else in your bed—that's *incredibly* mean. You're better off without someone who'd treat you like that.'

'I know,' he said. 'I asked her to leave, there and then.' He sighed. 'I'd bought the house before I met her, and it was convenient for work. I didn't want to sell up and move, so I tried to be fair about it.'

Whereas his ex, Joanne thought, hadn't been at all fair with him.

'I gave her her share of the increase in the house's value since she started paying towards the mortgage.'

Which was more than decent of him, Joanne thought.

'The night she left, I called a locksmith, got the locks changed and moved into the spare bedroom.' He grimaced. 'I got rid of the bed. And the duvet, the pillows and the bedlinen. I couldn't bear to have them in the house. Not after… Not after finding them together, there.'

'I would've burned the lot,' she said.

'I did think about doing that,' he admitted. 'But I figured it would be better to do something positive with the stuff than destroying it, so I gave the bedding to a local dog rescue centre, and the bed to a charity shop. Burning the lot might've given me a moment's satisfaction, but then I would've felt guilty about the waste of resources.'

'You're a better person than I am,' she said. 'And that's why you're in Hawaii? To forget her?'

'To give myself a bit of a reset. Start again,' he said. 'Because when the pity and the gossip finally stopped at work, the next thing was everyone trying to fix what they saw as my problem—loneliness—and find me Ms Right to fill the gap. Except I'm not looking for another relationship and I'm sick of people trying to fix me up with what they think is a suitable partner.'

She could understand that. In his shoes, she'd find it hard to trust again. And she definitely wouldn't want anyone else picking her next relationship for her—if she had one at all. How did you get over a betrayal like that? Your partner, in the intimate space you'd shared together, with someone else? 'Fair enough,' she said. 'Thank you for being honest with me.'

'Imogen liked a drink,' he said. 'She'd go out with the girls, have too many cocktails and come home plastered.'

Joanne winced. That night at the Pirate and Spear suddenly took on a whole new aspect. He'd seen her, drunk and incapable, and it had clearly brought back painful memories for him—of his ex, and her betrayal. Had he thought that she was the same kind of person? 'No wonder you were so fed up with me, the night we met. I'm sorry.'

'You weren't to know.' He paused. 'But you were telling me the truth, the morning after. You don't get drunk. You didn't even have a beer with our tacos, last weekend. You didn't know those cocktails were alcoholic—*and* you'd asked. It's not your fault you were given the wrong information.'

She shrugged. 'Now I understand why you reacted to me the way you did. In your shoes, I would probably have felt the same.'

'So what's your story?' he asked. 'Did you overdo it as a student and need a bit of help drying out?'

'No. I just always stick to just one drink.' He'd been honest with her; now it was her turn to be truthful with him. And she knew he wouldn't betray her confidence, just as she wouldn't betray his. 'I tell people it's because I can't hold my drink—' which was a fiction she'd cooked up with Jamie '—but it's actually to prove to myself I can stop.'

He frowned. 'Now I'm the one who doesn't understand.'

'My birth parents,' she said. 'I don't see them now. But my father was a raging alcoholic. And I mean raging in all senses of the word. When I was small, I learned not to make him angry. He was a mean drunk, and he'd lash out.'

Guy's eyes widened. 'He *hit* you?'

'A few times,' she said, doing her best to keep her voice neutral. 'And my mother.'

'She didn't have any friends who could help her get away, find her a refuge or something? She didn't have someone you could stay with, out of his way, when he got drunk and vicious?' Guy checked.

'She might've had friends. I don't know. But the thing is, she didn't *want* to get away,' Joanne said softly. 'She said she loved him, but she enabled him.' And she hadn't protected her small daughter. 'Looking back, I'm not sure they even meant to have me. I might've been a mistake.'

Guy reached out and squeezed her hand. 'That's not pity, either. It's solidarity, too, because I know how lucky I am with my family—Jordan might drive me bananas when he nags me about moving on or finding someone, but I know the nagging comes from a good place. It's because he cares. And I don't know where I'd be without them all.'

'I'm lucky,' she said. 'I had my grandparents. My mum's parents. They took me on and they brought me up.' She took a deep breath. 'That volcano experiment your mum did with you? Gran was a primary school teacher. She did that experiment with me, and I *loved* it. I was so excited. I tried to show my dad when he came home from work—well, I realise now he'd gone to the pub on the way home and had a few drinks. Some of the red food colouring got on his shirt and ruined it, and he went mad. He smashed up my volcano. Hit me. And my mum said it was my fault, too.'

Guy couldn't quite believe what he was hearing. Her father had hit her in an alcohol-fuelled rage when she'd been a child small enough to enjoy kitchen science? He'd *hit* her? And her mother had blamed her, instead of standing up for her? And Joanne could say that all out loud, so neutrally?

His heart bled for that small, scared child.

He wanted to wrap his arms round her, hold her tight and tell her he'd protect her—but he knew that wasn't what she needed. Smothering her would make her back away. Though he couldn't ignore this. She'd taken the risk of trusting him, and he wasn't going to let her down.

'I'm so sorry,' he said softly. 'Violence doesn't solve anything, but right now I think I'd like to punch your father. Very, very hard. And your mother…words fail me. How the hell can you treat a child like that?'

'Drink changes you,' she said, with the tiniest shrug of one shoulder.

Now he understood why she needed to have just one drink and stop. And to think he'd been pompous enough to lecture her about drinking too much. Even though he hadn't known about her past—he would never have said it if he'd had even the smallest clue—he hated himself for it. How much his words must've hurt. Scraping the top off a wound that went right to the bone.

'Your father hit you,' he said quietly. 'Didn't any of your teachers notice?'

'I don't think safeguarding was quite like it is today, back then. He hit me where the bruises didn't show,' Joanne said. 'And I couldn't tell anyone.' She took a deep breath. 'Because I thought it was my fault, and it would get worse if I told. You know, like when someone bullies you at school and steals your lunch, or drops your books in a puddle, or tells everyone not to sit with you because you smell. If they get a reaction, they do it even more. And I didn't want him to hit me again. I figured it was better to stay quiet.'

'It wasn't your fault. It really wasn't.' He paused. 'Did you tell someone, eventually?'

'Gran noticed,' Joanne said. 'She came over to see us, a couple of weeks later. My father was at work, and my mother was in the kitchen. Gran was playing a game with me. She asked me if I'd made any more lava in my volcano, and I couldn't help myself—I started crying. She gave me a cuddle and asked me what was wrong. I tried not to tell, I tried so hard, but the words bubbled out of my mouth, just like the lava. She hugged me and told me that nobody would ever, ever hit me again, and she'd make very sure of it. She told me to go upstairs and get my favourite teddy, because she was going to take me out for an ice cream. I don't know what she said to my mother, but when I came downstairs Gran was waiting. She put me in her car, but we didn't go to the ice cream shop. Instead, she drove me straight back to her house. She said Gramps would go and get the rest of my things, and I would live with her and Gramps in future. And my dad wouldn't be allowed near me without someone there to protect me. He'd never, ever get away with trying to hit me again.' She lifted a weary shoulder. 'And that's what happened. Gramps was a lawyer. I was too young to know what was happening, at the time, but he got special guardianship orders so he and my gran could bring me up. On the few occasions my parents saw me, it was under strict supervision.'

Her grandparents had kept her safe.

His shoulders sagged; he hadn't realised until that moment how tense he'd been, horrified by her story. 'I'm glad they had your back,' he said. 'I assume you don't see your parents now?'

'I haven't seen them since I was fourteen. There are only so many birthdays a child can take without their parents remembering to send a card,' she said dryly.

What? But—but birthdays were *important*, when you were a child.

'Or nativity plays where they were supposed to come to school to watch, but they were too hungover,' she added.

Something he'd taken for granted, whether he'd been a shepherd or a king—he'd look out and see his parents sitting there, watching the show and looking so proud of him. Joanne had clearly looked out but her parents hadn't been there.

'Or promised trips where they "forgot"—' she made speech marks with her fingers '—the arrangements and didn't turn up to take me out. What actually happened was they'd had a better offer. Usually involving alcohol.'

'That's—' He paused, not knowing what to say. 'That's rough,' he said, realising how inadequate the words were, but wanting her to know he was on her side.

'I had my grandparents,' she said softly. 'And then, as I got older, I realised I didn't need to keep waiting for my parents to love me enough to be there. They simply weren't capable of doing that. I would always come second to that bottle of vodka or gin or whatever. And I'm worth more than that.'

'Yes, you are,' he said. 'A lot more.'

'I talked to my grandparents about it and went no-contact with my parents,' she said. 'I think it was the best thing for all of us. They don't have the weight of my expectations, and I don't have the misery of them letting me down yet again.'

'You did the right thing,' he said. He was still trying to get his head round this, because it was so far from his own experience as a child. Her father was a drunk who'd hit her. Her grandparents had rescued her. And her mother had stayed with her father—had chosen a mean, violent drunk over the child she'd carried for nine months and given birth to. And every time Joanne had hoped they'd change, that they'd put her first, they'd crushed her. In her shoes, he would've reached the point where he'd had enough, too, and walked away.

'I'm the child of an addict, Guy,' she said. 'An addict and an enabler. That's why I stop at one drink. To prove to myself I'm not like my father.'

'You're not remotely like him. You heal people, not hurt them,' he said. 'And OK, I've known you all of two weeks. But the woman I've got to know is kind and caring. You don't ignore people who are in trouble—you try to help them. And I don't think you would ever hit anyone.'

'How do I *know* that, though? Maybe I've never been tested to that point. What if I get really stressed?' she asked.

Did she really think she was capable of the sort of harm her father had caused? He tried to think of a way to convince her. But he realised it would have to come from her, not him. 'OK. Say you've had the day from hell. It starts with half your department being off sick, so you're up to your eyes and you barely have time to chug down a glass of water and eat half a sandwich between appointments, and then you lose a patient—one who really matters because you've been treating them for years. When you finally leave your shift, three hours late, your car won't start. The recovery services take two hours to get there and then they tell you they can't fix it. And you finally get home to find the fridge is empty because your flatmate's boyfriend got the munchies and ate everything in sight. What do you do?' he asked.

'Put some music on, whack up the volume and sing very badly until I feel a bit better. And probably go to the open-all-hours corner shop to buy a ton of chocolate,' she said.

'There's your answer,' he pointed out. 'You wouldn't go and thump someone smaller than you, someone defenceless.'

She said nothing.

'Your grandparents brought you up to be the kind of woman they could be proud of,' he said softly. 'And *they're* your example. Not your parents. Your grandparents are the ones who nurtured you.'

'But what if nature overrides nurture?' she asked. 'I don't want to take that risk.'

'You have your grandparents' blood, too,' he pointed out. 'So you have their nature as well as their nurture, don't you?'

She grimaced. 'I still have my father's blood.'

'It's part of you,' he acknowledged. 'But only a part. And one that…' He raked a hand through his hair. 'Do you trust my judgement, Joanne? Even though I fell for someone who let me down?'

'Well, that wipes out my logical argument,' she said with a slightly crooked smile. 'I trust your clinical judgement. And you were right about the pineapple crème brûlée.'

Her tone was deceptively light, he thought. 'OK. Let's say you trust my judgement. I know how lucky I am with my family, and I love them to the end of the earth and back. And I would stake their lives on you never, ever becoming like your father.'

She blew out a breath. 'That's quite a compliment.'

'It's a fact,' he said. 'I like you, Joanne. And I think you like me.'

'I do. But I should warn you that I don't let people close,' she said.

After the way she'd been treated by the two people who should've loved her and protected her instead of hurting her and letting her down, that wasn't surprising. He'd find it hard to trust, too.

Well. He found it hard to trust anyway, since Imogen's betrayal. So he had to ask the question. 'What about Jamie?'

'He's my best friend. He has been since our first day at uni. Yes, he knows what happened when I was a kid,' she said. 'I had a meltdown in the first week of uni and told him about it. Then he appointed himself the brother I never had.'

'Uh-huh.' That wasn't quite what he'd meant, but he was glad she'd had someone looking out for her.

His silence clearly made her realise what he was really asking. 'As you told me about what Imogen did, I get why you're asking,' she said. 'You want to know if I ever had romantic feelings about him. I don't. I've truly never thought of him in that way. Gran said maybe the romance of Hawaii would make us both think differently, but when I saw him again I knew it wasn't going to happen, because we just don't feel that way about each other. We hug each other. He might hold my hand. He'll always answer my calls. But he's never been my boyfriend and never will be. He's my family—my brother,' she said. She gave a wry smile. 'Except he's way more laid-back than me. I'm a control freak.'

'So am I,' Guy said. 'I know I'm too serious. When someone makes a joke in the department, it often goes over my head.'

'Because you get other things, instead.' She flicked a hand up to indicate the sky. 'I bet you could name every star in the sky above us.'

'Not quite,' he said, 'but I could point out the planets and most of the constellations. Just as I bet you could pick up a bit of rock from any volcano around here and tell me all about the geology.'

'Yeah, I could,' she admitted, with a flash of that smile that made his heart turn over. 'We're both nerds. Or is it geeks?'

'I don't have a clue what the difference is,' he said. 'I'm sorry you had a rough time when you were tiny. But I'm glad you have the best grandparents ever.'

'Thank you. And I'm sorry your ex was so selfish. But it wasn't your fault.'

'It kind of was, for letting my heart get in the way of my head,' he said. 'I should've seen the signs.'

She looked shocked. 'Guy, you can't blame yourself for someone else's behaviour. It really wasn't your fault that Imogen cheated. It was her decision. She could've chosen to break up with you first, instead of stringing you along until she was sure of the other guy. And it wasn't your fault that you fell for someone who let you down. You weren't to know that she wasn't—well, who she seemed to be.'

He appreciated that she was on his side. 'I won't repeat that mistake.' He paused. He'd told her he liked her. She'd said she liked him. 'So what happens now?'

'I don't know,' she said. 'I'm a control freak. I don't let people into my life, not on more than a surface level.'

'I think we're on the same page,' he said. 'I don't want a relationship, and neither do you.'

'Agreed,' she said.

'But,' he added, 'we've already admitted we like each other.'

'We do.' She wrinkled her nose. 'But nothing's going to happen between us.'

'Except we kissed.'

'We're attracted to each other,' she allowed. 'But we can ignore that. Be professional. We're not teenagers.'

They could ignore the attraction. But it would drive him crazy, because he was so aware of her, and he rather thought it would be the same for her. 'Or,' he said, 'we could make life easier and not ignore it.'

She narrowed her eyes at him. 'How does not ignoring it make life easier?'

'Because,' he said, 'we're only here temporarily in Hawaii. There's a time limit. What's stopping us from having some kind of mad fling? We're both adults. Neither of us is committed elsewhere. We both feel the same way and we know we're going to walk away from each other at the end, so we can keep our hearts intact.'

'A mad fling,' she said.

'We get to spend time together. We date, we kiss, we make love—but there's no pressure because we already know there's an end and neither of us is looking for forever.' He shrugged. 'We have that trip to Big Island to plan, to see the volcanoes and the stars. That's going to happen, whether we're together or not—but I think it'll be more fun if we're *together* together.'

'*Together* together,' she echoed.

'For the rest of your time in Hawaii. And then we say goodbye.' He knew she was bright enough to work out what he meant: so it would be safe. For both of them.

'No pressure,' he said. 'Just think about it. And I'll walk you home.' He stood up, and reached down to help her to her feet.

'I don't need any more time to think about it,' she said.

She was going to turn him down flat? That swiftly?

But then she stood on tiptoe, slid her arms round his neck, and brushed her lips against his, making his mouth tingle. Her pupils were huge in the moonlight, and he couldn't help kissing her back.

'Last time we shared a bed was at your place,' she said.

Where he'd accused her of being a lush. How very wrong he'd been.

'This time,' she finished, 'I think it should be mine.'

Meaning that she'd feel in control of what was happening. Well, that was just fine by him. He smiled, and took her hand. 'Your place it is.'

CHAPTER TEN

ON SATURDAY MORNING, Guy woke, warm and comfortable, spooned against Joanne with his arms wrapped round her. Her hair smelled of vanilla, and he lay there, just enjoying the feeling of being close to her.

Last night had been amazing. Their first time making love should've been awkward and ungainly, but it had *worked*—almost as if they'd instinctively known how each other liked being touched, kissed.

And Joanne had been comfortable enough with him to ask him to stay for breakfast—which he thought was quite a big deal. She might be protecting herself by agreeing that this was a fling where they could walk away from each other at the end; but at the same time she wasn't keeping him at a distance.

Then again, it suited him, too, because it took out all the trust issues. He wasn't asking her to spend the rest of her life with him, the way he'd made himself vulnerable for Imogen. Getting properly involved with each other would be a terrible idea. Neither of them wanted to let someone that close. Neither of them wanted to risk their heart being broken again when the other let them down. They absolutely wouldn't let themselves fall in love with the other.

But they could still have fun together in a tropical paradise. Work hard at the hospital, and play hard outside. Three and a half months of enjoying each other's company, and no hurt feelings at the end.

It would do them both good, he thought. No risks, no angst, no promises—this was just for fun. A reset, for both of them.

A couple of minutes later, she woke, stretched, and turned to face him.

'Good morning.' Guy dropped a kiss on her forehead.

'Good morning.' She cuddled into him. 'Is it ridiculous that I feel all shy, right now?'

'No. Weirdly, so do I—though we really don't need to feel that way.' He brushed his lips against her. 'Can I make you a coffee?'

'You're my guest. I should be the one making coffee,' she pointed out.

'I've been awake longer than you have,' he countered.

She smiled. 'Then yes, please.'

He climbed out of bed, pulled on his underpants and chinos, and padded out of the bedroom to make coffee for both of them.

'Do you have anything planned for today?' he asked when he came back to bed.

'Thank you for this.' She took a sip. 'It's perfect. And no, I don't have any real plans. I thought I might do a bit of exploring. You?'

'I've got nothing planned,' he said. 'We could do some exploring together, if you like. A walk, perhaps, or a museum?'

'Either. Both,' she said. 'That'd be nice.'

'Though I need to go home and change, first.' He gave her a rueful smile. 'That shirt was fine for a luau, but it's not really...well, me.'

She smiled, and stroked his face. 'Do you have any idea how cute you are?'

He laughed. 'I'm dull.'

'You're not dull at all,' she corrected. 'I'll tell you what's dull—the kind of man who can't pass a mirror and insists on designer clothes. You know the sort: shallow as a puddle and can't talk about anything that's actually interesting, because he's too busy making sure he's seen in all the trendy places and wearing the most fashionable labels.'

Yeah. Imogen had been very keen on labels, too, and she'd never understood him. To him, a white T-shirt was a white T-shirt. 'I was thinking, maybe we can see if we can sync our off-duty,' he said. 'Because I have a trip in mind—and we'll need an overnight stay.'

'Overnight?' she asked.

'We have to fly to Big Island first—which takes the best part of an hour, if we get the fastest flight—and the trip itself is twelve hours or so.'

Her eyes brightened. 'Big Island. Does this mean volcanoes and stars, by any chance?'

He liked how quickly her mind worked. 'Yup. I'd already scoped out this one,' he said, and showed her the trip he'd bookmarked on his phone.

'Oh, that sounds amazing,' she said. 'We actually get to walk inside a lava tube! I'm definitely up for that.'

'Great. Once we've sorted the dates, I'll book it. My treat.'

She shook her head. 'It's very nice of you to offer, but no. We're going halves.'

'It's a date,' he said, 'and I was brought up to pay for dates.' Imogen had been happy enough about that. Joanne clearly wasn't, because again she shook her head.

'A date would be dinner, or maybe a show,' she said. 'This is a high-end trip, with a flight and two nights in a hotel. No way are you paying. Either we go halves, or we don't go at all.'

'I'm not exactly poor,' he said.

'That's got nothing to do with it.' She put her coffee on the bedside cabinet and folded her arms. 'I'm not looking to be a freeloader.'

'You,' he said, 'are the last person I'd consider to be a freeloader.' Thinking back, he realised Imogen had actually expected him to pay for everything and he'd just gone along with it. 'But OK. We'll go halves.' He paused. But there was independent, and there was stubborn. There was a fine line between the two, and he didn't want the hassle of constant fighting. 'Am I allowed to buy you dinner tonight?'

'Sure. As long as I can buy *you* dinner, the next time we eat out,' she said.

Independent, then. That was a relief. 'That works for me,' he said. 'So when do we book this trip?'

They checked their off-duty and discovered that they could make the following weekend; even better, there were spaces on the trip, there were seats on the flight they needed, and a room available at a nice-sounding hotel in Kona where the tour organisers could pick them up.

'This is going to be brilliant,' he said when he'd booked it.

And it was going to be special, because he'd be with her.

On Tuesday, the hospital chief called them both into his office for a meeting, and gave them the go-ahead to run the cardiac rehab project. 'I appreciate you're both using your free time to organise things,' he said.

Joanne was delighted. 'It'll make a difference to our patients,' she said. 'We give some guidance to people who've had surgery, but I think it would be helpful for those who've had a different cardiac procedure, too. The more we can get our patients to think about looking after themselves and come up with their own suggestions, the more likely they are to sustain the changes.'

'There's so much misinformation on the internet, and it's hard for them to know what to do for the best. A rehab class and a support group where they can ask for advice will make a huge difference,' Guy added.

For the rest of the week, they seemed to spend most of their off-duty planning the rehab classes together; but just being together felt good, Joanne thought. And the more time she spent with Guy, the more comfortable she was with him. He wasn't the judgy mansplainer she'd first thought him; he was quiet, thoughtful and measured. He noticed things. And he was trying to make the bits of the world around him a better place.

On Saturday, they caught an early flight to Big Island, took a taxi to their hotel and dropped off their overnight bags, and were ready waiting outside the hotel for the pickup for their tour.

They were the last to be picked up, joining two older couples and a couple with two children aged eight and ten in the back of the minibus. The guide introduced himself as Drew, and told them all stories of Hawaiian legends and culture on the way to their first stop, pointing out places of interest as they passed.

The first stop was at Punalu'u, to walk on the black sand beach.

'Basalt,' Joanne said. 'Like Reynisfjara beach in Iceland.'

He smiled. 'I knew you'd know.' And he really seemed to like her inner nerd, Joanne thought; he listened to what she said. Apart from Jamie—who teased her, half the time—she wasn't used to that, and she rather liked it.

'This is stunning,' she said. 'Last time I walked on a black sand beach, it was the Atlantic Ocean rolling in towards me—it was the most amazing turquoise blue, with the basalt stacks sticking up and being the only thing between us and Antarctica—a whole globe away.'

'Here, it's the Pacific,' Guy said. 'Also an amazing turquoise blue—except with coconut palms and lush green jungle as the backdrop, and I have no idea what the next land mass is.'

'Neither do I. Let's see.' She looked it up on her phone. 'Would you believe, *also* Antarctica, but only about half a globe away?'

'I love the fact you're comfortable with admitting a gap in your knowledge, and then you go and fill it,' he said.

'Well, hey. You get to learn more, that way. And what's the point of lying?' she asked.

'True,' he said.

His eyes darkened slightly. Was he remembering the way Imogen had lied to him? she wondered. Feeling guilty for trampling on a sore spot, even though it had been inadvertent, she squeezed his hand. 'Look—Drew was right. Green turtles, basking in the sun.'

They all kept a respectful distance of the turtles, taking pictures but making sure they didn't disturb the animals.

'This is just incredible,' Joanne said quietly. 'And I'm glad I'm sharing this with you.'

'Me, too,' Guy said, his blue eyes sincere.

They made friends with their fellow passengers, and chatted on their way to the Volcano National Park. They broke for lunch at a restaurant with a view over the Kīlauea caldera and the Halema'uma'u crater.

'Halema'uma'u is a lava lake—in legend, it's the home of Pele, the goddess of fire and volcanoes,' Drew told them. 'She's also the goddess of Hula. And they say if you see a beautiful young woman, dressed in red, with a white dog, who vanishes when you stop to help, it's Pele warning you of an eruption. We'll hike to the viewing spot where we might be lucky to see the lava. The red glow's visible at night, but not during the day.' He paused. 'Just a reminder that the volcano's sacred to Native Hawaiians, so if you wouldn't mind viewing quietly, with respect?'

'Of course,' they all reassured him.

'Is it all right to take photographs?' Joanne asked.

'If it's done with respect, yes,' Drew said.

From the viewing spot, Joanne was thrilled to see an eruption of bright red lava—something she'd always wanted to see. She took a couple of photographs, but then was content to stand and watch in silence, her fingers laced through Guy's as she was mesmerised by the eruptions. And it was so good to share her passion with someone else, to connect in a way she'd perhaps missed over the years by not letting people close to her.

This fling with Guy was pretty much a holiday romance, with a definite end date. But it was starting to make her see what a romance could feel like, the fizziness of sharing something new underpinned by the comfort of understanding each other. Part of her wondered what it would be like to have those feelings long-term, the warmth and the companionship and the fun all adding something extra to the pull of attraction. Though in a way it was pointless wishing, because she knew she'd always have those trust issues from her past and be too wary to open up completely to anyone.

On their trip through the National Park, Drew took them to see different craters and steam vents, and told them traditional *mo'olelo* stories of how the Hawaiian islands were formed. Joanne was delighted to see all the different textures of the lava flows, from swirling rocks to huge cracked bubbles. And Guy was indulgent when she went full-on nerd and talked about the different sorts of lava.

At one of the stops, the younger boy in their party found a stone. 'Look! It has rainbow colours in it,' he said, looking surprised.

'That's scoria—lava, to you and me,' she said. 'Can you see the holes in it? They formed when the hot lava met water and cooled down, and bubbles of gas tried to escape.'

He took the information in, nodding seriously. 'Why does it have rainbow colours?'

'Because it contains trace amounts of a mineral called cobalt, which gives things a rainbow sheen,' she explained.

'How do you know all this stuff?' his mother asked, looking interested. 'Guy said you were both doctors.'

'Because I've always been fascinated by volcanoes,' Joanne said with a smile. 'This trip is a big bucket list thing for me. I've always wanted to see Kīlauea and Mauna Loa. Seeing the actual lava today was the icing on the cake.'

'And now we get to walk through the lava tubes,' Drew said. 'So you'll get to see the places where the lava welled up, hundreds of years ago.'

When Drew had parked the minibus, their group walked through the rainforest towards Nāhuku lava tube, hearing the birds calling and the crickets trilling. The vegetation was lush and green; there were bright red needle-like blossoms on some of the shrubs, which Drew told them were ōhi'a lehua. 'It's the Hawaiian state tree,' he said, 'and it's usually the first plant to grow on new lava. It's sacred to Pele, the volcano goddess.'

'They're beautiful,' Joanne said.

'What are the red birds?' Guy asked.

'Apapane—a kind of honeycreeper, and they pollinate the shrubs,' Drew said. 'In the old days, lei used to be made for the nobility from apapane feathers.'

Finally they crossed a narrow bridge and went down into the lava tube. Despite Drew warning the group beforehand that it would be chilly in the lava tube, it was colder than Guy had expected, and he was glad of the sweater and waterproof he'd brought with him. Although there were lights, it was still very dark, cold and eerie—especially as they could see roots of trees coming through the roof, and water dripped down every so often, creating pools on the path.

'Amazing to think this was once a river of magma,' Joanne said to him.

'How did it form a tube?' Guy asked.

'The central current's fast enough to keep the core hot, while the edges cool and thicken—a bit like how ice forms on a river, crusting over from the sides,' Joanne explained. 'When the eruption stops, the lava drains away and leaves the tube behind.'

He loved how she knew things like this and explained them so clearly, yet without showing off. Wandering through natural wonders like this, hand in hand with her, was a real joy. He couldn't remember the last time he'd felt this happy. Not that he was going to jinx it by saying so.

They stopped for dinner of fresh local fish, simply cooked

with garlic butter and served with greens and rice. As they headed towards Mauna Kea, the sun set, turning the sky to flame: red, gold, orange and pink flared across the sky. Drew stopped to let them all take photos, and then told them to turn around.

Behind them was a red glow.

'Lava,' Drew said. 'We can get a bit closer, if you'd like to.'

'Oh, yes, *please*,' Joanne said, her voice filled with longing and awe. 'Twice in one day. How lucky is that?'

Guy tightened his hand round hers; he knew what this meant to her, and he loved the fact that he could share this moment with her.

And he couldn't resist taking a snap of her, her face lit by both the glow of the lava and the sheer joy of seeing something she'd always wanted to see.

Then, even though he'd enjoyed the volcanoes it was time for the bit of the tour he'd been looking forward to the most: stargazing.

'Mauna Kea—the White Mountain—is a sacred site,' Drew said, 'so I'd ask you to be really respectful here, too. In legend, Wakea, the god of the sky, married Papahanaumoku, the Earth Mother, and the ruling chiefs of Hawaii descended from them. The connection between earth and heaven makes it a bridge between the two realms, and at one point only the highest chiefs and priests were allowed to go to the top.'

'We're guests, so we need to be polite and be careful where we walk,' one of the other said.

'Exactly,' Drew agreed.

He parked the minibus; they all put on another layer, then went out to marvel at the night skies. There was a thin crescent moon, so the skies were dark; the Milky Way spread above them, a vast and luminous cloud of stars and gases.

'I've never seen so many stars in my entire life,' Joanne whispered, looking up.

'It's pretty special, out here,' he agreed. 'And it's the first time I've seen the southern hemisphere—constellations I've only ever seen in books or on videos.'

'I can't see anything I recognise,' she said.

Guy wanted to make this as special for her as it had been for him, hearing her talk about volcanoes and rocks. 'OK. Look up, and you'll see the Southern Cross,' he said. 'Follow where I'm pointing.'

They'd kissed on a tropical beach under the stars; but it had been at the edge of the city, where the streetlights dimmed out some of the stars. Here, there were no lights to affect their view; the skies were velvety, with glittering stars sprinkled liberally across every single part of the sky. And spread across the sky was the huge, glowing band of the Milky Way.

Guy stood behind her with one arm wrapped round her waist, resting his chin on her shoulder and his mouth very close to her ear. 'See the cross?' he asked.

'Yes.'

'Draw a line up left from that, and you'll see Beta Centauri.'

She followed where he pointed.

'Look to the left, and see that really bright star? That's Alpha Centauri,' he said. 'It's the closest star system to our sun, and the third brightest star in the sky after Sirius and Canopus.'

'How far away is it?' she asked.

'About 4.3 light years away. Which works out at a little over 25 trillion miles,' he said.

Numbers she could barely begin to process.

And she loved hearing the joy in his voice as he talked; he clearly felt the same way about the skies as she did about volcanoes.

'I say star,' he said, 'but I think Drew has a telescope we can look through, and you'll see it's a double star. Actually, it's a triple, but you can't see the third one very easily.'

'I'm still processing how far away it is, when you said it's the nearest star to our sun.'

'The Orion nebula—which you can see with the naked eye as the middle star of the sword—is about 1,350 light years away, or nearly eight thousand trillion miles away,' he said.

It was adorable, seeing him all lit up and excited about the stars—the same way that she felt about the volcanoes.

'While we're on silly numbers,' he said, 'go up and to the right of Alpha Centauri. See that bright fuzzy blob?'

'Yes.'

'That's Omega Centauri. It contains about ten million stars.'

'Ten million?' She blinked.

'Ten million,' he confirmed. 'And that's why I can't name every star in the sky for you. It's thought there are between a hundred and four hundred billion stars in the Milky Way alone.'

'That's mind-bending,' she said.

And so was standing here with him, his bodily warmth merging with hers. Right at that moment she felt warm and cherished, sharing a truly amazing sight with him. She slid her hand across the hand he'd wrapped round her waist, squeezing it gently.

'But you can't see them all,' he said. 'You can see maybe four and a half thousand with the naked eye per hemisphere.'

'It looks like more than that,' she said. 'And way, way more than I've ever seen before.'

'With all the light pollution in a city, only about thirty or forty stars are bright enough for you to see,' he said.

'If we were in London, could you name them?' she tested.

He chuckled. 'Most. I might need a prompt or two.' He held her closer, just for a moment.

This felt like more than just flirting—as if he'd actually been thinking about the possibility of meeting her in London when they were both back in England. Or was she kidding herself and he intended to stick to the letter of their agreement, so they'd simply walk away from each other when they walked away from Hawaii?

The thought of not being with him in the future actually hurt, shocking her. When had she got in so deep? This was dangerous. She needed to rein things back. Like, right now. They had a plan, and they both needed to stay within the boundaries. Or maybe she could let it go, just for tonight, and rebuild her defences tomorrow.

When she didn't say anything, he added, 'Binoculars gather more light, so they can help you see the fainter stars. You can see more than two hundred thousand stars with a pair of standard binoculars, and more than five million with a three-inch telescope. So with the sort of telescope they have in the observatory here…it's billions.' He squeezed her gently, and dropped his hand away. 'Anyway, we need to take some photographs—you can dazzle your grandparents, and I can turn my mum and my brother green with envy.'

Guy had brought a proper camera in his rucksack, along with a tripod, and although the photos on Joanne's phone were stunning enough, his were truly remarkable. And they were better still when he fitted the telephoto lens.

'Wow. And I thought my phone was good, picking up stars I couldn't see,' she said.

'Most of the time I use my phone as my camera,' he said. 'I did think about a telescope and buying the kit to attach my camera, a few years back, but it seemed a lot of faff. A telephoto lens is easier.'

'Still impressive,' she said.

On the way back to Kona, the children fell asleep while the adults, too tired to chat, looked out of the windows at the sky. Joanne had insisted on Guy taking the window seat, and rested her head on his shoulder.

'It's been an amazing day,' she said softly. 'Real bucket list stuff. Seeing turtles on the beach, walking through a lava tube, actually seeing lava—*twice*—and then the Milky Way and all those stars.'

'I'm glad I shared today with you,' he said, equally softly. 'It made the trip special. I completely get why you love volcanoes.'

'And I get why you love the stars,' she said. 'Maybe you can teach me what to look out for.'

'Sure. We can stargaze any night you want,' he said, holding her just a little bit closer.

CHAPTER ELEVEN

OVER THE NEXT few days, Joanne and Guy reached a new closeness and dropped into a kind of routine. On mornings when they hadn't spent the night together, she met him at the beach at the end of his run with a travel mug of coffee and a picnic breakfast of bagels and fruit, and they talked about everything under the sun. In the evenings, they met for dinner or grabbed a takeaway and streamed a movie.

Guy had never felt so in tune with anyone. Even in the early days with Imogen, when he'd thought he'd found The One, it hadn't been like this. Joanne, thankfully, wasn't into period dramas or the kind of slapstick comedies that Imogen had loved and did nothing for him; she preferred dramas with strong characters, and had a secret weakness for sci-fi that matched his own.

And gradually he started to realise that he'd taken Imogen's words the wrong way. True, he hadn't been enough for her—but that didn't mean he wasn't enough for anyone else. It simply meant that Imogen had changed her mind about what she wanted after she'd accepted his proposal of marriage. She'd wanted more than he could give her, and she hadn't taken what he wanted into account or been prepared to compromise. It wasn't because he was lacking. Imogen been the spoiled baby of the family, used to getting everything she wanted, whenever she demanded it.

Joanne, in sharp contrast, gave as well as took. She understood that running cleared his head and he needed to do it; although she didn't join him for the run itself, she was happy to sit watching the waves swoosh onto the shore or doing a crossword while she waited for him to finish. Just as he didn't want to go to a dance aerobics class with her, but he was happy to prepare dinner so it'd be ready when she came over after her class.

The evening he forgot to keep an eye on the sauce for the chicken dish he was making and burned it, Joanne didn't throw a hissy fit, the way Imogen would've done. She simply laughed. 'I've done that myself, a few times. I learned the hard way that if you're going to read an interesting journal while you're waiting for something to cook, you need to stick a timer on your phone, first.' Then she looked in his fridge, fished out a couple of simple ingredients and taught him one of her favourite quick recipes instead, so dinner wasn't ruined and it wasn't an issue. No sulking, no heavy silences; with Joanne, Guy found that he could be himself. And he was comfortable now with who he was, no longer worrying that he wasn't good enough.

Midway through the next week, Joanne finally had a chance to catch up with Jamie. It was ridiculous, she thought, that she'd travelled seven thousand miles to take a job where they were in the same city and would actually get to spend time together, and yet they'd spoken to each other less than they usually did back in England when they were miles and miles apart.

They'd arranged to meet in a bar near her apartment. She'd got there early, itching to talk to him and tell him about Guy, and had bought a beer for him and a soft drink for herself. She waited impatiently in the booth, and finally he slid in opposite her.

He started with his usual joking wisecracks, and she wondered how she was going to work round to telling him about the research project—and Guy.

Except she rather thought that Jamie had something to tell her.

It took a bit of nagging, but finally he came out with it. 'I might have met someone.'

Now that she hadn't expected. Since the whole drug-stealing mess at his last place—where she knew from the get-go that he was completely innocent, and she would've fought dragons for him to prove it—he'd been wary of getting involved with anyone.

And he looked nervous about this. What was he worried about? Her reaction? But why would he think she'd judge him?

To make him feel better, she said, 'I might have met someone, too.'

'What? Why didn't you tell me?'

Oh, that was rich. 'Why didn't *you* tell *me*?' she parried.

He sighed. 'OK. I need to know who he is, so I can decide if I like him, or want to kick his ass.'

Typical Jamie: he'd gone straight into big brother mode. Even though he was actually a month younger than she was.

They bickered a bit, as usual, and Joanne asked the killer question. 'Who is she?'

He looked awkward. 'That's the thing, and that's what makes this not so great. She's the doctor I'm training.'

A colleague. His junior. And funny how their situations were almost opposite, because Guy was technically her senior—even though he wasn't her boss. She lifted her glass towards his. 'And this is why we are best friends.'

Jamie clinked his glass against hers, looking confused. 'What are you talking about?'

'Guy is training me. Well.' She wrinkled her nose. 'Sort of.'

He frowned as he looked at her. 'So, it's Guy Sanders, the cardiothoracic surgeon you are seeing?'

She nodded. 'And what's your woman's name?'

'Piper. Piper Bronte.' He muttered a bit, and ran his fingers through his hair. 'I'm her boss. That isn't a good look. Which is why we'd prefer to keep things quiet.'

She got that. But she also agreed, it was kind of awkward. 'Are you sure about this?'

'Are you?'

'Stop.' They'd get nowhere if they just kept batting things back to each other. 'I want to know how she makes you feel.'

Jamie protested that he was taking the Fifth—which, considering he was Scottish, she disputed hotly—so it looked as if she'd have to start with the confessions.

'Guy. He annoyed me at first. I thought he might have taken advantage of me.'

'What?' His eyes widened.

Oh, now she'd really roused his protective instincts. 'Calm down,' she said, and explained how she'd mistaken the cocktail for an alcohol-free version and Guy had taken her back to his place to make sure she was OK. And, the next morning, she'd jumped to the wrong conclusions.

'Why didn't you tell me?' Jamie demanded.

'Because I got things wrong enough, without dragging anyone else into it. He's a good guy.' She rolled her eyes at the terrible pun. 'Anyway…we're seeing each other. But I wanted to mention it to you, before you noticed, or anyone else noticed something.' Because hospital gossip ran like lava…and it still surprised her that she and Guy had managed to disappear off for a weekend in Big Island to see the volcanoes and the stars without anyone noticing.

Jamie reached over and touched her hand. 'Thanks for telling me. I know you find it hard to trust people. But just know that I'm always going to have your back. No matter what else is going on.'

She reached over and put her hand over his. 'Thank you. I know that. Just as I'll always have yours.' Because Jamie counted as family. He'd tell her straight when she was being an idiot. Give her a hug when she needed one. Always pick up her calls. Just as she would with him.

And he was one of the people few people she felt she could be herself with. Along with her grandparents…and now Guy.

She lifted her glass again. 'So, we're good?'

He clinked his glass against hers. 'We're good.'

'Guy and I are setting up a joint cardiac rehab project, so my patients don't end up being his patients.' She smiled. 'Well, his patients come back to me for follow-up. Which works, but we don't want them needing more surgery. It's all so vague when we tell patients to pace themselves, to see how they go as they start to recover and do more. So we want to teach them about perceived exertion, and get them on board with making lifestyle changes. If they make the suggestions and feel we're listening to them, they're more likely to stick to the changes instead of being forced to do things and giving up.' She talked him through the project, and how they were involving other teams in the sessions.

'That sounds good,' Jamie said. 'Though the health systems are very different over here.'

'I know. So we ran it by the chief. He gave us the green light.'

'That's great,' Jamie said.

She smiled. 'And now I can tell you something else you might want to kill me for. I went to Big Island to see the volcanoes and do a bit of stargazing.'

'Without me? On your own?' he asked, looking shocked.

'Without you,' she said. 'Because you *know* your eyes start to glaze over when I start talking about geological faults and magma. But I'd also say think about taking Piper over to Big Island, because it's incredibly romantic.'

'Volcanoes. Romantic.' He rolled his eyes.

'The glow of the lava after sunset—there's nothing like it. Or seeing the stars out there. I mean, they're good here; but over there, with no light pollution—it's like nothing else you've ever seen. Just the two of you and the stars. Well, it's a small tour, so there are about ten of you, but it feels as if it's just the two of you.'

Jamie's eyes narrowed. 'You went with Guy?'

'He's as nerdy about astronomy as I am about volcanoes, so yes, I did,' she said. 'It's a long tour, plus a flight each way, so you need to stay overnight. And the hotel…'

'Stop,' Jamie said. 'I think that's about to become TMI.'

'I probably wasn't completely honest with you when I said I don't know where it's going between me and Guy. It ends when I leave Hawaii,' she said. 'I guess you could call it a fling. Almost a holiday romance. But we know where we stand, we don't have any false expectations, and it's all good.'

That wasn't strictly true, either. Over the last couple of

weeks, she'd started to reassess their agreement. Because she liked Guy. Really, *really* liked him. And that in itself was terrifying. No way could she let herself lose control of her feelings. She needed to stay strong. Independent. She couldn't risk the chance that he might let her down—or that she'd be the one to let him down. She would never betray him, the way his ex had done; but none of her previous relationships had lasted for more than a couple of months because she always ended up pushing her boyfriends away, to keep her heart safe.

Would she do that with Guy, too?

Or was he the one that could make her change?

And that in itself was even more terrifying.

She needed things to be clearer in her head before she discussed it with anyone, even her best friend. Right now, just thinking about it made her panic. Not to mention the fact that, even though she'd trust Jamie with her life, she didn't want to divulge any of the things Guy had told her in confidence. It wouldn't be fair to Guy.

So instead she changed the subject and kept everything light, chattering about people they'd trained with and what they were doing now, until they finished their drinks and Jamie walked her home.

The next morning, Guy was out for a run on the beach when his brother called.

'Is everything all right?' Guy asked, instantly concerned. 'It's a bit early for a social call.'

'It's almost dinnertime here,' Jordan reminded him. 'I knew you'd be up and out for a run by now. People could set their watch by you.' He paused. 'How's it going?'

Uh-oh. His brother sounded a little too casual. Was he

about to start nagging about how Guy needed a better work-life balance, and fish to see if his younger brother was actually dating? And then obviously he'd be reporting back to the rest of the family.

He sighed inwardly. He loved his family—and he appreciated them even more, now he knew what Joanne had been through with hers—but he wished sometimes they wouldn't smother him or try to live his life for him. That had been a major factor in his decision to come to Hawaii.

'It's all good,' Guy said, keeping his tone equally casual. 'I'm enjoying life in the tropics.' He couldn't resist adding, 'And checking out the southern constellations.'

To his relief, Jordan took the bait. 'I'm so envious of those pictures you sent from Mauna Kea. You actually saw Omega Centauri with the naked eye!'

'It was pretty cool. And chilly, actually—I've got used to the warm breezes here, but when you're halfway up a mountain at night you definitely need a coat.' And the bodily warmth he'd shared with Joanne, though he wasn't mentioning that.

'Mum's trying to talk Dad into coming over to visit you, and taking a tiny island-hop while they're there.'

'Sure. They can stay at my place, if they want. They'd love it out here—and so would you,' Guy added. 'The boys would be fascinated by the volcanoes, and Bex would adore the turtles. Hawaii's an incredible place.'

'So did you go on your own to Mauna Kea?' Jordan asked.

'No. I went with Joanne.' And then Guy remembered he hadn't actually told his brother about her. 'I went on a tour,' he added swiftly. 'The guide really knew his stuff—I learned tons about the Hawaiian culture.'

'Who's Joanne?' Jordan asked, his tone deceptively mild.

Guy knew he hadn't got away with it—how could he, when his chemistry teacher brother was a details man?—and sighed. 'The girl from the bar you noticed on that photo I sent you.'

'Oh, so you did dance with her, after all?' Jordan chuckled. 'I thought you'd just taken a random picture of the bar.'

'I did.'

'But you danced with her.'

'Yes. But, believe me, I didn't like her very much, that evening,' Guy said dryly, and explained about the cocktails and how he'd had to rescue her.

'Ouch. But that was, what, a month ago?' Jordan asked.

'Something like that,' Guy said.

'And you're still seeing her?'

'Well, yeah—she works with me,' Guy explained. 'She's a cardiologist.'

'I'm not talking about *work*. I'm talking about personal stuff,' Jordan said.

And this was where the nagging would start. 'I almost wish I hadn't told you, now,' Guy said.

'No, you don't. You told me because she's become important enough to you that you need reassurance that you're not making the same mistake you made with Imogen,' his brother said.

How come his older brother understood things that he hadn't quite yet worked out for himself?

He must've said it out loud, because Jordan said, 'Given the circumstances of how you met her, of course you're going to think of that—' He stopped, and blew out a cross breath. 'I can't say the word I want to use, in case the boys hear me, and I don't want them repeating it at school. But you know who I mean. I-me-again.'

Jordan wasn't usually one for vitriol, and Guy was slightly taken aback.

'Sorry,' Jordan muttered. 'Just—she did you a lot of damage. And I can't fix it. As your big brother, I should be able to fix it.'

'I appreciate you having my back,' Guy said, 'but getting over her…the only person who can fix that is me.' And, thanks to Joanne making him see things a different way, he was finally in a mental place where he really was getting over his past. 'I wasn't enough for Imogen,' he said. 'But that doesn't mean I won't be enough for someone else.'

'Well, I'm glad you're finally working that out for yourself. I've been saying it for long enough.' Jordan coughed. 'Sorry. Nagging again. Tell me about Joanne.'

'I already did,' Guy said. 'She's nice. I like her. She likes me. But.' And this was the rub. 'She's going back to England in a couple of months. End of story.'

'Not necessarily,' Jordan said. 'You're coming back to England, too, aren't you?'

'I haven't made my mind up when, yet,' Guy said. 'But, yes, that's the plan.'

'So, when you're back, you'll both be in the same country.'

'She lives in London. I live in Bristol. It's not really workable,' Guy said. 'It's hardly commuting distance.'

'But it's not that far. A little bit more than an hour, on the fast train. Two, in the car—well, out of rush hour. If you really like her, you can find a way round it. Or you could move and work in London. Or she could move and work in Bristol,' Jordan pointed out.

'It's a big ask.'

'If you moved to London,' Jordan said, 'OK, you wouldn't be just down the road from us any more, but you'd be near Mel.'

'It would be good to see more of Mel,' Guy admitted. 'But it's still early days between me and Joanne.' He added lightly, 'We might be thoroughly fed up with each other before we go back to England.'

'And you might not.' Jordan paused. 'She's the first person you've dated—or the first person you've admitted to dating, at least—since Imogen. But that doesn't mean it can't get serious. Not if you really like each other.'

'I like her, and she's definitely not like Imogen. She's kind. Thoughtful.' Guy told his brother about Geoff and Sally, and the way she'd cut their date short to help look after two vulnerable tourists. 'I like the way she is with people.'

'But?'

'Is it that obvious there's a but?' Guy asked.

'To me, yes,' Jordan said.

He sighed. 'She had a rough time as a kid. I'm not entirely sure she'll let me close enough for it to get properly serious between us.'

'But you'd like it to?'

'Honestly? I'm beginning to think so,' Guy said. 'I feel different when I'm with her. Lighter of spirit. There's just something about her. I'm not so…'

'Guy the Grouch?' Jordan suggested. 'Guy the Grumpy Gorilla?'

'If the boys start calling me Uncle Gorilla, you're in trouble,' Guy said, rolling his eyes.

Jordan laughed. 'It's good to hear you sounding more like yourself.'

Maybe. But the doubts still crept in. Would who he really was be enough for Joanne? After all, he hadn't been enough for Imogen.

Again, as if his brother had been able to read his mind, Jordan said, 'Stop worrying and just be you. If you're right for each other, then you'll find a way to be together. And if you're not, then at least you've made an effort to see someone, and next time it'll be easier.'

'Please don't set me up on any more dates,' Guy said. 'I can find my own dates.'

'Have some fun. That's all I want for you, little brother,' Jordan said.

Guy heard his brother's name being called in the background. 'I think you're wanted. I'll let you go. Give my love to Bex and the boys,' he said. 'And, Jordy? Thanks for checking on me. I know I never sound as if I appreciate it, but I'm grateful you have my back.'

'Just as you have mine, and if I hit a rough patch you'll be the one I'll talk to,' Jordan said. 'I'll speak to you soon.'

If you're right for each other, then you'll find a way to be together. The words echoed in Guy's head as he ran. He was beginning to think that they could be right for each other.

But could he convince Joanne?

CHAPTER TWELVE

As the weeks rushed past, Joanne and Guy continued to spend almost all of their free time together. They'd made a list of places they wanted to visit and started ticking them off in their spare time. Guy was delighted to discover that, like him, Joanne read up about the history of whatever they were going to visit before they went, to get the most out of the trip. And she always engaged with the staff at the museums, asking questions about the exhibits.

She was equally happy just chilling on the beach, watching the sun set and getting him to teach her some of the constellations in the darkening sky; or picking up stones on the beach as they wandered hand in hand along the shoreline, and pointing out which were bits of pumice polished by the sea, and which were bits of other minerals trapped in the lava, but she always left them where she found them. 'It means other people can enjoy them,' she said, when he commented. 'If everyone who came here took a shell or a stone, the place would be depleted pretty quickly.'

It was that kind of thoughtfulness that really drew him to her. Imogen, he reflected, would've wanted to take lava home as a souvenir. And she certainly wouldn't have shown the same respect to the islanders that Joanne did.

With Joanne, he could relax. Be himself, and know she wasn't judging him. And he'd noticed that she seemed more relaxed in his company, too, less guarded. It felt as if they'd known each other for years rather than a matter of weeks.

On a midweek day off, Joanne suggested that they should walk to Mānoa Falls. 'Apparently the valley is known as Rainbow Valley, because of how many you see there,' she said. 'And the rainforest has been used for film and TV locations—*Jurassic Park*, *Hawaii 5-0* and *Lost*,' she said. 'If we go early, we'll miss the crowds.'

Guy drove them to the car park; although it had been sunny in Honolulu, here in the rainforest—only a few minutes outside the city—it was drizzly, and clouds seemed to hug the tops of the trees. The valley seemed wreathed in mist rather than rainbows.

'Well, hey. No rainbows, but I guess at least we won't get too hot,' Joanne said as she pulled on her waterproof. She'd downloaded an information guide and a map, so they knew where to go and what they were looking at. Hand in hand, they followed a bridge over a narrow ravine with a stream gushing through the bottom, to the trail itself.

'It's structured like a series of different forests,' Joanne said. 'First the eucalyptus, and then the hau trees—and they're the really interesting ones. Apparently the early Hawaiian inhabitants used the wood to make the booms for outrigger canoes and fishing net floats, because the wood's really light; they used the bark for sandals, and the flower buds as laxatives. And they soaked the bark and drank the liquid to help with labour pains.'

'There are so many plants the ancient people knew about, and we don't have a clue,' Guy said. 'It makes you wonder what medical knowledge has been lost, over the years.'

'A lot, I reckon,' Joanne said. 'Those flowers are beautiful.' The blooms had five yellow heart-shaped petals with dark red centres. 'They're a kind of hibiscus and apparently the flowers only last for a day. But they bloom all year round.'

Tree roots snaked across the path in places, making them pick their way over; and then they came to a spot where the aerial roots had joined together naturally, forming a perfect circular arch. 'This is apparently a banyan tree arch,' she said, consulting her guide.

'This feels as if we're about to walk through a door into another world,' Guy said.

'Doesn't it just?' she asked, thinking of the mist they'd seen earlier in the valley. With a shiver, she added, 'There are all kinds of myths and legends here, about the Nightmarchers—the spirits of old warriors who guard sacred sites and the souls of ancient kings. If you hear chanting or see shadows, you're supposed to lie flat as a sign of respect.'

'Hopefully they'll let us pass because they know we're visitors and we pay attention to the places we travel through, their people and their history,' Guy said, and squeezed her hand.

He took a selfie of them together as they were about to step through.

Stepping into another world, she thought. One with all kinds of possibilities. That this wasn't just a fling, wasn't just having fun for now—that maybe, just maybe, they were starting to build a future. She wasn't sure if the prospect terrified her more, or excited her.

But she was overthinking it. Today was just a nice walk through gorgeous rainforest to a pretty waterfall, she reminded herself, in the company of someone she was starting to really like. And Guy had his own reasons for not wanting this to be any more complicated than it was. They needed to just let it be simple and enjoy the moment, she decided, instead of worrying about the what-ifs.

On the other side of the arch, they found themselves in the bamboo forest; jade-green bamboo stalks towered up to the sky on either side of a narrow path on the orangey-red earth. They could hear the bamboo stalks knocking against each other in the breeze as a kind of percussive counterpoint to the birds singing.

'The scientist in me knows that the stalks are hollow and that's why the bamboo makes those sounds,' Guy said, 'but I can also see how eerie this would sound at night.'

'Like drums beating or people marching—the Nightmarchers,' she said. 'You were right. This is like another world.'

'This is an incredible place,' Guy said. 'I'm really glad you suggested coming here.'

Finally, they climbed a set of rocky steps to a pool at the base of the waterfall; they could hear the water gushing down before they saw it. The long, narrow triangle of dark rock looked as if it had been carved through the lush vegetation on either side; water fell straight over the apex and fanned out as it dropped a hundred and fifty feet to the pool.

'It looks like the perfect place to swim,' she said. 'Except there's the risk of leptospirosis.' Otherwise known as Weil's disease, and one of the tropical diseases that Jamie specialised in. 'Which means swimming's way too dangerous, and the website warns not to let the water get into your nose, mouth, eyes or any open cuts.'

'The same as people are warned at home about canals and other waterways,' Guy reminded her. 'We have antibiotics to treat it, but it'd be better not to get it in the first place.' He looked at her, interested. 'Have you ever treated someone with a cardiac arrythmia caused by leptospirosis?'

'No,' she said. 'But I'll bear that in mind if any tourists come into my department who've ignored the notices not to swim.'

On their way back to the car park, the sun came out—and suddenly, through the mist, a rainbow started shimmering.

'That's the icing on the cake,' Guy said. 'And, speaking of cake—for lunch, we're on the hunt for malasadas.'

'Which are?' Joanne asked.

'Portuguese fried doughnuts with no hole in the middle,' he said. 'Ailani, my Theatre nurse, gave me the name of the best bakery to go to. She says her favourites are simply coated with cinnamon sugar; or, if we want one filled with custard, we need to try *liliko'i*. Passionfruit,' he added. 'Though apparently there are lots of different flavours.'

They found the bakery, which had an extensive menu.

'How are we meant to choose between them?' Joanne mock-grumbled.

'We don't. Especially as we're out for dinner again tonight. As cardiac specialists, we're sensible with cake. We order Ailani's favourites, and share them,' Guy said.

'Speak for yourself about being sensible with cake. We could have one of each, *each*,' she suggested with a grin.

'Yeah, but I want shave ice as well,' he countered. 'Which means one doughnut.'

'Or running twice as far tomorrow morning, to make up for it.'

'Coming for a run with me?' he teased.

'Not on your life,' she said with a grin. 'If you'd offered me a dance class, the answer would've been yes. But steady-state cardio...' She shook her head. 'That's so not my thing.

But you could come and join me in a dance class,' she added, teasing him back and knowing what his answer would be.

'I'm not coordinated enough for that,' Guy said. 'My hands, yes—my feet, no.'

He'd danced with her at the luau, she thought, but that had turned into something else entirely. 'Ben says there's a dance floor at the bar where he's playing tonight.'

'Then I'll dance with you tonight. You might want to wear hiking boots rather than pretty shoes, to protect your toes.'

'I'll teach you,' she said with a grin.

And it was fun, sitting in the bakery drinking coffee and sharing doughnuts, feeding each other forkfuls, teasing each other about their preferred exercise and sweet treats, with not a care in the world.

Hawaii, she thought, was a place that made you chill out just by being itself. Sharing her time here with Guy—who, like her, tended to be a little too serious—made it even better.

They spent the rest of the afternoon strolling about, seeing the sights; and later that evening they headed to the bar where Ben Palani's band played. 'Ben says the food is good, but we're here mainly for the music,' she said, and chose a table where they'd be able to see the band playing.

Guy scanned the menu. 'I'll order loco moco. I know you're not a fan of burgers, but at least it gives you a chance to try the gravy and the rice,' he said.

She smiled. 'I'll swap you for a taste of my coconut shrimp.'

Guy ordered a beer, and she chose blueberry lavender lemonade. When their waitress brought their drinks over, she was thrilled to see that her glass had an ombre effect with cloudy lemonade at the top and deep purple blueberry-lavender. It came garnished with a slice of lime and three blueberries spiked through with a lavender sprig.

Ben came over to their table, a few moments later. 'You made it! Aloha! Guys, this is the wonderful woman who fixed my heart,' he called to his bandmates.

'And he can still play. We all owe you for that,' one of the other members of the band said, coming over to join them.

'Can I buy you all a beer, Mr Palani?' she asked.

'It's Ben, to you,' he reminded her. 'Am I allowed beer?'

'The *occasional* glass,' she said. 'Everything in moderation.'

'Like you said in class, this week,' Ben said. 'My wife asked me to pass on her thanks. She said you've saved her nagging me.'

Joanne chuckled. 'Just doing my job. I assume the bar staff know what you all drink?'

'They do. We'd all love a beer. Thank you. And I haven't forgotten I promised to play a song for you tonight,' Ben said. He glanced at Guy. 'You're her young man?'

'Yes,' Guy said simply. 'Guy Sanders. Nice to meet you,' he said, shaking Ben's hand. 'I work with Joanne.'

'She's special,' Ben said.

Joanne cleared her throat noisily. 'I am *here*, you know.'

'Just making sure he knows your worth,' Ben said.

'I do,' Guy confirmed, and the flash of heat in his eyes made her pulse jump.

They'd agreed to have a fling—a just-for-now thing, not something that would last for ever. Though the more time she spent with Guy, the more she was starting to hope it might become something more than that.

Was it the same for him?

Though even discussing the possibility scared her. She

wasn't good at relationships. There were so many things that could go wrong. Although she was pretty sure that Guy was a decent man who wouldn't intentionally hurt her, the fear was still there. It might be decades ago now that her father had broken her ability to trust, but she knew that those early childhood experiences went deeper than anything else. Was Guy the one who'd help her finally to break the barriers down around her heart and learn to trust again? And could she in turn help to mend his broken heart?

'I'll order those beers,' she said, and beat a hasty retreat.

When she came back, Ben and the band were tuning up. She pasted a wide smile on her face and turned the subject of conversation to music, so she didn't have to talk about anything emotional with Guy.

As he'd promised back in the hospital, Ben played 'Albatross' for her—and she blushed when he introduced the song and told everyone in the bar, 'This one's especially for Joanne Meadows, the doctor who fixed my heart so I can keep playing my guitar. *Mahalo*, Joanne!'

She gave him a smile and a wave, and thoroughly enjoyed his playing.

'He's good,' Guy said appreciatively when the song ended. 'This is pretty much the perfect evening. Good food, good music and good company.'

'Seconded,' she said, and lifted her glass in a toast.

The band played a wide mix of tunes, some that were clearly original songs by the band, and some that were covers of well-known songs—as Ben had told Joanne, although in their jam sessions they tended to play seventies rock, at the bar they needed to appeal to a wider audience. The small dance floor in front of the band soon became crowded.

Guy was enjoying the music; although, as he'd told Joanne earlier, he wasn't great at dancing, he knew she loved dancing and he really wanted to dance with her. When they'd finished their main courses, he said, 'Shall we? I'll try not to tread on your toes *too* often.'

'Love to,' she said, smiling back at him, clearly pleased that he'd offered to do something she loved, even though she knew his limitations.

Together with everyone else on the dance floor, they danced and sang along with the band. It was the first time for a long while since Guy had really felt part of a crowd—even at the luau where he and Joanne had first got together, they'd left the party to talk rather than staying with everyone else. At work, they were meticulously professional with each other, with no hint of their personal relationship on show.

But right here, right now, he was part of the crowd, dancing with his girl, uncaring whether anyone they knew saw them together.

And then the band slowed everything down for the last dance of their set with Elvis's "Can't Help Falling in Love."

It was the perfect end to the set, Guy thought: one of the most famous songs from *Blue Hawaii*, being played live in Hawaii.

He drew Joanne into his arms, holding her close and dancing cheek to cheek with her. Around them, couples of all ages were crooning or humming along to the song, the lyrics clearly striking a chord with them.

This song's for us, he thought. Was Elvis right, and this thing between himself and Joanne was meant to be?

He was definitely starting to fall in love with her. Although the realisation shocked him—he'd vowed never to fall in love again, after Imogen—at the same time he realised that it had been inevitable. It had been a slow, steady slide since the moment they'd met. The more he got to know Joanne, the more he liked her. He liked everything about her: her warmth, her innate kindness, the way she smiled, the way she brought out the best in people around her. She was nothing like Imogen. He trusted her with their patients' hearts at work, and he was pretty sure he could trust her with his own heart, too.

But he didn't think she was ready to hear that just yet.

He'd be patient.

But, before she left Hawaii, he'd tell her how he felt. And he really hoped that she felt the same—so they'd have a future. Together.

CHAPTER THIRTEEN

THE FOLLOWING MONDAY AFTERNOON, Joanne went to see Guy in his office. 'Can I run a case by you, please?' she asked. 'Because I think this might end up being a joint case.'

'Sure,' he said. 'Would this be a good teaching case for Keanu?'

'Absolutely,' she said. 'Obviously I need to ask my patient if he can sit in, but I'm pretty sure she'll say yes.'

'Hit me with it,' he said.

'Maile, my patient, is seventy years old. She has kidney problems and coronary artery disease, has had atrial fibrillation and a stroke in the past, and when she came to see me she presented with symptoms of heart failure. I did an echo—actually, I did a transoesophageal echo as well, to give me better images. She's got a bicuspid aortic valve with a calcified raphe.'

A bicuspid aortic valve was where the valve on the left side of the heart had two flaps instead of the normal three, making it more difficult for the heart to pump blood. It was the most common congenital heart defect, though symptoms often didn't start until middle age—often a heart murmur, breathlessness, tiredness and swollen ankles.

'So we're looking at surgical aortic valve replacement?' he asked. Surgery was the most common method of replacing valves, either with a donated human valve or a mechanical valve.

'Given her kidney, CAD and heart failure, I think she's quite a high surgical risk,' Joanne said. 'I'd like to go for something minimally invasive—a transcatheter aortic valve implementation.'

'Even though her aortic valve is bicuspid?'

She nodded. 'I know there are challenges—the size and shape of the valve is tricky, and there's a high risk of conduction disturbances.'

'She might end up needing a permanent pacemaker,' he warned.

'And she might not. This is less invasive and she'll recover more quickly,' Joanne said. 'And obviously we'll need to convert it to open heart surgery if there are any problems on the day. But have a look at the scan results and see what you think.'

He liked the fact she was confident in her own judgement but was also prepared to listen if he made a different case. When she brought the two sets of scan results up onto his screen, he studied them thoughtfully.

'I think she's a good candidate,' Joanne said.

'I agree,' he said. 'Let's start with a TAVI, and I'll be there for backup if we need to convert it.'

'And I was thinking, we can get Keanu to explain the procedure—either to Maile, or to me. I could roleplay the patient and you can supervise.'

'That's an excellent idea. It'd be good to get him to explain it to you, for practice, and then maybe to your patient, if she's happy to help with some teaching,' he said. 'When works for you?'

'Give me twenty minutes. I want to talk to Maile first,' she said.

'OK. That gives me time to find Keanu and get him ready to talk you through it,' he said.

While Joanne was talking to her patient, Guy went to find his intern, and explained what they were going to do. 'Minimally invasive surgery means it's easier for the patient to recover. We'll be doing it under sedation, but if there are complications we'll switch to general anaesthetic and open heart surgery,' Guy said. 'It'll be Joanne's call.'

Right then, there was a knock on his office door and Joanne popped her head round the door. 'Is now a good time?'

'Perfect. Keanu's gone through the scans with me, and he's on board with what you're doing,' Guy said. 'I've told him it's your call, if you need to switch to open heart surgery tomorrow.'

'Great. And Maile's happy for you to observe tomorrow, Keanu.' She smiled and sat down. 'OK, Doctor. I'm your patient, lying on the couch, and you're going to talk me through the procedure for tomorrow. It's a TAVI.'

'TAVR, here,' Keanu said.

'Sorry.' She smiled at him. 'But it's the same procedure. OK. You've told me it's not going to be done under a general anaesthetic.'

She clearly enjoyed roleplay, Guy thought, because she looked anxious as she asked, 'How much is it going to hurt, Doctor? And if I'm awake—well, isn't it scary, hearing what's going on?

'It won't hurt, because you'll have a local anaesthetic, and you'll be given sedation for the procedures so you'll feel relaxed and you won't remember much about it afterwards. You might feel a bit of pressure when we fit the valve, but it shouldn't hurt. If you don't feel well, or you have any chest pain, just tell us,' Keanu said, 'and we'll do something about it.' He went on to explain how the catheter worked, and how they were going to fit a replacement valve inside her old one. Then he talked her through the monitoring procedure—her heart rate, her oxygen levels and her blood pressure—and what to expect when the catheter was taken out. 'We should be able to let you go home in a day or two,' he finished.

'And that's a wrap,' Joanne said. 'Well done. You've got a good bedside manner—you're clear, you don't use jargon, and you make eye contact with the patients. That's excellent; I've worked with doctors who huddle over their screen instead of looking at the patient, and that's where they miss important clues.'

Keanu went pink. 'Thank you. What could I do better?'

'Honestly?' She wrinkled her nose and shook her head. 'What you said was spot on. Some patients might want a few more details from you, but they're the sort who'll ask. The only thing I can think of is that you need to warn the patient if something doesn't go to plan, we might have to convert the operation to open heart surgery. Only make promises you know you'll definitely be able to keep,' she added. 'That way, your patients will know they can trust you and won't feel let down if anything doesn't go to plan.'

'Got it,' Keanu said.

'I've warned Maile already, but it wouldn't hurt to remind her when you talk her through the procedure,' she finished.

'I'll talk her through the procedure?' Keanu asked.

'Yes. This was a practice run,' she said with a smile.

'You'll be fine. We'll be there for backup, but I don't think you'll need us.'

Guy liked the way she'd encouraged the younger doctor and given him pointers. And he also liked the way she'd emphasised not making promises you couldn't keep. Joanne Meadows definitely had integrity. He could trust her with his patients—and with himself.

The following day, Joanne performed the valve replacement procedure with Guy and Keanu watching. She was delighted that everything went to plan and they didn't need to switch to traditional surgery. Guy was supportive throughout, asking questions which she realised were designed to widen Keanu's knowledge yet not trying to take over. He made it clear that he was there for backup and Joanne was in charge.

She really liked the way he worked with her professionally, supportive but respecting her own knowledge and experience. As a colleague, she trusted him absolutely. So could she trust him with herself? Could they both take the risk of making their fling more than just a temporary thing? When they both went back to England, could they find a way of making their relationship work on a more permanent basis?

It was a terrifying thought.

She'd never managed to keep a relationship going for more than a few weeks. Once it had been obvious that she wasn't going to let them close, her boyfriends had drifted away. She'd hurt a couple of people, without meaning to, because her feelings just hadn't been as strong as theirs. Guy had already been hurt in the past; Imogen had knocked his belief in himself so he thought he wasn't good enough for anyone. She'd helped him see that wasn't true—but if she let this thing between them carry on when they were back in England, what then? What if she ended up pushing him away, scared of relying on him? The last thing she wanted to do was reinforce how Imogen had made him feel.

They needed to talk.

But, until she'd sorted out the jumble in her head, she'd keep that particular conversation on hold.

A week later, Guy and Joanne visited the sunflower fields at Waimanalo. The massive fields were full of sunflowers, with a backdrop of forbidding, jagged mountain peaks. Colourful butterflies flitted everywhere, and honeybees were gathering pollen from the sunflowers.

'They're one of my favourite flowers,' Joanne said. 'They really live up to their name—they're like a burst of sunshine.'

'It's stunning to see so many of them, their faces all turned the same way,' Guy agreed. 'We need a selfie, I think.'

'Agreed.' She enjoyed posing against the flowers with him, and snapped some of him on his own as well as taking a selfie to send to her gran.

But later that evening, her phone beeped with a text from her gran.

Lovely pictures, darling xx

Thank you. The sunflowers were amazing, especially with the mountains as a backdrop, she texted back. They had a stall grilling sunflower heads on a barbecue, topped with parmesan and garlic—you scooped the seeds out with a fork. Never thought of doing that before! Gramps will have to up his barbecue game xx

Sounds as if you're having fun, her grandmother said. But then she added a line that Joanne really hadn't expected. *Your boyfriend looks nice xx.*

Boyfriend? But she hadn't sent a photograph of herself and Guy. She'd only sent the landscape shots, and one that Guy had taken from her—hadn't she?

She scrolled back up her phone to check, only to discover that she'd accidentally included a picture of Guy in the set of snaps she'd sent. Oh, no. Panic skittered through her. The last thing she wanted to do was talk relationships. Even though her grandmother had never put any pressure on her, Joanne knew she was secretly hoping that Joanne would settle down with someone who'd make her happy, and was maybe even more secretly hoping for great-grandchildren. And that was a whole can of worms Joanne definitely wasn't opening.

How did she do this without disappointing anyone?

That's Guy. He's my colleague and a good friend, she texted back eventually.

Which was true.

But she was uncomfortably aware that it was also less than the truth. He wasn't exactly her boyfriend, because they'd agreed a limit to their fling. When they left Hawaii, they would walk away from each other. That pretty much made him a friend with benefits; though that wasn't what she wanted to say to her grandmother, and it also wasn't very flattering to Guy.

So what exactly was he to her?

Colleague: tick. They worked well together, and he'd got her to sit in on some of his surgeries, really broadening her surgical knowledge in the same way that she'd got him to sit in on some of her procedures and broadened his knowledge of electrophysiology. She'd helped him to train his intern, too.

Friend: tick. She liked him. She was comfortable with him.

Lover: tick. Everything from a gentle squeeze of the hand through to a stolen kiss and spending the night together. Guy made her heart beat faster.

But she was starting to feel more than attraction and friendship towards him, and that unsettled her. She'd spent so many years with iron self-control, in charge of her own life. Having a proper relationship with Guy would mean having to learn to compromise—and the biggest compromise would be letting herself rely on him, trusting that he wouldn't let her down.

That was still the sticking point.

She wanted to trust him. He'd proved himself to her at work. She was pretty sure he'd never put any unfair pressure on her outside work.

But still the what-ifs pushed their way into her thoughts, sharp and insistent, as if she'd fallen into a patch of cacti.

What would happen when they went back to England? He lived in Bristol. She lived in London. It wasn't a commutable distance for either of them, which meant that one of them would have to give up their job and their home. Rely on the other. What if she went to Bristol and it didn't work out? She'd have to start all over again—a new home, a new job, finding a place where she fitted. Or if he moved in with her in London, and it went wrong, she'd feel guilty; even though she would never cheat on him, the way his ex had, she'd still feel that she'd let him down.

The only way to keep herself safe would be to end it between them.

But she didn't want to do that, either. Because a little part of her was starting wonder if her old life in London was just a little bit lonely, and all she had to do was reach out for what she wanted…

Maybe she should stop overthinking it. And the only way she could think of to balance herself again was to put her earbuds in, turn the volume up loud, and dance until the music filled her head, drowning out her thoughts.

The following week, Guy and Joanne had dinner out, then found a quiet corner of the beach so they could watch the sun set and the stars come out. They sat on the still-warm sand under the coconut palms and watched the waves trickling onto the shore, the reflections from the sky turning the azure waters pink and gold.

Sitting there, holding hands and chilling out together as the sky darkened to showcase the stars, Joanne felt at peace.

'I've been thinking,' Guy said. 'You're only here for another, what, three weeks?'

She nodded. 'The last three months have gone really quickly.'

'I've enjoyed exploring Hawaii with you,' he said. 'Spending time with you.'

Was this his way of starting to say goodbye? Reminding her that they'd agreed to a fling, just for her stay in Hawaii? Or was he thinking of making some last memories before they wished each other well and walked away?

'Me, too,' she said carefully. 'I'll never forget our trip to the Big Island and seeing lava.'

'And the stars, that night,' he said. He tightened his fingers through hers. 'Joanne. We said this was a fling—but we're both going back to England. Maybe we don't have to end this thing between us. We could maybe keep it going, back home.'

Her heart started to beat faster, though half of the adrenalin rush wasn't caused by delight but by sheer panic. She wanted to ask him to slow down because, even though she'd been thinking along similar lines, actually hearing the words out loud made it feel as if she was rushing into it. She tried to speak, but her mouth was so dry it felt as if her tongue had been glued to the roof of her mouth.

'I like you, Joanne. Really like you.'

She liked him, too. Really liked him.

But.

Having a relationship with him in England would be a whole different ball game. For a start, they didn't even live in the same city. They were *hours* apart. They couldn't just meet up for dinner after a shift, or make casual arrangements. Everything would have to be planned and accommodated between two different cities. It would be that much more difficult, and take that much more time. An extra barrier: she'd hadn't been able to make her previous relationships work, even when she'd lived in the same city as someone.

And although she'd never let anyone close enough to be really upset when the relationship fizzled out, she had a feeling that it would be different with Guy. This time, it would really hurt when things ended. So maybe it would be better to end things now. To keep the memories they'd made together so she could remember them as a happy time in her life without being tarnished by all the misery of a break-up when life got in the way—as it always had with her previous relationships.

As if he'd guessed at the objections she hadn't yet voiced,

he said, 'Bristol and London aren't exactly a commutable distance from each other.'

No. Because it wasn't just a case of driving or getting the train between the two cities. There was the journey from the west of London to Muswell Hill, too, which would involve several changes of Tube and a bus. It would be completely unworkable on a daily basis. So maybe they'd only be able to see each other at weekends—but if they spent the weekends as just the two of them together, they wouldn't have time to spend with their families and their friends, and those relationships would wither without being given proper attention. Hadn't he said that his brother had kids? Children grew up so quickly. Making him miss out on the fun of being an uncle would be unfair—to his family as well as to him.

'Logistically, one of us is going to have to move,' he said. 'Either I'll come to London, or you can come to Bristol.'

Finally she found her voice. Just to echo the one word. 'Move.' But she didn't want to move far from her grandparents, and she was pretty sure he didn't want to move away from his family. One of them was going to have to make the biggest compromise. Either option would mean a massive change in her life—one she wasn't sure she could cope with.

If she moved to Bristol, she'd be uprooting her whole life. She'd have to move away from her grandparents, away from the job she loved at the Muswell Hill Memorial Hospital, and try to fit into his life.

On the other hand, if he moved to London, she'd feel guilty about him being so far from his family; plus she'd still have to make a lot of changes to her life to accommodate him.

Bottom line, she'd have to trust him. Rely on him. Make herself vulnerable to being let down.

The total opposite of everything she'd done since she'd been a teenager. Give up control.

Even the thought of it made her mind blank with fear. It was the thing she'd always avoided—the reason she'd never let her relationships go past more than a few dates.

How stupid she'd been, thinking that putting an end date to their fling would make it safe.

It wasn't safe at all. Which terrified her.

And she didn't know how to tell him.

'We're both qualified and experienced. I don't think either of us will have much of a problem finding a job,' he said.

'I can't,' she said. 'I—it's too much. Too soon. Too fast.'

Guy stared at her. 'But I thought…'

'I'm sorry.' She shook her head. 'I'm not ready for this.'

'Joanne, what's the real issue?' he asked softly.

He was so sweet, so kind. Trying to understand, not riding roughshod over her feelings. Tears prickled her eyes and she wanted to bawl her heart out, explain that she was panicking. But the words just wouldn't come. 'I don't… I can't… It's not…' She dragged in a sobbing breath. Oh, for pity's sake! Since when was she this incoherent? The least he deserved was a proper explanation. 'It's not you. It's me.'

His expression turned impassive. 'I'm not enough for you.'

'No.'

He flinched, and she realised he'd completely mistaken what she'd meant. 'No, I don't mean it like *that*. The problem's not you. It's me,' she said again. 'If I could be with anyone, it'd be someone like you.'

'Someone like me.'

She knew she'd just hurt him even more, and all because her brain had turned into this hot incoherent mess and the words weren't coming out right. 'I didn't mean that how it sounded, either.' She blew out a breath. 'Look, I'm just not…' She shook her head. 'I've never been any good at relationships.'

'Given how capable and competent you are at work, that's surprising. Or are you just too scared to try?' he asked.

She deserved that. Because she *was* a coward, wasn't she? 'I just can't,' she said.

'I think,' he said, 'right now, you're panicking.'

Understatement of the year. She stared at him.

'And you don't have to,' he said quietly. 'I'm not going to pressure you.'

Oh, but he had. He'd asked her to make this thing between them *real*, not just a fun-for-now fling. And that was terrifying.

'But I'm going to be honest with you,' he said, 'so you know exactly what's in my head. I've fallen in love with you, Joanne. With *you*. With the person you are. I get that you're antsy about relationships—of course you are. You were let down, very badly, when you were small, and that's a hard thing to get over. But you're still capable of love and being loved. You let your grandparents love you. You love them back.'

Completely unable to speak, because she thought if she opened her mouth she might just start bawling her eyes out and never stop, she simply nodded.

'And I think you could learn to let me love you. Learn to love me back,' he said. 'I know that's scary. Just as it's scary for me to admit I've fallen for you, because I made such a huge mistake with Imogen and the idea of getting it wrong again makes my skin feel too tight. But,' he said, 'the idea of getting it even more wrong, by not asking you to give us a chance, is worse. So I'm going to be brave.' He took a deep breath. 'I love you, Joanne. You make the world feel like a better place. And I think we have a real chance of a future—but only if we communicate.'

He had a point.

But it was so *hard*. Letting someone close. Letting them see inside her head, inside her heart. Making herself vulnerable.

'I can see you're struggling with that,' he said, 'so I'm going to take the pressure off. I'm going to walk you home, and I'm going to say goodnight without even kissing you. But I'm not walking away from you, Joanne—be very clear about that. I'm just giving you a bit of space, a bit of time to think about things. I know you're self-reliant and capable, and that's a good thing. But don't think for one second that you always have to do every single thing on your own, because you don't. I'm here. I'm on your team. And I'll be here when you're ready to talk.'

And then he was as good as his word.

He walked her home, without so much as holding her hand: making sure she was all right, but also giving her space. When they got to her building, he didn't kiss her. He just said quietly, 'Goodnight, Joanne. Sweet dreams. And remember what I said: I'm not walking away from you. When you're ready to talk, come and find me. I'll be waiting.'

Except he wasn't actually sure that she'd come and find him. As he walked home, his old fears rose up. The memory of Imogen curling her lip at him as she said, 'You're not enough. You can't give me what I want so I've found someone who can.'

He shook himself. No. He'd moved past that. Imogen had blamed him because she refused to accept her share in the breakdown in their relationship. What she'd wanted—for him to give up the job he'd loved and spent years training for—wasn't reasonable. A good relationship was about *balance*. About good communication. Imogen hadn't understood that, but Joanne did.

At the same time, he knew that didn't mean Joanne would give them a chance. Because there was a world of difference between knowing something intellectually and knowing it in your heart. Joanne had suffered rejection, too, from the people who should've loved her and supported her. Even though she'd had her grandparents, her parents' behaviour had still caused damage. It was why she was so self-reliant and wouldn't let anyone close.

He could tell her over and over again that he wouldn't let her down. But, until she was ready to believe it, she simply wouldn't.

All he could do was hope that she'd give them both a chance. That she'd try.

Until then, he'd just have to be patient.

CHAPTER FOURTEEN

IT WAS STILL relatively early in the evening, and Joanne couldn't settle. She tried ringing Jamie, but his phone went to voicemail, and it wasn't something she wanted to leave a message about. Music for once didn't help; an online Pilates class helped to pass a bit of time but didn't relax her the way it usually would.

Was Guy right?

Did they have a future?

She couldn't think straight. Her mind was buzzing, spinning around the same few thoughts and going nowhere, like car tyres in a snowdrift.

Reading didn't help. She flicked through television channels, and they didn't help either. She could maybe ring her gran—but at this time of day in England her gran would be out for aqua-fit and coffee with her friends, and Joanne didn't want to worry her.

She was on her own.

Miserable.

And it was her own fault, for panicking and pushing Guy away.

It was much, much later when her phone beeped with a message.

Hi, this is Piper Bronte. You don't know me, but I work with Jamie and I got your number from his phone.

Piper. The woman Jamie was seeing and keeping it quiet, Joanne remembered, because he was training her and he didn't want people to think he was favouring her.

Just to let you know he was in an accident today, but he's OK and they're going to let him out in a couple of days. He says you're not to worry.

Accident? Hang on. It was late evening, now. When had the accident happened? What had happened? Deeply worried, Joanne rang Piper's number. But, just like Jamie's phone had earlier, it went to voicemail.

Thank you for letting me know. Tell him of *course* I'm worried, the stupid, stubborn, Scottish idiot! Joanne messaged quickly. What happened?

To her relief, Piper replied quickly. He was out surfing today when he rescued some teenagers in a riptide. He was thrown on some coral.

Joanne gasped in horror, knowing that if you scraped your skin on some kinds of coral it could actually kill you.

He nearly drowned, but they resuscitated him on the beach, and he's in Honolulu GMC right now. He's going to be OK.

Are *you* OK, Piper? Joanne texted swiftly. I can be there in 15 minutes. No, scratch that, I'll definitely be there in 15. What do you need me to bring you?

He's still very groggy from his injuries. Come tomorrow. But thank you. Jamie said you were special.

Ring me if you need anything, anything at all. Give him my love and tell him... Tell him I'll *kill* him if he pulls a stunt like that again.

Her best friend—one of the few people she loved enough to let close—had nearly drowned. She'd been so close to losing him. Close enough for the shock waves to ripple through her now and make her realise that Guy was also one of the people she really loved. What if Guy had been the one who'd gone to rescue those frightened teenagers—and she was pretty sure that was the sort of thing he would do—and he'd been thrown onto coral and needed resuscitating? What if he'd been badly hurt, maybe killed, and she hadn't had the chance to tell him how she felt about him? What if he'd died, believing she was too rigid in her thinking and set in her ways to allow herself to love him?

She'd nearly lost Jamie. And she was at risk of losing Guy, if she couldn't be brave enough to give them the chance of a future.

A tear leaked down from her eye and she scrubbed it away.

But then another one leaked down. And another. And she couldn't stop them. She cried and cried and cried, because she'd nearly lost her best friend in an accident, and she realised she was on the point of losing the man she loved because she'd given into fear and let it drive her away from him. Right at that moment there was nothing she could do to fix either problem.

When the tears finally stopped, feeling wrung-out and crumpled, she bathed her swollen eyes with a wet cloth.

Now wasn't the right time to get a cab and go over to Guy's and beg him to listen to her. She knew he had surgery tomorrow—a complicated aortic aneurysm repair where he'd need to be at the top of his game. Keeping him up talking all night would be selfish and unfair. But tomorrow, she'd be brave and take the risk that scared her most. She'd catch him before work, she'd apologise for pushing him away—and then she'd tell him how she really felt about him. She'd promise to talk properly when he was out of the operating theatre, but she needed him to know she loved him.

Even though she'd made the decision, she still slept badly. What if she'd left it too late? He'd promised to be patient, but what if he realised he needed someone brave enough to give him the love he deserved and changed his mind about waiting for her?

She was up early and rushed to the hospital, only to discover that Guy was already in the operating theatre. It was too late to grab those crucial moments with him. A moment of panic robbed her of her ability to breathe. What if she'd waited too long? Why hadn't she thrown caution to the wind and gone to see him last night, after all?

And it wasn't as if she could whisk him off to lunch, either—not when the operation would take around six hours. The irony struck her: Guy had promised to wait for her, but in the end she was the one who'd have to wait for him.

Maybe the fact she was prepared to wait would make him see that she wouldn't be like Imogen, expecting him to put her before his job. She left a message on Guy's phone that she wanted to talk, whenever he was ready, and left a bunch of messages with Jamie's secretary and dropped off the malasadas she'd bought on the way in with another message for Piper to call her if she needed anything.

And then she forced herself to focus on her morning rounds and then her clinic. To wait, without looking at her watch every ten seconds and wonder when Guy would be out of Theatre—or if he'd pick up her message and come to see her.

Knowing she wouldn't be good company for anyone at lunchtime, she settled for buying a sandwich at the canteen and eating it while she got to grips with the paperwork at her desk. Though this time she found herself clock-watching, wondering how time had seemed to slow down like treacle now she was so desperate to talk to Guy.

Then, at long last, there was a knock on her door. And there he was, all blond charm and blue eyes. And it felt as if the world had just tipped back into balance.

Joanne looked tired, as if she hadn't slept properly, Guy thought. And her eyes were puffy, as if she'd been crying. He wanted to wrap her in his arms and tell her that everything was going to be all right—that he'd make it all right—but he knew he needed to take this at her pace. And she'd made that first, all-important step. She'd left him that message saying she wanted to talk; that gave him hope

'Hi,' he said.

'Hi.' She smiled back, and his heart skipped. 'How did your aneurysm repair go?'

'There were a couple of complications, but it's fixed,' he said. And then he couldn't do the social niceties any more. 'You said you wanted to talk?'

'I do,' she admitted. 'But you're only just out of Theatre. An AA repair's a long op. You must be exhausted. I can't just—'

'I told you I'd be there when you were ready to talk,' he cut in, not wanting to give her the chance to back away again. 'And I am. And I'm on a break.' He looked at her desk. 'Can your paperwork wait?'

She nodded. 'I worked through my lunch break. I'm due some time.'

'All right. Let's go for a walk. Somewhere quiet,' he said.

They found a quiet seat in the hospital grounds.

'Jamie had an accident yesterday,' she said. 'They had to resuscitate him on the beach. He was rescuing some kids from a riptide.'

Her best friend. The man she'd said was like the brother she'd never had. She must be in bits. 'Is he OK?' he asked.

'I think so. They won't let me in until official visiting hours, even though I'm staff.'

That explained the puffy eyes. Of course she'd be worried sick until she had the chance to see him for herself.

'But it made me think—what if it had been you?' She swallowed hard. 'What if it had been you, and you'd died, and I hadn't told you that I love you?'

It took him a moment to process what she'd said.

What if... I hadn't told you that I love you?

And then it felt as if all the breath had been knocked out of him. If he hadn't been sitting down, he thought his knees might've given way. 'You...' The words came out in stupid lumps, as if they didn't quite fit together. 'Love? Me?'

'I'm making a mess of this,' she said, grimacing. 'You're right about me, Guy. I'm a coward. I've been running scared of relationships, letting fear stop me from trying in case whoever I fall for lets me down. I thought if I didn't let people close, that would keep me safe. But it hasn't. It's just left me lonely.'

He wanted to hold her and tell her she'd never be lonely again, because he'd always be there when she needed him. *Always.* But if he interrupted her, he'd side-track her and she wouldn't tell him what was in her head. And she needed to tell him. He needed to hear it.

So instead he just took her hand and said softly, 'I'm listening.'

'I don't want to be vulnerable. I hate taking risks,' she said. 'But if I don't take the risk of letting you close, it's only going to hurt both of us. If I walk away from Hawaii without you, I'm going to be miserable. I don't want to be miserable.'

'So walk away from Hawaii *with* me,' he said.

'It scares me stupid,' she told him. 'If I move to Bristol and it all goes wrong, what then? I'll have given up my job, my home and my family. And if you move to London and it all goes wrong, I'll have split you from your family and your job and your home, and that's horrible.'

She was on a panic loop. There was only one way he could think of to stop it. To shift her thinking. 'What if,' he asked mildly, 'it goes right?'

She stared at him as if she couldn't quite believe that could happen.

'Let me tell you what I see,' he said gently. 'Yes, it could go wrong. But we're on the same side, so we've got a good chance of making it work. It's not all going to be smooth sailing, because life isn't like that, but we'll get through all the bumpy bits because we'll talk and we'll be honest with each other.'

'That works for me,' she said.

She'd worried that she had to give up her job, her home and her family. He needed to reassure her about that. 'So we join our lives,' he said. 'That means we both get a bigger family. We both get to do a job we love—and, if we end up at the same hospital, with some patients, we'll even be working together. And, as for home: maybe we need to find a new place. Somewhere we choose together, so it's ours right from the start. Not yours or mine and awkward compromises as we try to fit the other in, but a place that feels right for both of us.'

She was silent for a moment, obviously thinking about it and trying to see what he saw.

'A new start,' she said.

'And we don't have to live in London or Bristol. We could find somewhere halfway, so we're near both of our families. Oxford, maybe,' he suggested.

Hope bloomed on her face. 'I never thought of that.'

'Nothing's set in stone. We can work things out, if we do it together,' he said. 'All we have to do is reach out. Talk to each other.'

'I want to be with you, Guy,' she said. 'Even saying this feels scary—but I love you. I really do. I love you.'

'The more you say it—and the more you hear it,' he said, 'the less scary it'll be. And I'm going to tell you every day, until you stop being scared. I love you, Joanne.' She'd admitted to her fears, so maybe it was time to admit to his. 'Even though it panics me that I'm not going to be enough for you, the way I wasn't enough for Imogen, I'm going to try my hardest to make sure I am.'

'You don't need to try. You *are* enough for me,' she said. 'You're what I want.' She smiled. 'Like you said, we're on the same side. A team. I love you.'

'I believe it's traditional to seal this sort of thing with a kiss,' he said.

'I agree,' she said, and kissed him.

And, under the bright sunshine, with the tropical breezes blowing round them, Guy knew that everything was going to be all right…

EPILOGUE

Nine months later

'YOU LOOK AMAZING,' Jamie told Joanne. 'And I'm happy for you. But it wouldn't be right, me being your groomsman of honour, to let you walk down the aisle—well, onto the beach—with your grandad and marry Guy without checking.'

She'd been kind of expecting this. As the man she thought of as her brother, he'd always had her back, and he'd video-called her to get a tour of her new house in Oxford, when she and Guy had decided to move halfway between their two families once they'd settled back in England. Thankfully it had all worked out well; they'd sold Guy's house in Bristol and Joanne's flat in Muswell Hill, and they'd both managed to get a job in the same hospital in Oxford. And Joanne had been thrilled to discover that their little bubble of Hawaiian happiness was just as strong in England.

'So I'm asking you now: is this what you truly want?' Jamie held her gaze. 'Because if it's not, tell me now and Piper will sneak you out of here while I go and sort everything else. You'll have nothing to worry about.'

'I'm sure.' She smiled. 'I love Guy. I want to marry him—to be with him for the rest of my life. Just like you and Piper.'

Joanne had been Jamie's best woman at his wedding to Piper in Scotland—where he'd worn the same kilt he was wearing today, as her groomsman of honour—and Jamie and Piper had flown in last night from Atlanta CDC, where they both had new jobs. Guy and Joanne had flown in from England with their respective families a couple of nights before, to let everyone get over the jetlag. And they'd all spent the evening together in Ben's bar with a joint hen and stag night, the previous night, including the children; they were holding the wedding breakfast there later, too.

'Let's get the show on the road,' Jamie said.

Piper handed Joanne her bouquet, full of traditional Hawaiian flowers: frangipani to signify new beginnings, hibiscus for love and passion, orchids for strength, and ti leaves for protectiveness and good luck.

'I hope you and Guy will be as happy as Jamie and me,' she said, giving Joanne a hug.

'Thank you. I'm pretty sure we will,' Joanne said, hugging her back. 'And I'm glad we decided to come back to Hawaii to get married.'

'Back where it all started. I get that,' Piper said.

Ailani, Guy's Theatre nurse, had become a close friend of both of them and had helped them to organise the wedding—everything from arranging the wedding licence to finding a wedding dress and a local florist to make the lei. The licence allowed them only a small wedding; her grandparents, Jamie and Piper from her side, his brother and sister and their partners and children on his; and a couple of their closest friends from the hospital, including Ailani and Keanu. Ben Palani was coming with his wife to play the guitar for them, and he'd arranged for Guy's sister, Melissa, to borrow a keyboard from his bandmate; and although neither of them would be drawn on what music they planned to play, apparently they'd rehearsed together over several video calls.

Ailani had helped Joanne choose a simple ivory raw silk tea-length dress with spaghetti straps; Joanne was also wearing a lei made of seashells, and knew Guy would be wearing a similar one, ready to exchange lei during the ceremony to respect the Hawaiian tradition of sharing love and strengthening their bond.

At the beach, her grandfather tucked her hand into the crook of his arm. 'You look beautiful. Your gran and I are so proud of you,' he said. 'And I'm glad you've found Guy. He's a good man and he'll never let you down.'

'And I'll never let him down, either,' she whispered.

'That's my girl,' her grandfather said, and walked her down the short aisle where their family and friends were sitting, accompanied by Ben and Melissa playing 'What a Wonderful World' on steel guitar and keyboard respectively, towards Guy, who was standing next to the arch of flowers and ribbons with the widest, widest smile on his face. In cream linen trousers and a white shirt, plus the seashell lei, he looked relaxed and handsome; and, like her, he was barefoot.

Kaleo, their officiant, was wearing a white orchid lei. He welcomed everyone to the wedding. 'I'll start by blowing the conch shell—this was important to the people of Hawaii because it called their families and friends and let them know something important was happening. And we have something important happening today—the union between Joanne and Guy. I'm calling you here to celebrate with them in mind, in heart and in love. The first two sounds are short, to drive away negative energy, and the third is long to symbolise our wish for a long life and a long, happy marriage.'

He held the conch shell to his lips and then blew the three blasts, producing a deep, mellow tone.

'And here in Hawaii at a wedding we ask the bride and groom to do the *honi*, sharing their life's breath. Take each other's hand, gently touch the tip of your nose and forehead together, close your eyes, take a deep breathe in, exhale, and say *aloha* to each other.'

Joanne gave her bouquet to Jamie, and together she and Guy followed Kaleo's directions.

Next was the exchanging of the lei. 'In Hawaii,' Kaleo said, 'we say *E lei no au i ko aloha.* That means "I'll wear your love as a wreath". When you place a lei upon someone's shoulders, you give them respect, honour, love and grace. Love and cherish each other with all your heart; and when you exchange your lei you tell us you want your love to last for all time.'

Carefully, Joanne and Guy removed the seashell lei from their own shoulders and replaced it on the other's.

Kaleo took them through the rest of the ceremony, guiding them to make their vows and exchange rings. And then, after they'd signed everything, it was time for the Sand Unity Ceremony. Kaleo had explained to them earlier that in Hawaiian tradition there was a unity candle ceremony, where the bride's and groom's mothers each lit a taper candle, which they passed to the bride and groom, who then used the tapers to light a single, larger pillar candle. To avoid the wind accidentally blowing out the candles on the beach, the sand ceremony was used instead.

'The bride and groom each have a small jar of sand,' he said. 'Guy's is from the beach where they first kissed, and

Joanne's is from the black basalt volcanic beach on Big Island. The separate sands symbolise their separate lives before they found each other. Today, they seal their bond by pouring the sand into one vessel, symbolising the joining of their lives into one.'

To the sound of Melissa and Ben playing 'Albatross' together, Guy and Joanne poured the sand into one container.

'Just as these grains of sand can never be separated and poured into the individual containers,' Kaleo said, 'so too will your marriage and your family for ever be intertwined.'

Everyone clapped when they'd finished, and together they put the stopper into the glass jar.

'As we say in Hawaii,' Kaleo finished, *'Aloha aku no, aloha mai no.* I give my love to you, you give your love to me.' He grinned broadly. 'I now pronounce you man and wife. You may now kiss the bride.'

And that was exactly what Guy did, to rapturous applause from their family and friends.

* * * * *

*If you enjoyed this story,
check out these other great reads from
Kate Hardy*

Paediatrician's Unexpected Second Chance
Sparks Fly with the Single Dad
An English Vet in Paris
Saving Christmas for the ER Doc

All available now!

MILLS & BOON®

Coming next month

FORBIDDEN FLING WITH THE PRINCESS
Amy Andrews

Dios! A man should not look that good in what were essentially blue pajamas.

'*Xio,*' he greeted as his gaze roved over her face and hair and neck and, god help her, lower.

She'd dressed this morning in her favourite form-fitting, v-necked, pink t-shirt with a glittery tiara stamped across the front, teaming it with a flowy, layered skirt of soft tulle that hid a multitude of sins and flirted with her ankles. For comfort, she'd told herself. Nothing stiff or formal for a long day sitting in the hospital keeping Phoebe company.

But in truth, she'd worn it for him, this man who seemed to have such a preoccupation with her clothes. Because she'd wanted him to look at her as he was now, his gaze brushing her neck and the swell of her breasts. She'd wanted to see his amber eyes darkening.

She'd wanted him to look at her like she wasn't some pretty, unattainable, untouchable princess on a pedestal but like she was a woman who knew her own power. A woman who craved his touch.

And in those long beats she totally forgot herself and their surroundings. And that two of the palace security detail were witnessing this mutual display of ogling that violated all kinds of royal protocols. Commoners should never look upon a royal princess with such unbridled lust. And the princess should definitely not be wondering how easy it was to get a man out of a pair of scrubs.

Continue reading

FORBIDDEN FLING WITH THE PRINCESS
Amy Andrews

Available next month
millsandboon.co.uk

Copyright © 2025 Amy Andrews

COMING SOON!

We really hope you enjoyed reading this book.
If you're looking for more romance
be sure to head to the shops when
new books are available on

Thursday 28th August

To see which titles are coming soon, please visit
millsandboon.co.uk/nextmonth

MILLS & BOON

afterglow BOOKS

Afterglow Books is a trend-led, trope-filled list of books with diverse, authentic and relatable characters, a wide array of voices and representations, plus real world trials and tribulations. Featuring all the tropes you could possibly want (think small-town settings, fake relationships, grumpy vs sunshine, enemies to lovers) and all with a generous dose of spice in every story.

@millsandboonuk
@millsandboonuk
afterglowbooks.co.uk
#AfterglowBooks

For all the latest book news, exclusive content and giveaways scan the QR code below to sign up to the Afterglow newsletter:

SCAN ME

afterglow BOOKS

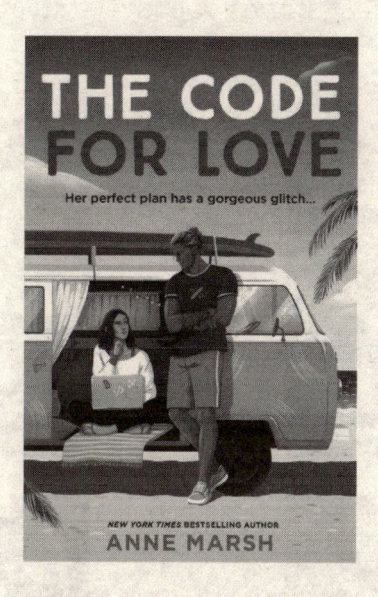

THE CODE FOR LOVE

Her perfect plan has a gorgeous glitch...

NEW YORK TIMES BESTSELLING AUTHOR
ANNE MARSH

✈ International

⛅ Grumpy/sunshine

🚻 Fake dating

OUT NOW

To discover more visit:
Afterglowbooks.co.uk

FOUR BRAND NEW BOOKS FROM
MILLS & BOON MODERN

The same great stories you love, a stylish new look!

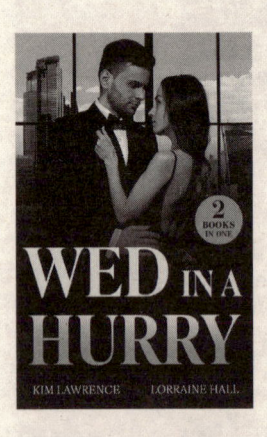

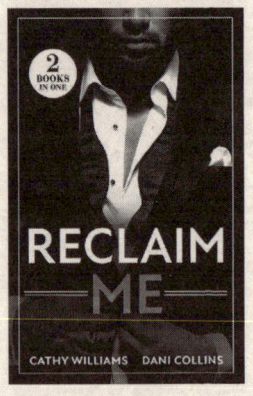

WED IN A HURRY
KIM LAWRENCE — LORRAINE HALL

BOUND & CROWNED
LOUISE FULLER — CLARE CONNELLY

LOVE TO HATE HIM
JULIA JAMES — MILLIE ADAMS

RECLAIM ME
CATHY WILLIAMS — DANI COLLINS

OUT NOW

Eight Modern stories published every month, find them all at:

millsandboon.co.uk

LET'S TALK
Romance

For exclusive extracts, competitions and special offers, find us online:

- **f** MillsandBoon
- **X** @MillsandBoon
- **◉** @MillsandBoonUK
- **♪** @MillsandBoonUK

Get in touch on 01413 063 232

For all the latest titles coming soon, visit
millsandboon.co.uk/nextmonth

OUT NOW!

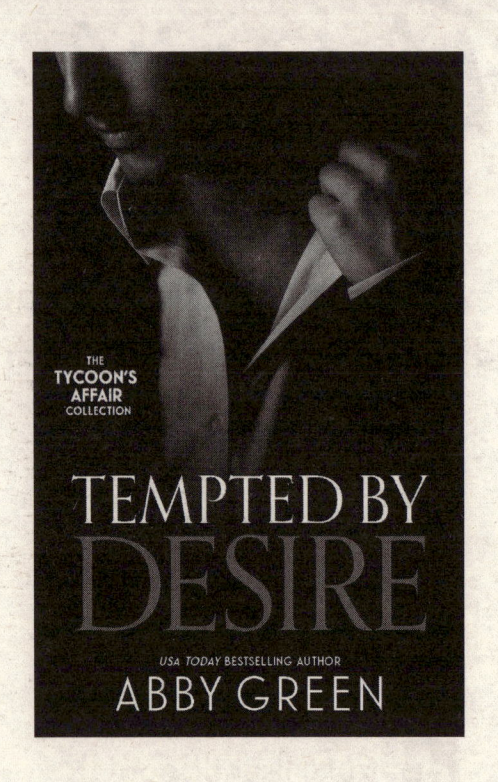

TEMPTED BY DESIRE

THE TYCOON'S AFFAIR COLLECTION

USA TODAY BESTSELLING AUTHOR
ABBY GREEN

Available at
millsandboon.co.uk

MILLS & BOON

OUT NOW!

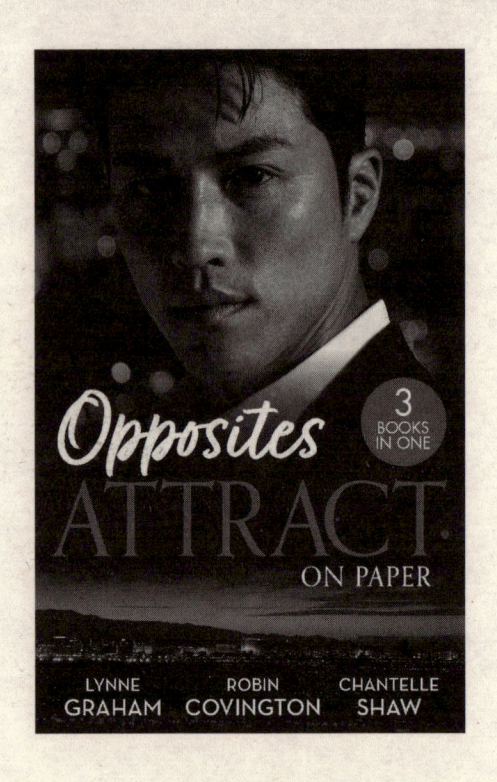

Opposites Attract On Paper

3 BOOKS IN ONE

LYNNE GRAHAM · ROBIN COVINGTON · CHANTELLE SHAW

Available at
millsandboon.co.uk

MILLS & BOON

OUT NOW!

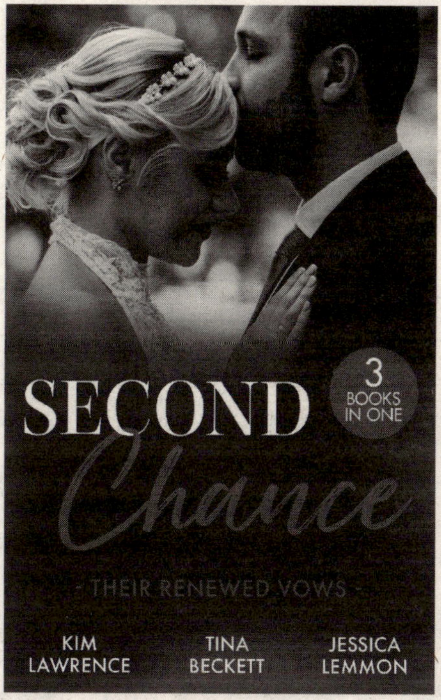

Available at
millsandboon.co.uk

MILLS & BOON

MILLS & BOON
A ROMANCE FOR EVERY READER

- **FREE** delivery direct to your door
- **EXCLUSIVE** offers every month
- **SAVE** up to 30% on pre-paid subscriptions

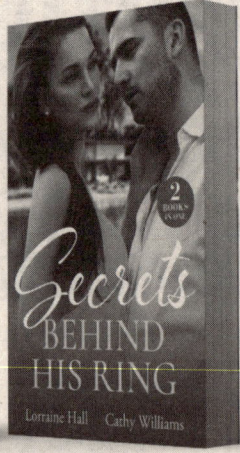

SUBSCRIBE AND SAVE

millsandboon.co.uk/Subscribe